Jane Austen's Sense and Sensibility for Teens

a simplified retelling of the classic original

Gerry Baird

Clearstone Publishing

PREFACE

Sense and Sensibility is one of my favorite Austen novels. If it were retitled using modern language, it might be something like, "Reason and Feeling," "Logic and Emotion," or "Head and Heart." Elinor believes that common sense and rational action are excellent guides for successful living, while her sister Marianne allows her strong feelings to guide her where they will. The contrasting storylines between the two, and the interactions between them, make for fascinating character studies as they each seek the happy marriage that is the goal of every Austen heroine.

To make this edition more accessible to a modern audience, I have broken long sentences into shorter ones, updated punctuation to improve clarity, and gently toned down the vocabulary while still honouring – to the degree possible – the author's intent. I have also, in certain cases, genericized references to very specific terms, such as the different types of carriages then in use. Words like *barouche* and *chaise-and-four* would have made perfect sense to Jane Austen's contemporaries, but as they serve no essential role in the plot they have been replaced in this version by the generic term "carriage." Most of the words in this book are Jane Austen's, and most remain exactly as she wrote them.

I am deeply indebted to David M. Shapard, who published "The Annotated Sense and Sensibility" (New York: Anchor, 2011). The valuable insights offered in this well-researched volume further expanded my knowledge and understanding of the words and world of Jane Austen.

If you enjoy this simplified retelling of Sense and Sensibility, you may also be interested in my other books: "Pride and Prejudice for Teens" and "Jane Austen's Emma for Teens. " They are both available on Amazon in Kindle and Paperback formats.

CHAPTER 1

The family of Dashwood had been long settled in Sussex. Their estate was large, and their residence was at Norland Park, in the centre of their property. For many generations they had lived so respectably as to ensure the general good opinion of their surrounding acquaintance. The late owner of this estate was a single man, who lived to a very advanced age, and who for many years of his life had a constant companion and housekeeper in his sister. But her death, which happened ten years before his own, produced a great alteration in his home. To replace her, he invited and received into his house the family of his nephew, Mr. Henry Dashwood, the legal inheritor of the Norland estate. In the company of his nephew and niece, and their children, the old gentleman's days were comfortably spent. His affection for them all increased. The constant attention of Mr. and Mrs. Henry Dashwood to his wishes, which proceeded not merely from financial interest, but from goodness of heart, gave him every degree of comfort which his age could receive; and the cheerfulness of the children added to his happiness.

By a former marriage, Mr. Henry Dashwood had one son; by his present wife, three daughters. The son, a steady, respectable young man, was well provided for by the fortune of his mother, which had been large, and half of which would be his when he became an adult. By his own marriage, likewise, which happened soon afterwards, he added to his wealth. To him, therefore, the inheritance of the Norland estate was not as important as to his sisters; for their fortune was rather small. Their mother had nothing, and their father only seven thousand pounds.

The old Gentleman died; his will was read, and like almost every other will, gave as much disappointment as pleasure. He was neither so unjust, nor so ungrateful, as to keep his estate from his nephew; but he left it to him on terms that destroyed half its value. Mr. Dashwood had wished for it more for the sake of his wife and daughters than for himself or his son; but to his son, and his son's son, a child of four years old, it was secured. He therefore had no power of providing for those who were most dear to him, although the three girls were given a thousand pounds each.

Mr. Dashwood's disappointment was at first severe; but his temper was cheerful, and he might reasonably hope to live many years. By economizing, he might set aside enough to support his wife and daughters. But the fortune was his for only a year. He died; and ten thousand pounds was all that remained for his widow and daughters.

His son was sent for, as soon as his danger was known, and the dying Mr. Dashwood begged him to care for his step-mother and half-sisters.

Mr. John Dashwood had not the strong feelings of the rest of the family; but he was affected by a request of such a nature at such a time, and he promised to do everything he could to make them comfortable. His father was gratified by such an assurance, and Mr. John Dashwood began to consider how much there might prudently be in his power to do for them.

He was not a man of poor character, unless to be rather cold-hearted, and rather selfish, is to have a poor character: but he was, in general, well respected; for he conducted himself with propriety in the discharge of his ordinary duties. Had he married a more amiable woman, he might have been made still more respectable than he was; he might even have been made amiable himself, for he was very young when he married, and very fond of his wife. But Mrs. John Dashwood was more narrow-minded and selfish than her husband.

When he gave his promise to his father, he thought that he might increase the fortunes of his sisters by the present of a thousand pounds each. He then really thought himself equal to it. The prospect of four thousand a year, in addition to his present income, besides the remaining half of his own mother's fortune, warmed his heart and made him feel capable of generosity. "Yes, he would give them three thousand pounds: it would be generous and charitable! It would be enough to make them completely comfortable. Three thousand pounds! He could spare such a large sum with little inconvenience." He thought of it all day long, and for many days successively, and he remained committed to this course of action.

No sooner was his father's funeral over than Mrs. John Dashwood, having given no prior notice, arrived with her child and their servants. No one could dispute her right to come; the house was her husband's from the moment of his father's decease. But her insensitivity was keenly felt. Mrs. John Dashwood had never been a favourite with any of her husband's family, but she had had no opportunity, till the present, of showing them with how little attention to the comfort of other people she could give when occasion required.

So acutely did Mrs. Dashwood feel this ungracious behaviour, and so earnestly did she despise her daughter-in-law for it, that, on the arrival of the latter, she would have left the house forever, had not the entreaty of her eldest girl induced her first to reflect on the possible consequences of a breach with their brother.

Elinor, this eldest daughter whose advice was so effectual, possessed a strength of understanding and coolness of judgment which qualified her, though only nineteen, to be the counsellor of her mother. She had an excellent heart; her disposition was affectionate, and her feelings were strong, but she knew how to govern them. It was a knowledge which her mother had yet to learn, and which one of her sisters had resolved never to be taught.

Marianne's abilities were, in many respects, quite equal to Elinor's. She was sensible and clever, but eager in everything: her sorrows, and her joys, could have no moderation. She was generous, amiable, interesting; she was everything but prudent. The similarities between her and her mother were striking.

Elinor saw, with concern, the excess of her sister's sensibility; but by Mrs. Dashwood it was valued and cherished. They encouraged each other now in their affliction. The agony of grief which overpowered them at first was voluntarily renewed, was sought for, was created again and again. They gave themselves up wholly to their sorrow, seeking increase of wretchedness in every reflection, and resolving against ever being consoled. Elinor, too, was deeply afflicted; but still she could make an effort, she could exert herself. She could consult with her brother, could receive her sister-in-law on her arrival, and treat her with proper attention; and she could encourage her mother to do the same.

Margaret, the other sister, was a good-humoured, well-disposed girl; but as she had already absorbed a good deal of Marianne's romance, without having much of her sense, she did not, at thirteen, appear to be on a course that would make her equal, at a future period, to her two sisters.

CHAPTER 2

Mrs. John Dashwood now installed herself as mistress of Norland, and her mother and sisters-in-law were downgraded to the condition of guests. As such, however, they were treated by her with quiet civility; and by her husband with as much kindness as he could feel towards anybody besides himself, his wife, and their child. He really encouraged them, with some earnestness, to consider Norland as their home; and, as she had no other alternative for the time being, his invitation was accepted.

Remaining in a place where everything reminded her of former delight was exactly what suited her. In seasons of cheerfulness, no temper could be more cheerful than hers, or possess, in a greater degree, that hope of happiness which is happiness itself. But in sorrow she must be equally carried away, to a place far beyond consolation.

Mrs. John Dashwood did not at all approve of what her husband intended to do for his sisters. To take three thousand pounds from the fortune of their dear little boy would, in her view, be impoverishing him to the most dreadful degree. She begged him to reconsider. How could he rob his child, and his only child too, of so large a sum? And what possible claim could the Miss Dashwoods, who were related to him only by half blood, which she considered as no relationship at all, have on his generosity? It was very well known that no affection was ever supposed to exist between the children of any man by different marriages; and why was he to ruin himself, and their poor little Harry, by giving away all his money to his half-sisters?

"It was my father's last request to me," replied her husband, "that I should assist his widow and daughters."

"He did not know what he was talking of, I dare say. Had he been in his right senses, he could not have thought of such a thing as begging you to give away half your own child's fortune."

"He did not mention any particular sum, my dear Fanny; he only requested me, in general terms, to assist them, and to make their situation more comfortable than he could do. Perhaps it would have been as well if he had said nothing. He could hardly suppose I would neglect them. But as he required the promise, I could do no less than give it: at least I thought so at the time. The promise, therefore, was given, and must be performed. Something must be done for them whenever they leave Norland and settle in a new home."

"Well, then, *let* something be done for them; but *that* something need not be three thousand pounds. Consider," she added, "that when the money is once parted with, it never can return. Your sisters will marry, and it will be gone forever."

"Why, to be sure," said her husband, very gravely, "the time may come when Harry will regret that so large a sum was parted with. If he should have a numerous family, for instance, it would be a very convenient addition."

"To be sure it would."

"Perhaps, then, it would be better for all parties if the sum were cut in half. Five hundred pounds would be a prodigious increase to their fortunes!"

"Oh! Certainly! What brother on earth would do half so much for his sisters, even his *full* sisters! You have such a generous spirit!"

"I do not wish to be miserly," he replied. "It is better, on such occasions, to do too much than too little. No one, at least, can think I have not done enough for them; even themselves, they can hardly expect more."

"There is no knowing what *they* may expect," said the lady, "but their expectations are none of *our* concern: the question is, what can you afford to do?"

"I think I can give them five hundred pounds each. As it is, without any addition of mine, they will individually have more than three thousand pounds on their mother's death; a very comfortable fortune for any young woman."

"To be sure it is: and, indeed, it strikes me that there is no need for any addition at all. They will have ten thousand pounds divided among them. If they marry, they will be sure of doing well; and if they do not, they may all live very comfortably together on the interest of ten thousand pounds."

"That is very true, and, therefore, I do not know whether, all things considered, it would not be more advisable to do something for their mother while she lives rather than for them; something of the annuity kind I mean. My sisters would feel the good effects of it as well as herself. A hundred a year would make them all perfectly comfortable."

His wife hesitated a little, however, in giving her consent to this plan.

"To be sure," said she, "it is better than parting with fifteen hundred pounds at once. But then, if Mrs. Dashwood should live fifteen years, think of the expense."

"Fifteen years! My dear Fanny; she is unlikely to live half that long."

"Certainly not; but people always see to live forever when there is any annuity to be paid. She is very healthy, and barely forty. An annuity is serious business; the payment must be made over and over every year, and there is no getting rid of it. You are not aware of what you are doing. I have known a great deal of the trouble of annuities, for my mother was burdened with the payment of three to former servants by my father's will, and it is amazing how disagreeable she found it. Twice every year, these annuities were to be paid, and there was no end of trouble getting it to them. Then one of them was said to have died, and afterwards it turned out to be false. My mother was quite sick of it. Her income was not her own, she said, with such perpetual claims on it. It has given me such an abhorrence of annuities that I am sure I would not burden myself with the payment of one for all the world."

"It is certainly an unpleasant thing," replied Mr. Dashwood, "to have those kind of yearly drains on one's income. One's fortune, as your mother justly says, is *not* one's own. To be tied down to the regular payment of such a sum, four times a year, is by no means desirable: it takes away one's independence."

"Undoubtedly; and, after all, you have no thanks for it. They are certain you will help them, so you do no more than what is expected, and it yields no gratitude at all. If I were you, whatever I did should be done at my own discretion entirely. I would not bind myself to allow them anything yearly. It may be very inconvenient some years to spare a hundred, or even fifty pounds from our own expenses."

"I believe you are right, my love; it will be better that there should be no annuity; whatever I may give them occasionally will be of far greater assistance than a yearly allowance, because they would only enlarge their style of living if they felt sure of a larger income, and would not be any richer for it at the end of the year. It will certainly be the best way. A present of fifty pounds, now and then, will prevent them from ever being distressed about money; and will, I think be amply fulfilling my promise to my father."

"To be sure it will. Indeed, to say the truth, I am convinced that your father had no intention of your giving them any money at all. The assistance he thought of, I dare say, was only such as might be reasonably expected of you; for instance, finding a comfortable small house for them, helping them move their things, and sending them presents of fish and game, whenever they are in season. I'll lay my life that he meant nothing farther; indeed, it would be very strange and unreasonable if he did. Do consider, my dear Mr. Dashwood, how excessively comfortable your mother-in-law and her daughters may live on the interest of seven thousand pounds, besides the thousand pounds belonging to each of the girls, which brings them fifty pounds a year, and, of course, they will pay their mother for their board out of it. Altogether, they will have five hundred a year among them, and what more can four women need than that? They will live so cheaply! Their housekeeping will be nothing at all. They will have no carriage, no horses, and hardly any servants; they will keep no company, and can have no expenses of any kind! Only think how comfortable they will be! Five hundred a year! I am sure I cannot imagine how they will spend half of it; and as to your giving them more, it is quite absurd to think of it. They will be much more able to give *you* something."

"Upon my word," said Mr. Dashwood, "I believe you are perfectly right. My father certainly could mean nothing more by his request to me than what you say. I clearly understand it now, and I will strictly fulfil my promise by such acts of assistance and kindness to them as you have described. When my mother moves into another house, my services shall be readily given to accommodate her as much as I can."

Thus he resolved that it would be absolutely unnecessary, if not highly inappropriate, to do more for the widow and children of his father than such kind and neighbourly acts as his wife pointed out.

CHAPTER 3

Mrs. Dashwood remained at Norland several months. When her spirits began to revive, and her mind became capable of some other exertion than that of heightening its affliction by melancholy remembrances, she was impatient to be gone. She began searching for a suitable dwelling in the neighbourhood of Norland; for to remove far from that beloved spot was impossible. But everything that suited her notions of comfort and ease was, in the opinion of her eldest daughter, too large for their income.

Mrs. Dashwood had been informed by her husband of the solemn promise on the part of his son in their favour, which gave comfort to his last earthly reflections. She believed, as had her husband, that the promise would be kept. She thought of it for her daughters' sake with satisfaction, though as for herself she was persuaded that a much smaller provision than seven thousand pounds would support her. His attentive behaviour to herself and his sisters convinced her that their welfare was dear to him, and, for a long time, she firmly relied on the promise of future generosity.

The contempt which she had, very early in their acquaintance, felt for her daughter-in-law, was very much increased by the farther knowledge of her character, which half a year's residence in her home afforded. Perhaps, in spite of every consideration of politeness or maternal affection on the side of the former, the two ladies might have found it impossible to have lived together so long, had not a particular circumstance occurred.

This circumstance was a growing attachment between her eldest girl and the brother of Mrs. John Dashwood, a gentlemanlike and pleasing young man, who was introduced to their acquaintance soon after his sister's establishment at Norland, and who had since spent the greatest part of his time there.

Some mothers might have encouraged the connection from motives of interest, for Edward Ferrars was the eldest son of a man who had died very rich. But for Mrs. Dashwood, it was enough for her that he appeared to be amiable, that he loved her daughter, and that Elinor returned the partiality. It was contrary to every doctrine of hers that difference of fortune should keep any couple apart who were attached to each other. That Elinor's good qualities should not be acknowledged by everyone who knew her, was to her understanding impossible.

Edward Ferrars was not recommended to their good opinion by any particular graces of person or address. He was not handsome, and his manners were not as refined as they might have been. He was too modest to do justice to himself; but when his natural shyness was overcome, his behaviour gave every indication of an open affectionate heart. He was intelligent and well-educated. But he was not distinguished enough. His mother wished to interest him in political concerns, to get him into parliament, or to see him connected with some of the great men of the day. Mrs. John Dashwood wished it likewise; but in the meanwhile, till one of these superior blessings could be attained, it would have quieted her ambition to see him driving a luxurious carriage. But Edward had no interest in great men or fancy carriages. All his wishes centered in domestic comfort and the quiet of private life. Fortunately, he had a younger brother who was more promising.

Edward had been staying several weeks in the house before he engaged much of Mrs. Dashwood's attention; for she was, at that time, in such affliction as rendered her insensible to her surroundings. She saw only that he was quiet and unobtrusive, and she liked him for it. He did not disturb the wretchedness of her mind by ill-timed conversation. She was first called to observe and approve him farther, by a reflection which Elinor chanced one day to make on the difference between him and his sister. It was a contrast which recommended him most powerfully to her mother.

"It is enough," said she; "to say that he is unlike Fanny is enough. It implies everything good. I love him already."

"I think you will like him," said Elinor, "when you know more of him."

"Like him!" replied her mother with a smile. "I can feel no sentiment less than love."

"You may esteem him."

"I have never yet known what it was to separate esteem and love."

Mrs. Dashwood now took pains to get acquainted with him. Her manners were warm and soon banished his reserve. She speedily understood all his merits—her belief of his regard for Elinor perhaps assisted her in this—but she really felt assured of his worth. Even the quietness of manner which went against all her established ideas of what a young man's behavior ought to be, was no longer uninteresting when she knew his heart to be warm and his temper affectionate.

No sooner did she perceive any symptom of love in his behaviour to Elinor, than she considered their serious attachment as certain, and looked forward to their marriage as rapidly approaching.

"In a few months, my dear Marianne," said she, "Elinor will in all probability be settled for life. We shall miss her; but *she* will be happy."

"Oh! Mama, how shall we do without her?"

"My love, it will be scarcely a separation. We shall live within a few miles of each other, and shall meet every day of our lives. You will gain a brother—a real, affectionate brother. I have the highest opinion in the world of Edward's heart. But you look grave, Marianne; do you disapprove your sister's choice?"

"Perhaps," said Marianne, "I may consider it with some surprise. Edward is very amiable, and I love him tenderly. But yet, he is not the kind of young man—there is a something wanting, his figure is not striking—it has none of that grace which I should expect in the man who could win my sister's heart. His eyes need that spirit, that fire, which at once announce virtue and intelligence. And besides all this, I am afraid, mama, he has no real taste. He cares little for music, and though he admires Elinor's drawings very much, it is not the admiration of a person who can understand their worth. It is evident, in spite of his frequent attention to her while she draws, that he knows nothing about it. He admires as a lover, not as a connoisseur. To satisfy me, those characters must be united. I could not be happy with a man whose taste did not in every point coincide with my own. The same books and the same music must charm us both. Oh mama! How spiritless, how tame was Edward's manner in reading to us last night! I felt for my sister most severely. Yet she bore it with so much composure, she seemed scarcely to notice it. I could hardly keep my seat. To hear those beautiful lines which have frequently almost driven me wild, pronounced with such impenetrable calmness, such dreadful indifference!"

"He would certainly have done more justice to simple and elegant prose. I thought so at the time; but you *would* give him Cowper."

"Nay, mama, if he is not to be animated by Cowper—but we must allow for difference of taste. Elinor has not my feelings, and therefore she may overlook it, and be happy with him. But it would have broken *my* heart, had I loved him, to hear him read with so little feeling. Mama, the more I know of the world, the more am I convinced that I shall never see a man whom I can really love. I require so much! He must have all Edward's virtues, and his person and manners must ornament his goodness with every possible charm."

"Remember, my love, that you are not seventeen. It is yet too early in life to despair of such happiness. Why should you be less fortunate than your mother? In one circumstance only, my Marianne, may your destiny be different from hers!"

CHAPTER 4

"What a pity it is, Elinor," said Marianne, "that Edward has no taste for drawing."

"No taste for drawing," replied Elinor; "why should you think so? He does not draw himself, indeed, but he has great pleasure in seeing the result. I assure you he is by no means deficient in natural taste, though he has not had opportunities of improving it. Had he been given a chance to learn, I think he would have drawn very well. He distrusts his own judgment in such matters, so much that he is always unwilling to give his opinion on any picture."

Marianne was afraid of offending, and said no more on the subject; but the kind of approval which Elinor described was very far from that rapturous delight, which, in her opinion, could alone be called taste. Yet, though smiling within herself at the mistake, she honoured her sister for that blind partiality to Edward which produced it.

"I hope, Marianne," continued Elinor, "you do not consider him as deficient in general taste. Indeed, I think I may say that you cannot, for your behaviour to him is perfectly cordial, and if *that* were your opinion, I am sure you could never be civil to him."

Marianne hardly knew what to say. She would not wound the feelings of her sister on any account, and yet to say what she did not believe was impossible. At length she replied –

"Do not be offended, Elinor, if my praise of him is not in everything equal to your sense of his merits. I have not had as many opportunities to assess his inclinations and tastes as you have; but I have the highest opinion in the world of his goodness and sense. I think him everything that is worthy and amiable."

"I am sure," replied Elinor with a smile, "that his dearest friends could not be dissatisfied with such commendation as that. I do not perceive how you could express yourself more warmly."

Marianne rejoiced to find her sister so easily pleased.

"Of his sense and his goodness," continued Elinor, "no one can, I think, be in doubt, who has seen him often enough to engage him in conversation. The excellence of his understanding and his principles can be concealed only by that shyness which too often keeps him silent. You know enough of him to do justice to his worth. But of his inclinations and tastes, you have from particular circumstances been kept more ignorant than myself. I have seen a great deal of him, have studied his sentiments and heard his opinion on subjects of literature and taste; and, upon the whole, I venture to pronounce that his mind is well-informed, his enjoyment of books exceedingly great, his imagination lively, his observation just and correct, and his taste delicate and pure. His abilities in every respect improve as much upon acquaintance as his manners and person. At first sight, his manners are certainly not striking; and his person can hardly be called handsome, till the expression of his eyes, which are uncommonly good, and the general sweetness of his countenance, is perceived. At present, I know him so well, that I think him really handsome; or, at least, almost so. What say you, Marianne?"

"I shall very soon think him handsome, Elinor, if I do not now. When you tell me to love him as a brother, I shall no more see imperfection in his face, than I now do in his heart."

Elinor started at this declaration, and was sorry for the warmth she had been betrayed into, in speaking of him. She felt that Edward stood very high in her opinion. She believed the regard to be mutual; but she required greater certainty of it before agreeing with Marianne's conviction. She knew that what Marianne and her mother conjectured one moment, they believed the next—that with them, to wish was to hope, and to hope was to expect. She tried to explain the real state of affairs to her sister.

"I do not attempt to deny," said she, "that I think very highly of him—that I greatly esteem, that I like him."

Marianne here burst forth with indignation –

"Esteem him! Like him! Cold-hearted Elinor! Oh! Worse than cold-hearted! Ashamed of being otherwise. Use those words again and I will leave the room this moment." Elinor could not help laughing.

"Excuse me," she said, "and be assured that I meant no offence to you, by speaking, in so subtle a way, of my own feelings. Believe them to be stronger than I have declared; believe them, in short, to be such as his merit, and the hope of his returned affection for me may warrant. But farther than this you must *not* believe. I am by no means assured of his regard for me. There are moments when the extent of it seems doubtful; and till his sentiments are fully known, you cannot wonder at my wishing to avoid any encouragement of my own partiality, by believing or calling it more than it is. In my heart I feel little—scarcely any doubt of his preference. But there are other points to be considered besides his preferences. He is very far from being independent. What his mother really is we cannot know; but, from Fanny's occasional mention of her conduct and opinions, we have never been disposed to think her amiable. I am very much mistaken if Edward is not himself aware that there would be many difficulties in his way if he were to wish to marry a woman who had neither great fortune nor high rank."

Marianne was astonished to find how much the imagination of her mother and herself had outstripped the truth.

"And you really are not engaged to him?" said she. "Yet it certainly soon will happen. But two advantages will proceed from this delay. *I* shall not lose you so soon, and Edward will have greater opportunity of improving his natural taste for drawing, which must be so indispensably necessary to your future felicity. Oh! If he should be so far stimulated by your abilities as to learn to draw himself, how delightful it would be!"

Elinor had given her real opinion to her sister. She could not consider her partiality for Edward in so good a state as Marianne had believed it. There was, at times, a lack of spirits about him, which, if it did not denote indifference, expressed something almost as unpromising. A doubt of her regard, supposing him to feel it, need not give him more than minor discomfort. It would not be likely to produce that dejection of mind which frequently attended him. A more reasonable cause might be found in his living situation, which kept him from the indulgence of his affection. She knew that his mother neither behaved to him so as to make his home comfortable at present, nor to give him any assurance that he might form a home for himself, without strictly attending to her views for his future. With such a knowledge as this, it was impossible for Elinor to feel easy on the subject. She was far from depending on that result of his preference of her, which her mother and sister still considered as certain. Nay, the longer they were together, the more doubtful seemed the nature of his regard; and sometimes, for a few painful minutes, she believed it to be no more than friendship.

But, whatever might really be its limits, is regard for Elinor was enough, when perceived by his sister, to make her uneasy; and at the same time (which was still more common), to make her uncivil. She took the first opportunity of confronting her mother-in-law, talking to her so expressively of her brother's great expectations, of Mrs. Ferrars's resolution that both her sons should marry well, and of the danger attaching any young woman who attempted to *draw him in*. Mrs. Dashwood could neither pretend to be uncertain of her meaning, nor endeavour to be calm. She gave her an answer which marked her contempt, and instantly left the room, resolving that, whatever might be the inconvenience or expense of so sudden a removal, her beloved Elinor should not be exposed another week to such insinuations.

In this state of her spirits, a letter was delivered to her from the post, which contained a proposal particularly well-timed. It was the offer of a small house, on very reasonable terms, belonging to a relation of her own, a gentleman of consequence and property in Devonshire. The letter was from this gentleman himself, and written in the true spirit of friendly accommodation. He understood that she was in need of a dwelling, and though the house he now offered her was merely a cottage, he assured her that everything should be done to it which she might think necessary, if the idea pleased her. He earnestly encouraged her, after giving the particulars of the house and garden, to come with her daughters to Barton Park, the place of his own residence, from whence she might judge, herself, whether Barton Cottage could be made comfortable to her. He seemed really anxious to accommodate them, and the whole of his letter was written in so friendly a style as could not fail to give pleasure to his cousin. She needed no time for deliberation or inquiry. Her resolution was formed as she read. The situation at Barton, in a county so far distant from Sussex as Devonshire, which, but a few hours before, would have been a sufficient objection to outweigh every possible advantage, was now its saving grace. To leave the neighbourhood of Norland was no longer an evil; it was an object of desire; it was a blessing when compared to the misery of remaining her daughter-in-law's guest. To leave forever that beloved place would be less painful than to inhabit or visit it while such a woman was its mistress. She instantly wrote Sir John Middleton her acknowledgment of his kindness, and her acceptance of his proposal. She then showed both letters to her daughters, so that she might be sure of their approval before the answer was sent.

Elinor had always thought it would be more prudent for them to settle at some distance from Norland than immediately amongst their present acquaintance. On *that* count, therefore, it was not for her to oppose her mother's intention of removing into Devonshire. The house, too, as described by Sir John, was on so simple a scale, and the rent so uncommonly moderate, as to leave her no right of objection on either point. Therefore, though she would miss Edward's company, she made no attempt to dissuade her mother from sending her letter of acceptance.

CHAPTER 5

No sooner was her answer dispatched than Mrs. Dashwood indulged herself in the pleasure of announcing to her son-in-law and his wife that she was planning to move. They heard her with surprise. Mrs. John Dashwood said nothing; but her husband civilly hoped that she would not be settled far from Norland. She had great satisfaction in replying that she was going all the way to Devonshire. Edward turned hastily towards her on hearing this, and in a voice of surprise and concern, which required no explanation to her, repeated, "Devonshire! Are you, indeed, going there? And to what part of it?" She explained the situation. It was within four miles northward of Exeter.

"It is but a cottage," she continued, "but I hope to see many of my friends in it. A room or two can easily be added; and if my friends find no difficulty in travelling so far to see me, I am sure I will find none in accommodating them."

She concluded with a very kind invitation to Mr. and Mrs. John Dashwood to visit her at Barton; and to Edward she gave one with still greater affection. Though her recent conversation with her daughter-in-law had made her resolve on leaving Norland, to separate Edward and Elinor was far from being her object. She wished to show Mrs. John Dashwood by this pointed invitation to her brother how completely she disregarded her disapproval of the match.

Mr. John Dashwood told his mother again and again how exceedingly sorry he was that she had taken a house at such a distance from Norland as to prevent his being of any service to her in moving her furniture. He really felt conscientiously vexed on the occasion; for the only gift he had actually planned to give in fulfillment of his promise to his father was by this arrangement rendered impossible, as the furniture was all sent round by water. It chiefly consisted of household linen, plate, china, and books, with a well-made piano of Marianne's. Mrs. John Dashwood saw the packages depart with a sigh; she could not help feeling it hard that as Mrs. Dashwood's income would be so trifling in comparison with their own, she should have any nice article of furniture.

Mrs. Dashwood took the house for a year; it was ready furnished, and she might have immediate possession. No difficulty arose on either side in the agreement; and she was soon ready to set off for the west. The horses which were left her by her husband had been sold soon after his death, and an opportunity now offering of disposing of her carriage, she agreed to sell that likewise at the earnest advice of her eldest daughter. For the comfort of her children, had she consulted only her own wishes, she would have kept it; but the discretion of Elinor prevailed. *Her* wisdom, too, limited the number of their servants to three; two maids and a man, with whom they were speedily provided from among the staff at Norland.

The man and one of the maids were sent off immediately into Devonshire, to prepare the house for their mistress's arrival. As Lady Middleton was entirely unknown to Mrs. Dashwood, she preferred going directly to the cottage to being a visitor at Barton Park. She relied so completely on Sir John's description of the house, as to feel no curiosity to examine it herself till she entered it as her own. Her eagerness to be gone from Norland was heightened by the evident satisfaction of her daughter-in-law at the prospect of her removal; a satisfaction which was poorly concealed under a cold invitation to her to delay her departure. Now was the time when her son-in-law's promise to his father might with particular propriety be fulfilled. Since he had neglected to do it on first coming to the estate, their leaving his house might be looked on as the most suitable period for it. But Mrs. Dashwood began shortly to give up every hope of the kind, and to be convinced, from the nature of his discourse, that his assistance extended no farther than their maintenance for six months at Norland. He so frequently talked of the increasing expenses of housekeeping, and of the perpetual demands upon his funds, which a man of any importance in the world was beyond calculation exposed to, that he seemed rather to stand in need of more money himself than to have any design of giving it away.

In a very few weeks from the day which brought Sir John Middleton's first letter to Norland, everything was so far settled as to enable Mrs. Dashwood and her daughters to begin their journey.

Many were the tears shed by them in their last goodbyes to a place so much beloved. "Dear, dear Norland!" said Marianne, as she wandered alone before the house, on the last evening of their being there, "when shall I cease to miss you?—when learn to feel at home elsewhere?—Oh happy house! Could you know what I suffer in now viewing you from this spot, from where perhaps I may view you no more!—And you, well-known trees!—but you will continue the same.—No leaf will decay because we are gone, nor any branch become motionless although we can observe you no longer!—No; you will continue the same, unconscious of the pleasure or the regret you cause, and insensible of any change in those who walk under your shade!—But who will remain to enjoy you?"

CHAPTER 6

The first part of their journey was performed in too melancholy a manner to be anything but tedious and unpleasant. As they drew towards the end of it, however, their interest in the appearance of the area they were to inhabit overcame their dejection, and a view of Barton Valley as they entered it gave them cheerfulness. It was a pleasant, fertile spot, well-wooded, and rich in pasture land. After winding along it for more than a mile, they reached their own house. A neat wicket gate admitted them into a small green yard.

As a house, Barton Cottage, though small, was comfortable and compact. A narrow passage led directly through the house into the garden behind. On each side of the entrance was a sitting room, about sixteen feet square; and beyond them were the kitchen, laundry room and stairs. Four bedrooms and two garrets formed the rest of the house. It had not been built many years ago and was in good repair. In comparison to Norland, it was poor and small indeed! But the tears which recollection called forth as they entered the house were soon dried away. They were cheered by the joy of the servants on their arrival, and each for the sake of the others resolved to appear happy. It was very early in September; the season was fine, and from first seeing the place under the advantage of good weather, they received additional impressions in its favour.

High hills rose immediately behind the house, and at no great distance on each side. The village of Barton was chiefly on one of these hills, and formed a pleasant view from the cottage windows.

The view in front was more extensive; it commanded the whole of the valley, and reached into the country beyond.

With the size and furniture of the house Mrs. Dashwood was upon the whole well-satisfied. "It is too small for our family," she said, "but we will make ourselves tolerably comfortable for the present, as it is too late in the year for improvements. Perhaps in the spring, if I have plenty of money, as I dare say I shall, we may think about building an addition. These sitting rooms are both too small for such parties of our friends as I hope to see often collected here. With a new drawing room, which may be easily added, and a bedroom and garret above, it will make a very snug little cottage. I wish the stairs were more elegant. But one must not expect everything; though I suppose it would be no difficult matter to widen them."

In the meantime, till all these alterations could be made from the savings of an income of five hundred a year by a woman who never saved in her life, they were wise enough to be contented with the house as it was. Each of them was busy arranging their particular concerns, and endeavouring, by placing around them their books and other possessions, to make themselves at home. Marianne's piano was unpacked, and Elinor's drawings were affixed to the walls of their sitting room.

In such employments as these they were interrupted soon after breakfast the next day by the entrance of their landlord, who called to welcome them to Barton, and to offer them every accommodation from his own house and garden in which theirs might at present be missing. Sir John Middleton was a good looking man of about forty. He had visited them before, but it was too long ago for his young cousins to remember him. His countenance was thoroughly good-humoured, and his manners were as friendly as the style of his letter. Their arrival seemed to give him real satisfaction, and their comfort was an object of real happiness to him. He said much of his earnest desire of them living on the most sociable terms with his family, and pressed them so cordially to dine at Barton Park every day till they were better settled at home, that they felt obliged to agree. His kindness was not limited to words alone, for within an hour after he left them, a large basket full of garden stuff and fruit arrived from the park, which was followed before the end of the day by a present of game. He insisted, moreover, on conveying all their letters to and from the post for them, and would not be denied the satisfaction of sending them his newspaper every day.

Lady Middleton had sent a very civil message by him, expressing her intention of waiting on Mrs. Dashwood as soon as she could be assured that her visit would be no inconvenience; and as this message was answered by an invitation equally polite, her ladyship was introduced to them the next day.

They were of course very anxious to see a person on whom so much of their comfort at Barton must depend; and the elegance of her appearance was favourable. Lady Middleton was not more than six or seven and twenty; her face was handsome, her figure tall and striking, and her address graceful. Her manners had all the elegance which her husband's lacked. But they would have been improved by some share of his frankness and warmth; for though she was perfectly well-bred, she was reserved, cold, and had nothing to say for herself beyond the most common-place inquiry or remark.

Conversation, however, was not wanted, for Sir John was very chatty, and Lady Middleton had taken the wise precaution of bringing with her their eldest child, a fine little boy about six years old, by which means there was one subject always to be brought up by the ladies in case of extremity. They had to inquire his name and age, and ask him questions, which his mother answered for him, while he hung about her and held down his head, to the great surprise of her ladyship, who wondered at his being so shy before company, as he could make plenty of noise at home. On every formal visit a child ought to be of the party, to provide material for discourse. In the present case it took ten minutes to determine whether the boy was most like his father or mother, and in what particular he resembled either; for of course everybody felt differently, and everybody was astonished at the opinion of the others.

An opportunity was soon to be given to the Dashwoods of debating about the rest of the children, as Sir John would not leave the house without securing their promise of dining at the park the next day.

CHAPTER 7

Barton Park was about half a mile from the cottage. The ladies had passed near it in their way along the valley, but it was screened from their view at home by a hill. The house was large and beautiful, and the Middletons lived in a style of equal hospitality and elegance. The former was for Sir John's gratification, the latter for that of his lady. They were scarcely ever without some friends staying with them in the house, and they kept more company of every kind than any other family in the neighbourhood. Sir John was a sportsman, Lady Middleton a mother. He hunted, and she humoured her children; these were their only pursuits. Lady Middleton had the advantage of being able to spoil her children all year long, while Sir John's were limited by the length of the hunting season. Continual engagements at home and abroad, however, supplied all the deficiencies of nature and education; supported the good spirits of Sir John, and gave exercise to the good-breeding of his wife. Lady Middleton prided herself upon the elegance of her table, and of all her domestic arrangements; and from this kind of vanity was her greatest enjoyment in any social gathering. But Sir John's satisfaction in society was much more real; he delighted in collecting about him more young people than his house would hold, and the noisier they were the happier he was. In summer he was forever forming parties to eat cold ham and chicken out of doors, and in winter his private balls were numerous enough for any but the most eager young lady.

The arrival of a new family in the country was always a matter of joy to him, and in every point of view he was charmed with the inhabitants he had now procured for his cottage at Barton. The Miss Dashwoods were young, pretty, and sincere. It was enough to secure his good opinion. The friendliness of his disposition made him happy in accommodating those whose situation might be considered, in comparison with the past, as unfortunate. In showing kindness to his cousins, therefore, he had the real satisfaction of a good heart; and in settling a family of females only in his cottage, he had brought no hunter who would compete with him for game.

Mrs. Dashwood and her daughters were met at the door of the house by Sir John, who welcomed them to Barton Park with great warmth. As he attended them to the drawing room, he repeated to the young ladies the concern which the same subject had drawn from him the day before, at being unable to get any eligible young men to meet them. They would see, he said, only one gentleman there besides himself; a particular friend who was staying at the park, but who was neither very young nor very lively. He hoped they would all excuse the smallness of the party, and could assure them it should never happen so again. He had been to several families that morning, in hopes of procuring some addition to their number, but everybody was busy. Luckily, Lady Middleton's mother had arrived at Barton within the last hour, and as she was a very cheerful, agreeable woman, he hoped the young ladies would not find it so very dull as they might imagine. The young ladies, as well as their mother, were perfectly satisfied with having two total strangers in the party, and wished for no more.

Mrs. Jennings, Lady Middleton's mother, was a good-humoured, merry, plump, elderly woman, who talked a great deal, seemed very happy, and was rather ill-mannered. She was full of jokes and laughter, and before dinner was over had said many witty things on the subject of lovers and husbands. She hoped they had not left their hearts behind them in Sussex, and pretended to see them blush whether they did or not. Marianne was upset for her sister's sake, and turned her eyes towards Elinor to see how she bore these attacks.

Colonel Brandon, the friend of Sir John, seemed no more suited by resemblance of manner to be his friend than Lady Middleton was to be his wife, or Mrs. Jennings to be Lady Middleton's mother. He was silent and grave. His appearance, however, was not unpleasing, in spite of his being in the opinion of Marianne and Margaret an absolute old bachelor, for he was on the wrong side of thirty-five; but though his face was not handsome, his countenance was pleasing, and his address was particularly gentlemanlike.

There was nothing in any of the party which could recommend them as companions to the Dashwoods; but the coldness of Lady Middleton was rather vexing. She seemed to be roused to enjoyment only by the entrance of her four noisy children after dinner, who pulled her about, tore her clothes, and put an end to every kind of discourse.

In the evening, as Marianne was discovered to be musical, she was invited to play. The instrument was unlocked, everybody prepared to be charmed, and Marianne, who sang very well, at their request went through most of the songs which Lady Middleton had brought into the family on her marriage, and which perhaps had lain ever since in the same position on the piano. Her ladyship had celebrated that event by giving up music, although by her mother's account she had played extremely well, and by her own was very fond of it.

Marianne's performance was highly applauded. Sir John was loud in his admiration at the end of every song, and as loud in his conversation with the others while she played. Lady Middleton frequently called him to order, wondered how anyone's attention could be diverted from music for a moment, and asked Marianne to sing a particular song which Marianne had just finished. Colonel Brandon alone, of all the party, heard her without being in raptures. He paid her only the compliment of attention; and she felt a respect for him on the occasion, which the others had reasonably forfeited by their shameless lack of taste. His pleasure in music, though it amounted not to that delight which alone could sympathize with her own, was estimable when contrasted against the horrible indifference of the others; and she was reasonable enough to allow that a man of five-and-thirty might well have outlived all intensity of feeling and every exquisite power of enjoyment. She was perfectly disposed to make every allowance for the colonel's advanced state of life which humanity required.

CHAPTER 8

Mrs. Jennings was a widow, with an ample income. She had only two daughters, both of whom she had lived to see respectably married, and she had now therefore nothing to do but be a matchmaker for all the rest of the world. In the promotion of this object, she was zealously active, as far as her ability reached, and missed no opportunity of projecting weddings among all the young people of her acquaintance. She was remarkably quick in the discovery of attachments, and had enjoyed the advantage of raising the blushes and the vanity of many a young lady by insinuations of her power over such a young man. This kind of discernment enabled her soon after her arrival at Barton decisively to pronounce that Colonel Brandon was very much in love with Marianne Dashwood. She rather suspected it to be so, on the very first evening of their being together, from his listening so attentively while she sang to them. When the visit was returned by the Middletons dining at the cottage, the fact was ascertained by his listening to her again. It must be so. She was perfectly convinced of it. It would be an excellent match, for *he* was rich and *she* was beautiful. Mrs. Jennings had been anxious to see Colonel Brandon well married ever since her connection with Sir John first brought him to her knowledge, and she was always anxious to get a good husband for every pretty girl.

The immediate advantage to herself was by no means inconsiderable, for it supplied her with endless jokes about them both. At the Park she laughed at the colonel, and in the cottage at Marianne. To the former her raillery was probably, as far as it regarded only himself, perfectly indifferent. But to the latter it was at first incomprehensible; and when it was understood, she hardly knew whether most to laugh at its absurdity, or censure its impoliteness, for she considered it as an unfeeling reflection on the colonel's advanced years, and on his forlorn condition as an old bachelor.

Mrs. Dashwood, who could not think a man five years younger than herself so exceedingly ancient as he appeared to the youthful fancy of her daughter, ventured to clear Mrs. Jennings from the probability of wishing to throw ridicule on his age.

"But at least, mama, you cannot deny the absurdity of the accusation, though you may not think it intentionally ill-natured. Colonel Brandon is certainly younger than Mrs. Jennings, but he is old enough to be *my* father; and if he were ever animated enough to be in love, must have long outlived every sensation of the kind. It is too ridiculous! When is a man to be safe from such wit, if age and infirmity will not protect him?"

"Infirmity!" said Elinor. "Do you call Colonel Brandon infirm? I can easily suppose that his age may appear much greater to you than to my mother; but you can hardly deceive yourself as to his having the use of his limbs."

"Did not you hear him complain of the rheumatism? And is not that the commonest infirmity of declining life?"

"My dearest child," said her mother laughing, "at this rate, you must be in continual terror of *my* decline; and it must seem to you a miracle that my life has been extended to the advanced age of forty."

"Mama, you are not doing me justice. I know very well that Colonel Brandon is not old enough to make his friends yet apprehensive of losing him in the course of nature. He may live twenty years longer. But thirty-five has nothing to do with matrimony."

"Perhaps," said Elinor, "thirty-five and seventeen had better not have anything to do with matrimony together. But if there should by any chance happen to be a woman who is single at twenty-seven, I should not think Colonel Brandon's being thirty-five any objection to his marrying *her*."

"A woman of seven-and-twenty," said Marianne, after pausing a moment, "can never hope to feel or inspire affection again; and if her home be uncomfortable, or her fortune small, I can suppose that she might bring herself to be his nurse, in exchange for the provision and security of being his wife. In his marrying such a woman, therefore, there would be nothing unsuitable. It would be a compact of convenience, and the world would be satisfied. In my eyes it would be no marriage at all, but that would be nothing. To me it would seem only a commercial exchange, in which each wished to be benefited at the expense of the other."

"It would be impossible, I know," replied Elinor, "to convince you that a woman of seven-and-twenty could feel for a man of thirty-five anything near enough to love to make him a desirable companion to her. But I must object to your dooming Colonel Brandon and his wife to the constant confinement of a sick chamber, merely because he chanced to complain yesterday (a very cold damp day) of a slight rheumatic feel in one of his shoulders."

"But he talked of flannel vests," said Marianne, "and with me a flannel vest is invariably connected with the aches, cramps, rheumatisms, and every species of ailment that can afflict the old and the feeble."

"Had he been only in a violent fever, you would not have despised him half so much. Confess, Marianne, is there nothing interesting to you in the flushed cheek, hollow eye, and quick pulse of a fever?"

Soon after this, upon Elinor's leaving the room,

"Mama," said Marianne, "I have an alarm on the subject of illness, which I cannot conceal from you. I am sure Edward Ferrars is not well. We have now been here almost a fortnight, and yet he does not come. Nothing but real indisposition could occasion this extraordinary delay. What else can detain him at Norland?"

"Had you any idea of his coming so soon?" said Mrs. Dashwood. "*I* had none. On the contrary, if I have felt any anxiety at all on the subject, it has been in recollecting that he sometimes showed a lack of pleasure and readiness in accepting my invitation, when I talked of his coming to Barton. Does Elinor expect him already?"

"I have never mentioned it to her; but of course she must."

"I rather think you are mistaken, for when I was talking to her yesterday of getting a new grate for the fireplace in the spare bedchamber, she observed that there was no immediate hurry for it, as it was not likely that the room would be wanted for some time."

"How strange this is! What can be the meaning of it? But the whole of their behaviour to each other has been unaccountable! How cold, how composed were their last goodbyes! How unenthusiastic their conversation the last evening of their being together! In Edward's farewell there was no distinction between Elinor and me: it was the good wishes of an affectionate brother to both. Twice did I leave them purposely together in the course of the last morning, and each time did he most unaccountably follow me out of the room. And Elinor, in leaving Norland and Edward, cried not as I did. Even now her self-command is invariable. When is she dejected or melancholy? When does she try to avoid society, or appear restless and dissatisfied in it?"

CHAPTER 9

The Dashwoods were now comfortably settled at Barton. The house and garden, with all the objects surrounding them, were now familiar; and the ordinary pursuits which had given Norland half its charms, were engaged in again with far greater enjoyment than Norland had been able to afford since the loss of their father. Sir John Middleton, who called on them every day for the first fortnight, and who was not in the habit of spending much time at home, could not conceal his amazement on finding them always busy.

Their visitors, except those from Barton Park, were not many; for, in spite of Sir John's urgent entreaties that they would mix more in the neighbourhood, and repeated assurances of his carriage being always at their service, Mrs. Dashwood declined to visit anyone beyond the distance of a walk.

About a mile and a half from the cottage, along the narrow winding valley of Allenham, the girls had, in one of their earliest walks, discovered an ancient respectable-looking mansion, which, by reminding them a little of Norland, interested their imagination, and made them wish to be better acquainted with it. But they learned, on inquiry, that its possessor, an elderly lady of very good character, was unfortunately too infirm to mix with the world, and never stirred from home.

The whole country about them abounded in beautiful walks. The high downs, which invited them from almost every window of the cottage to seek the exquisite enjoyment of air on their summits, were a happy alternative to walking in the valley. Towards one of these hills did Marianne and Margaret one memorable morning direct their steps, attracted by the partial sunshine of a showery sky, and unable to bear any longer the confinement which the settled rain of the two preceding days had occasioned. The weather was not tempting enough to draw the two others from their pencil and their book, in spite of Marianne's declaration that the day would be lastingly fair, and that every threatening cloud would be drawn off from their hills; so the two girls set off together.

They happily ascended the downs, rejoicing at every glimpse of blue sky, and pitying the fears which had prevented their mother and Elinor from sharing such delightful sensations.

"Is there a felicity in the world," said Marianne, "superior to this? Margaret, we will walk here at least two hours." Margaret agreed, and they pursued their way against the wind, resisting it with laughing delight for about twenty minutes longer, when suddenly the clouds united over their heads, and a driving rain began to fall. Chagrined and surprised, they were obliged, though unwillingly, to turn back, for no shelter was nearer than their own house. One consolation, however, remained for them; it was that of running with all possible speed down the steep side of the hill which led immediately to their garden gate.

They set off. Marianne had at first the advantage, but a false step brought her suddenly to the ground, and Margaret, unable to stop herself to assist her, was involuntarily hurried along, and reached the bottom in safety.

A gentleman carrying a gun, with two dogs playing round him, was passing up the hill and within a few yards of Marianne, when her accident happened. He put down his gun and ran to her assistance. She had raised herself from the ground, but her foot had been twisted in the fall, and she was scarcely able to stand. The gentleman offered his services, taking her up in his arms without farther delay, and carried her down the hill. Then passing through the garden, the gate of which had been left open by Margaret, he brought her directly into the house, where Margaret had just arrived, and seated Marianne in a chair in the parlour.

Elinor and her mother rose up in amazement at their entrance, and while the eyes of both were fixed on him with an evident wonder and a secret admiration which equally sprung from his appearance, he apologized for his intrusion by relating its cause, in a manner so frank and so graceful, that his person, which was uncommonly handsome, received additional charms from his voice and expression. Had he been even old, ugly, and vulgar, the gratitude and kindness of Mrs. Dashwood would have been secured by any act of attention to her child; but the influence of youth, beauty, and elegance, gave an interest to the action which came home to her feelings.

She thanked him again and again; and with a sweetness of address which always attended her, invited him to be seated. But this he declined, as he was dirty and wet. Mrs. Dashwood then begged to know to whom she was obliged. His name, he replied, was Willoughby, and his present home was at Allenham, from whence he hoped she would allow him the honour of calling tomorrow to inquire after Miss Dashwood. The honour was readily granted, and he then departed.

His charms and more than common gracefulness were instantly the theme of general admiration, and the laugh which his gallantry to Marianne raised received particular spirit from his attractiveness. Marianne herself had seen less of his person than the rest, for the confusion which crimsoned over her face, on his lifting her up, had robbed her of the power of looking at him after their entering the house. But she had seen enough of him to join in all the admiration of the others, and with an energy which always adorned her praise. His person and air were equal to what her fancy had always imagined for the hero of a favourite story. Every circumstance belonging to him was interesting. His name was good, and his residence was in their favourite village. Her imagination was busy, her reflections were pleasant, and the pain of a sprained ankle was disregarded.

Sir John called on them as soon as the next interval of fair weather that morning allowed him to get outdoors. Marianne's accident being related to him, he was eagerly asked whether he knew any gentleman of the name of Willoughby at Allenham.

"Willoughby!" cried Sir John; "What, is *he* in the country? That is good news, however; I will ride over tomorrow, and ask him to dinner on Thursday."

"You know him then," said Mrs. Dashwood. "Know him! to be sure I do. Why, he is down here every year."

"And what sort of a young man is he?" "As good a kind of fellow as ever lived, I assure you. A very decent shot, and there is not a bolder rider in England."

"And is *that* all you can say for him?" cried Marianne, indignantly. "But what are his manners on more intimate acquaintance? What of his pursuits, his talents?"

Sir John was rather puzzled.

"Upon my soul," said he, "I do not know much about him as to all *that*. But he is a pleasant, good-humoured fellow, and has got the nicest little black hunting dog I ever saw. Was she out with him today?"

But Marianne could no more satisfy him as to the colour of Mr. Willoughby's dog than he could describe to her the shades of his mind.

"But who is he?" said Elinor. "Where does he come from? Has he a house at Allenham?"

On this point Sir John could give more certain intelligence; and he told them that Mr. Willoughby had no property of his own in the country. He resided there only while he was visiting the old lady at Allenham Court, to whom he was related, and whose possessions he was to inherit; adding, "Yes, yes, he is very well worth catching, I can tell you, Miss Dashwood; he has a pretty little estate of his own in Somersetshire besides; and if I were you, I would not give him up to my younger sister in spite of all this tumbling down hills. Miss Marianne must not expect to have all the men to herself. Brandon will be jealous, if she does not take care."

"I do not believe," said Mrs. Dashwood, with a good-humoured smile, "that Mr. Willoughby will be inconvenienced by the attempts of either of *my* daughters towards what you call *catching him*. It is not an employment to which they have been brought up. Men are very safe with us, let them be ever so rich. I am glad to find, however, from what you say, that he is a respectable young man, and one whose acquaintance will not be ineligible."

"He is as good a sort of fellow, I believe, as ever lived," repeated Sir John. "I remember last Christmas, at a little ball at the Park, he danced from eight o'clock till four, without once sitting down."

"Did he indeed?" cried Marianne, with sparkling eyes, "and with elegance, with spirit?"

"Yes; and he was up again at eight to ride."

"That is what I like; that is what a young man ought to be. Whatever be his pursuits, his eagerness in them should know no moderation, and leave him no sense of fatigue."

"Aye, aye, I see how it will be," said Sir John, "I see how it will be. You will be thinking of Willoughby now. Poor Brandon! He is quite smitten already, and he is very worthy of consideration, I can tell you, in spite of all this tumbling about and spraining of ankles."

CHAPTER 10

Marianne's rescuer, as Margaret decided to call Willoughby, came to the cottage early the next morning to make his personal inquiries. He was received by Mrs. Dashwood with a kindness which Sir John's account of him and her own gratitude prompted. Everything that passed during the visit assured him of the sense, elegance, mutual affection, and domestic comfort of the family to whom accident had now introduced him. Of their personal charms he had not required a second interview to be convinced.

Miss Dashwood had a delicate complexion, regular features, and a remarkably pretty figure. Marianne was still more beautiful. Though shorter, her form was more striking; and her face was so lovely that when she was called a beautiful girl, truth was less violently outraged than usual. Her complexion was somewhat dark, but uncommonly brilliant; her features were all good, her smile was sweet and attractive, and in her eyes, which were very dark, there was a life, a spirit, an eagerness which could hardly be seen without delight. She, in her turn, saw that the perfect good-breeding of the gentleman was further enhanced by frankness and vivacity, and, above all, when she heard him declare that he was passionately fond of music and dancing, she gave him such a look of approval as secured the largest share of his conversation to herself for the rest of his stay.

It was only necessary to mention any favourite amusement to convince her to talk. She could not be silent when such points were introduced, and she had neither shyness nor reserve in their discussion. They speedily discovered that their enjoyment of dancing and music was mutual, and that it arose from a perfect unity of taste in all that related to either. Encouraged by this to a further examination of his opinions, she proceeded to question him on the subject of books. Her favourite authors were brought up and dwelt upon with so rapturous a delight that any young man of five-and-twenty must have been insensible indeed not to become an immediate convert to the excellence of such works, however little he may have thought of them before. Their taste was strikingly alike. The same books, the same passages were idolized by each—or, if any difference appeared, any objection arose, it lasted no longer than till the force of her arguments and the brightness of her eyes could be displayed. He acquiesced in all her decisions, caught all her enthusiasm, and long before his visit concluded, they conversed with the familiarity of long-established friends.

"Well, Marianne," said Elinor, as soon as he had left them, "for *one* morning I think you have done pretty well. You have already ascertained Mr. Willoughby's opinion in almost every matter of importance. You know what he thinks of Cowper and Scott; you are certain of his estimating their powers as he ought, and you have received every assurance of his admiring Pope no more than is proper. But how is your acquaintance to be long supported, under such extraordinary dispatch of every subject for discourse! You will soon have exhausted each favourite topic. Another meeting will suffice to explain his sentiments on picturesque beauty, and second marriages, and then you can have nothing farther to ask—"

"Elinor," cried Marianne, "Is this fair? Is this just? Are my ideas so scanty? But I see what you mean. I have been too much at ease, too happy, too frank. I have been open and sincere where I ought to have been reserved, spiritless, dull, and deceitful. Had I talked only of the weather and the roads, and had I spoken only once in ten minutes, this reproach would have been spared."

"My love," said her mother, "you must not be offended with Elinor—she was only in jest. I should scold her myself, if she were capable of wishing to check the delight of your conversation with our new friend." Marianne was softened in a moment.

Willoughby, on his side, gave every proof of his pleasure in their acquaintance, which an evident wish of improving it could offer. He came to them every day. To inquire after Marianne was at first his excuse; but the increasing warmth of his reception soon made such an excuse unnecessary. Due to her injured ankle she was confined for some days to the house: but never had any confinement been less irksome. Willoughby was a young man of good abilities, quick imagination, lively spirits, and open, affectionate manners. He was exactly designed to engage Marianne's heart; for, with all this, he joined not only a captivating person, but a natural strength of mind, which was now roused and increased by the example of her own, and which recommended him to her affection beyond everything else.

His company gradually became her most exquisite enjoyment. They read, they talked, they sang together; his musical talents were considerable; and he read with all the sensibility and spirit which Edward had unfortunately lacked.

In Mrs. Dashwood's estimation, he was as faultless as in Marianne's; and Elinor saw nothing to censure in him but a tendency to say exactly what he thought on every occasion, without attention to persons or circumstances. In hastily forming and giving his opinion of other people, he displayed a lack of caution which Elinor could not approve, in spite of all that he and Marianne could say in its defence.

Marianne began now to perceive that the desperation which had seized her at sixteen and a half, of ever seeing a man who could satisfy her ideas of perfection, had been rash and unjustifiable. Willoughby was all that all the she could have hoped for, and his behaviour declared his reciprocated interested in her.

Her mother, too, was led before the end of a week to hope and expect their engagement, and secretly to congratulate herself on having gained two such sons-in-law as Edward and Willoughby.

Colonel Brandon's partiality for Marianne, which had so early been discovered by his friends, now first became perceptible to Elinor, when it ceased to be noticed by them. Their attention was occupied by his more fortunate rival; and the teasing which the other had incurred before any partiality arose, was removed when his real feelings began. Elinor was obliged, though unwillingly, to believe that the sentiments which Mrs. Jennings had assigned him for her own satisfaction, were now actually excited by her sister. She saw it with concern; for what could a silent man of five-and-thirty hope, when opposed by a very lively one of five-and-twenty? As she could not even wish him successful, she heartily wished him indifferent. She liked him, and in spite of his gravity and reserve, she beheld in him an object of interest. His manners, though serious, were mild; and his reserve appeared rather the result of some oppression of spirits than of any natural gloominess of temper. Sir John had dropped hints of past injuries and disappointments which justified her belief of his being an unfortunate man, and she regarded him with respect and compassion.

Perhaps she pitied and esteemed him the more because he was slighted by Willoughby and Marianne, who, prejudiced against him for being neither lively nor young, seemed resolved to undervalue his merits.

"Brandon is just the kind of man," said Willoughby one day, when they were talking of him together, "whom everybody speaks well of, and nobody cares about; whom all are delighted to see, and nobody remembers to talk to."

"That is exactly what I think of him," cried Marianne.

"Do not boast of it, however," said Elinor, "for it is injustice in both of you. He is highly esteemed by all the family at the Park, and I never see him myself without taking pains to converse with him."

"That he is patronized by *you*," replied Willoughby, "is certainly in his favour; but as for the esteem of the others, it is a reproach in itself. Who would submit to the indignity of being approved by such women as Lady Middleton and Mrs. Jennings, that could command the indifference of anybody else?"

"But perhaps the abuse of such people as yourself and Marianne will make amends for the regard of Lady Middleton and her mother. If their praise is an insult, your insults may be praise; for they are not more undiscerning than you are prejudiced and unjust."

"This is a warm defence indeed."

"He is a sensible man; and sense will always have attraction for me. Yes, Marianne, even in a man between thirty and forty. He has seen a great deal of the world; has been abroad, has read, and has a thinking mind. I have found him capable of giving me much information on various subjects, and he has always answered my inquiries with the readiness of good-breeding and good nature."

"That is to say," cried Marianne contemptuously, "he has told you that in the East Indies the climate is hot, and the mosquitoes are troublesome."

"He *would* have told me so, I doubt not, had I made any such inquiries; but they happened to be points on which I had been previously informed. Why, Mr. Willoughby, should you dislike him so?"

"I do not dislike him. I consider him, on the contrary, to be a very respectable man, who has everybody's good word and nobody's notice; who has more money than he can spend, more time than he knows how to employ, and two new coats every year."

"Add to which," cried Marianne, "that he has neither ability, taste, nor spirit. That his understanding has no brilliancy, his feelings no strength, and his voice no expression."

"You seem to know him so well," replied Elinor, "that the defence I am able to give of him is comparatively cold. I can only pronounce him to be a sensible man, well-bred, well-informed, of gentle address, and, I believe, possessing an amiable heart."

"Miss Dashwood," cried Willoughby, "you are now using me unkindly. You are endeavouring to disarm me by reason, and to convince me against my will. But it will not do. You shall find me as stubborn as you can be artful. I have two unquestionable reasons for disliking Colonel Brandon: he has told me it will rain when I wanted it to be fine, and I cannot persuade him to buy my brown mare. If it will be any satisfaction to you, however, to be told that I believe his character to be in other respects irreproachable, I am ready to confess it. And in return for an acknowledgment, which must give me some pain, you cannot deny me the privilege of disliking him as much as ever."

CHAPTER 11

Little had Mrs. Dashwood or her daughters imagined, when they first came into Devonshire, that so many invitations would arrive to occupy their time as shortly presented themselves. Yet such was the case. When Marianne had recovered, the schemes of amusement at home and abroad, which Sir John had been previously forming, were put in execution. The private balls at the Park then began; and parties on the water were made and accomplished as often as a rainy October would allow. In every meeting of the kind, Willoughby was included; and the ease and familiarity which naturally attended these parties were exactly calculated to increase his acquaintance with the Dashwoods. They afforded him the opportunity of witnessing the excellencies of Marianne, of expressing his animated admiration of her, and of receiving, in her behaviour to himself, the most pointed assurance of her affection.

Elinor could not be surprised at their attachment. She only wished that it were less openly shown, and once or twice did venture to suggest the propriety of some self-command to Marianne. But Marianne abhorred all concealment. To restrain her sentiments appeared to her not merely an unnecessary effort, but a disgraceful subjection of reason to common-place and mistaken notions. Willoughby thought the same; and their behaviour, at all times, was an illustration of their opinions.

When he was present, she had no eyes for anyone else. Everything he did was right. Everything he said was clever. If their evenings at the park were concluded with cards, he cheated himself and all the rest of the party to get her a good hand. If dancing formed the amusement of the night, they were partners for half the time; and when obliged to separate for a couple of dances, were careful to stand together and scarcely spoke a word to anybody else. Such conduct made them of course most exceedingly laughed at; but ridicule could not shame, and seemed hardly to provoke them.

Mrs. Dashwood approved of all their feelings with a warmth which left her no inclination for checking this excessive display of them. To her it was but the natural consequence of strong affection on a young mind.

This was the season of happiness to Marianne. Her heart was devoted to Willoughby, and the fond attachment to Norland which she brought with her from Sussex, was more likely to be softened than she had thought it possible before, by the charms which his company bestowed on her present home.

Elinor's happiness was not so great. Her heart was not so much at ease, nor her satisfaction in their amusements so pure. They afforded her no companion that could make amends for what she had left behind, nor that could teach her to think of Norland with less regret than ever. Neither Lady Middleton nor Mrs. Jennings could supply to her the conversation she missed; although the latter was an everlasting talker, and from the first had regarded her with a kindness which ensured her a large share of her attentions. She had already repeated her own history to Elinor three or four times; and had Elinor's memory been better, she might have known very early in their acquaintance, all the particulars of Mr. Jennings's last illness, and what he said to his wife a few minutes before he died. Lady Middleton was more agreeable than her mother, only in being more silent. Towards her husband and mother she was the same as to them; and intimacy was therefore neither to be looked for nor desired. She had nothing to say one day that she had not said the day before. Though she did not oppose the parties arranged by her husband, provided everything were conducted in style and her two eldest children joined her, she never appeared to receive more enjoyment from them, than she might have experienced in sitting at home. So little did her presence add to the pleasure of the others, by any share in their conversation, that they were sometimes only reminded of her being among them by her attentions to her troublesome boys.

In Colonel Brandon alone, of all her new acquaintance, did Elinor find a person who could in any degree claim the respect of abilities, excite the interest of friendship, or give pleasure as a companion. Willoughby was out of the question. Her admiration and regard, even her sisterly regard, was all his own; but he was a lover, and his attentions were wholly Marianne's. A far less agreeable man might have been more generally pleasing. Colonel Brandon, unfortunately for himself, had no such encouragement to think only of Marianne, and in conversing with Elinor, he found the greatest consolation for the total indifference of her sister.

Elinor's compassion for him increased, as she had reason to suspect that the misery of disappointed love had already been known by him. This suspicion was given by some words which accidentally dropped from him one evening at the Park, when they were sitting and resting while the others were dancing. His eyes were fixed on Marianne, and, after a silence of some minutes, he said with a faint smile, "Your sister, I understand, does not approve of second attachments. Or rather, as I believe, she considers them impossible to exist."

"I believe that is the case. But how she can feel that way without reflecting on the character of her own father, who had himself two wives, I know not. A few years, however, will settle her opinions on the reasonable basis of common sense and observation."

"This will probably be the case," he replied; "and yet there is something so amiable in the prejudices of a young mind, that one is sorry to see them give way to the reception of more general opinions."

"I cannot agree with you there," said Elinor. "There are inconveniences attending such feelings as Marianne's, which all the charms of enthusiasm and ignorance of the world cannot atone for. Her views regularly cause her to set aside propriety; and a better acquaintance with the world is what I look forward to as her greatest possible advantage."

After a short pause, he resumed the conversation by saying—

"Does your sister make no distinction in her objections against a second attachment? Or is it equally criminal in everybody? Are those who have been disappointed in their first choice to be equally indifferent during the rest of their lives?"

"Upon my word, I am not acquainted with the minutia of her principles. I only know that I never yet heard her admit any instance of a second attachment's being pardonable."

"I once knew a lady who in temper and mind greatly resembled your sister, who thought and judged like her, but who from an enforced change—from a series of unfortunate circumstances—" Here he stopped suddenly; appeared to think that he had said too much, and by his countenance gave rise to conjectures which might not otherwise have entered Elinor's head. The lady would probably have passed without suspicion, had he not convinced Miss Dashwood that what concerned her ought not to escape his lips. As it was, it required little effort to connect his emotion with the tender recollection of past regard. Elinor attempted no more. But Marianne, in her place, would not have done so little. The whole story would have been speedily formed under her active imagination, and everything established in the most melancholy order of disastrous love.

CHAPTER 12

As Elinor and Marianne were walking together the next morning the latter communicated a piece of news to her sister, which, in spite of all that she knew before of Marianne's complete lack of practicality, still surprised her. Marianne told her, with the greatest delight, that Willoughby had given her a horse, one that he had bred himself on his estate in Somersetshire, and which had a delightful temperament. Without considering that it was not in her mother's plan to keep any horse—that they simply could not afford to care for it—she had accepted the present without hesitation, and told her sister of it in raptures.

"He intends to send his groom into Somersetshire immediately for it," she added, "and when it arrives, we will ride every day. You shall share its use with me. Imagine to yourself, my dear Elinor, the delight of a gallop on some of these downs."

Most unwilling was she to awaken from such a dream of felicity, to comprehend all the unhappy truths which attended the affair, and for some time she refused to submit to them. As to an additional servant to care for the horse, the expense would be a trifle; mama, she was sure, would never object to it. As to a stable, the merest shed would be sufficient. Elinor then ventured to doubt the propriety of her receiving such a present from a man so little, or at least so recently, known to her. This was too much.

"You are mistaken, Elinor," said she warmly, "in supposing I know very little of Willoughby. I have not known him long indeed, but I am much better acquainted with him than I am with any other creature in the world, except yourself and mama. It is not time or opportunity that is to determine intimacy; it is disposition alone. Seven years would be insufficient to make some people acquainted with each other, and seven days are more than enough for others. I should hold myself guilty of greater impropriety in accepting a horse from my brother than from Willoughby. Of John I know very little, though we have lived together for years; but of Willoughby my judgment has long been formed."

Elinor thought it wisest to discuss that point no more. She knew her sister's temper. Opposition on so tender a subject would only attach her more firmly to her own opinion. But by an appeal to her affection for her mother, by representing the inconveniences which that indulgent mother must draw on herself, if (as would probably be the case) she consented to this, Marianne was shortly subdued; and she promised not to tempt her mother to such imprudent kindness by mentioning the offer, and to tell Willoughby when she saw him next that it must be declined.

She was faithful to her word; and when Willoughby called at the cottage the same day, Elinor heard her express her disappointment to him in a low voice, on being obliged to forego the acceptance of his present. The reasons for this alteration were at the same time related, and they were such as to make further entreaty on his side impossible. His concern however was very apparent; and after expressing it with earnestness, he added in the same low voice— "But, Marianne, the horse is still yours, though you cannot use it now. I shall keep it only till you can claim it. When you leave Barton to form your own establishment in a more lasting home, you shall have your horse."

This was all overheard by Miss Dashwood; and in the whole of the sentence, in his manner of pronouncing it, and in his speaking to her sister by her Christian name alone, she instantly saw an intimacy so decided, a meaning so direct, as marked a perfect agreement between them. From that moment, she had no doubt that they were engaged to each other; and the belief of it created no other surprise than that she, or any of their friends, should be left by tempers so frank to discover it by accident.

Margaret related something to her the next day, which placed this matter in a still clearer light. Willoughby had spent the preceding evening with them, and Margaret, being left some time in the parlour with only him and Marianne, had observed something which she communicated to her eldest sister, when they were alone.

"Oh! Elinor," she cried, "I have such a secret to tell you about Marianne. I am sure she will be married to Mr. Willoughby very soon."

"You have said so," replied Elinor, "almost every day since they first met on High-church Down; and they had not known each other a week, I believe, before you were certain that Marianne wore his picture round her neck; but it turned out to be only the miniature of our great uncle."

"But indeed this is quite another thing. I am sure they will be married very soon, for he has got a lock of her hair."

"Take care, Margaret. It may be only the hair of some great uncle of *his*."

"But indeed, Elinor, it is Marianne's. I am almost sure it is, for I saw him cut it off. Last night after tea, when you and mama went out of the room, they were whispering and talking together as fast as could be, and he seemed to be begging something of her, and presently he took up her scissors and cut off a long lock of her hair, for it was all tumbled down her back; and he kissed it, and folded it up in a piece of white paper, and put it into his pocket-book."

With such particulars, stated with such authority, Elinor could not disagree. It was supported by everything she had heard and seen herself.

Margaret's wisdom was not always displayed in a way so satisfactory to her sister. When Mrs. Jennings attacked her one evening at the Park, to give the name of the young man who was Elinor's particular favourite, which had been long a matter of great curiosity to her, Margaret answered by looking at her sister, and saying, "May I tell her, Elinor?"

This of course made everybody laugh; and Elinor tried to laugh too. But the effort was painful. She was convinced that Margaret had fixed on a person, whose name she could not bear with composure to become a standing joke with Mrs. Jennings. Marianne felt for her most sincerely; but she did more harm than good to the cause, by turning very red, and saying in an angry manner to Margaret—

"Remember that whatever your guesses may be, you have no right to repeat them."

"I never had any guesses about it," replied Margaret; "it was you who told me of it yourself."

This increased the mirth of the company, and Margaret was eagerly pressed to say something more.

"Oh! Pray, Miss Margaret, let us know all about it," said Mrs. Jennings. "What is the gentleman's name?"

"I must not tell, ma'am. But I know very well what it is; and I know where he is, too."

"Yes, yes, we can guess where he is; at his own house at Norland to be sure. He is the curate of the parish I dare say."

"No, *that* he is not. He has no profession at all."

"Margaret," said Marianne, with great warmth, "you know that all this is an invention of your own, and that there is no such person in existence."

"Well, then, he is lately dead, Marianne, for I am sure there was such a man once, and his name begins with an E."

Most grateful did Elinor feel to Lady Middleton for observing at this moment, "that it rained very hard," though she believed the interruption to proceed less from any attention to her, than from her ladyship's great dislike of the inelegant teasing that delighted her husband and mother. Colonel Brandon, who was on every occasion mindful of the feelings of others, responded to her; and much was said on the subject of rain by both of them. Willoughby opened the piano, and asked Marianne to sit down to it; and thus, amidst the various endeavours of different people to drop the subject, it fell to the ground. But not so easily did Elinor recover from the alarm into which it had thrown her.

A party was formed this evening for going on the following day to see a very fine place about twelve miles from Barton, belonging to a brother-in-law of Colonel Brandon. The grounds were declared to be highly beautiful, and Sir John, who was particularly warm in their praise, might be allowed to be a tolerable judge, for he had formed parties to visit them at least twice every summer for the last ten years. They contained a noble piece of water; a sail on which was to form a great part of the morning's amusement, Cold provisions were to be taken, open carriages only to be employed, and everything conducted in the usual style of a complete party of pleasure.

To some few of the company, it appeared rather a bold undertaking, considering the time of year, and that it had rained every day for the last fortnight. Mrs. Dashwood, who already had a cold, was persuaded by Elinor to stay at home.

CHAPTER 13

Their intended excursion to Whitwell turned out very differently from what Elinor had expected. She was prepared to be wet through, fatigued, and frightened; but the event was still more unfortunate, for they did not go at all.

By ten o'clock the whole party were assembled at the Park, where they were to eat breakfast. The morning was rather favourable, though it had rained all night, as the clouds were then dispersing across the sky, and the sun frequently appeared. They were all in high spirits and good humour, determined to submit to the greatest inconveniences and hardships rather than be otherwise.

While they were at breakfast the letters were brought in. Among the rest there was one for Colonel Brandon. He took it, saw who it was from, changed colour, and immediately left the room.

"What is the matter with Brandon?" said Sir John.

Nobody knew.

"I hope he has not received any bad news," said Lady Middleton. "It must be something extraordinary that could make Colonel Brandon leave my breakfast table so suddenly."

In about five minutes he returned.

"No bad news, Colonel, I hope?" said Mrs. Jennings, as soon as he entered the room.

"None at all, ma'am, I thank you."

"Was it from Avignon? I hope it is not to say that your sister is worse."

"No, ma'am. It came from town, and is merely a letter of business."

"But how did it discompose you so much, if it was only a letter of business? Come, come, this won't do, Colonel; let us hear the truth of it."

"My dear madam," said Lady Middleton, "think of what you are saying."

"Perhaps it is to tell you that your cousin Fanny is married?" said Mrs. Jennings, ignoring her daughter's reproof.

"No, indeed, it is not."

"Well, then, I know who it is from, Colonel. And I hope she is well."

"Whom do you mean, ma'am?" said he, colouring a little.

"Oh! You know who I mean."

"I am particularly sorry, ma'am," said he, addressing Lady Middleton, "that I should receive this letter today, for it is on business which requires me to leave immediately for London."

"London!" cried Mrs. Jennings. "What can you have to do in town at this time of year?"

"My own loss is great," he continued, "in being obliged to leave so agreeable a party; but I am the more concerned, as I fear my presence is necessary to gain your admittance at Whitwell."

What a blow to them all this was!

"But if you write a note to the housekeeper, Mr. Brandon," said Marianne eagerly, "will it not be sufficient?"

He shook his head.

"We must go," said Sir John. "You cannot go to town till tomorrow, Brandon, that is all."

"I wish it could be so easily settled. But it is not in my power to delay my journey for one day!"

"If you would but let us know what your business is," said Mrs. Jennings, "we might see whether it could be put off or not."

"You would not be six hours later," said Willoughby, "if you were to defer your journey till our return."

"I cannot afford to lose *one* hour."

Elinor then heard Willoughby say in a low voice to Marianne, "There are some people who cannot bear a party of pleasure. Brandon is one of them. He was afraid of catching cold, I dare say, and invented this trick for getting out of it. I would bet fifty pounds the letter was of his own writing."

"I have no doubt of it," replied Marianne.

"There is no persuading you to change your mind," said Sir John, "when you are determined. But I hope you will think better of it. Consider, here are the two Miss Careys come over from Newton, the three Miss Dashwoods walked up from the cottage, and Mr. Willoughby got up two hours before his usual time, on purpose to go to Whitwell."

Colonel Brandon again repeated his sorrow at being the cause of disappointing the party, but at the same time declared it to be unavoidable.

"Well then, when will you come back again?"

"I hope we shall see you at Barton," added her ladyship, "as soon as you can conveniently leave town; and we must put off the party to Whitwell tell you return."

"You are very obliging. But it is so uncertain, when I may have it in my power to return, that I dare not make any commitment."

"Oh! He must and shall come back," cried Sir John. "If he is not here by the end of the week, I shall go after him."

"Aye, so do, Sir John," cried Mrs. Jennings, "and then perhaps you may find out what his business is."

"I do not want to pry into other men's concerns. I suppose it is something he is ashamed of."

Colonel Brandon's horses were announced.

"You are not going to town on horseback, are you?" added Sir John.

"Only to Honiton. I shall then go post."

"Well, as you are resolved to go, I wish you a good journey. But I think it would be much better if you changed your mind."

"I assure you it is not in my power."

He then took leave of the whole party.

"Is there no chance of my seeing you and your sisters in town this winter, Miss Dashwood?"

"None at all, I am afraid."

"Then I must bid you farewell for a longer time than I should wish to do."

To Marianne, he merely bowed and said nothing.

"Come, Colonel," said Mrs. Jennings, "before you go, do let us know what you are going about."

He wished her a good morning, and attended by Sir John, left the room.

The complaints and lamentations which politeness had hitherto restrained, now burst forth universally; and they all agreed again and again how provoking it was to be so disappointed.

"I can guess what his business is, however," said Mrs. Jennings exultingly.

"Can you, ma'am?" said almost everybody.

"Yes; it is about Miss Williams, I am sure."

"And who is Miss Williams?" asked Marianne.

"What! Do not you know who Miss Williams is? I am sure you must have heard of her before. She is a relation of the Colonel's, my dear—a very near relation. We will not say how near, for fear of shocking the young ladies." Then lowering her voice a little, she said to Elinor, "She is his illegitimate daughter."

"Indeed!"

"Oh! Yes; and as like him as she can be. I dare say the Colonel will leave her all his fortune."

When Sir John returned, he joined most heartily in the general regret on so unfortunate an event; concluding, however, by observing that as they were all together, they must do something enjoyable. After some consultation, it was agreed that although nothing could replace the joy that Whitwell would have brought them, they might procure a tolerable composure of mind by driving about the country. The carriages were then ordered; Willoughby's was first, and Marianne never looked happier than when she got into it. He drove through the park very fast, and they were soon out of sight. Nothing more of them was seen till their return, which did not happen till after the return of all the rest. They both seemed delighted with their drive, but said only in general terms that they had kept in the lanes, while the others went on the downs.

It was settled that there should be a dance in the evening, and that everybody should be extremely merry all day long. Some more of the Careys came to dinner, and they had the pleasure of dining with nearly people, which Sir John observed with great contentment. Willoughby took his usual place between the two elder Miss Dashwoods, and Mrs. Jennings sat on Elinor's right hand. They had not been long seated before she leaned behind her and Willoughby, and said to Marianne, loud enough for them both to hear, "I have found you out in spite of all your tricks. I know where you spent the morning."

Marianne coloured, and replied very hastily, "Where, pray?"

"Did not you know," said Willoughby, "that we had been out in my carriage?"

"Yes, yes, I know that very well, and I was determined to find out *where* you had been to in your carriage. I hope you like your house, Miss Marianne. It is a very large one I know, and when I come to see you, I hope you will have new furniture, for it is very much needed. At least it was when I was there six years ago."

Marianne turned away in great confusion. Mrs. Jennings laughed heartily; and Elinor found that in her resolution to know where they had been, she had actually made her own servant enquire of Mr. Willoughby's groom, and that she had by that method been informed that they had gone to Allenham, and spent a considerable time there walking about the garden and going all over the house.

Elinor could hardly believe this to be true, as it seemed very unlikely that Willoughby should propose, or Marianne consent, to enter the house while Mrs. Smith was in it, with whom Marianne had not the smallest acquaintance.

As soon as they left the dining room, Elinor enquired of her about it; and great was her surprise when she found that every circumstance related by Mrs. Jennings was perfectly true. Marianne was quite angry with her for doubting it.

"Why should you imagine, Elinor, that we did not go there, or that we did not see the house? Is not it what you have often wished to do yourself?"

"Yes, Marianne, but I would not go while Mrs. Smith was there, and with no other companion than Mr. Willoughby."

"Mr. Willoughby, however, is the only person who can have a right to show that house; and as we went in a two-seated carriage, it was impossible to have any other companion. I never spent a pleasanter morning in my life."

"I am afraid," replied Elinor, "that the pleasantness of an employment does not always correspond with its propriety."

"On the contrary, nothing can be a stronger proof of it, Elinor; for if there had been any real impropriety in what I did, I should have been sensible of it at the time, for we always know when we are acting wrong, and with such a conviction I could have had no pleasure."

"But, my dear Marianne, as it has already exposed you to some very impertinent remarks, do you not now begin to doubt the discretion of your own conduct?"

"If the impertinent remarks of Mrs. Jennings are to be the proof of impropriety in conduct, we are all offending every moment of our lives. I do not value her censure any more than her praise. I am not sensible of having done anything wrong in walking over Mrs. Smith's grounds, or in seeing her house. They will one day be Mr. Willoughby's, and—"

"If they were one day to be your own, Marianne, you would not be justified in what you have done."

She blushed at this hint, but it was even visibly gratifying to her. After ten minutes of earnest thought, she came to her sister again, and said with good humour, "Perhaps, Elinor, it *was* rather ill-judged in me to go to Allenham; but Mr. Willoughby wanted particularly to show me the place, and it is a charming house I assure you. There is one remarkably pretty sitting room upstairs; of a nice comfortable size for constant use, and with modern furniture it would be delightful. It is a corner room, and has windows on two sides. On one side you look across the lawn, behind the house, to a beautiful wood, and on the other you have a view of the church and village, and, beyond them, of those fine bold hills that we have so often admired. I did not see it to advantage, for nothing could be more forlorn than the furniture—but if it were newly fitted up—a couple hundred pounds, Willoughby says, would make it one of the pleasantest summer-rooms in England."

Could Elinor have listened to her without interruption from the others, she would have described every room in the house with equal delight.

CHAPTER 14

concealing its cause, filled the mind and sparked the curiosity of Mrs. Jennings for two or three days. She was greatly curious, as everyone must be who takes a very lively interest in all the comings and goings of all their acquaintance. She wondered without pause what could be the reason of it; was sure there must be some bad news, and thought over every kind of distress that could have befallen him, with a fixed determination that he should not escape them all.

"Something very melancholy must be the matter, I am sure," she said. "I could see it in his face. Poor man! I am afraid his circumstances may be bad. The estate at Delaford was never worth more than two thousand a year, and his brother was in quite a lot of debt prior to his passing. I do think he must have been sent for about money matters, for what else can it be? I wonder whether it is so. I would give anything to know the truth of it. Perhaps it is about Miss Williams—and, by the bye, I dare say it is, because he looked so self-conscious when I mentioned her. Maybe she is ill in town; nothing in the world more likely, for I have a notion she is always rather sickly. I would lay any wager it is about Miss Williams. It is not so very likely he should be distressed in his financial circumstances *now*, for he is a very prudent man, and to be sure must have paid the debts of the estate by this time. I wonder what it can be! Maybe his sister is worse at Avignon, and has sent for him. His setting off in such a hurry seems to indicate it. Well, I wish him out of all his trouble with all my heart, and a good wife into the bargain."

So wondered, so talked Mrs. Jennings; her opinion varying with every fresh conjecture, and all seeming equally probable as they arose. Elinor, though she felt really interested in the welfare of Colonel Brandon, could not bestow all the wonder on his going so suddenly away, which Mrs. Jennings was desirous of her feeling. Besides that the circumstance did not in her opinion justify such lasting amazement or variety of speculation, her curiosity was otherwise occupied. It was engrossed by the extraordinary silence of her sister and Willoughby on the subject of their engagement. As this silence continued, every day made it appear more strange and more incompatible with the disposition of both. Why they did not openly acknowledge to her mother and herself what their constant behaviour to each other declared to have taken place, Elinor could not imagine.

She could easily conceive that marriage might not be immediately in their power; for though Willoughby was independent, there was no reason to believe him rich. His estate had been rated by Sir John at about six or seven hundred a year; but he lived an expensive lifestyle, and he had himself often complained of his poverty. This strange kind of secrecy maintained by them relative to their engagement made no sense, and contradicted their general beliefs about sincerity, openness and honesty. Sometimes she thought that perhaps they were not engaged, though they certainly behaved as if they were. This doubt was enough to prevent her making any inquiry of Marianne.

Nothing could be more expressive of attachment to them all than Willoughby's behaviour. To Marianne it had all the distinguishing tenderness which a lover's heart could give, and to the rest of the family it was the affectionate attention of a son and a brother. The cottage seemed to be considered and loved by him as his home; many more of his hours were spent there than at Allenham. If no general engagement collected them at the park, the exercise which called him out in the morning was almost certain of ending with a visit to the Dashwoods, where the rest of the day was spent by himself at the side of Marianne, and by his favourite pointer at her feet.

One evening in particular, about a week after Colonel Brandon had left the country, his heart seemed more than usually open to every feeling of attachment to the objects around him. On Mrs. Dashwood's happening to mention her design of improving the cottage in the spring, he warmly opposed every alteration of a place which affection had established as perfect with him.

"What!" he exclaimed—"Improve this dear cottage! No—*that* I will never consent to. Not a stone must be added to its walls, not an inch to its size, if my feelings are regarded."

"Do not be alarmed," said Miss Dashwood, "nothing of the kind will be done; for my mother will never have money enough to attempt it."

"I am heartily glad of it," he cried. "May she always be poor, if she can employ her riches no better."

"Thank you, Willoughby. But you may be assured that I would not sacrifice one sentiment of local attachment of yours, or of anyone whom I loved, for all the improvements in the world. Depend upon it that whatever unemployed sum may remain, when I make up my accounts in the spring, I would even rather lay it uselessly by than dispose of it in a manner so painful to you. But are you really so attached to this place as to see no defect in it?"

"I am," said he. "To me it is faultless. Nay, more, I consider it as the only form of building in which happiness is attainable, and were I rich enough, I would instantly pull Combe down, and build it up again in the exact plan of this cottage."

"With dark narrow stairs, and a kitchen filled with smoke, I suppose," said Elinor.

"Yes," cried he in the same eager tone, "with all and everything belonging to it. Then, and then only, under such a roof, I might perhaps be as happy at Combe as I have been at Barton."

"I flatter myself," replied Elinor, "that even under the disadvantage of better rooms and a broader staircase, you will hereafter find your own house as faultless as you now do this one."

"There certainly are circumstances," said Willoughby, "which might greatly endear it to me; but this place will always have one claim on my affection, which no other can possibly share."

Mrs. Dashwood looked with pleasure at Marianne, whose fine eyes were fixed so expressively on Willoughby, as plainly denoted how well she understood him.

"How often did I wish," added he, "when I was at Allenham this time last year, that Barton Cottage were inhabited! I never passed within view of it without admiring it, and grieving that no one lived there. How little did I then think that the very first news I should hear from Mrs. Smith, when I next came into the country, would be that Barton cottage was taken! I felt an immediate satisfaction and interest in the event, which nothing but a kind of foreknowledge of what happiness I should experience from it, can account for. Must it not have been so Marianne?" speaking to her in a lowered voice. Then continuing his former tone, he said, "And yet this house you would spoil, Mrs. Dashwood! You would rob it of its simplicity by imaginary improvement! This dear parlour, in which our acquaintance first began, and in which so many happy hours have been since spent by us together, you would degrade to the condition of a common entrance, and everybody would be eager to pass through the room which has hitherto contained within itself more real accommodation and comfort than any other apartment containing whatever luxuries it might could possibly afford."

Mrs. Dashwood again assured him that no alteration of the kind should be attempted.

"You are a good woman," he warmly replied. "Your promise eases my concerns. Extend it a little farther, and it will make me happy. Tell me that not only your house will remain the same, but that I shall ever find you and yours as unchanged as your dwelling; and that you will always consider me with the kindness which has made everything belonging to you so dear to me."

The promise was readily given, and Willoughby's behaviour during the whole of the evening declared at once his affection and happiness.

"Shall we see you tomorrow to dinner?" said Mrs. Dashwood, when he was leaving them. "I do not ask you to come in the morning, for we must walk to the park, to call on Lady Middleton."

He promised to be with them by four o'clock.

CHAPTER 15

Mrs. Dashwood's visit to Lady Middleton took place the next day, and two of her daughters went with her; but Marianne excused herself from being of the party under some trifling pretext of employment. Her mother, who concluded that a promise had been made by Willoughby the night before of calling on her while they were absent, was perfectly satisfied with her remaining at home.

On their return from the park they found Willoughby's carriage and servant in waiting at the cottage, and Mrs. Dashwood was convinced that she had guessed correctly. So far it was all as she had foreseen; but on entering the house, she beheld what no foresight had taught her to expect. They were no sooner in the passage than Marianne came hastily out of the parlour, apparently in violent affliction, with her handkerchief at her eyes; and without noticing them ran upstairs. Surprised and alarmed, they proceeded directly into the room she had just left where they found only Willoughby, who was leaning against the mantle with his back towards them. He turned round on their coming in, and his countenance showed that he felt the same emotion which had overpowered Marianne.

"Is anything the matter with her?" cried Mrs. Dashwood as she entered. "Is she ill?"

"I hope not," he replied, trying to look cheerful; and with a forced smile, presently added, "It is I who may rather expect to be ill—for I am now suffering under a very heavy disappointment!"

"Disappointment!"

"Yes, for I am unable to keep my engagement with you. Mrs. Smith has this morning exercised her influence over me, by sending me on business to London. I must comply with her wishes if I am to receive my inheritance. I have taken my farewell of Allenham; and I am now come to take my farewell of you."

"To London! Are you going this morning?"

"Almost this moment."

"This is very unfortunate. But Mrs. Smith must be answered—and her business will not detain you from us long I hope."

He coloured as he replied, "You are very kind, but I have no plans to return to Devonshire anytime soon. My visits to Mrs. Smith are never repeated within the year."

"And is Mrs. Smith your only friend? Is Allenham the only house in the neighbourhood to which you will be welcome? For shame, Willoughby. You know you will always be welcome here."

His colour increased; and with his eyes fixed on the ground he only replied, "You are too good."

Mrs. Dashwood looked at Elinor with surprise. Elinor felt equal amazement. For a few moments everyone was silent. Mrs. Dashwood spoke first.

"I have only to add, my dear Willoughby, that at Barton cottage you will always be welcome; for I will not press you to return here immediately, because you only can judge how far *that* might be pleasing to Mrs. Smith."

"My engagements at present," replied Willoughby confusedly, "are of such a nature that—I dare not flatter myself—"

He stopped. Mrs. Dashwood was too much astonished to speak, and another pause succeeded. This was broken by Willoughby, who said with a faint smile, "It is folly to linger in this manner. I will not torment myself any longer by remaining among friends whose society it is impossible for me now to enjoy."

He then hastily took leave of them all and left the room. They saw him step into his carriage, and in a minute it was out of sight.

Mrs. Dashwood felt too much for speech, and instantly left the parlour, to give way in solitude to the concern and alarm which this sudden departure occasioned.

Elinor's uneasiness was at least equal to her mother's. She thought of what had just passed with anxiety and distrust. Willoughby's behaviour in taking leave of them, his embarrassment and false cheerfulness, and, above all, his unwillingness to accept her mother's invitation, greatly disturbed her. One moment she feared that no serious attachment had ever been formed on his side; and the next that some unfortunate quarrel had taken place between him and her sister. The distress in which Marianne had quitted the room was such as a serious quarrel could most reasonably account for, though when she considered what Marianne's love for him was, a quarrel seemed almost impossible.

But whatever might be the particulars of their separation, her sister's affliction could not be doubted. She thought with the tenderest compassion of that violent sorrow which Marianne was in all probability not merely giving way to as a relief, but feeding and encouraging as a duty.

In about half an hour her mother returned, and though her eyes were red, her countenance was not uncheerful.

"Our dear Willoughby is now some miles from Barton, Elinor," said she, as she sat down to work, "and with how heavy a heart does he travel?"

"It is all very strange. So suddenly to be gone! It seems but the work of a moment. And last night he was with us so happy, so cheerful, so affectionate. Now after only ten minutes' notice—gone too without intending to return? Something more than what he told us must have happened. He did not speak, he did not behave like himself. *You* must have seen the difference as well as I. What can it be? Can they have quarrelled? Why else should he have shown such unwillingness to accept your invitation here?"

"It was not inclination that made him refuse it, Elinor; I could plainly see *that*. He had not the power of accepting it. I have thought it all over, I assure you, and I can perfectly account for everything that at first seemed strange to me as well as to you."

"Can you indeed?"

"Yes. I have explained it to myself in the most satisfactory way. You, Elinor, who love to doubt where you can—it will not satisfy *you*, I know; but you shall not talk *me* out of my trust in it. I am persuaded that Mrs. Smith suspects his regard for Marianne, disapproves of it (perhaps because she has other views for him), and on that account is eager to get him away. The business which she sends him off to transact is an invented excuse to dismiss him. This is what I believe to have happened. He is moreover aware that she *does* disapprove the connection, he dares not therefore at present confess to her his engagement with Marianne, and he feels himself obliged, to preserve his inheritance, to give into her schemes, and leave Devonshire for a while. You will tell me, I know, that this may, or may *not* have happened; but can you offer a more fitting explanation than the one I have just given?"

"I certainly cannot, for how are we to know such details as you have described?"

"Then you would have told me, that it might or might not have happened. Oh! Elinor, how incomprehensible are your feelings! You had rather think the words—misery for Marianne and guilt for poor Willoughby, than make an apology for the latter. You are resolved to think him blameable, because he took leave of us with less affection than his usual behaviour has shown. And is no allowance to be made for the pain inflicted by recent disappointment? Are no probabilities to be accepted, merely because they are not certainties? Is nothing due to the man whom we have all so much reason to love, and no reason in the world to think ill of? And, after all, what is it you suspect him of?"

"I can hardly tell you myself. But suspicion of something unpleasant is the inevitable consequence of such an alteration as we have just witnessed in him. There is great truth, however, in what you have now urged of the allowances which ought to be made for him, and it is my wish to be fair in my judgment of everybody. Willoughby may undoubtedly have very sufficient reasons for his conduct, and I will hope that he has. But it would have been more like Willoughby to acknowledge them at once."

"Do not blame him, however, for departing from his character, where the deviation is necessary. But you really do admit the justice of what I have said in his defence? I am happy—and he is acquitted."

"Not entirely. It may be proper to conceal their engagement (if they *are* engaged) from Mrs. Smith—and if that is the case, it must be best for Willoughby to avoid Devonshire at present. But this is no excuse for their concealing it from us."

"Concealing it from us! My dear child, do you accuse Willoughby and Marianne of concealment? This is strange indeed, when your eyes have been reproaching them every day for their lack of caution."

"I have had proof enough of their affection," said Elinor, "but no proof at all of their engagement."

"I am perfectly satisfied of both."

"Yet not a syllable has been said to you on the subject, by either of them."

"I have not needed syllables where actions have spoken so plainly. Has not his behaviour to Marianne and to all of us, for at least the last fortnight, declared that he loved and considered her as his future wife, and that he felt for us the attachment of the nearest relation? Have we not perfectly understood each other? Has not my consent been daily asked by his looks, his manner, his attentive and affectionate respect? My Elinor, is it possible to doubt their engagement? How could such a thought occur to you? How is it to be supposed that Willoughby, persuaded as he must be of your sister's love, should leave her, and leave her perhaps for months, without telling her of his affection; that they should part without a mutual exchange of confidence?"

"I confess," replied Elinor, "that every circumstance except *one* is in favour of their engagement, but that *one* is the total silence of both on the subject, and with me it almost outweighs every other."

"How strange this is! You must think wretchedly indeed of Willoughby, if, after all that has openly passed between them, you can doubt the nature of the terms on which they are together. Has he been acting a part in his behaviour to your sister all this time? Do you suppose him really indifferent to her?"

"No, I cannot think that. He must and does love her, I am sure."

"But with a strange kind of tenderness, if he can leave her with such indifference, such carelessness of the future, as you attribute to him."

"You must remember, my dear mother, that I have never considered this matter as certain. I have had my doubts, I confess; but they are fainter than they were, and they may soon be entirely done away. If they write letters to each other, that will certainly prove that they are indeed engaged."

"A mighty concession indeed! If you were to see them at the altar, you would suppose they were going to be married. Ungracious girl! But *I* require no such proof. Nothing, in my opinion, has ever passed to justify doubt; no secrecy has been attempted, and all has been uniformly open and unreserved. You cannot doubt your sister's wishes. It must be Willoughby therefore whom you suspect. But why? Is he not a man of honour and feeling? Has there been any inconsistency on his side to create alarm? Can he be deceitful?"

"I hope not, I believe not," cried Elinor. "I love Willoughby, sincerely love him; and suspicion of his integrity cannot be more painful to yourself than to me. It has been involuntary, and I will not encourage it. I was startled, I confess, by the alteration in his manners this morning; he did not speak like himself, and did not return your kindness. But all this may be explained by such a situation of his affairs as you have supposed. He had just parted from my sister, had seen her leave him in the greatest affliction. If he felt obliged, from a fear of offending Mrs. Smith, to resist the temptation of returning here soon, and yet aware that by declining your invitation, by saying that he was going away for some time, he should seem to act ungenerous, he might well be embarrassed and disturbed. In such a case, a plain and open avowal of his difficulties would have been more to his honour, I think, as well as more consistent with his general character. But I will not raise objections against anyone's conduct on so weak a foundation."

"You speak very properly. Willoughby certainly does not deserve to be suspected. Though *we* have not known him long, he is no stranger in this part of the world; and who has ever spoken to his disadvantage? Had he been in a situation to act independently and marry immediately, it might have been odd that he should leave us without acknowledging everything to me at once; but this is not the case. It is an engagement in some respects not prosperously begun, for their marriage must be soon; and even secrecy, as far as it can be observed, may now be very advisable."

They were interrupted by the entrance of Margaret; and Elinor was then at liberty to think over the arguments of her mother, to acknowledge the probability of many, and hope for the justice of all.

They saw nothing of Marianne till dinner time, when she entered the room and took her place at the table without saying a word. Her eyes were red and swollen; and it seemed as if her tears were even then restrained with difficulty. She avoided the looks of them all, could neither eat nor speak, and after some time, on her mother's silently pressing her hand with tender compassion, her small degree of strength was quite overcome—she burst into tears and left the room.

This violent oppression of spirits continued the whole evening. She was inconsolable, because she had no desire to be consoled. The slightest mention of anything relative to Willoughby overpowered her in an instant; and though her family were most anxiously attentive to her comfort, it was impossible for them, if they spoke at all, to avoid every subject which her feelings connected with him.

CHAPTER 16

Marianne would have thought herself very inexcusable had she been able to sleep at all the first night after parting from Willoughby. She would have been ashamed to look her family in the face the next morning, had she not risen from her bed in more need of sleep than when she lay down in it. She was awake the whole night, and she wept the greatest part of it. She got up with a headache, was unable to talk, and unwilling to take any nourishment; giving pain every moment to her mother and sisters, and forbidding all attempt at consolation from either.

When breakfast was over, she walked out by herself, and wandered about the village of Allenham, indulging the recollection of past enjoyment and crying over the present change in her situation for the chief of the morning.

The evening passed in a similarly way. She played over every favourite song that she had played to Willoughby, every tune in which their voices had been oftenest joined, and sat at the instrument gazing on every line of music that he had written out for her, till her heart was so heavy that no farther sadness could be gained. This nourishment of grief was every day applied. She spent whole hours at the piano alternately singing and crying; her voice often totally suspended by her tears. In books, too, as well as in music, she courted the misery which a contrast between the past and present was certain of giving. She read nothing but what they had read together.

Such violence of affliction indeed could not be supported forever; it sunk within a few days into a calmer melancholy; but her solitary walks and silent meditations still produced occasional effusions of sorrow as lively as ever.

No letter from Willoughby came, and none seemed expected by Marianne. Her mother was surprised, and Elinor again became uneasy. But Mrs. Dashwood could find explanations whenever she wanted them, which at least satisfied herself.

"Remember, Elinor," said she, "how very often Sir John fetches our letters himself from the post, and carries them to it. We have already agreed that secrecy may be necessary, and we must acknowledge that it could not be maintained if their correspondence were to pass through Sir John's hands."

Elinor could not deny the truth of this, and she tried to find in it a motive sufficient for their silence. But there was one method so direct, so simple, that she could not help suggesting it to her mother.

"Why do you not ask Marianne at once," said she, "whether she is or is not engaged to Willoughby? From you, her mother, and so kind, so indulgent a mother, the question could not give offence. It would be the natural result of your affection for her. She used to be all openness, and to you more especially."

"I would not ask such a question for the world. Supposing it possible that they are not engaged, what distress would such an inquiry inflict! At any rate it would be most ungenerous. I should never deserve her confidence again, after forcing from her a confession of what is meant at present to be unacknowledged to anyone. I know Marianne's heart: I know that she dearly loves me, and that I shall not be the last to whom the truth is made known, when circumstances make the disclosure of it possible."

Elinor thought her mother overly cautious, and urged the matter farther, but in vain. Common sense, common care, and common prudence were nothing to Mrs. Dashwood's romantic delicacy.

It was several days before Willoughby's name was mentioned before Marianne by any of her family. Sir John and Mrs. Jennings, indeed, were not so nice; their witticisms added pain to many a painful hour—but one evening, Mrs. Dashwood, accidentally taking up a volume of Shakespeare, exclaimed,

"We have never finished Hamlet, Marianne; our dear Willoughby went away before we could get through it. We will set it aside, so when he comes again ... but it may be months, perhaps, before *that* happens."

"Months!" cried Marianne, with strong surprise. "I am sure it will be sooner."

Mrs. Dashwood was sorry for what she had said; but it gave Elinor pleasure, as it produced a reply from Marianne so expressive of confidence in Willoughby and knowledge of his intentions.

One morning, about a week after his leaving the country, Marianne was prevailed on to join her sisters in their usual walk, instead of wandering away by herself. Before this she had carefully avoided every companion in her rambles. If her sisters intended to walk on the downs, she directly stole away towards the lanes; if they talked of the valley, she was as speedy in climbing the hills, and could never be found when the others set off. But at length she was secured by the exertions of Elinor, who greatly disapproved such continual seclusion. They walked along the road through the valley, and chiefly in silence, for Marianne's *mind* could not be controlled, and Elinor, satisfied with gaining one point, would not then attempt more. Beyond the entrance of the valley, where the country, though still rich, was less wild and more open, a long stretch of the road which they had travelled on first coming to Barton lay before them. On reaching that point, they stopped to look around them. Among the objects in the scene, they soon discovered an animated one; it was a man on horseback riding towards them. In a few minutes they could distinguish him to be a gentleman; and in a moment afterwards Marianne rapturously exclaimed,

"It is he; it is indeed—I know it is!" She was hastening to meet him when Elinor cried out,

"Indeed, Marianne, I think you are mistaken. It is not Willoughby. The person is not tall enough to be him."

"He is, he is," cried Marianne, "I am sure he is! His manner of riding, his coat, his horse. I knew how soon he would come."

She walked eagerly on as she spoke; and Elinor, to protect Marianne from embarrassment, as she felt almost certain of its not being Willoughby, quickened her pace and kept up with her. They were soon within thirty yards of the gentleman. Marianne looked again; her heart sunk within her. She abruptly turned around and was hurrying back when the voices of both her sisters were raised to detain her. A third, almost as familiar as Willoughby's, joined them in begging her to stop, and she turned around with surprise to see and welcome Edward Ferrars.

He was the only person in the world who could at that moment be forgiven for not being Willoughby; the only one who could have gained a smile from her. In her sister's happiness she forgot for a time her own disappointment.

He dismounted, and giving his horse to his servant, walked back with them to Barton, where he was purposely coming to visit them.

He was welcomed by them all with great cordiality, but especially by Marianne, who showed more warmth of regard in her reception of him than even Elinor herself. To Marianne, indeed, the meeting between Edward and her sister was but a continuation of that unaccountable coldness which she had often observed at Norland in their mutual behaviour. On Edward's side, more particularly, there was a deficiency of all that a lover ought to look and say on such an occasion. He was confused, seemed scarcely to feel pleasure upon seeing them, looked neither rapturous nor happy, said little but what was forced from him by questions, and distinguished Elinor by no mark of affection. Marianne saw and listened with increasing surprise. She began almost to feel a dislike of Edward; and it ended, as every feeling must end with her, by carrying back her thoughts to Willoughby, whose manners formed a contrast sufficiently striking to Edward's.

After a short silence which followed the first surprise and inquiries of meeting, Marianne asked Edward if he came directly from London. No, he had been in Devonshire a fortnight.

"A fortnight!" she repeated, surprised at his being so long in the same county with Elinor without seeing her before.

He looked rather distressed as he added that he had been staying with some friends near Plymouth.

"Have you been in Sussex recently?" said Elinor.

"I was at Norland about a month ago."

"And how does dear, dear Norland look?" cried Marianne.

"Dear, dear Norland," said Elinor, "probably looks much as it always does at this time of year. The woods and walks thickly covered with dead leaves."

"Oh!" cried Marianne, "With what transporting sensations have I formerly seen them fall! How have I delighted, as I walked, to see them driven in showers about me by the wind! What feelings have they, the season, and the cool air altogether inspired! Now there is no one to regard them. They are seen only as a nuisance, swept hastily off, and driven as much as possible from sight."

"It is not everyone," said Elinor, "who has your passion for dead leaves."

"No; my feelings are not often shared, not often understood. But *sometimes* they are." As she said this, she sunk into a reverie for a few moments; but roused herself again. "Now, Edward," she said, calling his attention to the view, "here is Barton valley. Look up it, and be tranquil if you can. Look at those hills! Did you ever see their equals? To the left is Barton park, among those woods. You may see one end of the house. And there, beneath that farthest hill, which rises with such grandeur, is our cottage."

"It is a beautiful country," he replied; "but these roads must be dirty in winter."

"How can you think of dirt, with such objects before you?"

"Because," replied he, smiling, "among the rest of the objects before me, I see a very dirty lane."

"How strange!" said Marianne to herself as she walked on.

"Have you an agreeable neighbourhood here? Are the Middletons pleasant people?"

"No, not at all," answered Marianne, "we could not be more unfortunately situated."

"Marianne," cried her sister, "how can you say so? How can you be so unjust? They are a very respectable family, Mr. Ferrars, and towards us have behaved in the friendliest manner. Have you forgotten, Marianne, how many pleasant days we have owed to them?"

"No," said Marianne in a low voice, "nor how many painful moments."

Elinor took no notice of this, and directing her attention to their visitor, endeavoured to support something like conversation with him by talking of their present residence, its conveniences, etc., extorting from him occasional questions and remarks. His coldness and reserve mortified her severely: she was vexed and half angry; but resolving to allow her behaviour to him to be determined by the past rather than the present, she avoided every appearance of resentment or displeasure, and treated him as she thought he ought to be treated due to the family connection.

CHAPTER 17

Mrs. Dashwood was surprised only for a moment at seeing him; for his coming to Barton was, in her opinion, of all things the most natural. Her joy and expressions of regard long outlived her wonder. He received the kindest welcome from her; and shyness, coldness, and reserve could not stand against such a reception. They had begun to fail him before he entered the house, and they were quite overcome by the captivating manners of Mrs. Dashwood. Indeed a man could not very well be in love with either of her daughters, without extending the passion to her; and Elinor had the satisfaction of seeing him soon become more like himself. His affections seemed to reanimate towards them all, and his interest in their welfare again became perceptible. He was not in spirits however; he praised their house, was attentive and kind; but still he was not in spirits. The whole family perceived it, and Mrs. Dashwood attributed it to his mother.

"What are Mrs. Ferrars's views for you at present, Edward?" said she, when dinner was over and they had gathered round the fire. "Are you still to be a great orator against your wishes?"

"No. I hope my mother is now convinced that I have no more talents than inclination for a public life!"

"But how is your fame to be established? For famous you must be to satisfy all your family; and with no profession, and no assurance of one, you may find it a difficult matter."

"I shall not attempt it. I have no wish to be distinguished; and I have every reason to hope I never shall. Thank Heaven! I cannot be forced into genius and eloquence."

"You have no ambition, I well know. Your wishes are all moderate."

"As moderate as those of the rest of the world, I believe. I wish, as well as everybody else, to be perfectly happy; but, like everybody else, it must be in my own way. Greatness will not make me so."

"Strange if it would!" cried Marianne. "What have wealth or grandeur to do with happiness?"

"Grandeur has but little," said Elinor, "but wealth has much to do with it."

"Elinor, for shame!" said Marianne. "Money can only give happiness where there is nothing else to give it. Beyond taking care of basic needs, it can afford no real satisfaction."

"Perhaps," said Elinor, smiling, "we may come to the same point. *Your* definition of basic needs and *my* definition of wealth are very much alike, I dare say. How do you define basic need?"

"About eighteen hundred or two thousand a year; not more than *that*."

Elinor laughed. "*Two* thousand a year! *One* is my wealth! I guessed how it would end."

"And yet two thousand a year is a very moderate income," said Marianne. "A family cannot well be maintained on a smaller one. I am sure I am not extravagant in my demands. A proper establishment of servants, a carriage, perhaps two, and horses cannot be supported on less."

Elinor smiled again, to hear her sister describing so accurately their future expenses at Combe Magna.

"I wish," said Margaret, striking out a novel thought, "that somebody would give us all a large fortune apiece!"

"Oh that they would!" cried Marianne, her eyes sparkling with animation, and her cheeks glowing with the delight of such imaginary happiness.

"We are all unanimous in that wish, I suppose," said Elinor, "in spite of the insufficiency of wealth."

"Oh dear!" cried Margaret, "How happy I should be! I wonder what I should do with it?"

Marianne looked as if she had no doubt on that point.

"I would not know what to do with a large fortune myself," said Mrs. Dashwood, "if my children were all to be rich without my help."

"You could start by beginning your improvements on this house," observed Elinor.

"What magnificent orders would travel from this family to London," said Edward, "in such an event! What a happy day for booksellers, music sellers, and print shops! You, Miss Dashwood, would give a general order for every new book of merit to be sent you—and as for Marianne, I know her greatness of soul, there would not be music enough in London to content her. And books!—Thomson, Cowper, Scott—she would buy them all over and over again; she would buy up every copy, I believe, to prevent their falling into unworthy hands. Would you not, Marianne?"

"You are very right in supposing how my money would be spent—some of it, at least my loose cash, would certainly be employed in improving my collection of music and books."

"And the bulk of your fortune would be given to support the living expenses of those authors who produced such magnificent works."

"No, Edward, I should have something else to do with it."

"Perhaps, then, you would bestow it as a reward on that person who wrote the ablest defence of your favorite principle, that no one can ever be in love more than once in their life—for your opinion on that point is unchanged, I presume?"

"Undoubtedly. At my time of life, opinions are tolerably fixed. It is not likely that I should now see or hear anything to change them."

"Marianne is as steadfast as ever, you see," said Elinor, "she is not at all altered."

"She is only grown a little more melancholy than she was."

"Nay, Edward," said Marianne, "*you* need not reproach me. You are not in spirits yourself."

"Why should you think so!" replied he, with a sigh. "But exuberance never was a part of *my* character."

"Nor do I think it a part of Marianne's," said Elinor. "She is very earnest, very eager in all she does—sometimes talks a great deal and always with animation—but she is not often really merry."

"I believe you are right," he replied, "and yet I have always thought of her as a lively girl."

"I have frequently detected myself in such kind of mistakes," said Elinor, "in a total misjudgment of character in some point or other: fancying people so much more happy or grave, or ingenious or dull than they really are, and I can hardly tell how the deception originated. Sometimes one is guided by what they say of themselves, and very frequently by what other people say of them, without giving oneself time to deliberate and judge."

"But I thought it was right, Elinor," said Marianne, "to be guided wholly by the opinion of other people. I thought our judgments were given us merely to be subservient to those of our neighbours. This has always been your doctrine, I am sure."

"No, Marianne, never. My doctrine has never aimed at the repression of thoughts and feelings. All I have ever attempted to influence has been the behaviour. You must not confuse my meaning. I am guilty, I confess, of having often wished you to treat our acquaintance in general with greater attention; but when have I advised you to adopt their sentiments or conform to their judgment in serious matters?"

"You have not been able then to bring your sister over to your plan of general civility," said Edward to Elinor. "Do you gain no ground?"

"Quite the contrary," replied Elinor, looking expressively at Marianne.

"My judgment," he returned, "is all on your side of the question; but I am afraid my practice is much more on your sister's. I never wish to offend, but I am so foolishly shy, that I often seem negligent, when I am only kept back by my natural awkwardness."

"Marianne has not shyness to excuse any inattention of hers," said Elinor.

"She knows her own worth too well for false shame," replied Edward. "Shyness is only the effect of a sense of inferiority in some way or other. If I could persuade myself that my manners were perfectly easy and graceful, I would not be shy."

"But you would still be reserved," said Marianne, "and that is worse."

Edward stared—"Reserved! Am I reserved, Marianne?"

"Yes, very."

"I do not understand you," replied he, colouring. "Reserved! How? In what manner? What am I to say in my own defence?"

Elinor looked surprised at his emotion, but trying to laugh off the subject, she said to him, "Don't you know my sister well enough to understand what she means? She calls everyone reserved who does not talk as fast, and admire what she admires as rapturously as herself."

Edward made no answer. His gravity and thoughtfulness returned on him in their fullest extent—and he sat for some time silent and dull.

CHAPTER 18

Elinor saw with great uneasiness the low spirits of her friend. His visit afforded her only very limited satisfaction, while his own enjoyment in it appeared so imperfect. It was evident that he was unhappy; she wished it were equally evident that he still distinguished her with the same affection which once she had felt no doubt of inspiring. But the reservedness of his manner towards her contradicted one moment what a more animated look had hinted at the preceding one.

He joined her and Marianne in the breakfast room the next morning before the others were down; and Marianne, who was always eager to promote their happiness as far as she could, soon left them to themselves. But before she was halfway upstairs she heard the parlour door open, and, turning round, was astonished to see Edward himself come out.

"I am going into the village to see my horses," said he, "as you are not yet ready for breakfast; I shall be back again presently."

Edward returned to them with fresh admiration of the surrounding country; in his walk to the village, he had seen many parts of the valley to advantage. The village itself afforded a general view of the whole area, which had exceedingly pleased him. This was a subject which ensured Marianne's attention, and she was beginning to describe her own admiration of these scenes, and to question him more minutely on the objects that had particularly struck him, when Edward interrupted her by saying, "You must not inquire too far, Marianne—remember, I have no knowledge in the picturesque, and I shall offend you by my ignorance and want of taste, if we come to particulars. I shall call hills steep, which ought to be bold! Surfaces strange and uncouth, which ought to be irregular and rugged; and distant objects out of sight, which ought only to be indistinct through the soft medium of a hazy atmosphere. You must be satisfied with such admiration as I can honestly give. I call it a very fine country— the hills are steep, the woods seem full of fine timber, and the valley looks comfortable and snug—with rich meadows and several neat farm houses scattered here and there. It exactly answers my idea of a fine country, because it unites beauty with practicality—and I dare say it is a picturesque one too, because you admire it. I can easily believe it to be full of rocks and promontories, grey moss and brush wood, but these are all lost on me. I know nothing of the picturesque."

"I am afraid it is but too true," said Marianne, "but why should you boast of it?"

"I suspect," said Elinor, "that because he believes many people pretend to admire the beauties of nature, and is disgusted with such pretensions, he affects greater indifference and less discrimination in viewing them himself than he possesses."

"It is very true," said Marianne, "that admiration of landscape scenery has become cliché. Everybody pretends to feel and tries to describe with the taste and elegance of him who first defined what picturesque beauty was. I detest such unoriginality, and sometimes I have kept my feelings to myself because I could find no language to describe them except what was worn out with overuse."

"I am convinced," said Edward, "that you really feel all the delight in a fine prospect which you profess to feel. But, in return, your sister must allow me to feel no more than I profess. I like a fine prospect, but not on picturesque principles. I do not like crooked, twisted trees. I admire them much more if they are tall, straight and flourishing. I do not like ruined, tattered cottages. I am not fond of nettles, or thistles, or heath blossoms. I have more pleasure in a snug farmhouse than a watch-tower—and a troop of tidy, happy villagers please me better than the finest gypsies in the world."

Marianne looked with amazement at Edward, and with compassion at her sister. Elinor only laughed.

The subject was continued no farther; and Marianne remained thoughtfully silent till a new object suddenly engaged her attention.

She was sitting by Edward, and as he took his tea from Mrs. Dashwood, his hand passed so closely in front of her as to make a ring, with a lock of hair in the centre, very conspicuous on one of his fingers.

"I never saw you wear a ring before, Edward," she cried. "Is that Fanny's hair? I remember her promising to give you some. But I would have thought her hair would be darker."

Marianne spoke inconsiderately—but when she saw how much she had pained Edward, her own vexation at her blunt manner could not be surpassed by his. He coloured very deeply, and giving a momentary glance at Elinor, replied, "Yes, it is my sister's hair. The setting always casts a different shade on it, you know."

Elinor had met his eye, and looked self-conscious likewise. That the hair was her own, she instantaneously felt as well satisfied as Marianne. The only difference in their conclusions was, that what Marianne considered as a free gift from her sister, Elinor was conscious must have been procured by some theft or contrivance unknown to herself. She was not disposed, however, to take offence, and pretending to take no notice of what passed, by instantly talking of something else, she internally resolved henceforward to catch every opportunity of eyeing the hair, and satisfying herself, beyond all doubt, that it was exactly the shade of her own.

Edward's embarrassment lasted some time, and it ended in an absence of mind still more pronounced. He was particularly grave the whole morning. Marianne severely censured herself for what she had said; but her own forgiveness might have been more speedy, had she known how little offence it had given her sister.

Before the middle of the day, they were visited by Sir John and Mrs. Jennings, who, having heard of the arrival of a gentleman at the cottage, came to meet the guest. With the assistance of his mother-in-law, Sir John was not long in discovering that the name of Ferrars began with an F, and this prepared a future line of raillery against the devoted Elinor, which nothing but the newness of their acquaintance with Edward could have prevented from being immediately begun.

Sir John never came to the Dashwoods without either inviting them to dine at the Park the next day, or to drink tea with them that evening. On the present occasion, for the better entertainment of their visitor, towards whose amusement he felt himself bound to contribute, he wished to engage them for both.

"You *must* drink tea with us tonight," said he, "for we shall be quite alone—and tomorrow you must absolutely dine with us, for we shall be a large party."

"And who knows but that we may have a dance," said Mrs. Jennings. "That will surely tempt *you*, Miss Marianne."

"A dance!" cried Marianne. "Impossible! Who will be dancing?"

"Who! Why yourselves, and the Careys, and Whitakers to be sure. What! You thought nobody could dance because a certain person that shall be nameless is gone!"

"I wish with all my soul," cried Sir John, "that Willoughby were among us again."

This, and Marianne's blushing, gave new suspicions to Edward. "And who is Willoughby?" he whispered to Miss Dashwood, by whom he was sitting.

She gave him a brief reply. Marianne's countenance was more communicative. Edward saw enough to comprehend not only the meaning of others, but such of Marianne's expressions as had puzzled him before. When their visitors left them, he went immediately round to her and said, in a whisper, "I have been guessing. Shall I tell you my guess?"

"What do you mean?"

"Shall I tell you?"

"Certainly."

"Well, then, I guess that you greatly admire this Mr. Willoughby."

Marianne was surprised and confused, yet she could not help smiling at the quiet archness of his manner, and, after a moment's silence, said,

"Oh! Edward! How can you?—But the time will come, I hope ... I am sure you will like him."

"I do not doubt it," replied he, rather astonished at her earnestness and warmth.

CHAPTER 19

Edward remained a week at the cottage; he was earnestly pressed by Mrs. Dashwood to stay longer, but he seemed resolved to be gone just when his enjoyment among his friends was at its height. His spirits during the last two or three days, though still not fully restored, were greatly improved. He grew more and more attached to the house and neighbourhood—never spoke of going away without a sigh—declared his time to be wholly disengaged—even doubted to what place he should go when he left them—but still, go he must. Never had any week passed so quickly—he could hardly believe it to be gone. He had no pleasure at Norland; he detested being in town; but either to Norland or London, he must go. He valued their kindness beyond anything, and his greatest happiness was in being with them. Yet he must leave them at the end of a week, in spite of their wishes and his own, though he could give no pressing reason for his departure.

Elinor attributed all that could not be explained in this way of acting to his mother's interference. It was happy for her that he had a mother whose character was so imperfectly known to her, as to be the general excuse for everything strange on the part of her son. Disappointed, however, and vexed as she was, and sometimes displeased with his uncertain behaviour to herself, she was very willing to make allowances for him. His low spirits, lack of openness, and inconsistency, must be the result of his dependence on Mrs. Ferrars. The shortness of his visit, and the steadiness of his purpose in leaving them, originated from the same source, the same inevitable necessity of pleasing his mother. She would have been glad to know when these difficulties were to cease, and her son could be happy. But from such vain wishes, she was forced to turn for comfort to the renewal of her confidence in Edward's affection. She thought with fondness about the flattering proof of it which he constantly wore round his finger.

"I think, Edward," said Mrs. Dashwood, as they were at breakfast the last morning, "you would be a happier man if you had a profession to engage your time. Some inconvenience to your friends, indeed, might result from it—you would not be able to be with the so much. But," she said with a smile, "you would be materially benefited in one particular at least—you would know where to go when you left them."

"I do assure you," he replied, "that I have long thought on this point as you think now. It has been, and is, and probably will always be a heavy misfortune to me, that I have had no necessary business to engage me, no profession to give me employment or offer me anything like independence. But, unfortunately, my mother and I could never agree in our choice of profession. I always preferred the church, as I still do. But that was not good enough for my family. They recommended the army, which was entirely against my inclination. The law was admitted to be genteel enough; many young barristers made a very good appearance in the first circles, and drove about town in very smart carriages. But I had no inclination for the law. As for the navy, I was too old when the subject was first started to enter it—and, at length, as there was no necessity for my having any profession at all, idleness was pronounced on the whole to be the most advantageous and honourable. I was therefore entered at Oxford and have been properly idle ever since."

"The consequence of which, I suppose, will be," said Mrs. Dashwood, "since leisure has not promoted your own happiness, that your sons will be brought up to many pursuits, employments, professions, and trades."

"They will be brought up," said he, in a serious accent, "to be as unlike myself as is possible—in feeling, in action, in condition, in everything."

"Come, come; this is all a result of low spirits, Edward. You are in a melancholy humour, and assume that anyone unlike yourself must be happy. But remember that the pain of parting from friends will be felt by everybody at times, whatever their education or profession. You only need patience—or give it a more fascinating name, call it hope. Your mother will give you the inheritance you deserve, in time, that independence you are so anxious for; it is her duty, and it will, it must ere long become her happiness to prevent your whole youth from being wasted in discontent. How much may not a few months do?"

"I think," replied Edward, "that many months will not do me any good."

This desponding turn of mind, though it could not be communicated to Mrs. Dashwood, gave additional pain to them all in the parting, which shortly took place, and left an uncomfortable impression on Elinor. But as it was her determination to subdue it, and to prevent herself from appearing to suffer more than what all her family suffered on his going away, she did not adopt the method so judiciously employed by Marianne, to wilfully augment her sorrow. Their means were as different as their objects, and equally suited to the advancement of each.

Elinor sat down to her drawing table as soon as he was out of the house, busily employed herself the whole day, neither sought nor avoided the mention of his name, and appeared to interest herself almost as much as ever in the general concerns of the family. If, by this conduct, she did not lessen her own grief, it was at least prevented from unnecessary increase, and her mother and sisters were spared much concern on her account.

Such behaviour as this, so exactly the reverse of her own, appeared no more heroic to Marianne than her own had seemed faulty to her. The business of self-command she settled very easily; with strong affections it was impossible, with calm ones it could have no merit. That her sister's affections *were* calm, she dared not deny, though she blushed to acknowledge it; and of the strength of her own, she gave a very striking proof, by still loving and respecting that sister in spite of this mortifying conviction.

Without shutting herself up from her family, or leaving the house in determined solitude to avoid them, or lying awake the whole night, Elinor found every day afforded her leisure enough to think of Edward, and of Edward's behaviour. There were moments in abundance, when, if not by the absence of her mother and sisters, at least by the nature of their employments, conversation among them was limited, and every effect of solitude was produced. Her mind was inevitably at liberty; her thoughts could not be occupied elsewhere; and the past and the future, on a subject so interesting, must be before her, must force her attention, and engross her memory, her reflection, and her imagination.

From a reverie of this kind, as she sat at her drawing table, she was roused one morning, soon after Edward's leaving them, by the arrival of company. She happened to be quite alone. The closing of the little gate, at the entrance of the small lawn in front of the house, drew her eyes to the window, and she saw a large party walking up to the door. Among them were Sir John and Lady Middleton, and Mrs. Jennings; but there were two others, a gentleman and lady, who were quite unknown to her. She was sitting near the window, and as soon as Sir John saw her, he left the rest of the party to the ceremony of knocking at the door, and stepping across the turf, obliged her to open the window to speak to him, though the space was so short between the door and the window, as to make it hardly possible to speak at one without being heard at the other.

"Well," said he, "we have brought you some strangers. How do you like them?"

"Hush! They will hear you."

"Never mind if they do. It is only the Palmers. Charlotte is very pretty, I can tell you. You may see her if you look this way."

As Elinor was certain of seeing her in a couple of minutes, without taking that liberty, she begged to be excused.

"Where is Marianne? Has she run away because we have come? I see her piano is open."

"She is walking, I believe."

They were now joined by Mrs. Jennings, who had not patience enough to wait till the door was opened before she told *her* story. She came to the window. "How do you do, my dear? How is Mrs. Dashwood? And where are your sisters? What! All alone? You will be glad of a little company to sit with you. I have brought my other son and daughter to see you. Only think of their coming so suddenly! I thought I heard a carriage last night, while we were drinking our tea, but it never entered my head that it could be them. I thought Colonel Brandon had come back again; so I said to Sir John, 'I do think I hear a carriage; perhaps it is Colonel Brandon come back again—'"

Elinor was obliged to turn from her, in the middle of her story, to receive the rest of the party. Lady Middleton introduced the two strangers, and Mrs. Dashwood and Margaret came downstairs at the same time. They all sat down to look at one another, and Mrs. Jennings continued her story as she walked through the passage into the parlour, attended by Sir John.

Mrs. Palmer was several years younger than Lady Middleton, and totally unlike her in every respect. She was short and plump, had a very pretty face, and the finest expression of good humour in it that could possibly be. Her manners were by no means as elegant as her sister's, but she was much friendlier. She came in with a smile— smiled all the time of her visit, except when she laughed, and smiled when she went away. Her husband was a grave looking young man of twenty-five or twenty-six, with an air of more fashion and sense than his wife, but of less willingness to please or be pleased. He entered the room with a look of self-importance, slightly bowed to the ladies without speaking a word, and after briefly surveying them and their apartments, took up a newspaper from the table and continued to read it as long as he stayed.

Mrs. Palmer, on the contrary, was hardly seated before her admiration of the parlour and everything in it burst forth.

"Well! What a delightful room this is! I never saw anything so charming! Only think, mama, how it is improved since I was here last! I always thought it such a sweet place, ma'am!" She turned to Mrs. Dashwood and continued, "But you have made it so charming! Only look, sister, how delightful everything is! How I should like such a house for myself! Would you not, Mr. Palmer?"

Mr. Palmer made her no answer, and did not even raise his eyes from the newspaper.

"Mr. Palmer does not hear me," said she, laughing, "he never does. It is so ridiculous!"

This was quite a new idea to Mrs. Dashwood. She had never before found humour in the inattention of anyone, and could not help looking with surprise at them both.

Mrs. Jennings, in the meantime, talked on as loudly as she could, and continued her account of their surprise, the evening before, on seeing their friends, without ceasing till everything was told. Mrs. Palmer laughed heartily at the recollection of their astonishment, and everybody agreed, two or three times over, that it had been quite an agreeable surprise.

"You may believe how glad we all were to see them," added Mrs. Jennings, leaning forward towards Elinor, and speaking in a low voice as if she meant to be heard by no one else, though they were seated on different sides of the room. "But I can't help wishing they had not travelled quite so fast, nor made such a long journey of it, for they came all round by London upon account of some business, for you know," she nodded significantly and pointed to her daughter, "it was wrong in her situation. I wanted her to stay at home and rest this morning, but she would come with us; she longed so much to see you all!"

Mrs. Palmer laughed, and said it would not do her any harm.

"She is pregnant, and expects to be confined in February," continued Mrs. Jennings.

Lady Middleton exerted herself to ask Mr. Palmer if there was any news in the paper.

"No, none at all," he replied, and read on.

"Here comes Marianne," cried Sir John. "Now, Palmer, you shall see a very pretty girl."

He immediately went into the passage, opened the front door, and ushered her in himself. Mrs. Jennings asked her, as soon as she appeared, if she had been to Allenham; and Mrs. Palmer laughed so heartily at the question as to show she understood it. Mr. Palmer looked up on her entering the room, stared at her some minutes, and then returned to his newspaper. Mrs. Palmer's eye was now caught by the drawings which hung round the room. She got up to examine them.

"Oh! Dear, how beautiful these are! Well, how delightful! Do look, mama, how sweet! I declare they are quite charming; I could look at them forever." And then, sitting down again, she very soon forgot that there were any such things in the room.

When Lady Middleton rose to go away, Mr. Palmer rose also, laid down the newspaper, stretched himself, and looked at them all around.

"My love, have you been asleep?" said his wife, laughing.

He made her no answer; and only observed, after again examining the room, that the ceiling was crooked. He then made his bow and departed with the rest.

Sir John had urged them all to spend the next day at the park. Mrs. Dashwood, who did not choose to dine with them oftener than they dined at the cottage, absolutely refused on her own account; her daughters might do as they pleased. But they had no curiosity to see how Mr. and Mrs. Palmer ate their dinner, and no expectation of pleasure from them in any other way. They attempted, therefore, likewise to excuse themselves; the weather was uncertain and not likely to be good. But Sir John would not be satisfied—the carriage should be sent for them, and they must come. Lady Middleton too, though she did not press their mother, pressed them. Mrs. Jennings and Mrs. Palmer joined their entreaties, all seemed equally anxious to avoid a family party; and the young ladies were obliged to yield.

CHAPTER 20

As the Miss Dashwoods entered the drawing room of the park the next day, Mrs. Palmer came running up to them, looking as good-humoured and merry as before. She took them all most affectionately by the hand.

"I am so glad to see you!" she said, seating herself between Elinor and Marianne, "for it is so bad a day I was afraid you might not come, which would be a shocking thing, as we are going away again tomorrow. We must go, for the Westons come to us next week, you know. It was quite a sudden thing our coming at all, and I knew nothing of it till the carriage was coming to the door, and then Mr. Palmer asked me if I would go with him to Barton. He is so funny! He never tells me anything! I am so sorry we cannot stay longer; however we shall meet again in town very soon, I hope."

They were obliged to put an end to such an expectation.

"Not go to town!" cried Mrs. Palmer, with a laugh. "I shall be quite disappointed if you do not. I could get the nicest house in the world for you, next door to ours, in Hanover Square. You must come, indeed. I am sure I shall be very happy to chaperon you at any time till I am confined, if Mrs. Dashwood does not like to go out."

They thanked her, but were obliged to resist all her entreaties.

"Oh! My love," cried Mrs. Palmer to her husband, who just then entered the room. "You must help me persuade the Miss Dashwoods to go to town this winter."

Her love made no answer, and after slightly bowing to the ladies, began complaining of the weather.

"How horrid all this is!" said he. "Such weather makes everything and everybody disgusting. Dullness is as much produced within doors as without by rain. It makes one detest all one's acquaintance. What the devil does Sir John mean by not having a billiard room in his house? How few people know what comfort is!"

The rest of the company soon dropped in.

"I am afraid, Miss Marianne," said Sir John, "that you have not been able to take your usual walk to Allenham today."

Marianne looked very grave and said nothing.

"Oh! Don't be so secretive," said Mrs. Palmer: "for we know all about it, I assure you; and I admire your taste very much, for I think he is extremely handsome. We do not live a great way from him in the country, you know—not above ten miles, I dare say."

"Much nearer thirty," said her husband.

"Ah! Well! There is not much difference. I never was at his house; but they say it is a sweet, pretty place."

"As vile a spot as I ever saw in my life," said Mr. Palmer.

Marianne remained perfectly silent, though her countenance betrayed her interest in what was being said.

"Is it very ugly?" continued Mrs. Palmer. "Then it must be some other place that is so pretty, I suppose."

When they were seated in the dining room, Sir John observed with regret that they were only eight altogether.

"My dear," said he to his lady, "it is very provoking that we should be so few. Why did you not ask the Gilberts to come to us today?"

"Did not I tell you, Sir John, when you spoke to me about it before, that it could not be done? They dined with us last."

"You and I, Sir John," said Mrs. Jennings, "should not stand upon such ceremony."

"Then you would be very ill-bred," cried Mr. Palmer.

"My love, you contradict everybody," said his wife with her usual laugh. "Do you know that you are quite rude?"

"I did not know I contradicted anybody in calling your mother ill-bred."

"Aye, you may abuse me as you please," said the good-natured old lady, "you have taken Charlotte off my hands, and cannot give her back again. So there I have the advantage over you."

Charlotte laughed heartily to think that her husband could not get rid of her, and exultingly said she did not care how cross he was to her, as they must live together. It was impossible for anyone to be more thoroughly good-natured or more determined to be happy than Mrs. Palmer. The studied indifference, insolence, and discontent of her husband gave her no pain; and when he scolded her, she was highly amused.

"Mr. Palmer is so droll!" said she, in a whisper, to Elinor. "He is always out of humour."

Elinor was not inclined, after a little observation, to give him credit for being so genuinely and unaffectedly ill-natured or ill-bred as he wished to appear. His temper might perhaps be a little soured by finding, like many other men, that through some unaccountable bias in favour of beauty, he was the husband of a very silly woman—but she knew that this kind of blunder was too common for any sensible man to be lastingly hurt by it. It was rather a wish of distinction she believed, which produced his contemptuous treatment of everybody. It was the desire of appearing superior to other people. The motive was too common to be wondered at; but the means, however they might succeed by establishing his superiority in ill-breeding, were not likely to attach anyone to him except his wife.

"Oh! My dear Miss Dashwood," said Mrs. Palmer soon afterwards, "I have got such a favour to ask of you and your sister. Will you come and spend some time at Cleveland this Christmas? Now, pray do—and come while the Westons are with us. You cannot think how happy I shall be! It will be quite delightful! — My love," applying to her husband, "don't you long to have the Miss Dashwoods come to Cleveland?"

"Certainly,"—he replied with a sneer—"I came into Devonshire with no other view."

"There now," said his lady. "You see Mr. Palmer expects you; so you cannot refuse to come."

They both eagerly and resolutely declined her invitation.

"But indeed, you must and shall come. I am sure you will like it. The Westons will be with us, and it will be quite delightful. You cannot think what a sweet place Cleveland is; and we are so happy now, for Mr. Palmer is always going about the country canvassing for the election; and so many people come to dine with us that I never saw before, it is quite charming! But, poor fellow! It is very fatiguing to him, for he is forced to make everybody like him."

Elinor could hardly keep her from laughing as she acknowledged the hardship of such an obligation.

"How charming it will be," said Charlotte, "when he is in Parliament! Won't it? How I shall laugh! It will be so ridiculous to see all his letters directed to him with an M.P. Won't it, Mr. Palmer?"

Mr. Palmer took no notice of her.

"He cannot stand writing letters, you know," she continued.

"No," said he, "I never said anything so irrational. Don't palm all your abuses of language off on me."

"There now; you see how droll he is. This is always the way with him! Sometimes he won't speak to me for half a day together, and then he comes out with something so droll."

She surprised Elinor very much as they returned into the drawing room, by asking her whether she did not like Mr. Palmer excessively.

"Certainly," said Elinor. "He seems very agreeable."

"Well—I am so glad you do. I thought you would, he is so pleasant; and Mr. Palmer is excessively pleased with you and your sisters I can tell you, and you can't think how disappointed he will be if you don't come to Cleveland. I can't imagine why you should object to it."

Elinor was again obliged to decline her invitation; and by changing the subject, put a stop to her entreaties. She thought it probable that as they lived in the same country, Mrs. Palmer might be able to give some more particular account of Willoughby's general character than could be gathered from the Middletons' partial acquaintance with him. She was eager to gain from anyone such a confirmation of his merits as might remove the possibility of fear for Marianne. She began by inquiring if they saw much of Mr. Willoughby at Cleveland, and whether they were intimately acquainted with him.

"Oh! Dear, yes; I know him extremely well," replied Mrs. Palmer. "Not that I ever spoke to him, indeed; but I have seen him often in town. Somehow or other, I never happened to be staying at Barton while he was at Allenham. Mama saw him here once before, but I was with my uncle at Weymouth. However, I dare say we should have seen a great deal of him in Somersetshire, if it had not happened very unluckily that we should never have been in the country together. He is very little at Combe, I believe. If he were ever so much there, I do not think Mr. Palmer would visit him, for he is in the opposition you know, and besides it is such a way off. I know why you inquire about him, very well; your sister is to marry him. I am very glad of it, for then I shall have her for a neighbour you know."

"Upon my word," replied Elinor, "you know much more of the matter than I do, if you have any reason to expect such a match."

"Don't pretend to deny it, because you know it is what everybody talks of. I assure you I heard of it on my way through town."

"My dear Mrs. Palmer!"

"Upon my honour I did. I met Colonel Brandon Monday morning in Bond Street, just before we left town, and he told me of it."

"You surprise me very much. Colonel Brandon tell you of it! Surely you must be mistaken. To give such intelligence to a person who could not be interested in it, even if it were true, is not what I would expect Colonel Brandon to do."

"But I do assure you it was so, for all that, and I will tell you how it happened. When we met him, he turned back and walked with us; and so we began talking of my brother and sister. One thing led to another, and I said to him, 'So, Colonel, there is a new family at Barton Cottage, I hear, and mama sends me word they are very pretty, and that one of them is going to be married to Mr. Willoughby, of Combe Magna. Is it true, pray? For of course you must know, as you have been in Devonshire so lately.'"

"And what did the Colonel say?"

"Oh!—he did not say much; but he looked as if he knew it to be true, so from that moment I set it down as certain. It will be quite delightful, I declare! When is it to take place?"

"Mr. Brandon was very well, I hope."

"Oh! Yes, quite well; and so full of your praises, he did nothing but say fine things of you."

"I am flattered by his commendation. He seems an excellent man; and I think him uncommonly pleasing."

"So do I. He is such a charming man that it is quite a pity he should be so grave and so dull. Mama says *he* was in love with your sister too. I assure you it was a great compliment if he was, for he hardly ever falls in love with anybody."

"Is Mr. Willoughby much known in your part of Somersetshire?" said Elinor.

"Oh! Yes, extremely well; that is, I do not believe many people are acquainted with him, because Combe Magna is so far off;. But they all think him extremely agreeable, I assure you. Nobody is more liked than Mr. Willoughby wherever he goes, and so you may tell your sister. She is a very lucky girl to get him, upon my honour."

Mrs. Palmer's information respecting Willoughby was not very material; but any testimony in his favour, however small, was pleasing to her.

"I am so glad we have become acquainted at last," continued Charlotte. "And now I hope we shall always be great friends. You can't think how much I longed to see you! It is so delightful that you should live at the cottage! Nothing can be like it, to be sure! And I am so glad your sister is going to be well married! I hope you will be a great deal at Combe Magna. It is a sweet place by all accounts."

"You have been long acquainted with Colonel Brandon, have you not?"

"Yes, a great while; ever since my sister married. He was a particular friend of Sir John's. I believe," she added in a low voice, "he would have been very glad to have had me, if he could. Sir John and Lady Middleton wished it very much. But mama did not think the match good enough for me, otherwise Sir John would have mentioned it to the colonel, and we would have been married immediately."

"Did Colonel Brandon know of Sir John's proposal to your mother before it was made? Had he never admitted his affection to you?"

"Oh! no; but if mama had not objected to it, I dare say he would have liked it of all things. He had not seen me then above twice, for it was before I left school. However, I am much happier as I am. Mr. Palmer is just the kind of man I like."

CHAPTER 21

The Palmers returned to Cleveland the next day, and the two families at Barton were again left to entertain each other. But this did not last long; Elinor had hardly got their last visitors out of her head—had hardly finished wondering at Charlotte's being so happy without a cause, at Mr. Palmer's acting so foolishly with good abilities, and at the strange unsuitableness which often existed between husband and wife, before Sir John's and Mrs. Jennings's active zeal in the cause of society procured her some other new acquaintances to see and observe.

In a morning's excursion to Exeter, they had met with two young ladies, whom Mrs. Jennings had the satisfaction of discovering to be her relations, and this was enough for Sir John to invite them directly to the Park, as soon as their present engagements at Exeter were over. Their engagements at Exeter instantly gave way before such an invitation, and Lady Middleton was thrown into no little alarm on the return of Sir John, by hearing that she was very soon to receive a visit from two girls whom she had never seen in her life, and of whose elegance—whose tolerable gentility even—she could have no proof. The assurances of her husband and mother on that subject meant nothing at all. Their being her relations too, made it so much the worse; and Mrs. Jennings's attempts at consolation—when she advised her daughter not to care about their being so fashionable, because they were all cousins and must put up with one another—utterly failed.

As it was impossible now to prevent their coming, Lady Middleton resigned herself to the idea of it with all the philosophical acceptance of a well-bred woman, contenting herself with merely giving her husband a gentle reprimand on the subject five or six times every day.

The young ladies arrived, their appearance was by no means ungenteel or unfashionable. Their clothing was very elegant, their manners very civil, they were delighted with the house and in raptures with the furnishings. They happened to be so dotingly fond of children that Lady Middleton's good opinion was engaged in their favour before they had been an hour at the Park. She declared them to be very agreeable girls indeed, which for her ladyship was enthusiastic admiration. Sir John's confidence in his own judgment rose with this animated praise, and he set off directly for the cottage to tell the Miss Dashwoods of the Miss Steeles' arrival, and to assure them of their being the sweetest girls in the world. From such commendation as this, however, there was not much to be learned. Elinor well knew that the sweetest girls in the world were to be met with in every part of England, under every possible variation of form, face, temper, and understanding. Sir John wanted the whole family to walk to the Park directly and look at his guests. Benevolent, philanthropic man! It was painful to him even to keep a third cousin to himself.

"Do come now," said he. "Pray come—you must come—I declare you shall come. You can't think how you will like them. Lucy is monstrous pretty, and so good-humoured and agreeable! The children are all hanging about her already, as if she was an old acquaintance. And they both long to see you of all things, for they have heard at Exeter that you are the most beautiful creatures in the world; and I have told them it is all very true, and a great deal more. You will be delighted with them, I am sure. They have brought the whole coach full of playthings for the children. How can you be so cross as not to come? Why they are your cousins, you know, after a fashion. *You* are my cousins, and they are my wife's, so you *must* be related."

But Sir John could not prevail. He could only obtain a promise of their calling at the Park within a day or two, and then left them in amazement at their indifference, to walk home and boast anew of their attractions to the Miss Steeles, as he had been already boasting of the Miss Steeles to them.

When their promised visit to the Park and introduction to these young ladies took place, they found little to admire in the appearance of the eldest. She was nearly thirty, with a very plain and not a sensible face. But in the other, who was not more than twenty-two or twenty-three, they acknowledged considerable beauty. Her features were pretty, and she had a sharp, quick eye, and a smartness of air, which though it did not give actual elegance or grace, gave distinction to her person. Their manners were particularly civil, and Elinor soon gave them credit for having some kind of sense, when she saw with what constant and judicious attentions they were making themselves agreeable to Lady Middleton. With her children they were in continual raptures, extolling their beauty, courting their notice, and humouring all their whims. Such of their time as could be spared from the importunate demands which this politeness made on it, was spent in admiration of whatever her ladyship was doing, if she happened to be doing anything. Fortunately for those who engage in such foibles, a fond mother, in pursuit of praise for her children, will believe anything. The excessive affection of the Miss Steeles towards her offspring was viewed therefore by Lady Middleton without the smallest surprise or distrust. It suggested no other surprise than that Elinor and Marianne should sit so composedly by, without claiming a share in what was passing.

"John is in such spirits today!" she said, on his taking Miss Steele's pocket handkerchief and throwing it out of the window. "He is full of monkey tricks."

And soon afterwards, on the second boy's violently pinching one of the same lady's fingers, she fondly observed, "How playful William is!"

"And here is my sweet little Annamaria," she added, tenderly caressing a little girl of three years old, who had not made a noise for the last two minutes. "She is always so gentle and quiet—never was there such a quiet little thing!"

But unfortunately, in bestowing these embraces, a pin in her ladyship's head-dress slightly scratching the child's neck, produced from this pattern of gentleness a series of violent screams. The mother's consternation was excessive; but it could not surpass the alarm of the Miss Steeles, and everything was done by all three, in so critical an emergency, to assuage the agonies of the little sufferer. She was seated in her mother's lap, covered with kisses, her wound bathed with lavender-water by one of the Miss Steeles, who was on her knees to attend her, and her mouth stuffed with sugar plums by the other. With such a reward for her tears, the child was too wise to cease crying. She still screamed and sobbed lustily, kicked her two brothers for offering to touch her, and all their united soothings were ineffectual till Lady Middleton luckily remembering that in a scene of similar distress, last week, some apricot marmalade had been successfully applied for a bruised temple. The same remedy was eagerly proposed for this unfortunate scratch, and a slight intermission of screams in the young lady on hearing it, gave them reason to hope that it would not be rejected. She was carried out of the room therefore in her mother's arms, in quest of this medicine, and as the two boys chose to follow, though earnestly entreated by their mother to stay behind, the four young ladies were left in a quietness which the room had not known for many hours.

"Poor little creature!" said Miss Steele, as soon as they were gone. "It might have been a very sad accident."

"Yet I hardly know how," cried Marianne, "unless it had been under totally different circumstances. But this is the usual way of heightening alarm, where there is nothing to be alarmed at in reality."

"What a sweet woman Lady Middleton is," said Lucy Steele.

Marianne was silent; it was impossible for her to say what she did not feel, however trivial the occasion. Upon Elinor, therefore, the whole task of telling lies when politeness required it always fell. She did her best when thus called on by speaking of Lady Middleton with more warmth than she felt, though with far less than Miss Lucy.

"And Sir John, too," cried the elder sister, "what a charming man he is!"

Here, too, Miss Dashwood's commendation being only simple and just, came in without any flair. She merely observed that he was perfectly good-humoured and friendly.

"And what a charming little family they have! I never saw such fine children in my life. I declare I quite dote upon them already, and indeed I am always distractedly fond of children."

"I should guess so," said Elinor with a smile, "from what I have witnessed this morning."

"I have a notion," said Lucy, "you think the little Middletons rather too much indulged. Perhaps they may be; but it is so natural in Lady Middleton. For my part, I love to see children full of life and spirits; I cannot bear them if they are tame and quiet."

"I confess," replied Elinor, "that while I am at Barton Park, I never think of tame and quiet children with any abhorrence."

A short pause succeeded this speech, which was first broken by Miss Steele, who seemed very much disposed for conversation, and who now said rather abruptly, "And how do you like Devonshire, Miss Dashwood? I suppose you were very sorry to leave Sussex."

In some surprise at the familiarity of this question, or at least of the manner in which it was spoken, Elinor replied that she was.

"Norland is a prodigious beautiful place, is it not?" added Miss Steele.

"We have heard Sir John admire it excessively," said Lucy, who seemed to think some apology necessary for the familiarity of her sister's conversation.

"I think everyone *must* admire it," replied Elinor, "who ever saw the place; though it is not to be supposed that anyone can esteem its beauties as we do."

"And had you a great many smart beaux there? I suppose you have not so many in this part of the world; for my part, I think they are a vast addition always."

"But why should you think," said Lucy, looking ashamed of her sister, "that there are not as many genteel young men in Devonshire as Sussex?"

"Nay, my dear, I'm sure I don't pretend to say that there an't. I'm sure there's a vast many smart beaux in Exeter; but you know, how could I tell what smart beaux there might be about Norland? I was only afraid the Miss Dashwoods might find it dull at Barton, if they had not as many as they used to have. But perhaps you young ladies may not care about the beaux, and could just as well be without them as with them. For my part, I think they are vastly agreeable, provided they dress smart and behave civil. But I can't bear to see them dirty and nasty. Now, there's Mr. Rose at Exeter, a prodigious smart young man, quite a beau, clerk to Mr. Simpson, you know, and yet if you do but meet him in the morning, he is not fit to be seen. I suppose your brother was quite a beau, Miss Dashwood, before he married, as he was so rich?"

"Upon my word," replied Elinor, "I cannot tell you, for I do not perfectly comprehend the meaning of the word. But this I can say, that if he ever was a beau before he married, he is one still, for there is not the smallest alteration in him."

"Oh dear! One never thinks of married men being beaux—they have something else to do."

"Lord! Anne," cried her sister, "you can talk of nothing but beaux—you will make Miss Dashwood believe you think of nothing else." And then to turn the discourse, she began admiring the house and the furniture.

This specimen of the Miss Steeles was enough. The vulgar freedom and folly of the eldest left her no recommendation, and as Elinor was not blinded by the beauty or the shrewd look of the youngest, to her lack of real elegance and artlessness, she left the house without any wish of knowing them better.

Not so the Miss Steeles. They came from Exeter well-provided with admiration for the use of Sir John Middleton, his family, and all his relations, including his fair cousins, whom they declared to be the most beautiful, elegant, accomplished and agreeable girls they had ever beheld, and with whom they were particularly anxious to be better acquainted. To be better acquainted, therefore, Elinor soon found was their inevitable lot; for as Sir John was entirely on the side of the Miss Steeles, their party would be too strong for opposition, and that kind of intimacy must be submitted to, which consists of sitting an hour or two together in the same room almost every day. Sir John could do not more; but he did not know that any more was required. To be together was, in his opinion, to be intimate, and while his continual schemes for their meeting were effectual, he had not a doubt of their being established friends.

To do him justice, he did everything in his power to promote their unreserve by making the Miss Steeles acquainted with whatever he knew or supposed of his cousins' situations in the most delicate particulars. Elinor had not seen them more than twice, before the eldest of them wished her joy on her sister's having been so lucky as to make a conquest of a very smart beau since she came to Barton.

"'Twill be a fine thing to have her married so young, to be sure," said she, "and I hear he is quite a beau, and prodigious handsome. And I hope you may have as good luck yourself soon—but perhaps you may have a friend in the corner already."

Elinor could not suppose that Sir John would be more nice in proclaiming his suspicions of her regard for Edward than he had been with respect to Marianne; indeed it was rather his favourite joke of the two, as being somewhat newer Since Edward's visit, they had never dined together, without his drinking to her best affections with so many nods and winks as to excite general attention. The letter F had been likewise invariably brought forward, and found productive of such countless jokes, that its character as the wittiest letter in the alphabet had been long established with Elinor.

The Miss Steeles, as she expected, had now all the benefit of these jokes, and in the eldest of them they raised a curiosity to know the name of the gentleman alluded to, which, though often impertinently expressed, was perfectly in line with her general inquisitiveness into the concerns of their family. But Sir John did not sport long with the curiosity which he delighted to raise, for he had at least as much pleasure in telling the name as Miss Steele had in hearing it.

"His name is Ferrars," said he, in a very audible whisper; "but pray do not tell it, for it is a great secret."

"Ferrars!" repeated Miss Steele; "Mr. Ferrars is the happy man, is he? What! Your sister-in-law's brother, Miss Dashwood? A very agreeable young man to be sure; I know him very well."

"How can you say so Anne?" cried Lucy, who generally made an amendment to all her sister's assertions. "Though we have seen him once or twice at my uncle's, it is rather too much to pretend to know him very well."

Elinor heard all this with attention and surprise. "And who was this uncle? Where did he live? How came they to be acquainted?" She wished very much to have the subject continued, though she did not choose to join in it herself; but nothing more of it was said, and, for the first time in her life, she thought Mrs. Jennings deficient in curiosity after petty information. The manner in which Miss Steele had spoken of Edward increased her curiosity, for it struck her, as being rather ill-natured, and suggested the suspicion of that lady's knowing something to his disadvantage. But her curiosity was unavailing, for no farther notice was taken of Mr. Ferrars's name by Miss Steele when alluded to or even openly mentioned by Sir John.

CHAPTER 22

Marianne, who had little tolerance for anything like vulgarity or difference of taste from herself, was at this time particularly ill-disposed, from the state of her spirits, to be pleased with the Miss Steeles, or to encourage their advances. To the invariable coldness of her behaviour towards them, which prevented every endeavour at intimacy on their side, Elinor principally attributed that preference of herself which soon became evident in the manners of both, but especially of Lucy, who missed no opportunity of engaging her in conversation, or of striving to improve their acquaintance by an easy and frank communication of her sentiments.

Lucy was naturally clever; her remarks were often just and amusing, and as a companion for half an hour Elinor frequently found her agreeable. But her abilities had received no aid from education: she was ignorant and illiterate, and her deficiency of all mental improvement, her lack of information in the most common particulars, could not be concealed from Miss Dashwood, in spite of her constant endeavour to appear to advantage. Elinor saw, and pitied her for, the neglect of abilities which education might have rendered so respectable; but she saw, with less tenderness of feeling, the thorough lack of delicacy and integrity which her attentions and flatteries at the Park betrayed. She could have no lasting satisfaction in the company of a person who joined insincerity with ignorance, and whose conduct towards others made every show of attention and deference towards herself perfectly valueless.

"You will think my question an odd one, I dare say," said Lucy to her one day as they were walking together from the park to the cottage—"but, pray, are you personally acquainted with your sister-in-law's mother, Mrs. Ferrars?"

Elinor *did* think the question a very odd one, and her countenance expressed it, as she answered that she had never seen Mrs. Ferrars.

"Indeed!" replied Lucy; "I wonder at that, for I thought you must have seen her at Norland sometimes. Then perhaps you cannot tell me what sort of a woman she is?"

"No," returned Elinor, cautious of giving her real opinion of Edward's mother, and not very desirous of satisfying what seemed pointless curiosity, "I know nothing of her."

"I am sure you think me very strange for inquiring about her in such a way," said Lucy, eyeing Elinor attentively as she spoke, "but perhaps there may be reasons—I wish I could say what they were, but I hope you will do me the justice of believing that I do not mean to be impertinent."

Elinor made her a civil reply, and they walked on for a few minutes in silence. It was broken by Lucy, who renewed the subject again by saying with some hesitation,

"I cannot bear to have you think me impertinently curious. I am sure I would rather do anything in the world than be thought so by a person whose good opinion is as well worth having as yours. And I am sure I should not have the smallest fear of trusting *you*; indeed I should be very glad of your advice about how to manage an uncomfortable situation. But there is no occasion to trouble *you*. I am sorry you do not happen to know Mrs. Ferrars."

"I am sorry I do *not*," said Elinor in great astonishment, "if it could be of any use to *you* to know my opinion of her. But really, I never understood that you were at all connected with that family, and therefore I am a little surprised, I confess, at so serious an inquiry into her character."

"I dare say you are, and I am sure I do not at all wonder at it. But if I told you all, you would not be so much surprised. Mrs. Ferrars is certainly nothing to me at present—but the time *may* come—how soon it will come must depend upon herself— when we may be very intimately connected."

She looked down as she said this, amiably bashful, with only one side glance at her companion to observe its effect on her.

"Good heavens!" cried Elinor, "What do you mean? Are you acquainted with Mr. Robert Ferrars? Can you be—?" She did not feel much delighted with the idea of such a sister-in-law.

"No," replied Lucy, "not to Mr. *Robert* Ferrars—I never saw him in my life; but," fixing her eyes upon Elinor, "to his elder brother."

What Elinor felt at that moment! She turned towards Lucy in silent amazement, unable to divine the reason or object of such a declaration; and though her complexion varied, she stood firm, and felt in no danger of a hysterical fit, or a swoon.

"You may well be surprised," continued Lucy; "for to be sure, you could have had no idea of it before; for I dare say he never dropped the smallest hint of it to you or any of your family. It was always meant to be a great secret, and I am sure it has been faithfully kept so by me to this hour. Not a soul of all my relations know of it but Anne, and I never should have mentioned it to you, if I had not felt the greatest dependence in the world upon your secrecy; and I really thought my behaviour in asking so many questions about Mrs. Ferrars must seem so odd that it ought to be explained. And I do not think Mr. Ferrars can be displeased when he learns I have told you, because I know he has the highest opinion in the world of all your family, and looks upon yourself and the other Miss Dashwoods quite as his own sisters." She paused.

Elinor for a few moments remained silent. Her astonishment at what she heard was at first too great for words; but at length forcing herself to speak, and to speak cautiously. She said with a calmness of manner which tolerably well concealed her surprise and solicitude—"May I ask if your engagement is of long standing?"

"We have been engaged these four years."

"Four years!"

"Yes."

Elinor, though greatly shocked, still felt unable to believe it.

"I did not know," said she, "that you were even acquainted till the other day."

"Our acquaintance, however, is of many years' date. He was under my uncle's care, you know, a considerable while."

"Your uncle!"

"Yes; Mr. Pratt. Did you never hear him talk of Mr. Pratt?"

"I think I have," replied Elinor, with an exertion of spirits which increased with her heightened emotions.

"He was four years with my uncle, who lives at Longstaple, near Plymouth. It was there our acquaintance begun, for my sister and me was often staying with my uncle, and it was there our engagement was formed, though not till a year after he had quitted as a pupil; but he was almost always with us afterwards. I was very unwilling to enter into it, as you may imagine, without the knowledge and approval of his mother; but I was too young and loved him too well to be as prudent as I ought to have been. Though you do not know him as well as me, Miss Dashwood, you must have seen enough of him to be sensible he is very capable of making a woman sincerely attached to him."

"Certainly," answered Elinor, without knowing what she said; but after a moment's reflection, she added with revived security of Edward's honour and love, and her companion's falsehood— "Engaged to Mr. Edward Ferrars!—I confess myself so totally surprised at what you tell me, that really—I beg your pardon; but surely there must be some mistake of person or name. We cannot mean the same Mr. Ferrars."

"We can mean no other," cried Lucy smiling. "Mr. Edward Ferrars, the eldest son of Mrs. Ferrars of Park Street, and brother of your sister-in-law, Mrs. John Dashwood, is the person I mean; you must allow that *I* am not likely to be deceived as to the name of the man on who all my happiness depends."

"It is strange," replied Elinor, in a most painful perplexity, "that I should never have heard him even mention your name." "No; considering our situation, it was not strange. Our first care has been to keep the matter secret. You knew nothing of me or my family, and therefore there could be no *occasion* for ever mentioning my name to you; and as he was always particularly afraid of his sister's suspecting anything, *that* was reason enough for his not mentioning it."

She was silent. Elinor's confidence sank; but her self-command did not sink with it.

"Four years you have been engaged," said she with a firm voice.

"Yes; and Heaven knows how much longer we may have to wait. Poor Edward! It puts him quite out of spirits." Then taking a small miniature from her pocket, she added, "To prevent the possibility of mistake, be so good as to look at this face. It does not do him justice to be sure, but yet I think you cannot be deceived as to the person it represents. I have had it for three years."

She put it into her hands as she spoke, and when Elinor saw the painting, whatever other doubts her fear of a too hasty decision, or her wish of detecting falsehood might suffer to linger in her mind, she could have none of its being Edward's face. She returned it almost instantly, acknowledging the likeness.

"I have never been able," continued Lucy, "to give him my picture in return, which I am very much vexed at, for he has been always so anxious to get it! But I am determined to sit for it at the very first opportunity."

"You are quite in the right," replied Elinor calmly. They then proceeded a few paces in silence. Lucy spoke first.

"I am sure," said she, "I have no doubt in the world of your faithfully keeping this secret, because you must know of what importance it is to us not to have it reach his mother; for she would never approve of it, I dare say. I shall have no fortune, and I fancy she is an exceeding proud woman."

"I certainly did not seek your confidence," said Elinor; "but I may be depended on. Your secret is safe with me; but pardon me if I express some surprise at so unnecessary a communication. You must at least have felt that my being acquainted with it could not add to its safety."

As she said this, she looked earnestly at Lucy, hoping to discover something in her countenance—perhaps the falsehood of the greatest part of what she had been saying; but Lucy's countenance did not change.

"I was afraid you would think I was taking a great liberty with you," said she, "in telling you all this. I have not known you long to be sure, personally at least, but I have known you and all your family by description a great while. As soon as I saw you, I felt almost as if you was an old acquaintance. Besides, in the present case, I really thought some explanation was due to you after my making such particular inquiries about Edward's mother; and I am so unfortunate, that I have not a creature whose advice I can ask. Anne is the only person that knows of it, and she has no judgment at all; indeed she does me a great deal more harm than good, for I am in constant fear of her betraying me. She does not know how to hold her tongue, as you must perceive; and I am sure I was in the greatest fright in the world t'other day, when Edward's name was mentioned by Sir John, lest she should out with it all. You can't think how much I go through in my mind from it altogether. I only wonder that I am alive after what I have suffered for Edward's sake these last four years. Everything in such suspense and uncertainty, and seeing him so seldom—we can hardly meet more than twice a year. I am sure I wonder my heart is not quite broke."

Here she took out her handkerchief; but Elinor did not feel very compassionate.

"Sometimes," continued Lucy, after wiping her eyes, "I think whether it would not be better for us both, to break off the matter entirely." As she said this, she looked directly at her companion. "But then at other times I have not resolution enough for it. I cannot bear the thought of making him so miserable, as I know the very mention of such a thing would do. And on my own account too—as dear as he is to me—I don't think I could be equal to it. What would you advise me to do in such a case, Miss Dashwood? What would you do yourself?"

"Pardon me," replied Elinor, startled by the question; "but I can give you no advice under such circumstances. Your own judgment must direct you."

"To be sure," continued Lucy, after a few minutes silence on both sides, "his mother must provide for him some time or other; but poor Edward is so cast down about it! Did not you think him dreadful low-spirited when he was at Barton? He was so miserable when he left us at Longstaple, to go to you, that I was afraid you would think him quite ill."

"Did he come from your uncle's then, when he visited us?"

"Oh! Yes; he had been staying a fortnight with us. Did you think he came directly from town?"

"No," replied Elinor, sensible of every fresh circumstance in favour of Lucy's honesty. "I remember he told us that he had been staying a fortnight with some friends near Plymouth." She remembered, too, her own surprise at the time, at his mentioning nothing farther of those friends, at his total silence with respect even to their names.

"Did not you think him sadly out of spirits?" repeated Lucy.

"We did indeed, particularly so when he first arrived."

"I begged him to exert himself for fear you should suspect what was the matter; but it made him so melancholy, not being able to stay more than a fortnight with us, and seeing me so much affected. Poor fellow! I am afraid it is just the same with him now; for he writes in wretched spirits. I heard from him just before I left Exeter;" taking a letter from her pocket and carelessly showing the direction to Elinor. "You know his hand, I dare say, a charming one it is; but that is not written as well as usual. He was tired, I dare say, for he had just filled the sheet to me as full as possible."

Elinor saw that it *was* his hand, and she could doubt no longer. The picture, she had allowed herself to believe, might have been accidentally obtained; it might not have been Edward's gift; but a correspondence between them by letter could subsist only under a positive engagement, could be authorised by nothing else. For a few moments, she was almost overcome—her heart sunk within her, and she could hardly stand; but exertion was indispensably necessary, and she struggled so resolutely against the oppression of her feelings, that her success was speedy, and for the time complete.

"Writing to each other," said Lucy, returning the letter into her pocket, "is the only comfort we have in such long separations. Yes, *I* have one other comfort in his picture; but poor Edward has not even *that*. If he had but my picture, he says he would feel so much better. I gave him a lock of my hair set in a ring when he was at Longstaple last, and that was some comfort to him, he said, but not equal to a picture. Perhaps you might have noticed the ring when you saw him?"

"I did," said Elinor, with a composure of voice under which was concealed an emotion and distress beyond anything she had ever felt before. She was mortified, shocked, confounded.

Fortunately for her they had now reached the cottage, and the conversation could be continued no farther. After sitting with them a few minutes, the Miss Steeles returned to the Park, and Elinor was then at liberty to think and be wretched.

CHAPTER 23

However small Elinor's general trust in Lucy's honesty might be, it was impossible for her on serious reflection to believe that she was being lied to in the present case, as nothing could explain the folly of inventing a falsehood of such a description. What Lucy had asserted to be true, therefore, Elinor could not doubt; supported as it was too on every side by such probabilities and proofs, and contradicted by nothing but her own wishes. Their opportunity of acquaintance in the house of Mr. Pratt was a foundation for the rest, at once indisputable and alarming. Edward's visit near Plymouth, his melancholy state of mind, his dissatisfaction at his own prospects, his uncertain behaviour towards herself, the intimate knowledge of the Miss Steeles as to Norland and their family connections, which had often surprised her, the picture, the letter, the ring, formed altogether such a body of evidence, as overcame every fear of condemning him unfairly, and established as a fact for which no excuse could be made, his ill-treatment of herself. Her resentment of such behaviour, her indignation at having been its dupe, for a short time made her feel only for herself; but other ideas, other considerations soon arose. Had Edward been intentionally deceiving her? Had he feigned a regard for her which he did not feel? Did he truly love Lucy? No; whatever it might once have been, she could not believe it such at present. His affection was all her own. She could not be deceived in that. Her mother, sisters, Fanny, all had been aware of his regard for her at Norland; it was not an illusion of her own vanity. He certainly loved her. What a softener of the heart was this persuasion! How much could it not tempt her to forgive! He had been blameable, highly blameable, in remaining at Norland after he felt her influence over him to be more than it ought to be. In that, he could not be defended; but if he had injured her, how much more had he injured himself! If her case were pitiable, his was hopeless. His imprudence had made her miserable for a while; but it seemed to have deprived himself of all chance of ever being otherwise. She might in time regain tranquillity; but *he*, what had he to look forward to? Could he ever be tolerably happy with Lucy Steele? Could he, were his affection for herself out of the question, with his integrity, his delicacy, and well-informed mind, be satisfied with a wife like her— uneducated, scheming, and selfish?

The youthful infatuation of nineteen would naturally blind him to everything but her beauty and good nature; but the four succeeding years—years, which if rationally spent, give such improvement to the understanding, must have opened his eyes to her defects of education. The same period of time, spent on her side in inferior society and more frivolous pursuits, had perhaps robbed her of that simplicity which might once have given an interesting character to her beauty.

If his difficulties from his mother had seemed great, when a match between him and herself had been in question, how much greater were they now likely to be, when the object of his engagement was undoubtedly inferior in connections, and probably inferior in fortune to herself! These difficulties, indeed, with a heart so alienated from Lucy, might not press very hard upon his patience; but sad indeed was the state of the person whose only hope for rescue was the opposition of family!

As these considerations occurred to her in painful succession, she wept for him more than for herself. Supported by the conviction of having done nothing to merit her present unhappiness, and consoled by the belief that Edward had done nothing to forfeit her esteem, she thought she could even now, under the first sting of the heavy blow, command herself enough to guard every suspicion of the truth from her mother and sisters. So well was she able to answer her own expectations, that when she joined them at dinner only two hours after she had first suffered the extinction of all her dearest hopes, no one would have supposed from the appearance of the sisters that Elinor was mourning in secret over obstacles which must divide her forever from the object of her love, and that Marianne was internally dwelling on the perfections of a man, of whose whole heart she felt thoroughly possessed, and whom she expected to see in every carriage which drove near their house.

The necessity of concealing from her mother and Marianne what had been entrusted in confidence to herself, though it obliged her to unceasing exertion, was no aggravation of Elinor's distress. On the contrary, it was a relief to her, to be spared the communication of what would give such affliction to them, and to be saved likewise from hearing that condemnation of Edward, which would probably flow from the excess of their affection for herself, and which was more than she felt equal to support.

From their counsel or their conversation she knew she could receive no assistance; their tenderness and sorrow must add to her distress, while her self-command would neither receive encouragement from their example nor from their praise. She was stronger alone, and her own good sense so well supported her, that her firmness was as unshaken, her appearance of cheerfulness as invariable, as, with regrets so poignant and so fresh, it was possible for them to be.

Much as she had suffered from her first conversation with Lucy on the subject, she soon felt an earnest wish of renewing it, and this for more reasons than one. She wanted to hear many particulars of their engagement repeated again, she wanted more clearly to understand what Lucy really felt for Edward, whether there were any sincerity in her declaration of tender regard for him, and she particularly wanted to convince Lucy, by her readiness to enter on the matter again, and her calmness in conversing on it, that she had no other interest in it than as a friend, which she very much feared her involuntary agitation, in their morning discussion, must have left at least doubtful. That Lucy was disposed to be jealous of her appeared very probable; it was plain that Edward had always spoken highly in her praise, not merely from Lucy's assertion, but from her venturing to trust her on so short a personal acquaintance, with a secret so confessedly and evidently important. And even Sir John's joking intelligence must have had some weight. But indeed, while Elinor remained so well assured within herself of being really beloved by Edward, it required no other consideration of probabilities to make it natural that Lucy should be jealous; and that she was so, her confiding the secret of their engagement was a proof. What other reason for the disclosure of the affair could there be, but that Elinor might be informed by it of Lucy's superior claims on Edward, and be taught to avoid him in future? She had little difficulty in understanding this much of her rival's intentions, and while she was firmly resolved to act by her as every principle of honour and honesty directed, to combat her own affection for Edward and to see him as little as possible, she could not deny herself the comfort of endeavouring to convince Lucy that her heart was unwounded. And as she could now have nothing more painful to hear on the subject than had already been told, she did not mistrust her own ability of going through a repetition of particulars with composure.

But it was not immediately that an opportunity of doing so was offered, though Lucy was as well-disposed as herself to take advantage of any that occurred. The weather was not often fine enough to allow of their joining in a walk, where they might most easily separate themselves from the others; and though they met at least every other evening either at the Park or cottage, and chiefly at the former, they could not be supposed to meet for the sake of conversation. Such a thought would never enter either Sir John or Lady Middleton's head, and therefore very little leisure was ever given for general chat, and none at all for private conversation. They met for the sake of eating, drinking, and laughing together, playing at cards or any other game that was sufficiently noisy.

One or two meetings of this kind had taken place without affording Elinor any chance of engaging Lucy in private, when Sir John called at the cottage one morning, to beg in the name of charity, that they would all dine with Lady Middleton that day, as he was obliged to attend the club at Exeter, and she would otherwise be quite alone, except her mother and the two Miss Steeles. Elinor, who foresaw an opportunity to talk to Lucy, immediately accepted the invitation; Margaret, with her mother's permission, was equally compliant, and Marianne, though always unwilling to join any of their parties, was persuaded by her mother, who could not bear to have her seclude herself from any chance of amusement, to go likewise.

The young ladies went, and Lady Middleton was happily preserved from the frightful solitude which had threatened her. The dullness of the meeting was exactly such as Elinor had expected; it produced not one novelty of thought or expression, and nothing could be less interesting than the whole of their conversation both in the dining parlour and drawing-room. To the latter, the children accompanied them, and while they remained there, she was too well convinced of the impossibility of engaging Lucy's attention to attempt it. They left it only with the removal of the tea things. The card table was then placed, and Elinor began to wonder at herself for having ever entertained a hope of finding time for conversation at the Park. They all rose up in preparation for a game.

"I am glad," said Lady Middleton to Lucy, "you are not going to finish poor little Annamaria's basket this evening; for I am sure it must hurt your eyes to work by candlelight. And we will make the dear little love some amends for her disappointment tomorrow, and then I hope she will not much mind it."

This hint was enough; Lucy recollected herself instantly and replied, "Indeed you are very much mistaken, Lady Middleton; I am only waiting to know whether you can make your party without me, or I should have been at my work already. I would not disappoint the little angel for all the world; and if you want me at the card table now, I am resolved to finish the basket after supper."

"You are very good. I hope it won't hurt your eyes—will you ring the bell for some candles? My poor little girl would be sadly disappointed, I know, if the basket was not finished tomorrow, for though I told her it certainly would not, I am sure she depends upon having it done."

Lucy directly drew her work table near her and reseated herself with a cheerfulness which seemed to infer that she could taste no greater delight than in making a basket for a spoiled child.

Lady Middleton proposed a round of casino to the others. No one made any objection but Marianne, who, with her usual inattention to the forms of general civility, exclaimed, "Your ladyship will have the goodness to excuse *me*—you know I detest cards. I shall go to the piano; I have not touched it since it was tuned." And without farther ceremony, she turned away and walked to the instrument.

Lady Middleton looked as if she thanked heaven that *she* had never made so rude a speech.

"Marianne can never keep long from that instrument you know, ma'am," said Elinor, endeavouring to smooth away the offence; "and

I do not much wonder at it, for it is the very best-toned piano I ever heard."

The remaining five were now to draw their cards.

"Perhaps," continued Elinor, "if I did not join the game, I may be of some use to Miss Lucy Steele; there is so much still to be done to the basket, that it must be impossible, I think, for her labour alone and finish it this evening. I should like the work exceedingly, if she would allow me a share in it."

"Indeed I shall be very much obliged to you for your help," cried Lucy, "for I find there is more to be done to it than I thought there was; and it would be a shocking thing to disappoint dear Annamaria after all."

"Oh! That would be terrible indeed," said Miss Steele "Dear little soul, how I do love her!"

"You are very kind," said Lady Middleton to Elinor. "As you really like the work, perhaps you could join the game when you have finished?"

Elinor joyfully profited by this proposal, and thus, by a little of that address which Marianne could never condescend to practise, gained her own end, and pleased Lady Middleton at the same time. Lucy made room for her with ready attention, and the two fair rivals were thus seated side by side at the same table, and with the utmost harmony engaged in the same work. The piano, at which Marianne, wrapped up in her own music and her own thoughts, had by this time forgotten that anybody was in the room besides herself, was luckily so near them that Miss Dashwood now judged she might safely, under the shelter of its noise, introduce the subject in question without any risk of being heard at the card table.

CHAPTER 24

In a firm, though cautious tone, Elinor thus began —

"I should be undeserving of the confidence you have honoured me with, if I felt no desire for its continuance, or no farther curiosity on its subject. I will not apologize therefore for bringing it forward again."

"Thank you," cried Lucy warmly, "for breaking the ice; you have set my heart at ease by it. I was somehow or other afraid I had offended you by what I told you that Monday."

"Offended me! How could you suppose so? Believe me," and Elinor spoke it with the truest sincerity, "nothing could be farther from my intention than to give you such an idea. Could you have a motive for the trust that was not honourable and flattering to me?"

"And yet I do assure you," replied Lucy, her little sharp eyes full of meaning, "there seemed to me to be a coldness and displeasure in your manner that made me quite uncomfortable. I felt sure that you was angry with me; and have been quarrelling with myself ever since, for having took such a liberty as to trouble you with my affairs. But I am very glad to find it was only my own fancy, and that you do not really blame me. If you knew what a consolation it was to me to relieve my heart by speaking to you of what I am always thinking of every moment of my life, your compassion would make you overlook everything else, I am sure."

"Indeed I can easily believe that it was a very great relief to you, to acknowledge your situation to me, and be assured that you shall never have reason to regret it. Your case is a very unfortunate one;

you seem to me to be surrounded with difficulties, and you will have need of all your mutual affection to support you under them. Mr. Ferrars, I believe, is entirely dependent on his mother."

"He has only two thousand pounds of his own; it would be madness to marry upon that, though for my own part I could give up every prospect of more without a sigh. I have been always used to a very small income, and could struggle with any poverty for him. But I love him too well to be the selfish means of robbing him, perhaps, of all that his mother might give him if he married to please her. We must wait, it may be for many years. With almost every other man in the world, it would be an alarming prospect; but I know nothing can deprive me of Edward's affection and constancy."

"That conviction must be everything to you; and he is undoubtedly supported by the same trust in yours. If the strength of your reciprocal attachment had failed, as between many people and under many circumstances it naturally would during a four years' engagement, your situation would have been pitiable indeed."

Lucy here looked up; but Elinor was careful in guarding her countenance from every expression that could give her words a suspicious tendency.

"Edward's love for me," said Lucy, "has been pretty well put to the test, by our long, very long absence since we were first engaged, and it has stood the trial so well, that I should be unpardonable to doubt it now. I can safely say that he has never gave me one moment's alarm on that account from the first."

Elinor hardly knew whether to smile or sigh at this assertion.

Lucy went on. "I am rather of a jealous temper, too, by nature, and from our different situations in life, from his being of so much more consequence in the world than me, and our continual separation, I was enough inclined for suspicion, to have found out the truth in an instant, if there had been the slightest alteration in his behaviour to me when we met, or any lowness of spirits that I could not account for, or if he had talked more of one lady than another, or seemed in any respect less happy at Longstaple than he used to be. I do not mean to say that I am particularly observant or quick-sighted in general, but in such a case I am sure I could not be deceived."

"But what," said Elinor, after a short silence, "are your views? Or have you none but that of waiting for Mrs. Ferrars's death, which is a melancholy and shocking extremity? Is her son determined to submit to this, and to all the tediousness of the many years of suspense in which it may involve you, rather than run the risk of her displeasure for a while by confessing the truth?"

"If we could be certain that it would be only for a while! But Mrs. Ferrars is a very headstrong, proud woman, and in her first fit of anger upon hearing it, would very likely secure everything to Robert; and the idea of that, for Edward's sake, frightens away all my inclination for hasty measures."

"And for your own sake too, as a marriage of relative poverty would hardly be ideal."

Lucy looked at Elinor again, and was silent.

"Do you know Mr. Robert Ferrars?" asked Elinor.

"Not at all—I never saw him; but I fancy he is very unlike his brother—pompous and vain."

"Pompous and vain!" repeated Miss Steele, whose ear had caught those words by a sudden pause in Marianne's music. "Oh! they are talking of their favourite beaux, I dare say."

"No, sister," cried Lucy, "you are mistaken there, our favourite beaux are *not* pompous and vain."

"I can answer for it that Miss Dashwood's is not," said Mrs. Jennings, laughing heartily; "for he is one of the modestest, best behaved young men I ever saw. But as for Lucy, she is such a sly little creature, there is no finding out who *she* likes."

"Oh!" cried Miss Steele, looking significantly round at them, "I dare say Lucy's beau is quite as modest and well-behaved as Miss Dashwood's."

Elinor blushed in spite of herself. Lucy bit her lip, and looked angrily at her sister. A mutual silence took place for some time. Lucy first put an end to it by saying in a lower tone, though Marianne was then giving them the powerful protection of a very magnificent piece of music —

"I will honestly tell you of one scheme which has lately come into my head, for bringing matters to bear; indeed I am bound to let you into the secret, for you are a party concerned. I dare say you have seen enough of Edward to know that he would prefer the church to every other profession. Now, my plan is that he should take orders as soon as he can, and then through your recommendation, which I am sure you would be kind enough to make out of friendship for him, and I hope, out of some regard to me, your brother might be persuaded to give him the Norland living; which I understand is a very good one, and the present occupant not likely to live a great while. That would be enough for us to marry upon, and we might trust to time and chance for the rest."

"I should be always happy," replied Elinor, "to show any mark of my esteem and friendship for Mr. Ferrars; but do not you perceive that my recommendation on such an occasion would be perfectly unnecessary? He is the brother of Mrs. John Dashwood—*that* must be recommendation enough for her husband."

"But Mrs. John Dashwood would not much approve of Edward's going into orders."

"Then I rather suspect that my recommendation would do very little."

They were again silent for many minutes. At length Lucy exclaimed with a deep sigh —

"I believe it would be the wisest way to put an end to the business at once by dissolving the engagement. We seem so beset with difficulties on every side, that though it would make us miserable for a time, we should be happier perhaps in the end. But you will not give me your advice, Miss Dashwood?"

"No," answered Elinor, with a smile which concealed very agitated feelings, "on such a subject I certainly will not. You know very well that my opinion would have no weight with you, unless it were on the side of your wishes."

"Indeed, you wrong me," replied Lucy with great solemnity. "I know nobody of whose judgment I think so highly as I do of yours; and I do really believe that if you was to say to me, 'I advise you by all means to put an end to your engagement with Edward Ferrars, it will be more for the happiness of both of you,' I should resolve upon doing it immediately."

Elinor blushed for the insincerity of Edward's future wife, and replied, "This compliment would frighten me from giving any opinion on the subject, had I formed one. It raises my influence much too high; the power of dividing two people so tenderly attached is too much for an indifferent person."

"'Tis because you are an indifferent person," said Lucy, with some heat, and laying a particular stress on those words, "that your judgment might justly have such weight with me. If you could be supposed to be biased in any respect by your own feelings, your opinion would not be worth having."

Elinor thought it wisest to make no answer to this, lest they might provoke each other to an unsuitable increase of incivility; and was even partly determined never to mention the subject again. Another pause therefore of many minutes' duration succeeded this speech, and Lucy was still the first to end it.

"Shall you be in town this winter, Miss Dashwood?" she asked.

"Certainly not."

"I am sorry for that," returned the other, while her eyes brightened at the information. "It would have gave me such pleasure to meet you there! But I dare say you will go in the end. To be sure, your brother and sister will ask you to come to them."

"It will not be in my power to accept their invitation if they do."

"How unlucky that is! I had quite depended upon meeting you there. Anne and me are to go the latter end of January to some relations who have been wanting us to visit them these several years! But I only go for the sake of seeing Edward. He will be there in February; otherwise London would have no charms for me, I have not spirits for it."

Elinor was soon called to the card table by the conclusion of the first game, and the confidential discussion of the two ladies was therefore at an end, to which both of them submitted without any reluctance, for nothing had been said on either side to make them dislike each other less than they had done before. Elinor sat down to the card table with the melancholy persuasion that Edward was not only without affection for the person who was to be his wife, but that he had not even the chance of being tolerably happy in marriage, which sincere affection on *her* side would have given, for self-interest alone could induce a woman to keep a man to an engagement, of which she seemed so thoroughly aware that he was weary.

From this time the subject was never brought up by Elinor; and when entered on by Lucy, who seldom missed an opportunity of introducing it, and was particularly careful to inform her confidante of her happiness whenever she received a letter from Edward, it was treated by the former with calmness and caution, and dismissed as soon as civility would allow. She felt such conversations to be an indulgence which Lucy did not deserve, and which were dangerous to herself.

The visit of the Miss Steeles at Barton Park was lengthened far beyond what the first invitation implied. Their favour increased, and they could not be spared; Sir John would not hear of their going. In spite of their numerous and long arranged engagements in Exeter, in spite of the absolute necessity of their returning to fulfil them immediately, which was in full force at the end of every week, they were prevailed on to stay nearly two months at the Park.

CHAPTER 25

Though Mrs. Jennings was in the habit of spending a large portion of the year at the houses of her children and friends, she was not without a settled habitation of her own. Since the death of her husband, who had traded with success in a less elegant part of town, she had resided every winter in a house in one of the streets near Portman Square. As January drew near, she began to think it was time for her to go to London. One day she abruptly, and very unexpectedly by them, asked the elder Miss Dashwoods to accompany her. Elinor, without seeing the animated look of her sister, which indicated her approval of the plan, immediately gave a grateful but absolute denial for both, in which she believed herself to be speaking their united inclinations. The reason alleged was their determined resolution of not leaving their mother at that time of year. Mrs. Jennings received the refusal with some surprise, and repeated her invitation immediately.

"Oh Lord! I am sure your mother can spare you very well, and I *do* beg you will favour me with your company, for I've quite set my heart upon it. Don't think you will be any inconvenience to me, for I shan't put myself at all out of my way for you. We shall be able to go very well in my carriage; and when we are in town, if you do not want to go wherever I do, you can always go with one of my daughters. I am sure your mother will not object to it; for I have had such good luck in getting my own children married off, that she will think me a very fit person to be in charge of you. If I don't get one of you at least well married before I am finished with you, it shall not be my fault. I shall speak a good word for you to all the young men, you may depend upon it."

"I have a notion," said Sir John, "that Miss Marianne would not object to such a scheme, if her elder sister would agree to it. It is very hard indeed that she should not have a little pleasure, because Miss Dashwood does not wish it. So I would advise you two to set off for town, when you are tired of Barton, without saying a word to Miss Dashwood about it."

"Nay," cried Mrs. Jennings, "I am sure I shall be monstrous glad of Miss Marianne's company, whether Miss Dashwood will go or not, only the more the merrier say I, and I thought it would be more comfortable for them to be together. If they get tired of me, they might talk to one another, and laugh at my odd ways behind my back. But one or the other, if not both of them, I must have. Lord bless me! How do you think I can live all alone this winter, when I have always had my Charlotte with me before. Come, Miss Marianne, let us strike hands upon the bargain, and if Miss Dashwood will change her mind, why, so much the better."

"I thank you, ma'am, sincerely thank you," said Marianne, with warmth. "Your invitation has ensured my gratitude forever, and it would give me such happiness, yes almost the greatest happiness I am capable of, to be able to accept it. But my mother, my dearest, kindest mother—I feel the justice of what Elinor has urged, and if she were to be made less happy, less comfortable by our absence— Oh! No, nothing should tempt me to leave her. It should not, must not be a struggle."

Mrs. Jennings repeated her assurance that Mrs. Dashwood could spare them perfectly well; and Elinor, who now understood her sister, and saw that she was simply eager to be with Willoughby again, made no farther direct opposition to the plan, and merely referred it to her mother's decision.

On being informed of the invitation, Mrs. Dashwood, persuaded that such an excursion would produce much amusement to both her daughters, and perceiving through all her affectionate attention to herself, how much the heart of Marianne was in it, would not hear of their declining the offer upon *her* account. She insisted on their both accepting it immediately, and then began to foresee with her usual cheerfulness a variety of advantages that this separation would bring to them all.

"I am delighted with the plan," she cried, "it is exactly what I could wish. Margaret and I shall be as much benefited by it as yourselves. When you and the Middletons are gone, we shall go on so quietly and happily together with our books and our music! You will find Margaret so improved when you come back again! And I have a little plan of alteration for your bedrooms too, which may now be performed without inconvenience to anyone. It is very right that you *should* go to town; I would have every young woman of your condition in life acquainted with the manners and amusements of London. You will be under the care of a motherly, good sort of woman, of whose kindness to you I can have no doubt. And in all probability you will see your brother, and whatever may be his faults, or the faults of his wife, when I consider whose son he is, I cannot bear to have you so wholly estranged from each other."

"Though, with your usual anxiety for our happiness," said Elinor, "you have been ignoring every impediment to the present scheme which occurred to you, there is still one objection which, in my opinion, cannot be so easily removed."

Marianne's countenance sunk.

"And what," said Mrs. Dashwood, "is my dear prudent Elinor going to suggest? What formidable obstacle is she now to bring forward? Do not let me hear a word about the expense of it."

"My objection is this; though I think very well of Mrs. Jennings' heart, she is not a woman whose company can afford us pleasure, and her manners and social status could reflect poorly on us."

"That is very true," replied her mother; "but of her company, separately from that of other people, you will scarcely have anything at all, and you will almost always appear in public with Lady Middleton."

"If Elinor is frightened away by her dislike of Mrs. Jennings," said Marianne, "at least it need not prevent *my* accepting her invitation. I have no such scruples, and I am sure I could put up with every unpleasantness of that kind with very little effort."

Elinor could not help smiling at this display of indifference towards the manners of a person to whom she had often had difficulty in persuading Marianne to behave with tolerable politeness. She therefore resolved within herself, that if her sister persisted in going, she would go likewise, as she did not think it proper that Marianne should be left to the sole guidance of her own judgment, or that Mrs. Jennings should be abandoned to the mercy of Marianne for all the comfort of her domestic hours. To this determination she was the more easily reconciled by recollecting that Edward Ferrars, by Lucy's account, was not to be in town before February, and that their visit, might be finished before then.

"I will have you *both* go," said Mrs. Dashwood. "These objections are nonsensical. You will have much pleasure in being in London, and especially in being together; and if Elinor would ever condescend to anticipate enjoyment, she would foresee it there from a variety of sources. She would perhaps expect some from improving her acquaintance with her sister-in-law's family."

Elinor had often wished for an opportunity of attempting to weaken her mother's dependence on the attachment of Edward and herself, that the shock might be less when the whole truth was revealed. She began her design by saying, as calmly as she could, "I like Edward Ferrars very much, and shall always be glad to see him; but as to the rest of the family, it is a matter of perfect indifference to me, whether I am ever known to them or not."

Mrs. Dashwood smiled and said nothing, but Marianne lifted up her eyes in astonishment.

After very little farther discourse, it was finally settled that the invitation should be fully accepted. Mrs. Jennings received the information with a great deal of joy, and many assurances of kindness and care; nor was it a matter of pleasure merely to her. Sir John was delighted; for to a man whose prevailing anxiety was the dread of being alone, adding two more to the number of inhabitants in London was something. Even Lady Middleton took the trouble of being delighted, which was putting herself rather out of her way; and as for the Miss Steeles, especially Lucy, they had never been so happy in their lives as this intelligence made them.

With less reluctance than she had expected to feel, Elinor submitted to the arrangement which counteracted her wishes. With regard to herself, it was now a matter of unconcern whether she went to town or not; and when she saw her mother so thoroughly pleased with the plan, and her sister exhilarated by it in look, voice, and manner, restored to all her usual animation, and elevated to more than her usual spirits, she could not be dissatisfied with the cause.

Marianne's joy was almost a degree beyond happiness, so great was her spirits and her impatience to be gone. Her unwillingness to leave her mother was her only regret; and at the moment of parting her grief on that score was excessive. Her mother's affliction was hardly less, and Elinor was the only one of the three who seemed to consider the separation as anything short of eternal.

Their departure took place in the first week in January. The Middletons were to follow in about a week. The Miss Steeles kept their station at the Park, and were to leave it only with the rest of the family.

CHAPTER 26

Elinor could not find herself in the carriage with Mrs. Jennings, and beginning a journey to London under her protection, without wondering at her own situation, so short had their acquaintance with that lady been. But this objection had, with that happy excess of youth which Marianne and her mother equally shared, been overcome or overlooked. Elinor, in spite of every occasional doubt of Willoughby's constancy, could not witness the rapture of delightful expectation which filled the whole soul and beamed in the eyes of Marianne, without feeling how cheerless her own prospects were by comparison, and how gladly she would like to feel similarly hopeful. A very short time, however, must now decide what Willoughby's intentions were: in all probability he was already in town. Marianne's eagerness to be gone declared her belief of finding him there. Elinor was resolved not only upon gaining new insight about his character, but likewise upon watching his behaviour to her sister, to ascertain his true intentions before many meetings had taken place. Should the result of her observations be unfavourable, she was determined at all events to open the eyes of her sister. If it were otherwise, her exertions would be of a different nature—she must then learn to avoid every selfish comparison, and banish every regret which might lessen her satisfaction in the happiness of Marianne.

They were three days on their journey, and Marianne's behaviour as they travelled was a happy specimen of what her future complaisance and companionableness to Mrs. Jennings might be expected to be. She sat in silence almost all the way, wrapped in her own meditations, and scarcely ever voluntarily speaking, except when any object of picturesque beauty within their view drew from her an exclamation of delight exclusively addressed to her sister. To make up for the poor conduct of her sister, therefore, Elinor took immediate possession of the post of civility which she had assigned herself. She talked with Mrs. Jennings, laughed with her, and listened to her whenever she could. Mrs. Jennings, on her side, treated them both with all possible kindness. She was concerned on every occasion about their comfort and enjoyment, and only worried that she could not make them choose their own dinners at the inn, nor extort a confession of their preferring salmon to cod, or boiled fowls to veal cutlets. They reached town by three o'clock the third day, glad to be released, after such a journey, from the confinement of a carriage, and ready to enjoy all the luxury of a good fire.

The house was nice and well-furnished, and the young ladies were immediately put in possession of a very comfortable room. It had formerly been Charlotte's, and over the mantlepiece still hung a landscape, proof of her having spent seven years at a great school in town to some effect.

As dinner was not to be ready for two hours after their arrival, Elinor determined to spend her time writing to her mother, and sat down for that purpose. In a few moments Marianne did the same. "*I* am writing home, Marianne," said Elinor. "Perhaps you had better defer your letter for a day or two."

"I am *not* going to write to mother," replied Marianne hastily, as if wishing to avoid any farther inquiry. Elinor said no more. It immediately struck her that she must be writing to Willoughby, and the conclusion which as instantly followed was, that however mysteriously they might wish to conduct the affair, they must be engaged. This conviction, though not entirely satisfactory, gave her pleasure, and she continued her letter. Marianne's was finished in a very few minutes; in length it could be no more than a note: it was then folded up, sealed and directed with eager rapidity. Elinor thought she could distinguish a large W in the address, and no sooner was it finished than Marianne rang the bell to get her letter conveyed at once.

Her spirits still continued very high, but there was a flutter in them which prevented their giving much pleasure to her sister, and this agitation increased as the evening drew on. She could scarcely eat any dinner, and when they afterwards returned to the drawing room, seemed anxiously listening to the sound of every carriage.

It was a great satisfaction to Elinor that Mrs. Jennings, by being busy in her own room, could see little of what was passing. The tea things were brought in, and already had Marianne been disappointed more than once by a rap at a neighbouring door, when a loud one was suddenly heard which could not be mistaken for one at any other house. Elinor felt sure of its announcing Willoughby's approach, and Marianne starting moving towards the door. Everything was silent; this could not be borne many seconds. She opened the door, advanced a few steps towards the stairs, and after listening half a minute, returned into the room in all the agitation which a conviction of having heard him would naturally produce. In the ecstasy of her feelings at that instant she could not help exclaiming, "Oh Elinor, it is Willoughby, indeed it is!" and seemed almost ready to throw herself into his arms, when Colonel Brandon appeared.

It was too great a shock to be borne with calmness, and she immediately left the room. Elinor was disappointed too; but at the same time her regard for Colonel Brandon ensured his welcome with her, and she felt particularly hurt that a man so partial to her sister should perceive that she experienced nothing but grief and disappointment on seeing him. She instantly saw that it was not unnoticed by him, that he even observed Marianne as she left the room, with such astonishment and concern that he hardly retained the ability to engage in common civilities.

"Is your sister ill?" said he. Elinor answered in some distress that she was, and then talked of headaches, low spirits, and fatigues; and of everything to which she could decently attribute her sister's behaviour.

He heard her with the most earnest attention, but seeming to recollect himself, said no more on the subject, and began directly to speak of his pleasure at seeing them in London, making the usual inquiries about their journey and the friends they had left behind.

In this calm kind of way, with very little interest on either side, they continued to talk, both of them out of spirits, and the thoughts of both engaged elsewhere. Elinor wished very much to ask whether Willoughby were then in town, but she was afraid of giving him pain by any inquiry after his rival. At length by way of saying something, she asked if he had been in London ever since she had seen him last.

"Yes," he replied with some embarrassment, "almost ever since; I have been once or twice at Delaford for a few days, but it has never been in my power to return to Barton."

This, and the manner in which it was said, immediately brought back to her remembrance all the circumstances of his leaving that place, with the uneasiness and suspicions they had caused to Mrs. Jennings, and she was fearful that her question had implied much more curiosity on the subject than she had ever felt.

Mrs. Jennings soon came in. "Oh Colonel!" said she, with her usual noisy cheerfulness, "I am monstrous glad to see you—sorry I could not come before—beg your pardon, but I have been forced to look about me a little, and settle my matters. It is a long while since I have been at home, and you know one has always a world of little odd things to do after one has been away for any time. I have been as busy as a bee ever since dinner! But pray, Colonel, how did you know I would be arriving in town today?"

"I had the pleasure of hearing it at Mr. Palmer's, where I have been dining."

"Oh! You did; well, and how do they all do at their house? How is Charlotte? I am sure she is a fine size by this time."

"Mrs. Palmer appeared quite well, and asked me to tell you that you will certainly see her tomorrow."

"Aye, to be sure, I thought as much. Well, Colonel, I have brought two young ladies with me, you see—that is, you see but one of them now, but there is another somewhere. Your friend Miss Marianne, too—which you will not be sorry to hear. I do not know what you and Mr. Willoughby will do between you about her. Aye, it is a fine thing to be young and beautiful. Well! I was young once, but I never was very beautiful—worse luck for me. However, I got a very good husband, and I don't know that the greatest beauty could have done any better. Ah! Poor man! He has been dead these eight years. But, Colonel, where have you been to since we parted? Come, come, let's have no secrets among friends."

He replied with his usual mildness to all her inquiries, but without satisfying her in any. Elinor now began to make the tea, and Marianne was obliged to appear again.

After her entrance, Colonel Brandon became more thoughtful and silent than he had been before, and Mrs. Jennings could not prevail on him to stay long. No other visitor appeared that evening, and the ladies were unanimous in agreeing to go to bed early.

Marianne rose the next morning with recovered spirits and happy looks. The disappointment of the evening before seemed forgotten in the expectation of what was to happen that day. They had not long finished their breakfast before Mrs. Palmer's carriage stopped at the door, and in few minutes she came laughing into the room; so delighted to see them all, that it was hard to say whether she received most pleasure from meeting her mother or the Miss Dashwoods again. So surprised at their coming to town, though it was what she had rather expected all along; so angry at their accepting her mother's invitation after having declined her own, though at the same time she would never have forgiven them if they had not come!

"Mr. Palmer will be so happy to see you," said she. "What do you think he said when he heard of your coming with mama? I forget what it was now, but it was something so droll!"

After an hour or two spent in what her mother called comfortable chat, or in other words, in every variety of inquiry concerning all their acquaintance on Mrs. Jennings's side, and in laughter without cause on Mrs. Palmer's, it was proposed by the latter that they should all accompany her to some shops where she had business that morning. Mrs. Jennings and Elinor readily consented, as having likewise some purchases to make themselves; and Marianne, though declining it at first, was induced to go likewise.

Wherever they went, she was evidently always on the watch. In Bond Street especially, where much of their business lay, her eyes were in constant inquiry; and in whatever shop the party were engaged, her mind was equally distracted from everything actually before them. Restless and dissatisfied everywhere, her sister could never obtain her opinion of any article of purchase, however it might equally concern them both. Marianne received no pleasure from anything; was only impatient to be at home again, and could with difficulty govern her vexation at the tediousness of Mrs. Palmer, whose eye was caught by everything pretty, expensive, or new; who was wild to buy all, could determine on none, and dawdled away her time in rapture and indecision.

It was late in the morning before they returned home, and no sooner had they entered the house than Marianne flew eagerly upstairs, and when Elinor followed, she found her turning from the table with a sorrowful countenance, which declared that no Willoughby had been there.

"Has no letter been left here for me since we went out?" said she to the footman who then entered with the parcels. She was answered in the negative. "Are you quite sure of it?" she replied. "Are you certain that no servant, no porter has left any letter or note?"

The man replied that none had.

"How very odd!" said she in a low and disappointed voice, as she turned away to the window.

"How odd indeed!" repeated Elinor within herself, regarding her sister with uneasiness. "If she had not known him to be in town, she would not have written to him as she did; she would have written to Combe Magna; and if he *was* in town, how odd that he should neither come nor write! O my dear mother, you must be wrong in permitting an engagement between a daughter so young, a man so little known, to be carried on in so doubtful, so mysterious a manner! *I* long to inquire; but how will *my* interference be tolerated!"

She determined, after some consideration, that if appearances continued many days longer as unpleasant as they now were, she would represent in the strongest manner to her mother the necessity of some serious inquiry into the affair.

Mrs. Palmer and two elderly ladies of Mrs. Jennings's acquaintance, whom she had met and invited in the morning, dined with them. The former left them soon after tea to fulfil her evening engagements, and Elinor was obliged play cards with the others. Marianne was of no use on these occasions, as she would never learn to play; but though her time was therefore at her own disposal, the evening was by no means more productive of pleasure to her than to Elinor, for it was spent in all the anxiety of expectation and the pain of disappointment. She sometimes endeavoured for a few minutes to read; but the book was soon thrown aside, and she returned to the more interesting employment of walking backwards and forwards across the room, pausing for a moment whenever she came to the window, in hopes of distinguishing the long-expected rap.

CHAPTER 27

"If this good weather holds much longer," said Mrs. Jennings, when they met at breakfast the following morning. "Sir John will not like leaving Barton next week. 'Tis a sad thing for sportsmen to lose a day's pleasure. Poor souls! I always pity them when they do—they seem to take it so much to heart."

"That is true," cried Marianne in a cheerful voice, and walking to the window as she spoke, to examine the day. "I had not thought of *that*. This weather will keep many sportsmen in the country."

It was a lucky recollection, and all her good spirits were restored by it. "It is charming weather for *them* indeed," she continued, as she sat down to the breakfast table with a happy countenance. "How much they must enjoy it! But," she said with a little return of anxiety, "it cannot be expected to last long. At this time of year, and after so much rain, we shall certainly have very little more of it. Frosts will soon set in, and in all probability with severity. In another day or two, perhaps; this extreme mildness can hardly last longer—nay, perhaps it may freeze tonight!"

"At any rate," said Elinor, wishing to prevent Mrs. Jennings from seeing her sister's thoughts as clearly as she did, "I dare say we shall have Sir John and Lady Middleton in town by the end of next week."

"Aye, my dear, I'm certain we shall. Mary always has her own way."

"And now," silently conjectured Elinor, "she will write to Combe by this day's post."

But if she *did*, the letter was written and sent away with a privacy which eluded all her watchfulness. Whatever the truth of it might be, and far as Elinor was from feeling thorough contentment about it, while she saw Marianne in spirits, she could not be very uncomfortable herself. And Marianne was in spirits, happy in the mildness of the weather, and still happier in her expectation of a frost.

The morning was chiefly spent in leaving cards at the houses of Mrs. Jennings's acquaintances to inform them of her being in town; and Marianne was all the time busy in observing the direction of the wind, watching the variations of the sky, and imagining an alteration in the air.

"Don't you find it colder than it was in the morning, Elinor? There seems to me a very decided difference. I can hardly keep my hands warm even in my muff. It was not so yesterday, I think. The clouds seem to be parting, too; the sun will be out in a moment, and we shall have a clear afternoon."

Elinor was alternately amused and pained; but Marianne persevered, and saw every night in the brightness of the fire, and every morning in the appearance of the atmosphere, the certain symptoms of approaching frost.

The Miss Dashwoods had no greater reason to be dissatisfied with Mrs. Jennings's style of living and social connections than with her behaviour to themselves, which was invariably kind. Excepting a few old city friends, whom, to Lady Middleton's regret, she had never dropped, she visited no one to whom an introduction could at all discompose the feelings of her young companions. Pleased to find herself more comfortably situated in that regard than she had expected, Elinor was very willing to endure the lack of much real enjoyment from any of their evening parties, which, whether at home or abroad, formed only for cards, could have little to amuse her.

Colonel Brandon, who had a general invitation to the house, was with them almost every day; he came to look at Marianne and talk to Elinor, who often derived more satisfaction from conversing with him than from any other daily occurrence, but who saw at the same time with much concern his continued regard for her sister. She feared it was a strengthening regard. It grieved her to see the earnestness with which he often watched Marianne, and his spirits were certainly worse than when at Barton.

About a week after their arrival it became certain that
Willoughby had also arrived. His card was on the table, when they
came in from the morning's drive.

"Good God!" cried Marianne. "He has been here while we were
out." Elinor, rejoiced to be assured of his being in London, now
ventured to say, "Depend upon it, he will call again tomorrow." But
Marianne seemed hardly to hear her, and on Mrs. Jennings's entrance,
escaped with the precious card.

This event, while it raised the spirits of Elinor, restored to those
of her sister all, and more than all, their former agitation. From this
moment, her mind was never quiet; the expectation of seeing him
every hour of the day made her unfit for anything. She insisted on
being left behind the next morning, when the others went out.

Elinor's thoughts were full of what might be passing in Berkeley
Street during their absence; but a moment's glance at her sister when
they returned was enough to inform her that Willoughby had paid no
second visit there. A note was just then brought in and laid on the
table.

"For me?" cried Marianne, stepping hastily forward.

"No, ma'am, for my mistress."

But Marianne, not convinced, took it instantly up.

"It is indeed for Mrs. Jennings; how provoking!"

"You are expecting a letter then?" said Elinor, unable to be
longer silent.

"Yes, a little—not much."

After a short pause, "You do not trust me, Marianne."

"Nay, Elinor, this reproach from *you*!—you who can trust no
one!"

"Me!" returned Elinor in some confusion. "Indeed, Marianne, I
have nothing to tell."

"Nor I," answered Marianne with energy. "Our situations then
are alike. We have neither of us anything to tell; you, because you
communicate, and I, because I conceal nothing."

Elinor, distressed by this charge of reserve in herself, which she
was not at liberty to defend, knew not how, under such
circumstances, to press for greater openness in Marianne.

Mrs. Jennings soon appeared, and the note being given her, she
read it aloud. It was from Lady Middleton, announcing their arrival in
Conduit Street the night before, and requesting the company of her

mother and cousins the following evening. Business on Sir John's part, and a violent cold on her own, prevented their calling in Berkeley Street. The invitation was accepted, but when the hour of appointment drew near, necessary as it was in common civility to Mrs. Jennings that they should both attend her on such a visit, Elinor had some difficulty in persuading her sister to go. Marianne still had seen nothing of Willoughby, and therefore was not disposed for amusement abroad, unwilling to run the risk of his calling again in her absence.

Elinor found, when the evening was over, that disposition is not materially altered by a change of abode, for although scarcely settled in town, Sir John had contrived to collect around him nearly twenty young people, and to amuse them with a ball. This was an affair, however, of which Lady Middleton did not approve. In the country, an impromptu dance was very allowable; but in London, where the reputation of elegance was more important and less easily attained, it was risking too much, for the gratification of a few girls, to have it known that Lady Middleton had given a small dance to eight or nine couples, with only two violins, and no formal meal.

Mr. and Mrs. Palmer were of the party. From the former, whom they had not seen before since their arrival in town, as he was careful to avoid the appearance of any attention to his mother-in-law, they received no mark of recognition on their entrance. He looked at them without seeming to know who they were, and merely nodded to Mrs. Jennings from the other side of the room. Marianne gave one glance round the apartment as she entered; it was enough, *he* was not there—and she sat down, equally ill-disposed to receive or communicate pleasure. After they had been assembled about an hour, Mr. Palmer sauntered towards the Miss Dashwoods to express his surprise on seeing them in town, though Colonel Brandon had been first informed of their arrival at his house, and he had himself said something very droll on hearing that they were to come.

"I thought you were both in Devonshire," said he.

"Did you?" replied Elinor.

"When do you go back again?"

"I do not know." And thus ended their discourse.

Never had Marianne been so unwilling to dance in her life as she was that evening, and never so much fatigued by the exercise. She complained of it as they returned to Berkeley Street.

"Aye, aye," said Mrs. Jennings, "we know the reason of all that very well; if a certain person who shall be nameless had been there, you would not have been a bit tired; and to say the truth, it was not very nice of him not to appear when he was invited."

"Invited!" cried Marianne.

"So my daughter Middleton told me, for it seems Sir John met him somewhere in the street this morning."

Marianne said no more, but looked exceedingly hurt. Impatient in this situation to be doing something that might lead to her sister's relief, Elinor resolved to write the next morning to her mother, and hoped by awakening her fears for the health of Marianne, to encourage her to ask her daughter if she were engaged or not. She was still more eagerly bent on this measure by perceiving after breakfast on the morrow that Marianne was again writing to Willoughby, for she could not suppose it to be to any other person.

About the middle of the day, Mrs. Jennings went out by herself on business, and Elinor began her letter directly; while Marianne, too restless for employment, too anxious for conversation, walked from one window to the other, or sat down by the fire in melancholy meditation. Elinor was very earnest in her application to her mother, relating all that had passed, her suspicions of Willoughby's inconstancy, urging her by every plea of duty and affection to demand from Marianne an account of her real situation with respect to him.

Her letter was scarcely finished when a rap foretold a visitor, and Colonel Brandon was announced. Marianne, who had seen him from the window, and who hated company of any kind, left the room before he entered it. He looked more than usually grave, and though expressing satisfaction at finding Miss Dashwood alone, as if he had something particular to tell her, sat for some time without saying a word. Elinor, persuaded that he had some communication to make in which her sister was concerned, waited impatiently. It was not the first time of her feeling the same kind of conviction; for more than once before, beginning with the observation of "Your sister looks unwell today," or "Your sister seems out of spirits," he had appeared on the point, either of disclosing, or of inquiring, something particular about her. After a pause of several minutes, their silence was broken by his asking her in a voice of some agitation, when he was to congratulate her on the acquisition of a brother? Elinor was not prepared for such a question, and having no answer ready, was obliged to adopt the simple and common expedient, of asking what he meant. He tried to smile as he replied, "your sister's engagement to Mr. Willoughby is very generally known."

"It cannot be generally known," returned Elinor, "for her own family do not know it."

He looked surprised and said, "I beg your pardon, I am afraid my inquiry has been impertinent; but I had not supposed any secrecy intended, as they openly correspond, and their marriage is universally talked of."

"How can that be? By whom can you have heard it mentioned?"

"By many—by some of whom you know nothing, by others with whom you are most intimate—Mrs. Jennings, Mrs. Palmer, and the Middletons. But still I might not have believed it, for where the mind is perhaps rather unwilling to be convinced, it will always find something to support its doubts, if I had not, when the servant let me in today, accidentally seen a letter in his hand, directed to Mr. Willoughby in your sister's writing. I came to inquire, but I was convinced before I could ask the question. Is everything finally settled? Is it impossible to—? But I have no right, and I could have no chance of succeeding. Excuse me, Miss Dashwood. I believe I have been wrong in saying so much, but I hardly know what to do, and on your prudence I have the strongest dependence. Tell me that it is all absolutely resolved on, that any attempt—that in short concealment, if concealment be possible, is all that remains."

These words, which conveyed to Elinor a direct avowal of his love for her sister, affected her very much. She was not immediately able to say anything, and even when her spirits were recovered, she debated for a short time on the answer it would be most proper to give. The real state of things between Willoughby and her sister was so little known to herself, that in endeavouring to explain it, she might be as liable to say too much as too little. Yet as she was convinced that Marianne's affection for Willoughby could leave no hope of Colonel Brandon's success, whatever the event of that affection might be, and at the same time wished to shield her conduct from censure, as it would be wrong to correspond in the absence of an engagement, she thought it most prudent and kind, after some consideration, to say more than she really knew or believed. She acknowledged, therefore, that though she had never been informed of the terms on which they stood with each other, of their mutual affection she had no doubt, and of their correspondence she was not astonished to hear.

He listened to her with silent attention, and on her ceasing to speak, rose directly from his seat, and after saying in a voice of emotion, "To your sister I wish all imaginable happiness; to Willoughby that he may endeavour to deserve her," he took his leave.

Elinor derived no comfortable feelings from this conversation to lessen the uneasiness of her mind on other points; she was left, on the contrary, with a melancholy impression of Colonel Brandon's unhappiness, and was prevented even from wishing it removed, by her anxiety for the very event that must confirm it.

CHAPTER 28

Nothing occurred during the next three or four days to make Elinor regret what she had done in applying to her mother; for Willoughby neither came nor wrote. They were invited about the end of that time to join Lady Middleton at a party, from which Mrs. Jennings was kept away by the state of her youngest daughter, who was about to give birth. For this party, Marianne, wholly dispirited, careless of her appearance, and seeming equally indifferent whether she went or stayed, prepared, without one look of hope, or one expression of pleasure. She sat by the drawing room fire after tea, till the moment of Lady Middleton's arrival, without once stirring from her seat, or altering her attitude, lost in her own thoughts and insensible of her sister's presence. When at last they were told that Lady Middleton waited for them at the door, she started as if she had forgotten that anyone was expected.

They arrived in due time at the place of destination, and as soon as the string of carriages before them would allow, alighted, ascended the stairs, heard their names announced, and entered a room splendidly lit up, quite full of company, and insufferably hot. When they had paid their tribute of politeness by curtsying to the lady of the house, they were permitted to mingle in the crowd, and take their share of the heat and inconvenience, to which their arrival must necessarily add. After some time spent in saying little and doing less, Lady Middleton sat down to cards, and as Marianne was not in spirits for moving about, she and Elinor, luckily finding chairs, placed themselves at no great distance from the table.

They had not remained in this manner long before Elinor perceived Willoughby standing within a few yards of them, in earnest conversation with a very fashionable looking young woman. She soon caught his eye, and he immediately bowed, but without attempting to speak to her, or to approach Marianne, though he had surely seen her. Then he continued his discourse with the same lady. Elinor turned involuntarily to Marianne, to see whether it had been observed by her. At that moment she perceived him, and her whole countenance glowing with sudden delight, she would have moved towards him instantly, had not her sister caught hold of her.

"Good heavens!" she exclaimed. "He is there—he is there—Oh! why does he not look at me? why cannot I speak to him?"

"Pray, pray be composed," cried Elinor, "and do not betray what you feel to everybody present. Perhaps he has not observed you yet."

This, however, was more than she could believe herself, and to be composed at such a moment was not only beyond the reach of Marianne, it was beyond her wish. She sat in an agony of impatience which affected every feature.

At last he turned round again, and looked at them both; she started up, and pronouncing his name in a tone of affection, held out her hand to him. He approached, and addressing himself rather to Elinor than Marianne, as if wishing to avoid her eye, and determined not to observe her attitude, inquired in a hurried manner after Mrs. Dashwood, and asked how long they had been in town. Elinor was robbed of all presence of mind by such an address, and was unable to say a word. But the feelings of her sister were instantly expressed. Her face was crimsoned over, and she exclaimed in a voice of the greatest emotion, "Good God! Willoughby, what is the meaning of this? Have you not received my letters? Will you not shake hands with me?"

He could not then avoid it, but her touch seemed painful to him, and he held her hand only for a moment. During all this time he was evidently struggling for composure. Elinor watched his countenance and saw its expression becoming more tranquil. After a moment's pause, he spoke with calmness.

"I did myself the honour of calling in Berkeley Street last Tuesday, and very much regretted that I was not fortunate enough to find yourselves and Mrs. Jennings at home. My card was not lost, I hope."

"But have you not received my notes?" cried Marianne in the wildest anxiety. "Here is some mistake, I am sure—some dreadful mistake. What can be the meaning of it? Tell me, Willoughby—for heaven's sake, tell me, what is the matter?"

He made no reply; his complexion changed and all his embarrassment returned; but on catching the eye of the young lady with whom he had been previously talking, he felt the necessity of instant exertion, and recovered himself again, saying, "Yes, I had the pleasure of receiving the information of your arrival in town, which you were so good as to send me." He then turned hastily away with a slight bow and joined his friend.

Marianne, now looking dreadfully white and unable to stand, sunk into her chair, and Elinor, expecting every moment to see her faint, tried to screen her from the observation of others, while reviving her with lavender water.

"Go to him, Elinor," she cried, as soon as she could speak, "and force him to come to me. Tell him I must see him again—must speak to him instantly. I cannot rest—I shall not have a moment's peace till this is explained—some dreadful misapprehension or other. Oh go to him this moment."

"How can that be done? No, my dearest Marianne, you must wait. This is not a place for explanations. Wait only till tomorrow."

With difficulty, however, could she prevent her from following him herself; and to persuade her to check her agitation—to wait with at least the appearance of composure—till she might speak to him with more privacy and more effect, was impossible. Marianne continued incessantly to give way in a low voice to the misery of her feelings, by exclamations of wretchedness. In a short time Elinor saw Willoughby leave the room by the door towards the staircase, and telling Marianne that he was gone, urged the impossibility of speaking to him again that evening, as a fresh argument for her to be calm. She instantly begged her sister to entreat Lady Middleton to take them home, as she was too miserable to stay a minute longer.

Lady Middleton, though in the middle of a game, on being informed that Marianne was unwell, was too polite to object for a moment to her wish of going away, and giving her cards to a friend, they departed as soon as the carriage could be found. Scarcely a word was spoken during their return to Berkeley Street. Marianne was in a silent agony, too much oppressed even for tears; but as Mrs. Jennings was luckily not yet home, they could go directly to their own room. She was soon undressed and in bed, and as she seemed desirous of being alone, her sister then left her, and while she awaited the return of Mrs. Jennings, had leisure enough for thinking.

That some kind of engagement had existed between Willoughby and Marianne, she could not doubt; and that Willoughby was weary of it, seemed equally clear; for however Marianne might still feed her own wishes, *she* could not attribute such behaviour to a mistake or misunderstanding of any kind. Nothing but a thorough change of sentiment could account for it. Her indignation would have been still stronger than it was, had she not witnessed that embarrassment which seemed to speak a consciousness of his own misconduct, and prevented her from believing him so unprincipled as to have been playing with the affections of her sister from the first, without any design to marry her. Absence might have weakened his regard, but that such a regard had formerly existed she could not bring herself to doubt.

As for Marianne, on the pangs which so unhappy a meeting must already have given her, and on those still more severe which might await her in its probable consequence, she could not reflect without the deepest concern. Her own situation was better by comparison, for she could still think well of Edward, however they might be divided in future. But every circumstance that could embitter such an evil seemed uniting to heighten the misery of Marianne in a final separation from Willoughby—in an immediate and irreconcilable rupture with him.

CHAPTER 29

Before the maid had lit their fire the next day, Marianne, only half dressed, was kneeling against one of the window-seats for the sake of all the little light she could command from it, and writing as fast as a continual flow of tears would permit her. In this situation, Elinor, roused from sleep by her agitation and sobs, first perceived her. After observing her for a few moments with silent anxiety, she said, in a tone of the most considerate gentleness,

"Marianne, may I ask—?"

"No, Elinor," she replied, "ask nothing; you will soon know all."

The sort of desperate calmness with which this was said lasted no longer than while she spoke, and was immediately followed by a return of the same excessive affliction. It was some minutes before she could go on with her letter, and the frequent bursts of grief which still obliged her, at intervals, to withhold her pen, were proofs enough of her feeling how likely it was that she was writing for the last time to Willoughby.

Elinor would have tried to calm her still more had not Marianne entreated her, with all the eagerness of the most nervous irritability, not to speak to her for the world. In such circumstances, it was better for both that they should not be long together. The restless state of Marianne's mind not only prevented her from remaining in the room a moment after she was dressed, but requiring at once solitude and continual change of place, made her wander about the house till breakfast, avoiding the sight of everybody.

At breakfast, she neither ate nor attempted to eat anything; and Elinor's attention was then all employed, not in urging her, not in pitying her, nor in appearing to regard her, but in endeavouring to keep Mrs. Jennings from noticing anything out of the ordinary.

As this was a favourite meal with Mrs. Jennings, it lasted a considerable time, and they were only just gathering in the parlour when a letter was delivered to Marianne, which she eagerly caught from the servant, and, turning pale, instantly ran out of the room. Elinor, who knew that it must have come from Willoughby, felt immediately such a sickness at heart as made her hardly able to hold up her head, and she sat in such a general tremour that she feared it impossible to escape Mrs. Jennings's notice. That good lady, however, saw only that Marianne had received a letter from Willoughby, which appeared to her a very good joke, and which she treated accordingly, by hoping, with a laugh, that she would find it to her liking. Of Elinor's distress, she noticed nothing at all, and calmly continuing her talk. As soon as Marianne disappeared, she said —

"Upon my word, I never saw a young woman so desperately in love in my life! *My* girls were nothing to her, and yet they used to be foolish enough; but as for Miss Marianne, she is quite an altered creature. I hope, from the bottom of my heart, he won't keep her waiting much longer, for it is quite grievous to see her look so ill and forlorn. Pray, when are they to be married?"

Elinor, though never less disposed to speak than at that moment, obliged herself to answer such an attack as this, and, therefore, trying to smile, replied, "And have you really, ma'am, talked yourself into a persuasion of my sister's being engaged to Mr. Willoughby? I thought it had been only a joke, but so serious a question seems to imply more; and I must beg, therefore, that you will not deceive yourself any longer. I do assure you that nothing would surprise me more than to hear of their upcoming marriage."

"For shame, for shame, Miss Dashwood! How can you talk so! Don't we all know that it must be a match—that they were head over heels in love with each other from the first moment they met? Did not I see them together in Devonshire every day, and all day long? And did I not know that your sister came to town with me on purpose to buy wedding clothes? Come, come, this won't do. Because you are so sly about it yourself, you think nobody else has any awareness; but it is not so, I can tell you, for it has been known all over town this ever so long. I tell everybody of it, and so does Charlotte."

"Indeed, ma'am," said Elinor very seriously, "you are mistaken. Indeed, you are doing a very unkind thing in spreading such news."

Mrs. Jennings laughed again, but Elinor had not spirits to say more, and eager at all events to know what Willoughby had written, hurried away to their room, where, on opening the door, she saw Marianne stretched on the bed, almost choked by grief, one letter in her hand, and two or three others lying by her. Elinor drew near, but without saying a word; and seating herself on the bed, took her hand, kissed her affectionately several times, and then gave way to a burst of tears, which at first was scarcely less violent than Marianne's. The latter, though unable to speak, seemed to feel all the tenderness of this behaviour, and after some time thus spent in joint affliction, she put all the letters into Elinor's hands; and then covering her face with her handkerchief, almost screamed with agony. Elinor, who knew that such grief, shocking as it was to witness it, must be expressed, watched by her till this excess of suffering had somewhat spent itself, and then turning eagerly to Willoughby's letter, read as follows:

Bond Street, January.

MY DEAR MADAM,—I have just had the honour of receiving your letter, for which I beg to return my sincere acknowledgments. I am much concerned to find there was anything in my behaviour last night that did not meet your approval; and though I am quite at a loss to discover in what point I could be so unfortunate as to offend you, I entreat your forgiveness of what I can assure you to have been perfectly unintentional. I shall never reflect on my former acquaintance with your family in Devonshire without the most grateful pleasure, and flatter myself it will not be broken by any mistake or misunderstanding of my actions. My esteem for your whole family is very sincere; but if I have been so unfortunate as to give rise to a belief of more than I felt, or meant to express, I shall reproach myself for not having been more guarded in my professions of that esteem. That I should ever have meant more you will allow to be impossible, when you understand that my affections have been long engaged elsewhere. It will not be many weeks, I believe, before I am married. It is with great regret that I obey your commands of returning the letters, with which I have been honoured from you, and the lock of hair, which you so obligingly bestowed on me.

I am, dear Madam,

Your most obedient humble Servant,

JOHN WILLOUGHBY

With what indignation such a letter as this must be read by Miss Dashwood may be imagined. Though aware, before she began it, that it must bring a confession of his inconstancy, and confirm their separation forever, she was not aware that such formal and indifferent language would be used to announce it! Nor could she have supposed Willoughby capable of departing so far from the appearance of every honourable and delicate feeling—so far from the common decorum of a gentleman, as to send a letter so cruel: a letter which acknowledged no wrong, nor contained any professions of regret. It denied all particular affection whatsoever! Every line was an insult, and proclaimed its writer to be deep in hardened villainy.

She paused over it for some time with indignant astonishment, then read it again and again; but every perusal only served to increase her abhorrence of the man, and so bitter were her feelings against him that she dared not trust herself to speak, lest she might wound Marianne still deeper by treating their separation as an escape from the worst and most irremediable of all evils: a connection, for life, with an unprincipled man.

In her earnest meditations on the contents of the letter, on the depravity of that mind which could author it, Elinor forgot the immediate distress of her sister, forgot that she had three letters on her lap yet unread, and so entirely forgot how long she had been in the room, that upon hearing a carriage drive up to the door, she went to the window to see who could be coming so unreasonably early. She was all astonishment to perceive Mrs. Jennings's carriage, which she knew had been requested at one o'clock. Determined not to leave Marianne, though hopeless of contributing, at present, to her ease, she hurried away to excuse herself from attending Mrs. Jennings, on account of her sister being indisposed. Mrs. Jennings, with a thoroughly good-humoured concern for its cause, accepted the excuse most readily. Elinor, after seeing her safely off, returned to Marianne, whom she found attempting to rise from the bed, and whom she reached just in time to prevent her from falling on the floor, faint from a lack of proper rest and food; for it was many days since she had any appetite, and many nights since she had really slept. Now, when her mind was no longer supported by the fever of suspense, the consequence of all this was felt in an aching head, a weakened stomach, and a general nervous faintness. A glass of wine, which Elinor procured for her directly, made her more comfortable, and she was at last able to express some sense of her kindness, by saying —

"Poor Elinor! How unhappy I must make you!"

"I only wish," replied her sister, "there was something I could do which might be of comfort to you."

This, as everything else would have been, was too much for Marianne, who could only exclaim, in the anguish of her heart, "Oh! Elinor, I am miserable indeed," before her voice was entirely lost in sobs.

Elinor could no longer witness this torrent of unrestrained grief in silence.

"Exert yourself, dear Marianne," she cried, "if you would not kill yourself and all who love you. Think of your mother; think of her misery while *you* suffer; for her sake you must exert yourself."

"I cannot, I cannot," cried Marianne; "leave me, leave me, if I distress you; leave me, hate me, forget me; but do not torture me so. Oh! How easy for those who have no sorrow of their own to talk of exertion! Happy, happy Elinor, *you* cannot have an idea of what I suffer."

"Do you call *me* happy, Marianne? Ah; if you knew! And can you believe me to be so while I see you so wretched!"

"Forgive me, forgive me," throwing her arms round her sister's neck. "I know you feel for me; I know what a heart you have; but yet you are—you must be happy; Edward loves you—what, oh! what can do away such happiness as that?"

"Many, many circumstances," said Elinor, solemnly.

"No, no, no," cried Marianne wildly. "He loves you, and only you. You can have no grief."

"I can have no pleasure while I see you in this state."

"And you will never see me otherwise. Mine is a misery which nothing can do away."

"You must not talk so Marianne. Have you no comforts? No friends? Is your loss such as leaves no opening for eventual consolation? As much as you suffer now, think what you would have suffered if the discovery of his character had been delayed to a later period—if your engagement had been carried on for months and months, as it might have been, before he chose to put an end to it.

Every additional day of unhappy confidence on your side would have made the blow more dreadful."

"Engagement!" cried Marianne. "There has been no engagement."

"No engagement!"

"No, he is not as unworthy as you believe him. He has broken no faith with me."

"But he told you that he loved you?"

"Yes—no—never absolutely. It was every day implied, but never declared. Sometimes I thought it had been—but it never was."

"Yet you wrote to him?"

"Yes—could that be wrong after all that had passed? But I cannot talk."

Elinor said no more, and turning again to the three letters which now raised a much stronger curiosity than before, immediately ran over the contents of all. The first, which was what her sister had sent him on their arrival in town, was to this effect.

"Berkeley Street, January.

"How surprised you will be, Willoughby, on receiving this! I think you will feel something more than surprise when you know that I am in town. An opportunity of coming hither, though with Mrs. Jennings, was a temptation we could not resist. I wish you may receive this in time to come here to-night, but I will not depend on it. At any rate I shall expect you tomorrow. For the present, adieu. M. D."

Her second note, which had been written on the morning after the dance at the Middletons', was in these words —

"I cannot express my disappointment in having missed you the day before yesterday, nor my astonishment at not having received any answer to a note which I sent you over a week ago. I have been expecting to hear from you, and still more to see you, every hour of the day. Pray call again as soon as possible, and explain the reason of my having expected this in vain. You had better come earlier another time, because we are generally out by one. We were last night at Lady Middleton's where there was a dance. I have been told that you were invited. But could it be so? You must be very much altered indeed since we parted, if that could be the case, and you not there. But I will not suppose this possible, and I hope very soon to receive your personal assurance of its being otherwise. M. D."

148

The contents of her last note to him were these:

"What am I to imagine, Willoughby, by your behaviour last night? Again I demand an explanation of it. I was prepared to meet you with the pleasure which our separation naturally produced, with the familiarity which our intimacy at Barton appeared to me to justify. I was repulsed indeed! I have spent a wretched night endeavouring to excuse conduct which can scarcely be called less than insulting; but though I have not yet been able to form any reasonable explanation for your behaviour, I am perfectly ready to hear your justification of it. You have perhaps been misinformed, or purposely deceived, in something concerning me, which may have lowered me in your opinion. Tell me what it is, explain the grounds on which you acted, and I shall be satisfied in being able to satisfy you. It would grieve me indeed to be obliged to think ill of you; but if I am to do it, if I am to learn that you are not what we have hitherto believed you, that your regard for us all was insincere, that your behaviour to me was intended only to deceive, let it be told as soon as possible. My feelings are at present in a state of dreadful indecision; I wish to exonerate you, but certainty on either side will be ease to what I now suffer. If your sentiments are no longer what they were, you will return my notes, and the lock of my hair which is in your possession. M. D."

That such letters, so full of affection and confidence, could have been so answered, Elinor, for Willoughby's sake, would have been unwilling to believe. But her condemnation of him did not blind her to the impropriety of their having been written at all. Marianne, perceiving that she had finished the letters, observed to her that they contained nothing but what anyone would have written in the same situation.

"I felt myself," she added, "to be as solemnly engaged to him as if the strictest legal covenant had bound us to each other."

"I can believe it," said Elinor; "but unfortunately, he did not feel the same."

"He *did* feel the same, Elinor—for weeks and weeks he felt it. I know he did. Whatever may have changed him now (and nothing but the blackest art employed against me can have done it), I was once as dear to him as my own soul could wish. This lock of hair, which now he can so readily give up, was begged of me with the most earnest supplication. Had you seen his look, his manner, had you heard his voice at that moment! Have you forgotten the last evening of our being together at Barton? The morning that we parted, too! When he told me that it might be many weeks before we meet again—his distress—can I ever forget his distress!"

For a moment or two she could say no more; but when this emotion had passed away, she added, in a firmer tone —

"Elinor, I have been cruelly used, but not by Willoughby."

"Dearest Marianne, who but Willoughby could be responsible for such actions as this?"

"Anyone, anyone else rather than him. It would be easier to believe every creature of my acquaintance had banded together to ruin me in his opinion than to believe him capable of such cruelty. This woman of whom he writes—whoever she is—or anyone, in short, but your own dear self, mama, and Edward, may have been barbarous enough to sink me in his eyes. Beyond you three, is there a creature in the world whom I would not rather suspect of evil than Willoughby, whose heart I know so well?"

Elinor would not argue with her, and only replied, "Whoever may have been so detestably your enemy, let them be cheated of their malignant triumph, my dear sister, by seeing how nobly the consciousness of your own innocence and good intentions supports your spirits. It is a reasonable and praiseworthy pride which resists an attack such as this."

"No, no," cried Marianne, "misery such as mine has no pride. I care not who knows that I am wretched. The triumph of seeing me so may be open to all the world. Elinor, Elinor, they who suffer little may be as proud and independent as they like—they may resist insult, or return mortification—but I cannot. I must feel—I must be wretched—and they are welcome to enjoy the consciousness of it."

"But for my mother's sake and mine—"

"I would do more than for my own. But to appear happy when I am so miserable—Oh! who can require it?"

Again they were both silent. Elinor was employed in walking thoughtfully from the fire to the window, from the window to the fire, without knowing that she received warmth from one, or discerning objects through the other. Marianne, seated at the foot of the bed, with her head leaning against one of its posts, again took up Willoughby's letter, and after shuddering over every sentence, exclaimed—

"It is too much! Oh! Willoughby, Willoughby, could this be yours! Cruel, cruel—nothing can excuse you. Elinor, nothing can. Whatever he might have heard against me—ought he not to have disbelieved it? Should he not have told me of it and given me the opportunity to defend myself? 'The lock of hair which you so obligingly bestowed on me'—That is unpardonable. Willoughby, where was your heart when you wrote those words? Oh! Barbarously insolent!—Elinor, can he be justified?"

"No, Marianne, in no possible way."

"And yet this woman—who knows what her art may have been—how long it may have been premeditated, and how deeply contrived by her! Who is she?—Who can she be?—Whom did I ever hear him talk of as young and attractive among his female acquaintance?—Oh! No one, no one—he talked to me only of myself."

Another pause ensued; Marianne was greatly agitated, and it ended thus—

"Elinor, I must go home. I must go and comfort mama. Cannot we be gone tomorrow?"

"Tomorrow, Marianne!"

"Yes; why should I stay here? I came only for Willoughby's sake—and now who cares for me? Who notices me?"

"It would be impossible to go tomorrow. We owe Mrs. Jennings much more than civility; and civility of the commonest kind must prevent such a hasty removal as that."

"Well, then, another day or two, perhaps; but I cannot stay here long, I cannot stay to endure the questions and remarks of all these people. The Middletons and Palmers—how am I to bear their pity? The pity of such a woman as Lady Middleton! Oh! What would *he* say to that!"

Elinor advised her to lie down again, and for a moment she did so; but nothing could make her relax; and in restless pain of mind and body she moved from one posture to another, till growing more and more hysterical, her sister could with difficulty keep her on the bed at all, and for some time was fearful of being constrained to call for assistance. Some lavender drops, however, which she was at length persuaded to take, were of use; and from that time till Mrs. Jennings returned, she continued on the bed quiet and motionless.

CHAPTER 30

Mrs. Jennings came immediately to their room on her return, and without waiting to have her request of admittance answered, opened the door and walked in with a look of real concern.

"How are you feeling, my dear?" she asked, in a voice of great compassion.

Marianne turned away without attempting to answer.

"How is she, Miss Dashwood? Poor thing! she looks very bad. No wonder. Aye, it is but too true. He is to be married very soon—a good-for-nothing fellow! Mrs. Taylor told me of it half an hour ago, and she was told it by a particular friend of Miss Grey herself, else I am sure I should not have believed it. I was almost ready to faint as it was. Well, said I, all I can say is, that if it is true, he has used a young lady of my acquaintance abominably ill, and I wish with all my soul his wife may make him miserable. And so I shall always say, my dear, you may depend on it. I have no notion of men's going on in this way: and if ever I meet him again, I will give him such a talking to as he has not had this many a day. But there is one comfort, my dear Miss Marianne; he is not the only young man in the world worth having. With your pretty face you will have plenty of suitors. Well, poor thing! I won't disturb her any longer, for she had better have her cry out at once and be done with it. The Parrys and Sandersons luckily are coming tonight, you know, and that will amuse her."

She then went away, walking on tiptoe out of the room, as if she supposed her young friend's affliction could be increased by noise.

Marianne, to the surprise of her sister, determined to dine with them. Elinor even advised her against it. But she insisted she would go down; said she could bear it very well, and that the bustle about her would be a helpful distraction. Elinor, pleased to have her governed for a moment by such a motive, though believing it hardly possible that she could sit through the dinner, said no more; and adjusting her dress for her as well as she could, while Marianne still remained on the bed, was ready to assist her into the dining room as soon as they were summoned to it.

When there, though looking most wretched, she ate more and was calmer than her sister had expected. Had she tried to speak, or had she been conscious of half Mrs. Jennings's well-meant but ill-judged attentions to her, this calmness could not have been maintained; but not a syllable escaped her lips, and being absorbed in thought she remained ignorant of everything that was passing before her.

Elinor, who did justice to Mrs. Jennings's kindness, though its forms were often distressing, and sometimes almost ridiculous, made her those acknowledgments, and returned her those civilities, which her sister could not make or return for herself. Their good friend saw that Marianne was unhappy, and felt that everything was due to her which might make her at all less so. She treated her, therefore, with all the indulgent fondness of a parent towards a favourite child on the last day of the holidays. Marianne was to have the best place by the fire, was to be encouraged to eat by every delicacy in the house, and to be amused by the relation of all the news of the day. Had not Elinor been worried about her sister, she could have been very entertained by Mrs. Jennings's endeavours to cure a disappointment in love with a variety of sweetmeats and olives, and a good fire. As soon, however, as the consciousness of all this was forced by continual repetition on Marianne, she could stay no longer. With a hasty exclamation of misery, and a sign to her sister not to follow her, she directly got up and hurried out of the room.

"Poor soul!" cried Mrs. Jennings, as soon as she was gone, "How it grieves me to see her! She has gone away without finishing her wine! And the dried cherries too! Lord! Nothing seems to do her any good. I am sure if I knew anything she would like, I would send all over the town for it. Well, it is the oddest thing to me that a man should use such a pretty girl so ill! But when there is plenty of money on one side, and next to none on the other, Lord bless you! They care no more about such things!"

"The lady then—Miss Grey I think you called her—is very rich?"

"Fifty thousand pounds, my dear. Did you ever see her? A smart, stylish girl they say, but not beautiful. I remember her aunt very well, Biddy Henshawe; she married a very wealthy man. But the family are all rich together. Fifty thousand pounds! By all accounts it won't come before it's needed, for they say he is very indebted. No wonder! Dashing about with his fancy carriage and horses! Well, it don't signify talking, but when a young man, be he whom he will, courts a pretty girl, and promises marriage, he has no business to fly off from his word only because he grows poor, and a richer girl is ready to have him. Why don't he, in such a case, sell his horses, rent his house, turn out his servants, and make a thorough reform at once? I warrant you, Miss Marianne would have been ready to wait till matters came round. But that won't do, now-a-days; nothing in the way of pleasure can ever be given up by the young men of this age."

"Do you know what kind of a girl Miss Grey is? Is she said to be amiable?"

"I never heard any harm of her; indeed I hardly ever heard her mentioned, except that Mrs. Taylor did say this morning that one day Miss Walker hinted to her that she believed Mr. and Mrs. Ellison would not be sorry to have Miss Grey married, for she and Mrs. Ellison could never agree."

"And who are the Ellisons?"

"Her guardians, my dear. But now she is of age and may choose for herself; and what a choice she has made!" Then, after pausing a moment—"Your poor sister is gone to her own room, I suppose, to moan by herself. Is there nothing one can get to comfort her? Poor dear, it seems quite cruel to let her be alone. Well, soon we shall have a few friends, and that will amuse her a little. What shall we play? She hates whist I know; but is there no other game she cares for?"

"Dear ma'am, this kindness is quite unnecessary. Marianne, I dare say, will not leave her room again this evening. I shall persuade her if I can to go early to bed, for I am sure she needs rest."

"Aye, I believe that will be best for her. Let her name her own supper, and go to bed. Lord! No wonder she has been looking so bad and so cast down this last week or two, for this matter I suppose has been hanging over her head as long as that. And so the letter that came today finished it! Poor soul! I am sure if I had had a notion of it, I would not have joked with her about it for all my money. But then you know, how should I guess such a thing? I was sure it was nothing but a common love letter, and you know how young people like to be laughed at about them. Lord! How concerned Sir John and my daughters will be when they hear it! If I had had my senses about me, I might have called in Conduit Street in my way home, and told them of it. But I shall see them tomorrow."

"It would be unnecessary, I am sure, for you to caution Mrs. Palmer and Sir John against ever naming Mr. Willoughby, or making the slightest allusion to what has passed, before my sister. Their own good-nature must point out to them the real cruelty of appearing to know anything about it when she is present; and the less that may ever be said to myself on the subject, the more my feelings will be spared, as you, my dear madam, will easily believe."

"Oh Lord! Yes, that I do indeed. It must be terrible for you to hear it talked of; and as for your sister, I am sure I would not mention a word about it to her for the world. You saw I did not all dinner time. No more would Sir John nor my daughters, for they are all very thoughtful and considerate—especially if I give them a hint, as I certainly will. For my part, I think the less that is said about such things, the sooner 'tis blown over and forgot. And what good does talking ever do, you know?"

"In this affair it can only do harm—more so perhaps than in many cases of a similar kind, for it has been attended by circumstances which, for the sake of everyone concerned in it, make it unfit to become public conversation. I must do *this* justice to Mr. Willoughby—he has broken no positive engagement with my sister."

"Law, my dear! Don't pretend to defend him. No positive engagement indeed! after taking her all over Allenham House, and fixing on the very rooms they were to live in hereafter!"

Elinor, for her sister's sake, could not press the subject farther, and she hoped it was not required of her for Willoughby's; since, though Marianne might lose much, he could gain very little if the real truth became generally known. After a short silence on both sides, Mrs. Jennings, with all her natural boisterousness, burst forth again—

"Well, my dear, it will be all the better for Colonel Brandon. He will have her at last; aye, that he will. Mind me, now, if they ain't married by midsummer. Lord! How he'll chuckle over this news! I hope he will come tonight. It will be a much better match for your sister. Two thousand a year without debt or drawback—except his daughter, indeed; aye, I had forgot her. But she may be apprenticed out at a small cost. Delaford is a nice place, I can tell you; exactly what I call a nice old-fashioned place, full of comforts and conveniences; quite enclosed with great garden walls that are covered with the best fruit trees in the country: and such a mulberry tree in one corner! Lord! How Charlotte and I did gorge ourselves the only time we were there! Then there are some delightful ponds, and a very pretty canal; and everything, in short, that one could wish for: and, moreover, it is close to the church, and only a quarter of a mile from the turnpike-road, so 'tis never dull, for if you only go and sit up in an old tree behind the house, you may see all the carriages that pass along. Oh! 'tis a nice place! A butcher in the nearby village, and the parsonage house within a stone's throw. In my view it is a thousand times prettier than Barton Park, where they are forced to send three miles for their meat, and have not a neighbour nearer than your mother. Well, I shall cheer up the Colonel as soon as I can. If we *can* but put Willoughby out of her head!"

"Aye, if we can but do *that*, Ma'am," said Elinor, "we shall do very well with or without Colonel Brandon." And then rising, she went away to join Marianne, whom she found, as she expected, in her own room, leaning, in silent misery, over the small remains of a fire, which, till Elinor's entrance, had been her only light.

"You had better leave me," was all the notice that her sister received from her.

"I will leave you," said Elinor, "if you will go to bed." At first she refused, but her sister's earnest, though gentle persuasion, soon softened her. Elinor saw her lay her aching head on the pillow, and saw her, as she hoped, ready to get some quiet rest before she left her.

In the drawing room, where she then went, she was soon joined by Mrs. Jennings, with a wine glass, full of something, in her hand.

"My dear," said she, entering, "I have just recollected that I have some of the finest wine in the house that ever was tasted—so I have brought a glass of it for your sister. My poor husband! How fond he was of it! Do take it to your sister."

"Dear ma'am," replied Elinor, "how good you are! But I have just left Marianne in bed, and I hope she is nearly asleep. As I think nothing will be of so much service to her as rest, if you will give me leave, I will drink the wine myself."

Mrs. Jennings, though regretting that she had not been five minutes earlier, was satisfied with the compromise; and Elinor, as she swallowed it, reflected that its healing powers on a disappointed heart might be as reasonably tried on herself as on her sister.

Colonel Brandon came in while the party were at tea, and by his manner of looking round the room for Marianne, Elinor immediately fancied that he neither expected nor wished to see her there, and, in short, that he was already aware of what caused her absence. Mrs. Jennings was not struck by the same thought; for, soon after his entrance, she walked across the room to the tea table where Elinor presided, and whispered—"The Colonel looks as grave as ever, you see. He knows nothing of it; do tell him, my dear."

He shortly afterwards drew a chair close to hers, and, with a look which perfectly assured her of his knowledge, inquired after her sister.

"Marianne is not well," said she. "She has been indisposed all day, and we have persuaded her to go to bed."

"Perhaps, then," he hesitatingly replied, "what I heard this morning may be true—there may be more truth in it than I could believe possible at first."

"What did you hear?"

"That a gentleman, whom I had reason to think—in short, that a man, whom I *knew* to be engaged—but how shall I tell you? If you know it already, as surely you must, I may be spared."

"You mean," answered Elinor, with forced calmness, "Mr. Willoughby's marriage with Miss Grey. Yes, we *do* know it all. This seems to have been a day of general illumination, for we only discovered it this very morning. Mr. Willoughby is unfathomable! Where did you hear it?"

"In a shop where I had business. Two ladies were waiting for their carriage, and one of them was giving the other an account of the intended match in a very loud voice. The name of Willoughby, John Willoughby, frequently repeated, first caught my attention, and what followed was a positive assertion that everything was now finally settled respecting his marriage with Miss Grey—it was no longer to be a secret—it would take place even within a few weeks, with many particulars of preparations and other matters. One thing, especially, I remember, because it served to identify the man still more—as soon as the ceremony was over, they were to go to Combe Magna, his home in Somersetshire. My astonishment! It would be impossible to describe what I felt. The communicative lady, I learned on inquiry, for I stayed in the shop till they were gone, was a Mrs. Ellison, and that, as I have been since informed, is the name of Miss Grey's guardian."

"It is. But have you likewise heard that Miss Grey has fifty thousand pounds? In that, if in anything, we may find an explanation."

"It may be so; but Willoughby is capable—at least I think—" He stopped a moment; then added in a voice which seemed to distrust itself, "And your sister—how did she—"

"Her sufferings have been very severe. I have only to hope that they may be proportionately short. It has been, it is a most cruel affliction. Till yesterday, I believe, she never doubted his regard; and even now, perhaps—but *I* am almost convinced that he never was really attached to her. He has been very deceitful! In some points, there seems a hardness of heart about him."

"Ah!" said Colonel Brandon, "there is, indeed! But your sister does not—I think you said so—she does not consider it quite as you do?"

"You know her disposition, and may believe how eagerly she would still defend him if she could."

He made no answer; and soon afterwards, by the removal of the tea things, and the arrangement of the card parties, the subject was necessarily dropped.

Mrs. Jennings, who had watched them with pleasure while they were talking, expected to see the effect of Miss Dashwood's communication in such an instantaneous happiness on Colonel Brandon's side as might have become a man in the bloom of youth. Instead she saw him, with amazement, remain the whole evening more serious and thoughtful than usual.

CHAPTER 31

From a night of more sleep than she had expected, Marianne awoke the next morning to the same consciousness of misery in which she had closed her eyes.

Elinor encouraged her as much as possible to talk of what she felt; and before breakfast was ready, they had gone through the subject again and again; with the same steady conviction and affectionate counsel on Elinor's side, the same feelings and varying opinions on Marianne's, as before. Sometimes she could believe Willoughby to be as unfortunate and as innocent as herself, and at other times she felt he was very blamable. At one moment she was absolutely indifferent to the observation of all the world, at another she would seclude herself from it forever. In one thing, however, she was uniform: she could not endure the presence of Mrs. Jennings, and remained in determined silence whenever they were in the same room. Her heart was hardened against the belief of Mrs. Jennings's entering into her sorrows with any compassion.

"No, no, no, it cannot be," she cried. "She cannot feel. Her kindness is not sympathy; her good-nature is not tenderness. All that she wants is gossip, and she only likes me now because I supply it."

Marianne, though with excellent abilities and a good disposition, was neither reasonable nor fair. She expected from other people the same opinions and feelings as her own, and she judged their motives by the immediate effect of their actions on herself. Thus a circumstance occurred, while the sisters were together in their own room after breakfast, which lowered Mrs. Jennings still more in

Marianne's estimation, even though Mrs. Jennings was governed by an impulse of the utmost goodwill.

With a letter in her outstretched hand, and countenance happily smiling, from the persuasion of bringing comfort, she entered their room, saying—

"Now, my dear, I bring you something that I am sure will do you good."

Marianne heard enough. In one moment her imagination placed before her a letter from Willoughby, full of tenderness and contrition, explanatory of all that had passed, satisfactory, convincing; and instantly followed by Willoughby himself, rushing eagerly into the room to enforce, at her feet, by the eloquence of his eyes, the assurances of his letter. The work of one moment was destroyed by the next. The handwriting of her mother, never till then unwelcome, was before her; and, in the acuteness of the disappointment which followed such an ecstasy of more than hope, she felt as if, till that instant, she had never suffered.

The cruelty of Mrs. Jennings was inexpressible; and now she could reproach her only by the tears which streamed from her eyes with passionate violence—a reproach, however, so entirely lost on its object, that after many expressions of pity, she withdrew, still referring her to the letter for comfort. But the letter, when she was calm enough to read it, brought little comfort. Willoughby filled every page. Her mother was still confident of their engagement, and relied as warmly as ever on his constancy. Her affection for Willoughby, and her conviction of their future happiness together, made Marianne weep in agony as she read.

All her impatience to be at home again now returned; her mother was dearer to her than ever—dearer through the very excess of her mistaken confidence in Willoughby. Elinor, unable herself to determine whether it were better for Marianne to be in London or at Barton, offered no counsel of her own except of patience till their mother's wishes could be known; and at length she obtained her sister's consent to wait for that knowledge.

Mrs. Jennings left them earlier than usual, for she could not be easy till the Middletons and Palmers were able to grieve as much as herself. Positively refusing Elinor's offered attendance, she went out alone for the rest of the morning. Elinor, with a very heavy heart, much aware of the pain she was going to communicate, sat down to write her mother an account of what had passed, and ask for her advice. Marianne, who had come into the drawing room on Mrs. Jennings's going away, remained fixed at the table where Elinor wrote, watching the advancement of her pen, grieving over the hardship of such a task, and grieving still more fondly over its effect on her mother.

In this manner they continued about a quarter of an hour, when Marianne, whose nerves could not then bear any sudden noise, was startled by a rap at the door.

"Who can this be?" cried Elinor. "So early too!"

Marianne moved to the window.

"It is Colonel Brandon!" said she, with vexation. "We are never safe from *him*."

"He will not come in, as Mrs. Jennings is out."

"I will not trust *that*," she said, retreating to her own room. "A man who has nothing to do with his own time has no conscience in his intrusion on that of others."

The event proved her conjecture right, though it was founded on injustice and error, for Colonel Brandon *did* come in. Elinor, who was convinced that concern for Marianne brought him there, could not forgive her sister for thinking so little of him.

"I met Mrs. Jennings in Bond Street," he said after greeting her, "and she encouraged me to visit you. I was the more easily encouraged, because I thought it probable that I might find you alone, which I was very desirous of doing. My object—my wish—my sole wish in desiring it—I hope, I believe it is—is to be a means of giving comfort; no, I must not say comfort—not present comfort—but conviction, lasting conviction to your sister's mind. My regard for her, for yourself, for your mother—will you allow me to prove it, by relating some circumstances, which nothing but a *very* sincere regard—nothing but an earnest desire of being useful—I think I am justified—though where so many hours have been spent in convincing myself that I am right, is there not some reason to fear I may be wrong?" He stopped.

"I understand you," said Elinor. "You have something to tell me of Mr. Willoughby, that will open his character farther. Your telling it will be the greatest act of friendship that can be shown Marianne. *My* gratitude will be ensured immediately by any information tending to that end, and *hers* must be gained by it in time. Pray, pray let me hear it."

"You shall; and, to be brief, when I left Barton last October— but this will give you no idea—I must go farther back. You will find me a very awkward narrator, Miss Dashwood; I hardly know where to begin. A short account of myself, I believe, will be necessary, and it *shall* be a short one. On such a subject," sighing heavily, "I can have little temptation to be long-winded."

He stopped a moment for recollection, and then, with another sigh, went on.

"You have probably entirely forgotten a conversation (it is not to be supposed that it could make any impression on you) between us one evening at Barton Park—it was the evening of a dance—in which I alluded to a lady I had once known, as resembling, in some measure, your sister Marianne."

"Indeed," answered Elinor, "I have *not* forgotten it." He looked pleased by this remembrance, and added—

"There is a very strong resemblance between them, in mind as well as in person—the same warmth of heart, the same eagerness of fancy and spirits. This lady was one of my nearest relations, an orphan from her infancy, and under the guardianship of my father. Our ages were nearly the same, and from our earliest years we were playfellows and friends. I cannot remember the time when I did not love Eliza; and my affection for her, as we grew up, was such as perhaps, judging from my present forlorn and cheerless gravity, you might think me incapable of having ever felt. Hers, for me, was, I believe, fervent as the attachment of your sister to Mr. Willoughby, and it was, though from a different cause, no less unfortunate. At seventeen, she was married against her inclination to my brother. Her fortune was large, and our family was deeply in debt. My brother did not deserve her; he did not even love her. I had hoped that her regard for me would support her under any difficulty, and for some time it did; but at last the misery of her situation, for she experienced great unkindness, overcame all her resolution, and though she had promised me that nothing—but how blindly I relate! I have never told you how this was brought on. We were within a few hours of eloping together for Scotland, but my cousin's maid betrayed us. I was banished to the house of a relation far distant, and she was allowed no freedom, no company, no amusement, till my father's point was gained. I had depended on her fortitude too far, and the blow was a severe one—but had her marriage been happy, so young as I then was, a few months must have reconciled me to it, or at least I should not have now to lament it. This, however was not the case. My brother had no regard for her; his pleasures were not what they ought to have been, and from the first he treated her unkindly. The consequence of this, upon a mind so young, so lively, so inexperienced as Mrs. Brandon's, was but too natural. With such a husband, and without a friend to advise or restrain her (my father lived only a few months after their marriage, and I was with my regiment in the East Indies), she was unfaithful, and my brother divorced her for it, leaving her with very little to live upon. It was *that* which threw this gloom—even now the recollection of what I suffered—"

He could say no more, and rising hastily walked for a few minutes about the room. Elinor, affected by his relation, and still more by his distress, could not speak. He saw her concern, and coming to her, took her hand, pressed it, and kissed it with grateful respect. A few minutes more of silent exertion enabled him to proceed with composure.

"It was nearly three years after this unhappy period before I returned to England. My first care, when I *did* arrive, was of course to look for her; but the search was as fruitless as it was melancholy. I could not trace her beyond her first seducer, and there was every reason to fear that she had left him only to sink deeper into a life of sin. At last, however, and after I had been six months in England, I *did* find her. Regard for a former servant of my own, who had since fallen into misfortune, carried me to visit him in debtors prison; and there, in the same house, under a similar confinement, was my unfortunate sister. So altered—so faded—worn down by acute suffering of every kind! Hardly could I believe the melancholy and sickly figure before me to be the remains of the lovely, blooming, healthful girl on whom I had once doted. What I endured in thus beholding her—but I have no right to wound your feelings by attempting to describe it—I have pained you too much already. That she was, to all appearances, in the last stages of consumption was— yes, in such a situation it was my greatest comfort. Life could do nothing for her beyond giving time for a better preparation for death; and that was given. I saw her placed in comfortable lodgings, and under proper attendants; I visited her every day during the rest of her short life, and I was with her in her last moments."

Again he stopped to recover himself, and Elinor spoke her feelings in an exclamation of tender concern at the fate of his unfortunate friend.

"Your sister, I hope, cannot be offended," said he, "by the resemblance I have fancied between her and my poor disgraced relation. Their fates, their fortunes cannot be the same; and had the natural sweet disposition of the one been guarded by a firmer mind, or a happier marriage, she might have been all that you will live to see the other be. But to what does all this lead? I seem to have been distressing you for nothing. Ah! Miss Dashwood—a subject such as this—untouched for fourteen years—it is dangerous to handle it at all! I *will* be more collected—more concise. She left to my care her only child, a little girl, the offspring of her first guilty connection, who was then about three years old. She loved the child dearly. It was a valued, precious trust to me; but I had no family, no home. So my little Eliza was placed at school. I saw her there whenever I could, and after the death of my brother (which happened about five years ago, and which left to me the possession of the family property), she frequently visited me at Delaford. I called her a distant relation, but I know people suspect she is my own illegitimate child. It is now three years ago (she had just reached her fourteenth year), that I removed her from school and placed her under the care of a very respectable woman. For two years, I had every reason to be pleased with her situation. But last February, almost a year ago, she suddenly disappeared. I had allowed her (imprudently, as it has since turned out), at her earnest desire, to go to Bath with one of her young friends, who was attending her father there for his health. I knew him to be a very good sort of man, and I thought well of his daughter— better than she deserved. Her father had been generally confined to the house while the girls were ranging over the town and making what acquaintance they chose; and he tried to convince me, as thoroughly as he was convinced himself, of his daughter's being entirely unconcerned in the business. In short, I could learn nothing but that she was gone; all the rest, for eight long months, was left to conjecture. What I thought, what I feared, may be imagined; and what I suffered too."

"Good heavens!" cried Elinor, "Could it be! Could Willoughby—"

"The first news that reached me of her," he continued, "came in a letter from herself last October. It was forwarded to me from Delaford, and I received it on the very morning of our intended party to Whitwell; and this was the reason of my leaving Barton so suddenly, which I am sure must at the time have appeared strange to everybody, and which I believe gave offence to some. Little did Mr. Willoughby imagine, I suppose, when his looks censured me for incivility in breaking up the party, that I was called away to the relief of one whom he had made poor and miserable. But *had* he known it, what good would it have done? Would he have been less happy in the smiles of your sister? No, he had already done that which no man who *can* feel for another would do. He had left the girl whose youth and innocence he had seduced, in a situation of the utmost distress, with no creditable home, no help, no friends! He had left her, promising to return; he neither returned, nor wrote, nor relieved her."

"This is beyond everything!" exclaimed Elinor.

"His character is now before you. Knowing all this, as I have now known it many weeks, guess what I must have felt on seeing your sister as fond of him as ever, and on being assured that she was to marry him; guess what I must have felt for all your sakes. When I came to you last week and found you alone, I came determined to know the truth, though irresolute what to do when it *was* known. My behaviour must have seemed strange to you then; but now you will understand it. To suffer you all to be so deceived; to see your sister— but what could I do? I had no hope of convincing her, and sometimes I thought your sister's influence might yet reclaim him. But now, after such dishonourable usage, who can tell what were his designs on her? Whatever they may have been, however, she may now, and hereafter doubtless *will*, turn with gratitude towards her own condition, when she compares it with that of my poor Eliza. She will feel her own sufferings to be nothing. They proceed from no misconduct, and can bring no disgrace. On the contrary, every friend must be made still more her friend by them. Concern for her unhappiness, and respect for her fortitude under it, must strengthen every attachment. Use your own discretion, however, in communicating to her what I have told you. You must know best what will be its effect; but had I not seriously and from my heart believed it might be of service, might lessen her regrets, I would not have suffered myself to trouble you with this account of my family afflictions."

Elinor's thanks followed this speech with grateful earnestness; attended too with the assurance of her expecting material advantage to Marianne, from the communication of what had passed.

"I have been more pained," said she, "by her endeavours to defend him than by all the rest; for it irritates her mind more than the most perfect conviction of his unworthiness can do. Now, though at first she will suffer much, I am sure she will soon become easier. Have you," she continued, after a short silence, "seen Mr. Willoughby since you left him at Barton?"

"Yes," he replied gravely, "once I have. One meeting was unavoidable."

Elinor, startled by his manner, looked at him anxiously, saying—

"What? Have you met him to duel?"

"I could meet him in no other way. Eliza had confessed to me, though most reluctantly, the name of her lover; and when he returned to town, which was within a fortnight after myself, we met by appointment: he to defend, and I to punish his conduct. We returned unwounded, and the meeting, therefore, was never publicized."

Elinor sighed over the fancied necessity of this; but to a man and a soldier, it had perhaps seemed the only honourable course of action.

"Such," said Colonel Brandon, after a pause, "has been the unhappy resemblance between the fate of mother and daughter! And so imperfectly have I discharged my trust!"

"Is she still in town?"

"No; as soon as she had recovered from giving birth, I moved her and her child into the country, and there she remains."

Recollecting, soon afterwards, that he was probably dividing Elinor from her sister, he put an end to his visit, receiving from her again the same grateful acknowledgments, and leaving her full of compassion and esteem for him.

CHAPTER 32

When the particulars of this conversation were repeated by Miss Dashwood to her sister, as they very soon were, the effect on her was not entirely such as her sister had hoped to see. Not that Marianne appeared to distrust the truth of any part of it, for she listened to it all with the most steady and submissive attention. She made neither objection nor remark, attempted no vindication of Willoughby, and seemed to show by her tears that such conduct was indefensible. This behaviour assured Elinor that the conviction of his guilt *was* carried home to her mind. She saw with satisfaction the effect of it, in her no longer avoiding Colonel Brandon when he visited, in her speaking to him, even voluntarily speaking, with a kind of compassionate respect. Though she saw her spirits less violently irritated than before, she did not see her less wretched. Her mind did become settled, but it was settled in a gloomy dejection. She felt the loss of Willoughby's good character more heavily than she had felt the loss of his heart. His seduction and desertion of Miss Williams, the misery of that poor girl, and the doubt of what his designs might *once* have been on herself, preyed altogether so much on her spirits, that she could not bring herself to speak of what she felt even to Elinor. Brooding over her sorrows in silence gave more pain to her sister than could have been communicated by the most open and most frequent confession of them.

To give the feelings or the language of Mrs. Dashwood on receiving and answering Elinor's letter, would be only to give a repetition of what her daughters had already felt and said. Long letters from her, one after the other, arrived to tell all that she suffered and thought; to express her anxious concern for Marianne, and to encourage her to bear with fortitude this misfortune.

Against the interest of her own individual comfort, Mrs. Dashwood had determined that it would be better for Marianne to be anywhere at that time than at Barton, where everything within her view would be bringing back the past in the strongest and most afflicting manner. She recommended it to her daughters, therefore, by all means not to shorten their visit to Mrs. Jennings; the length of which, though never exactly fixed, had been expected by all to comprise at least five or six weeks. A variety of occupations, of objects, and of company, which could not be procured at Barton, would be inevitable there, and might yet, she hoped, distract Marianne.

From all danger of seeing Willoughby again, her mother considered her to be at least equally safe in town as in the country, since his acquaintance must now be dropped by all who called themselves her friends. A chance meeting was less likely in the crowd of London than even in the seclusion of Barton, where it might force him before her while paying the expected visit to Allenham after his marriage.

She had yet another reason for wishing her children to remain where they were; a letter from her son-in-law had told her that he and his wife were to be in town before the middle of February, and she judged it right that they should sometimes see their brother.

Marianne had promised to be guided by her mother's opinion, and she submitted to it therefore without opposition, though it was not what she wished and expected. By requiring her longer continuance in London, it deprived her of the only possible alleviation of her wretchedness, the personal sympathy of her mother, and doomed her to such society and such scenes as must prevent her ever knowing a moment's rest.

But it was a matter of great consolation to her, that what brought trouble to herself would bring good to her sister. Elinor, on the other hand, suspecting that it would not be in her power to avoid Edward entirely, comforted herself by thinking, that though their longer stay would do little for her own happiness, it would be better for Marianne than an immediate return to Devonshire.

Her carefulness in guarding her sister from ever hearing Willoughby's name mentioned, was not without benefit. Marianne, though without knowing it herself, reaped all its advantage; for neither Mrs. Jennings, nor Sir John, nor even Mrs. Palmer herself, ever spoke of him before her. Elinor wished that the same forbearance could have extended towards herself, but that was impossible, and she was obliged to listen day after day to the indignation of them all.

Sir John could not have thought it possible. A man of whom he had always had such reason to think well! Such a good-natured fellow! He did not believe there was a bolder rider in England! It was an unaccountable business. He would not speak another word to him, meet him where he might, for all the world! Such a scoundrel of a fellow! Such a deceitful dog!

Mrs. Palmer, in her way, was equally angry. She was determined to drop his acquaintance immediately, and she was very thankful that she had never been acquainted with him at all. She wished with all her heart Combe Magna was not so near Cleveland; but it did not matter, for it was a great deal too far off to visit. She hated him so much that she was resolved never to mention his name again, and she would tell everybody she saw, how good-for-nothing he was.

The rest of Mrs. Palmer's sympathy was shown in procuring all the particulars of the approaching marriage, and communicating them to Elinor. She could soon tell at what coachmaker's the new carriage was being built, by what painter Mr. Willoughby's portrait was taken, and from what shop Miss Grey's clothes would be acquired.

The calm and polite unconcern of Lady Middleton on the occasion was a happy relief to Elinor's spirits, oppressed as they often were by the clamorous kindness of the others. Every qualification is raised at times, by the circumstances of the moment, to more than its real value; and she sometimes even felt that good manners were superior to good nature.

Lady Middleton expressed her sense of the affair about once every day, or twice, if the subject occurred very often, by saying, "It is very shocking indeed!" and by the means of this continual though gentle vent, was able not only to see the Miss Dashwoods from the first without the smallest emotion, but very soon to see them without recollecting a word of the matter. Having thus supported the dignity of her own sex, and spoken her decided censure of what was wrong in the other, she thought herself at liberty to attend to social graces, and therefore determined (though rather against the opinion of Sir John), that as Mrs. Willoughby would at once be a woman of elegance and fortune, to leave her card with her as soon as she married.

Colonel Brandon's delicate inquiries were never unwelcome to Miss Dashwood. He had abundantly earned the privilege of discussing her sister's disappointment, by the friendly zeal with which he had endeavoured to soften it, and they always conversed with confidence. His chief reward for the painful exertion of disclosing past sorrows and present humiliations, was given in the pitying eye with which Marianne sometimes observed him, and the gentleness of her voice whenever (though it did not often happen) she was obliged, or could oblige herself to speak to him. *These* assured him that his exertion had produced an increase of good will towards himself, and gave Elinor hopes of its being farther augmented hereafter; but Mrs. Jennings, who knew nothing of all this—who knew only that the Colonel continued as grave as ever, and that she could neither prevail on him to make the offer himself, nor commission her to make it for him—began at the end of two days to think that, instead of Midsummer, they would not be married till September, and by the end of a week that it would not be a match at all. The good understanding between the Colonel and Miss Dashwood seemed rather to declare that the honours of the mulberry tree, and the canal, would all be made over to *her*; and Mrs. Jennings had for some time ceased to think at all of Mr. Ferrars.

Early in February, within a fortnight of the receipt of Willoughby's letter, Elinor had the painful office of informing her sister that he was married. She had taken care to have the intelligence conveyed to herself, as soon as it was known that the ceremony was over, as she was desirous that Marianne should not receive the first notice of it from the public papers, which she saw her eagerly examining every morning.

She received the news with resolute composure; made no observation on it, and at first shed no tears; but after a short time they burst out, and for the rest of the day, she was in a state hardly less pitiable than when she first learned to expect the event.

The Willoughbys left town as soon as they were married; and Elinor now hoped, as there could be no danger of her seeing either of them, to prevail on her sister, who had never yet left the house since the blow first fell, to go out again as she had done before.

About this time, the two Miss Steeles, recently arrived at their cousin's house, presented themselves again before their wealthier relations in Conduit and Berkeley Street; and were welcomed by them all with great cordiality.

Elinor only was sorry to see them. Their presence always gave her pain, and she hardly knew how to make a very gracious return to the overpowering delight of Lucy in finding her *still* in town.

"I should have been quite disappointed if I had not found you here *still*," said she repeatedly, with a strong emphasis on the word. "But I always thought I *would*. I was almost sure you would not leave London yet awhile; though you *told* me, you know, at Barton, that you should not stay for longer than a *month*. But I thought, at the time, that you would most likely change your mind. It would have been such a great pity to have gone away before your brother and sister came. And now, to be sure, you will be in no *hurry* to be gone. I am amazingly glad you did not keep *your word*."

Elinor perfectly understood her, and was forced to use all her self-command to make it appear that she did *not*.

"Well, my dear," said Mrs. Jennings, "and how did you travel?"

"We came post all the way," replied Miss Steele, with quick exultation, "and had a very smart beau to attend us. Dr. Davies was coming to town, and so we thought we'd join him. He behaved very genteelly, and paid ten or twelve shillings more than we did."

"Oh, oh!" cried Mrs. Jennings. "Very nice, indeed! And the Doctor is a single man?"

"There now," said Miss Steele, "everybody laughs at me so about the Doctor, and I cannot think why. My cousins say they are sure I have made a conquest; but for my part I declare I never think about him from one hour's end to another. 'Lord! Here comes your beau, Nancy,' my cousin said t'other day, when she saw him crossing the street to the house. 'My beau, indeed!' said I, 'I cannot think who you mean. The Doctor is no beau of mine.'"

"Aye, aye, that is all very nice—but it won't do—the Doctor is the man, I see."

"No, indeed!" replied her cousin, with affected earnestness, "and I beg you will contradict it, if you ever hear it talked of."

Mrs. Jennings directly gave her the gratifying assurance that she certainly would *not*, and Miss Steele was made completely happy.

"I suppose you will go and stay with your brother and sister, Miss Dashwood, when they come to town," said Lucy, returning, after a cessation of hostile hints, to their original subject.

"No, I do not think we shall."

"Oh, yes, I dare say you will."

Elinor would not humour her by farther opposition.

"What a charming thing it is that Mrs. Dashwood can spare you both for so long a time together!"

"Long time, indeed," said Mrs. Jennings. "Why, their visit has just begun!"

Lucy was silenced.

"I am sorry we cannot see your sister, Miss Dashwood," said Miss Steele. "I am sorry she is not well." (Marianne had left the room on their arrival.)

"You are very good. My sister will be equally sorry to miss the pleasure of seeing you; but she has been very much plagued lately with headaches, which make her unfit for company or conversation."

"Oh, dear, that is a great pity! But such old friends as Lucy and me!—I think she might see *us*; and I am sure we would not speak a word."

Elinor, with great civility, declined the proposal. Her sister was perhaps laid down upon the bed, or in her dressing gown, and therefore not able to come to them.

"Oh, if that's all," cried Miss Steele, "we can just as well go and see *her.*"

Elinor began to find this insistence too much for her temper; but she was saved the trouble of checking it, by Lucy's sharp reprimand, which now, as on many occasions, though it did not give much sweetness to the manners of one sister, was helpful in governing those of the other.

CHAPTER 33

After some opposition, Marianne yielded to her sister's entreaties, and consented to go out with her and Mrs. Jennings one morning for half an hour. She expressly requested, however, that they pay no visits. She would do no more than accompany them to Gray's, where Elinor was carrying on a negotiation for the exchange of a few old-fashioned jewels of her mother.

When they stopped at the door, Mrs. Jennings recollected that there was a lady at the other end of the street on whom she ought to call; and as she had no business at Gray's, it was resolved that while her young friends transacted theirs, she should pay her visit and return for them.

On ascending the stairs, the Miss Dashwoods found so many people before them in the room, that there was not a person at liberty to attend them, and they were obliged to wait. All that could be done was to sit down at the end of the counter which appeared least busy. One gentleman only was standing there, and Elinor hoped her presence would cause him to finish his business quickly. But the correctness of his eye, and the delicacy of his taste, proved to be beyond his politeness. He was giving orders for a toothpick case for himself, and till its size, shape, and ornaments were determined—all of which, after examining and debating for a quarter of an hour over every toothpick-case in the shop, were finally arranged by his own inventive fancy—he had no leisure to bestow any other attention on the two ladies than what was comprised in three or four very broad stares.

Marianne was spared from the troublesome feelings of contempt and resentment, on this impertinent examination of their features, and on the shallowness of his manner in deciding on all the different horrors of the various toothpick cases presented to him, by remaining unconscious of it all. She was as able to become lost in her thoughts, and be as ignorant of what was passing around her, in Mr. Gray's shop as in her own bedroom.

At last the affair was decided. The ivory, the gold, and the pearls, all received their appointment, and the gentleman having named the last day on which his existence could be continued without the possession of the toothpick case, drew on his gloves with leisurely care, and bestowing another glance on the Miss Dashwoods, but such a one as seemed rather to demand than express admiration, walked off with a happy air of real conceit and affected indifference.

Elinor lost no time in bringing her business forward, and was on the point of concluding it, when another gentleman presented himself at her side. She turned her eyes towards his face, and found him with some surprise to be her brother.

Their affection and pleasure in meeting was just enough to make a very creditable appearance in Mr. Gray's shop. John Dashwood was really far from being sorry to see his sisters again; it rather gave them satisfaction, and his inquiries after their mother were respectful and attentive.

Elinor found that he and Fanny had been in town two days.

"I wished very much to call upon you yesterday," said he, "but it was impossible, for we were obliged to take Harry to see the wild beasts at the zoo: and we spent the rest of the day with Mrs. Ferrars. Harry was vastly pleased. *This* morning I had fully intended to call on you, if I could possibly find a spare half-hour, but one has always so much to do on first coming to town. I am come here to buy Fanny a seal. But tomorrow I think I shall certainly be able to call in Berkeley Street, and be introduced to your friend Mrs. Jennings. I understand she is a woman of very large fortune. And the Middletons too, you must introduce me to *them*. As my mother-in-law's relations, I shall be happy to show them every respect. They are excellent neighbours to you in the country, I understand."

"Excellent indeed. Their attention to our comfort, their friendliness in every particular, is more than I can express."

"I am extremely glad to hear it, upon my word; extremely glad indeed. But so it ought to be; they are people of great wealth, they are related to you, and every civility and accommodation that can serve to make your situation pleasant, might be reasonably expected. And so you are most comfortably settled in your little cottage and have no need for anything! Edward brought us a most charming account of the place; the most complete thing of its kind, he said, that ever was, and you all seemed to enjoy it beyond anything. It was a great satisfaction to us to hear it, I assure you."

At that moment, Mrs. Jennings's servant came to tell her that his mistress waited for them at the door.

Mr. Dashwood attended them downstairs, was introduced to Mrs. Jennings at the door of her carriage, and repeating his hope of being able to call on them the next day, took leave.

His visit was duly paid. He came with an apology from their sister-in-law, for not coming too; she was so much engaged with her mother, that really she had no leisure for going anywhere. Mrs. Jennings, however, assured him directly that she should not stand upon ceremony, for they were all cousins, or something like it, and she would certainly visit Mrs. John Dashwood very soon, and bring her sisters to see her. His manners to *them*, though calm, were perfectly kind; to Mrs. Jennings, most attentively civil; and on Colonel Brandon's coming in soon after himself, he eyed him with a curiosity which seemed to say that he only needed to know him to be rich to be equally civil to *him*.

After staying with them half an hour, he asked Elinor to walk with him to Conduit Street and introduce him to Sir John and Lady Middleton. The weather was remarkably fine, and she readily consented. As soon as they were out of the house, his inquiries began.

"Who is Colonel Brandon? Is he a man of fortune?"

"Yes; he has very good property in Dorsetshire."

"I am glad of it. He seems a most gentlemanlike man; and I think, Elinor, I may congratulate you on the prospect of a very respectable establishment in life."

"Me, brother—what do you mean?"

"He likes you. I observed him narrowly, and am convinced of it. What is the amount of his fortune?"

"I believe about two thousand a year."

"Two thousand a year;" and then working himself up to a pitch of enthusiastic generosity, he added:

"Elinor, I wish, with all my heart, it were *twice* as much, for your sake."

"Indeed I believe you," replied Elinor; "but I am very sure that Colonel Brandon has not the smallest wish of marrying *me.*"

"You are mistaken, Elinor; you are very much mistaken. A very little trouble on your side secures him. Perhaps just at present he may be undecided; the smallness of your fortune may make him hang back; his friends may all advise him against it. But some of those little attentions and encouragements which ladies can so easily give, will win him over, in spite of himself. And there can be no reason why you should not try for him. It is not to be supposed that any prior attachment on your side—in short, you know, to Edward—can stand in your way. Colonel Brandon must be the man; and no civility shall be wanting on my part, to make him pleased with you and your family. It is a match that must give universal satisfaction. In short, it is a kind of thing that"—lowering his voice to an important whisper—"will be exceedingly welcome to *all parties.*" Recollecting himself, however, he added, "That is, I mean to say—your friends are all truly anxious to see you well settled, Fanny particularly, for she has your interest very much at heart, I assure you. And her mother too, Mrs. Ferrars, a very good-natured woman, I am sure it would give her great pleasure; she said as much the other day."

Elinor did not trust herself to make an answer.

"It would be something remarkable now," he continued, "something droll, if Fanny should have a brother and I a sister settling at the same time. And yet it is not very unlikely."

"Is Mr. Edward Ferrars," said Elinor with resolution, "going to be married?"

"It is not actually settled, but there is such a thing in discussion. He has a most excellent mother. Mrs. Ferrars, with the utmost liberality, will come forward, and settle on him a thousand a year, if the match takes place. The lady is the Honorable Miss Morton, only daughter of the late Lord Morton, with thirty thousand pounds. A very desirable connection on both sides, and I have not a doubt of its taking place in time. A thousand a year is a great deal for a mother to give away, to make over forever; but Mrs. Ferrars has a noble spirit. To give you another instance of her liberality, the other day, as soon as we came to town, aware that money could not be very abundant with us just now, she put bank notes into Fanny's hands to the amount of two hundred pounds. And extremely acceptable it is, for we must live at a great expense while we are here."

He paused for her assent and compassion; and she forced herself to say—

"Your expenses both in town and country must certainly be considerable, but your income is a large one."

"Not as large, I dare say, as many people suppose. I do not mean to complain, however; it is undoubtedly a comfortable one, and I hope, will in time be better. The fencing of Norland Common, now in progress, is a most serious drain. And then I have made a little purchase within this half year—East Kingham Farm, you must remember the place, where old Gibson used to live. The land was so very desirable for me in every respect, so immediately adjoining my own property, that I felt it my duty to buy it. I could not have answered it to my conscience to let it fall into any other hands. A man must pay for his convenience, and it *has* cost me a vast deal of money."

"More than you think it really worth?"

"Why, I hope not that. I might have sold it again the next day for more than I gave, but with regard to the purchase money, I might have been very unfortunate indeed; for the stocks were at that time so low, that if I had not happened to have the necessary sum in my banker's hands, I must have sold at a very great loss."

Elinor could only smile.

"Other great and inevitable expenses too we have had on first coming to Norland. Our respected father, as you well know, bequeathed all the Stanhill effects that remained at Norland (and very valuable they were) to your mother. Far be it from me to complain about his doing so; he had an undoubted right to dispose of his own property as he chose. But, in consequence of it, we have been obliged to make large purchases of linen, china, etc., to supply the place of what was taken away. You may guess, after all these expenses, how very far we must be from being rich, and how acceptable Mrs. Ferrars's kindness is."

"Certainly," said Elinor; "and assisted by her liberality, I hope you may yet live to be in easy circumstances."

"Another year or two may do much towards it," he gravely replied; "but there is still a great deal to be done. There is not a stone laid of Fanny's greenhouse, and nothing but the plan of the flower-garden marked out."

"Where is the greenhouse to be?"

"Upon the knoll behind the house. The old walnut trees are all come down to make room for it. It will be a very fine object from many parts of the park, and the flower-garden will slope down just before it, and be exceedingly pretty. We have cleared away all the old thorns that grew in patches over the brow."

Elinor kept her concern and her censure to herself; and was very thankful that Marianne was not present, to share the provocation.

Having now said enough to make his poverty clear, and to do away the necessity of buying a pair of earrings for each of his sisters, in his next visit at Gray's, his thoughts took a cheerfuller turn, and he began to congratulate Elinor on having such a friend as Mrs. Jennings.

"She seems a most valuable woman indeed. Her house, her style of living, all bespeak an exceeding good income, and it is an acquaintance that has not only been of great use to you hitherto, but in the end may prove materially advantageous. Her inviting you to town is certainly in your favour; and indeed, it speaks altogether so great a regard for you, that in all probability when she dies you will not be forgotten. She must have a great deal to leave."

"Nothing at all, I should rather suppose; for she has only her annuity, which will descend to her children."

"But it is not to be imagined that her expenses match her income. Few people of common prudence will do *that*; and whatever she saves, she will be able to dispose of."

"And do you not think it more likely that she should leave it to her daughters, than to us?"

"Her daughters are both exceedingly well married, and therefore I cannot perceive the necessity of her remembering them farther. Whereas, in my opinion, by her taking so much notice of you, and treating you in this kind of way, she has given you a sort of claim on her future consideration, which a conscientious woman would not disregard. Nothing can be kinder than her behaviour; and she can hardly do all this, without being aware of the expectation she raises."

"But she raises none in those most concerned. Indeed, brother, your anxiety for our welfare and prosperity carries you too far."

"Why to be sure," said he, seeming to recollect himself. "What is the matter with Marianne? She looks very unwell, has lost her colour, and is grown quite thin. Is she ill?"

"She is not well; she has had a nervous complaint for several weeks."

"I am sorry for that. At her time of life, any illness destroys the bloom forever! Hers has been a very short one! She was as beautiful a girl last September as any I ever saw, and as likely to attract the men. There was something in her style of beauty, to please them particularly. I remember Fanny used to say that she would marry sooner and better than you did; not that she isn't exceedingly fond of *you*—but so it happened to strike her. She will be mistaken, however. I question whether Marianne *now*, will marry a man worth more than five or six hundred a year, at the most, and I am very much deceived if *you* do not do better. Dorsetshire! I know very little of Dorsetshire, but, my dear Elinor, I shall be exceedingly glad to know more of it; and I think I can answer for your having Fanny and myself among the earliest and best pleased of your visitors."

Elinor tried very seriously to convince him that there was no likelihood of her marrying Colonel Brandon; but it was an expectation of too much pleasure to himself to be relinquished, and he was really resolved on seeking an intimacy with that gentleman, and promoting the marriage by every possible attention. He had just conscience enough for having done nothing for his sisters himself, to be exceedingly anxious that everybody else should do a great deal; and an offer from Colonel Brandon, or a legacy from Mrs. Jennings, was the easiest means of atoning for his own neglect.

They were lucky enough to find Lady Middleton at home, and Sir John came in before their visit ended. Civilities passed on all sides. Sir John was ready to like anybody, and though Mr. Dashwood did not seem to know much about horses, he soon determined him to be a very good-natured fellow: while Lady Middleton saw enough of fashion in his appearance to think his acquaintance worth having, and Mr. Dashwood went away delighted with both.

"I shall have a charming account to carry to Fanny," said he, as he walked back with his sister. "Lady Middleton is really a most elegant woman! Such a woman as I am sure Fanny will be glad to know. And Mrs. Jennings too, an exceeding well-behaved woman, though not as elegant as her daughter. Your sister need not have any scruple even of visiting *her*, which, to say the truth, has been a little the case, and very naturally; for we only knew that Mrs. Jennings was the widow of a man who had obtained all his money in a common way. Fanny and Mrs. Ferrars were both strongly convinced that neither she nor her daughters were such kind of women Fanny would like to associate with. But now I can carry her a most satisfactory account of both."

CHAPTER 34

Mrs. John Dashwood had so much confidence in her husband's judgment that she visited Mrs. Jennings and her daughter the very next day. Her confidence was rewarded by finding even the former, even the woman with whom her sisters were staying, by no means unworthy of her notice; and as for Lady Middleton, she found her to be one of the most charming women in the world!

Lady Middleton was equally pleased with Mrs. Dashwood. There was a kind of cold-hearted selfishness on both sides which mutually attracted them.

The same manners however, which recommended Mrs. John Dashwood to the good opinion of Lady Middleton, did not suit the fancy of Mrs. Jennings, and to *her* she appeared nothing more than a little proud-looking woman who met her husband's sisters without any affection, and almost without having anything to say to them. Of the quarter of an hour bestowed on Berkeley Street, she sat at least seven and a half minutes in silence.

Elinor wanted very much to know, though she did not choose to ask, whether Edward was then in town; but nothing would have induced Fanny voluntarily to mention his name before her, till able to tell her that his marriage with Miss Morton was settled on. The intelligence however, which *she* would not give, soon flowed from another quarter. Lucy came very shortly to claim Elinor's compassion on being unable to see Edward, though he had arrived in town with Mr. and Mrs. Dashwood. He dared not come to Bartlett's Buildings for fear of detection, and though their mutual impatience to meet was great, they could do nothing at present but write.

Edward assured them himself of his being in town, within a very short time, by twice calling in Berkeley Street. Twice was his card found on the table when they returned from their morning's engagements. Elinor was pleased that he had called, and still more pleased that she had not been at home when he came.

The Dashwoods were so delighted with the Middletons, that though not much in the habit of giving anything, they determined to give them a dinner, and soon after their acquaintance began, invited them to dine in Harley Street, where they had taken a very good house for three months. Their sisters and Mrs. Jennings were invited likewise, and John Dashwood was careful to secure Colonel Brandon, who, always glad to be where the Miss Dashwoods were, received his eager civilities with some surprise, but much more pleasure. They were to meet Mrs. Ferrars; but Elinor could not learn whether her sons were to be there. The expectation of seeing *her*, however, was enough to make her interested in the dinner; for though she could now meet Edward's mother without that strong anxiety which had once promised to accompany such an introduction, her curiosity to know what she was like was as strong as ever.

The interest with which she thus anticipated the party was soon afterwards increased, more powerfully than pleasantly, by her hearing that the Miss Steeles were also to be in attendance.

So well had they recommended themselves to Lady Middleton, so agreeable had their flatteries made them to her, that though Lucy was certainly not elegant, and her sister not even genteel, she was as ready as Sir John to ask them to spend a week or two in Conduit Street. It happened to be particularly convenient to the Miss Steeles, as soon as the Dashwoods' invitation was known, that their visit would begin a few days before the party took place.

Their claims to the notice of Mrs. John Dashwood, as the nieces of the gentleman who for many years had had the care of her brother, might not have done much towards procuring them seats at her table. As Lady Middleton's guests, however, they must be welcome. Lucy, who had long wanted to be personally known to the family, had seldom been happier in her life than she was on receiving Mrs. John Dashwood's card.

On Elinor its effect was very different. She began immediately to determine that Edward, who lived with his mother, must be invited, as his mother was, to a party given by his sister; and to see him for the first time after all that had passed, in the company of Lucy! She hardly knew how she could bear it!

These fears perhaps were not founded entirely on reason, and certainly not at all on truth. They were relieved however, not by her own remembrance, but by the good will of Lucy, who believed herself to be inflicting a severe disappointment when she told her that Edward certainly would not be in Harley Street on Tuesday. She then attempted to persuade Elinor that he was kept away by that extreme affection for herself, which he could not conceal when they were together.

The important Tuesday came that was to introduce the two young ladies to this formidable mother-in-law.

"Pity, dear Miss Dashwood!" said Lucy, as they walked up the stairs together—for the Middletons arrived so directly after Mrs. Jennings, that they all followed the servant at the same time—"There is nobody here but you that knows what I am about to go through. I declare I can hardly stand. Good gracious! In a moment I shall see the person that all my happiness depends on—that is to be my mother!"

Elinor could have given her immediate relief by suggesting the possibility of its being Miss Morton's mother, rather than her own, whom they were about to see; but instead of doing that, she assured her, and with great sincerity, that she did pity her—to the utter amazement of Lucy, who, though really uncomfortable herself, hoped at least to be an object of envy to Elinor.

Mrs. Ferrars was a little, thin woman, upright, even to formality, in her figure, and serious, even to sourness, in her aspect. Her complexion was sallow: and her features small, without beauty, and naturally without expression. She was not a woman of many words: for, unlike people in general, she proportioned them to the number of her ideas. Of the few syllables that did escape her, not one fell to the share of Miss Dashwood, whom she eyed with the spirited determination of disliking her.

Elinor could not *now* be made unhappy by this behaviour. A few months ago it would have hurt her exceedingly; but it was not in Mrs. Ferrars's power to distress her by it now; and the difference of her manners to the Miss Steeles—a difference which seemed purposely made to humble her more—only amused her. She could not but smile to see the graciousness of both mother and daughter towards the very person—for Lucy was particularly distinguished—whom of all others, had they known as much as she did, they would have been most anxious to mortify; while she herself, who had comparatively no power to wound them, was purposely slighted by both. But while she smiled at a graciousness so misapplied, she could not reflect on the mean-spirited folly from which it sprung, nor observe the studied attentions with which the Miss Steeles courted its continuance, without thoroughly despising all four of them.

Lucy was all exultation on being so honourably distinguished; and Miss Steele needed only to be teased about Dr. Davies to be perfectly happy.

The dinner was a grand one, the servants were numerous, and everything highlighted the Mistress's inclination for show, and the Master's ability to support it. In spite of the improvements and additions which were being made to the Norland estate, and in spite of its owner having once been within some thousand pounds of being obliged to sell at a loss, nothing gave any symptom of those desperate financial circumstances which he had tried to infer from it. No poverty of any kind, except of conversation, appeared—but there, the deficiency was considerable. John Dashwood had not much to say that was worth hearing, and his wife had still less.

When the ladies withdrew to the drawing room after dinner, this lack of discussion topics was particularly evident, for the gentlemen *had* supplied the discourse with some variety—the variety of politics, fencing land, and breaking horses—but then it was all over, and one subject only engaged the ladies till coffee came in, which was the comparative heights of Harry Dashwood and Lady Middleton's second son William, who were nearly of the same age.

Had both the children been there, the affair might have been determined too easily by measuring them at once; but as Harry only was present, it was all guessing on both sides, and everybody had a right to be equally positive in their opinion, and to repeat it over and over again as often as they liked.

The parties stood thus:

The two mothers, though each really convinced that her own son was the tallest, politely decided in favour of the other.

The two grandmothers, with not less partiality, but more sincerity, were equally earnest in support of their own descendant.

Lucy, who was hardly less anxious to please one parent than the other, thought the boys were both remarkably tall for their age, and could not conceive that there could be the smallest difference in the world between them; and Miss Steele gave it, as fast as she could, in favour of each.

Elinor, having once delivered her opinion on William's side, by which she offended Mrs. Ferrars and Fanny still more, did not see the necessity of enforcing it by any farther comment; and Marianne, when called on for hers, offended them all by declaring that she had no opinion to give, as she had never thought about it.

Before leaving Norland, Elinor had painted a very pretty pair of screens for her sister-in-law, which being now just mounted and brought home, ornamented her present drawing room. These screens, catching the eye of John Dashwood on his following the other gentlemen into the room, were officiously handed by him to Colonel Brandon for his admiration.

"These are done by my eldest sister," said he, "and you, as a man of taste, will, I dare say, be pleased with them. I do not know whether you ever happened to see any of her performances before, but it is said that she draws extremely well."

The Colonel, though disclaiming all pretensions to fine taste, warmly admired the screens, as he would have done anything painted by Miss Dashwood. The curiosity of the others being of course excited, they were handed round for general inspection. Mrs. Ferrars, not aware of their being Elinor's work, particularly requested to look at them. After they had received the gratifying testimony of Lady Middleton's approval, Fanny presented them to her mother, considerately informing her at the same time that they were done by Miss Dashwood.

"Hmm"—said Mrs. Ferrars—"very pretty,"—and without looking at them at all, returned them to her daughter.

Perhaps Fanny thought for a moment that her mother had been too rude—for, colouring a little, she immediately said,

"They are very pretty, ma'am—ain't they?" But then again, the dread of having been too civil, too encouraging herself, probably came over her, for she presently added,

"Do you not think they are similar to Miss Morton's style of painting, ma'am? *She does* paint most delightfully. How beautifully her last landscape was done!"

"Beautifully indeed! But she does everything well."

Marianne could not bear this. She was already greatly displeased with Mrs. Ferrars; and such ill-timed praise of another, at Elinor's expense, though she had not any notion of what was principally meant by it, provoked her immediately to say with warmth,

"This is admiration of a very peculiar kind! What is Miss Morton to us? Who knows or who cares for her? It is Elinor of whom *we* think and speak."

And so saying, she took the screens out of her sister-in-law's hands to admire them herself as they ought to be admired.

Mrs. Ferrars looked exceedingly angry, and drawing herself up more stiffly than ever, pronounced in retort: "Miss Morton is Lord Morton's daughter."

Fanny looked very angry too, and her husband was all in a fright at his sister's audacity. Elinor was much more hurt by Marianne's reaction than she had been by what produced it; but Colonel Brandon's eyes, as they were fixed on Marianne, declared that he noticed only what was amiable in it; the affectionate heart which could not bear to see a sister slighted in the smallest degree.

Marianne's feelings did not stop here. The coldness of Mrs. Ferrars's general behaviour to her sister seemed, to her, to foretell such difficulties and distresses to Elinor, as her own wounded heart taught her to think of with horror. Urged by a strong impulse of affectionate sensibility, she moved, after a moment, to her sister's chair, and putting one arm round her neck, and one cheek close to hers, said in a low, but eager voice:

"Dear, dear Elinor, don't mind them. Don't let them make *you* unhappy."

She could say no more; her spirits were quite overcome, and hiding her face on Elinor's shoulder, she burst into tears. Everybody's took notice, and almost everybody was concerned. Colonel Brandon rose up and went to them. Mrs. Jennings, with a very intelligent "Ah! Poor dear," immediately gave her her salts. Sir John felt so desperately enraged against the author of this nervous distress that he instantly changed his seat to one close by Lucy Steele, and gave her, in a whisper, a brief account of the whole shocking affair.

In a few minutes, however, Marianne was recovered enough to put an end to the bustle, and sit down among the rest; though her spirits retained the impression of what had passed the whole evening.

"Poor Marianne!" said her brother to Colonel Brandon in a low voice, as soon as he could secure his attention, "Her health is not as good as her sister's—she has not Elinor's constitution—and one must allow that there is something very trying to a young woman who *has been* a beauty, in the loss of her personal attractions. You would not think it perhaps, but Marianne *was* remarkably beautiful a few months ago—quite as beautiful as Elinor. Now you see it is all gone."

CHAPTER 35

Elinor's curiosity to see Mrs. Ferrars was satisfied. She had found in her everything that could tend to make a farther connection between the families undesirable. She had seen enough of her pride, and her determined prejudice against herself, to foretell all the difficulties that must have accompanied the engagement, and hindered the marriage plans of Edward and herself, had he been otherwise free. She had seen almost enough to be thankful for her *own* sake that one greater obstacle preserved her from suffering under any other of Mrs. Ferrars's creation. Or at least, if she did not bring herself quite to rejoice in Edward's being fettered to Lucy, she determined, that had Lucy been more amiable, she *ought* to have rejoiced.

She wondered that Lucy's spirits could be so very much elevated by the civility of Mrs. Ferrars; that her interest and her vanity should so very much blind her, as to make the attention which seemed only paid her because she was *not Elinor*, appear a compliment to herself. Had her real situation been known, she would have been treated very differently. But Lucy was delighted by everything that had occurred, as she declared the next morning; for at her particular desire, Lady Middleton sent her down to Berkeley Street on the chance of seeing Elinor alone, to tell her how happy she was.

The chance proved a lucky one, for a message from Mrs. Palmer soon after she arrived took Mrs. Jennings away.

"My dear friend," cried Lucy as soon as they were by themselves, "I come to talk to you of my happiness. Could anything be so flattering as Mrs. Ferrars's way of treating me yesterday? So exceeding affable as she was! You know how I dreaded the thoughts of seeing her; but the very moment I was introduced, there was such an affability in her behaviour as really should seem to say, she had quite took a fancy to me. Now was not it so? You saw it all; and was not you quite struck with it?"

"She was certainly very civil to you."

"Civil! Did you see only civility? I saw a vast deal more—such kindness as fell to the share of nobody but me!"

Elinor wished to talk of something else, but still Lucy pressed on, and Elinor was obliged state her true opinion.

"Undoubtedly, if they had known about your engagement," said she, "nothing could be more flattering than their treatment of you; but as that was not the case—"

"I guessed you would say so," replied Lucy quickly, "but there was no reason in the world why Mrs. Ferrars should seem to like me, if she did not—and her liking me is everything. You shan't talk me out of my satisfaction. I am sure it will all end well, and there will be no difficulties at all, to what I used to think. Mrs. Ferrars is a charming woman, and so is your sister. They are both delightful women indeed! I wonder I should never hear you say how agreeable Mrs. Dashwood was!"

To this, Elinor had no answer to make, and did not attempt any.

"Are you ill, Miss Dashwood? You seem low—you don't speak—sure you ain't well."

"I never was in better health."

"I am glad of it with all my heart, but really you did not look it. I should be so sorry to have *you* ill—you, that have been the greatest comfort to me in the world! Heaven knows what I should have done without your friendship."

Elinor tried to make a civil answer, though doubting her own success. But it seemed to satisfy Lucy, for she directly replied:

"Indeed I am perfectly convinced of your regard for me, and next to Edward's love, it is the greatest comfort I have. Poor Edward! But now, there is one good thing—we shall be able to meet, and meet pretty often, for Lady Middleton's delighted with Mrs. Dashwood, so we shall be a good deal in Harley Street, I dare say. Edward spends half his time with his sister—besides, Lady Middleton and Mrs. Ferrars will visit now—and Mrs. Ferrars and your sister were both so good to say more than once, they should always be glad to see me. They are such charming women! I am sure if you ever tell your sister what I think of her, you cannot speak too high."

But Elinor would not give her any encouragement to hope that she *should* tell her sister. Lucy continued:

"I am sure I should have seen it in a moment, if Mrs. Ferrars had took a dislike to me. If she had only made me a formal curtsey, for instance, without saying a word, and never after had took any notice of me, and never looked at me in a pleasant way—you know what I mean—if I had been treated in that forbidding sort of way, I should have gave it all up in despair. I could not have stood it. For where she *does* dislike, I know it is most violent."

Elinor was prevented from making any reply to this civil triumph by the door's being thrown open, the servant's announcing Mr. Ferrars, and Edward's immediately walking in.

It was a very awkward moment; and the countenance of each showed that it was so. They all felt exceedingly foolish; and Edward seemed to have as great an inclination to walk out of the room again, as to advance farther into it. The very circumstance, in its unpleasantest form, which they would each have been most anxious to avoid, had fallen on them. They were not only all three together, but were together without the relief of any other person. The ladies recovered themselves first. It was not Lucy's business to put herself forward, and the appearance of secrecy must still be kept up. She could therefore only *look* her tenderness, and after greeting him, said no more.

But Elinor had more to do; and so anxious was she, for his sake and her own, to do it well, that she forced herself, after a moment's recollection, to welcome him, with a look and manner that were almost easy and almost open; and another struggle, another effort still improved them. She would not allow the presence of Lucy, nor the consciousness of some injustice towards herself, to deter her from saying that she was happy to see him, and that she had very much regretted being away from home when he called before in Berkeley Street. She would not be frightened from paying him those attentions which, as a friend and near relation, were his due.

Her manners gave some reassurance to Edward, and he had courage enough to sit down; but his embarrassment still exceeded that of the ladies, for his heart had not the indifference of Lucy's, nor could his conscience have quite the ease of Elinor's.

Lucy seemed determined to make no contribution to the comfort of the others, and would not say a word; and almost everything that *was* said, proceeded from Elinor, who was obliged to volunteer all the information about her mother's health, their coming to town, etc., which Edward ought to have inquired about, but never did.

Her exertions did not stop here; for she soon afterwards felt herself so heroically disposed as to determine, under pretense of fetching Marianne, to leave the others by themselves. She loitered away several minutes on the landing before she went to her sister. When that was done, however, it was time for the raptures of Edward to cease; for Marianne's joy brought her into the drawing room immediately. Her pleasure in seeing him was like every other feeling she had: strong in itself, and strongly expressed. She met him with a voice that expressed the affection of a sister.

"Dear Edward!" she cried. "This is a moment of great happiness! This would almost make amends for everything!"

Edward tried to return her kindness as it deserved, but before such witnesses he dared not say half what he really felt. Again they all sat down, and for a moment or two all were silent. Marianne was looking with great tenderness, sometimes at Edward and sometimes at Elinor, regretting only that their delight in each other should be checked by Lucy's unwelcome presence. Edward was the first to speak, and it was to notice Marianne's altered looks, and express his fear of her not finding London agreeable.

"Oh! Don't think of me!" she replied, with spirited earnestness, though her eyes filled with tears as she spoke. "Don't think of *my* health. Elinor is well, you see. That must be enough for us both."

This remark did not make Edward or Elinor more easy, nor did it invite the good will of Lucy, whose face told all that words could not.

"Do you like London?" said Edward, willing to say anything that might introduce another subject.

"Not at all. I expected much pleasure in it, but I have found none. The sight of you, Edward, is the only comfort it has afforded; and, thank Heaven! You are what you always were!"

She paused—no one spoke.

"I think, Elinor," she presently added, "we must employ Edward to take care of us in our return to Barton. In a week or two, I suppose, we shall be going; and, I trust, Edward will not be very unwilling to accept the charge."

Poor Edward muttered something; but what it was, nobody knew, not even himself. Marianne, who saw his agitation, and could easily trace it to whatever cause best pleased herself, was perfectly satisfied, and soon talked of something else.

"We spent such a day, Edward, in Harley Street yesterday! So dull, so wretchedly dull! But I have much to say to you which cannot be said now."

And with this admirable discretion did she defer the assurance of her finding their mutual relatives more disagreeable than ever, and of her being particularly disgusted with his mother, till they were more in private.

"But why were you not there, Edward? Why did you not come?"

"I was busy elsewhere."

"Busy! But what was that, when such friends were to be met?"

"Perhaps, Miss Marianne," cried Lucy, eager to take some revenge on her, "you think young men never keep commitments, small as well as big."

Elinor was very angry, but Marianne seemed entirely insensible of the sting; for she calmly replied,

"Not so, indeed; for, seriously speaking, I am very sure that conscience only kept Edward from Harley Street. And I really believe he *has* the most delicate conscience in the world; the most scrupulous in keeping every commitment however trivial, and however much he may dislike it. He is the most fearful of giving pain, of wounding expectation, and the most incapable of being selfish of anybody I ever saw. Edward, it is so, and I will say it. What! Are you never to hear yourself praised? Then, you must be no friend of mine; for those who will accept of my love and esteem must submit to my praise."

The nature of her commendation, in the present case, however, happened to be particularly ill-suited to the feelings of two-thirds of her listeners, and was so very unexhilarating to Edward, that he very soon got up to go away.

"Going so soon!" said Marianne. "My dear Edward, this must not be."

Drawing him a little aside, she whispered her persuasion that Lucy could not stay much longer. But even this encouragement failed, for he must go; and Lucy, who would have outstayed him had his visit lasted two hours, soon afterwards went away.

"What can bring her here so often!" said Marianne, on her leaving them. "Could she not see that we wanted her gone? How provoking to Edward!"

"Why so? We were all his friends, and Lucy has known him longer than us. It is but natural that he should like to see her as well as ourselves."

Marianne looked at her steadily, and said "You know, Elinor, this is a kind of talking which I cannot bear. If you only hope to have your assertion contradicted, as I must suppose to be the case, you ought to recollect that I am the last person in the world to do it. I cannot descend to be tricked out of assurances that are not really wanted."

She then left the room; and Elinor dared not follow her to say more, for bound as she was by her promise of secrecy to Lucy, she could give no information that would convince Marianne; and painful as the consequences of her still continuing in an error might be, she was obliged to submit to it. All that she could hope was that Edward would not often expose her or himself to the distress of hearing Marianne's mistaken warmth, nor to the repetition of any other part of the pain that had attended their recent meeting—and this she had every reason to expect.

CHAPTER 36

Within a few days after this meeting, the newspapers announced to the world that the wife of Thomas Palmer, Esq., had safely delivered a son and heir; a very interesting and satisfactory paragraph, at least to all those who already knew of it.

This event, highly gratifying to Mrs. Jennings, produced a temporary alteration in her habits, and influenced in a like degree the engagements of her young friends. As she wished to be as much as possible with Charlotte, she went there every morning as soon as she was dressed, and did not return till late in the evening; and the Miss Dashwoods, at the particular request of the Middletons, spent the whole of every day in Conduit Street. For their own comfort, they would much rather have remained, at least all the morning, in Mrs. Jennings's house; but it was not a thing to be done against the wishes of everybody. Their hours were therefore spent with Lady Middleton and the two Miss Steeles, by whom their company was as little valued as it was sought.

They had too much sense to be desirable companions to Lady Middleton; and by the Miss Steeles they were considered with a jealous eye, as intruding on *their* ground, and sharing the kindness which they wanted to monopolise. Though nothing could be more polite than Lady Middleton's behaviour to Elinor and Marianne, she did not really like them at all. Because they neither flattered herself nor her children, she could not believe them good-natured. Their presence was a strain both on her and on Lucy. It checked the idleness of one, and the busyness of the other. Lady Middleton was ashamed of doing nothing before them, and the flattery which Lucy was proud to think of and administer at other times, she feared they would despise her for offering. Miss Steele was the least affected by their presence; and it was in their power to reconcile her to it entirely. If either of them would have given her a full account of the whole affair between Marianne and Mr. Willoughby, she would have thought herself amply rewarded for sacrificing the best place by the fire after dinner, which was their due as guests. But this was not granted; for though she often threw out expressions of pity for her sister to Elinor, and more than once dropped a hint about the inconstancy of beaux before Marianne, no effect was produced, but a look of indifference from the former, or of disgust in the latter. An effort even yet lighter might have made her their friend. Would they only have laughed at her about the Doctor! But so little were they inclined to oblige her, that if Sir John dined away from home, she might spend a whole day without hearing any other raillery on the subject than what she was kind enough to bestow on herself.

All these jealousies, however, were so totally unsuspected by Mrs. Jennings, that she thought it a delightful thing for the girls to be together; and generally congratulated her young friends every night, on having escaped the company of a boring old woman for so long. She joined them sometimes at Sir John's, and sometimes at her own house; but wherever it was, she always came in excellent spirits, full of delight, attributing Charlotte's well-doing to her own care, and ready to give so exact, so minute a detail of her situation, as only Miss Steele had curiosity enough to desire. One thing *did* disturb her; and of that she made her daily complaint. Mr. Palmer maintained the common, but unfatherly opinion among his sex, of all infants being alike. Though she could plainly perceive at different times, the most striking resemblance between this baby and every one of his relations on both sides, there was no convincing his father of it. He could not even be brought to acknowledge the simple proposition of its being the finest child in the world.

About this time, a misfortune befell Mrs. John Dashwood. It so happened that while her two sisters and Mrs. Jennings were first calling on her in Harley Street, another of her acquaintances had dropped in—a circumstance in itself not apparently likely to produce trouble for her. But in this particular instance, the lady allowed her fancy so far to outrun truth and probability, that on merely hearing the name of the Miss Dashwoods, and understanding them to be Mr. Dashwood's sisters, she immediately concluded that they were staying in Harley Street. This produced invitations for them as well as for their brother and sister to attend a small musical party at her house. The consequence of which was, that Mrs. John Dashwood was obliged to submit not only to the exceedingly great inconvenience of sending her carriage for the Miss Dashwoods, but, what was still worse, must be subject to all the unpleasantness of appearing to pay attention to them. Who could tell that they might not expect to go out with her a second time? The power of disappointing them, it was true, must always be hers. But that was not enough; for when people are determined on a mode of conduct which they know to be wrong, they feel injured by the expectation of anything better from them.

Marianne had now been brought by degrees so much into the habit of going out every day that it was become a matter of indifference to her whether she went or not. She prepared quietly and mechanically for every evening's engagement, though without expecting even the smallest amusement, and very often without knowing till the last moment where it was to take her.

To her dress and appearance she was grown so perfectly indifferent as not to bestow half the consideration on it, during the whole of her preparation, which it received from Miss Steele in the first five minutes of their being together. Nothing escaped *her* minute observation and general curiosity; she saw everything, and asked everything; never rested till she knew the price of every part of Marianne's attire; could have guessed the number of her gowns altogether with better judgment than Marianne herself, and was not without hopes of finding out before they parted, how much her washing cost per week, and how much she had every year to spend upon herself. The impertinence of this, moreover, was generally concluded with a compliment, which though meant as kind, was considered by Marianne as the greatest impertinence of all; for after undergoing an examination into the value and make of her gown, the colour of her shoes, and the arrangement of her hair, she was almost sure of being told that she looked vastly smart, and would make a great many conquests.

With such encouragements, she was sent on the present occasion to her brother's carriage. They were ready to enter five minutes after it stopped at the door, a punctuality not very agreeable to their sister-in-law. She had preceded them to the house of her acquaintance, and was there hoping for some delay on their part that might inconvenience either herself or her coachman.

The events of the evening were not very remarkable. The party, like other musical parties, included a great many people who had musical taste, and a great many more who had none at all. The performers themselves were, as usual, in their own estimation, and that of their immediate friends, the best musicians in England.

As Elinor was neither musical, nor pretending to be so, she turned away her eyes from the grand piano whenever it suited her, and unrestrained even by the presence of a harp, and a cello, fixed them at pleasure on any other object in the room. In one of these glances she perceived among a group of young men, the very man who had given them a lecture on toothpick cases at Gray's. She perceived him soon afterwards looking at herself, and speaking familiarly to her brother; and had just determined to find out his name from the latter, when they both came towards her, and Mr. Dashwood introduced him to her as Mr. Robert Ferrars.

He addressed her with easy civility, and twisted his head into a bow. She wondered at the difference of the two young men, but she did not find that the emptiness and conceit of the one affected her feelings of charity for the other. Why they *were* different, Robert explained to her himself in the course of a quarter of an hour's conversation; for, talking of his brother, he generously attributed it much less to any natural deficiency, than to the misfortune of private tutoring. He himself, though probably without any material superiority by nature, merely from the advantage of attending school, was as well fitted to mix in the world as any other man.

"Upon my soul," he added, "I believe it is nothing more; and so I often tell my mother, when she is grieving about it. 'My dear madam,' I always say to her, 'you must make yourself easy. The evil is now done, and it has been entirely your own doing. Why would you be persuaded by my uncle, Sir Robert, against your own judgment, to place Edward under private tuition, at the most critical time of his life? If you had only sent him to Westminster as well as myself, instead of sending him to Mr. Pratt's, all this would have been prevented.' This is the way in which I always consider the matter, and my mother is perfectly convinced of her error."

Elinor would not disagree with him, because whatever might be her general estimation of the advantage of attending a school, she could not think of Edward's abode in Mr. Pratt's family with any satisfaction.

"You reside in Devonshire, I think," was his next observation.

Elinor told him of their cottage, and he bestowed his hearty approval.

"For my own part," said he, "I am excessively fond of a cottage; there is always so much comfort, so much elegance about them. And I protest, if I had any money to spare, I would buy a little land and build one myself, within a short distance of London, where I might drive myself down at any time, and collect a few friends about me, and be happy. I advise everybody who is going to build, to build a cottage. My friend Lord Courtland came to me the other day to ask my advice, and laid before me three different plans of Bonomi's. I was to decide on the best of them. 'My dear Courtland,' said I, immediately throwing them all into the fire, 'do not adopt any of them, but by all means build a cottage.' And that, I fancy, will be the end of it.

"Some people imagine that there can be no accommodations, no space in a cottage; but this is all a mistake. I was last month at my friend Elliott's near Dartford. Lady Elliott wished to give a dance. 'But how can it be done?' said she. 'My dear Ferrars, do tell me how it is to be managed. There is not a room in this cottage that will hold ten couples, and where can the supper be?'" *I* immediately saw that there could be no difficulty in it, so I said, 'My dear Lady Elliott, do not be uneasy. The dining parlour will admit eighteen couples with ease; card tables may be placed in the drawing room; the library may be open for tea and other refreshments; and let the supper be set out in the living room.' Lady Elliott was delighted with the thought. We measured the dining room, and found it would hold exactly eighteen couples, and the event was arranged precisely by my plan. So that in fact, you see, if people do but know how to go about it, every comfort may be as well enjoyed in a cottage as in the most spacious dwelling."

Elinor agreed to it all, for she did not think he deserved the compliment of rational opposition.

As John Dashwood had no more pleasure in music than his eldest sister, his mind was equally at liberty to think about anything else; and a thought struck him during the evening, which he communicated to his wife, for her approval, when they got home. Mrs. Dennison's mistake, in supposing his sisters their guests, had suggested the propriety of their being really invited to become such, while Mrs. Jennings's engagements kept her from home. The expense would be nothing, the inconvenience not more; and it was altogether an attention which the delicacy of his conscience pointed out to be required to completely fulfill his promise to his father. Fanny was startled at the proposal.

"I do not see how it can be done," said she, "without affronting Lady Middleton, for they spend every day with her; otherwise I should be exceedingly glad to do it. You know I am always ready to pay them any attention in my power, as my taking them out this evening shows. But they are Lady Middleton's visitors. How can I ask them to leave her?"

Her husband, with great humility, pointed out that they had already spent a week in this manner in Conduit Street, and Lady Middleton could not be displeased at their giving the same number of days to such near relations.

Fanny paused a moment, and then, with fresh vigour, said—

"My love, I would ask them with all my heart, if it was in my power. But I had just settled within myself to ask the Miss Steeles to spend a few days with us. They are very well behaved, good kind of girls; and I think the attention is due, as their uncle did so very well by teaching Edward. We can ask your sisters some other year, you know; but the Miss Steeles may not be in town anymore. I am sure you will like them; indeed, you *do* like them, you know, very much already, and so does my mother; and they are such favourites with Harry!"

Mr. Dashwood was convinced. He saw the necessity of inviting the Miss Steeles immediately, and his conscience was pacified by the resolution of inviting his sisters another year. At the same time, however, he suspected that another year would make the invitation needless, by bringing Elinor to town as Colonel Brandon's wife, and Marianne as *their* visitor.

Fanny, rejoicing in her narrow escape, wrote the next morning to Lucy, to request her company and her sister's for some days in Harley Street, as soon as Lady Middleton could spare them. This was enough to make Lucy happy. Such an opportunity of being with

Edward and his family was most desirable, and such an invitation most gratifying to her feelings! It was an advantage that could not be too gratefully acknowledged, and the visit to Lady Middleton, which had not before had any precise limits, was instantly discovered to have been always meant to end in two days' time.

When the note was shown to Elinor, as it was within ten minutes after its arrival, it gave her, for the first time, some insight into the expectations of Lucy. Such a mark of uncommon kindness, made after so short an acquaintance, might be brought to do everything that Lucy wished. Her flattery had already subdued the pride of Lady Middleton, and made an entry into the closed heart of Mrs. John Dashwood; and these were effects that laid open the probability of greater.

The Miss Steeles moved to Harley Street, and all that reached Elinor of their influence there strengthened her expectation of the event. Sir John, who called on them more than once, brought home such accounts of the favour they were in, as must be universally striking. Mrs. Dashwood had never been so pleased with any young women in her life as she was with them; had given each of them a needle case, called Lucy by her Christian name, and did not know whether she would ever be able to part with them.

CHAPTER 37

Mrs. Palmer was so well at the end of a fortnight, that her mother felt it no longer necessary to give all her time to her. Contenting herself with visiting her once or twice a day, she returned from that period to her own home, and her own habits, and she found the Miss Dashwoods very ready to reassume their former routine.

About the third or fourth morning after their being thus re-settled in Berkeley Street, Mrs. Jennings, on returning from her regular visit to Mrs. Palmer, entered the drawing room, where Elinor was sitting by herself, with an air of such hurrying importance as prepared her to hear something remarkable. Giving her time only to form that idea, Mrs. Jennings began directly to justify it by saying,

"Lord! My dear Miss Dashwood! have you heard the news!"

"No, ma'am. What is it?"

"Something so strange! But you shall hear it all. When I got to Mr. Palmer's, I found Charlotte quite in a fuss about the child. She was sure it was very ill—it cried, and fretted, and had red spots. So I looked at it directly, and, "Lord! My dear," says I, "it is nothing but a rash," and nurse said just the same. But Charlotte, she would not be satisfied, so Mr. Donavan was sent for. Luckily he happened to be just coming in from Harley Street, so he walked over directly, and as soon as he saw the child, he said just as we did, that it was nothing in the world but a rash, and then Charlotte felt at ease. And so, just as he was going away again, it came into my head, I am sure I do not know how I happened to think of it, but it came into my head to ask him if there was any news. So upon that, he looked grave, and said, 'I have recently been to see Mrs. Dashwood.'"

"What! Is Fanny ill?"

"That is exactly what I said, my dear. 'Lord!' says I, 'Is Mrs. Dashwood ill?' So then it all came out; and here is the long and the short of the matter, by all I can learn. Mr. Edward Ferrars, the very young man I used to joke with you about (but, however, as it turns out, I am monstrous glad there never was any thing in it), Mr. Edward Ferrars, it seems, has been engaged for more than a year to my cousin Lucy!—There's something for you, my dear!—And not a creature knowing a syllable of the matter except her sister!—Could you have believed such a thing possible?—There is no great wonder in their liking one another; but to be engaged, and nobody suspect it! *That* is strange!—I never happened to see them together, or I am sure I would have discovered the secret myself. Well, and so they told no one, for fear of Mrs. Ferrars; and neither she nor your brother or sister suspected a word of the matter;—till this very morning, when poor Miss Steele, who, you know, is a well-meaning creature, told all. 'Lord!' thinks she to herself, 'They are all so fond of Lucy, to be sure there will be no difficulty;' and so, away she went to your sister, who was sitting all alone at her needlework, little suspecting what was to come—for she had just been saying to your brother, only five minutes before, that she thought to make a match between Edward and some Lord's daughter or other, I forget who. So you may think what a blow it was to all her vanity and pride. She fell into violent hysterics immediately, with such screams as reached your brothers ears, as he was sitting in his study downstairs, thinking about writing a letter to his steward in the country. So up he flew directly, and a terrible scene took place, for Lucy had come to them by that time, little dreaming what was going on. Poor soul! I pity *her*. And I must say, I think she was treated very harshly; for your sister scolded like any fury, and soon drove her into a fainting fit. Miss Steele fell upon her knees, and cried bitterly; and your brother, he walked about the room, and said he did not know what to do. Mrs. Dashwood declared they should not stay a minute longer in the house, and your brother was forced to go down upon *his* knees too, to persuade her to let them stay till they had packed up their clothes. *Then* she fell into hysterics again, and he was so frightened that he sent for Mr. Donavan, and Mr. Donavan found the house in all this uproar. The carriage was at the door ready to take my poor cousins away, and they were just stepping in as he came off. Poor Lucy was in such a condition, he says, that she could hardly walk; and her sister was almost as bad. I declare, I have no patience with your sister; and I hope, with all my heart, it will be a match in spite of her. Lord! How poor Mr. Edward will feel when he hears of it! To have his love used so scornfully! They say he is monstrous fond of her. Mr. Donovan and I had a great deal of talk about it, and he has gone back again to Harley Street, that he may be within call when Mrs. Ferrars is told of it, for she was sent for as soon as my cousins left the house, for your sister was sure *she* would be in hysterics too. I have no pity for either of them. I have no notion of people's making such a to-do about money and greatness. There is no reason on earth why Mr. Edward and Lucy should not marry; for I am sure Mrs. Ferrars may afford to do very well by her son; and though Lucy has next to nothing herself, she knows better than anybody how to make the most of everything. I dare say, if Mrs. Ferrars would only allow him five hundred a year, she would make as good an appearance with it as anybody else would with eight. Lord! How cozily they might live in such a cottage as yours—or a little bigger—with two maids and two men; and I believe I could help them find a housemaid, for my Betty has a sister out of work, that would fit them exactly."

Here Mrs. Jennings ceased, and as Elinor had had time enough to collect her thoughts, she was able to give such an answer, and make such observations, as the subject might naturally be supposed to produce. Happy to find that she was not suspected of any extraordinary interest in it; that Mrs. Jennings (as she had hoped might be the case) had ceased to imagine her at all attached to Edward; and happy above all the rest that Marianne was not there. She therefore felt very well able to speak of the affair without embarrassment, and to give her opinion, as she believed, with impartiality on the conduct of everyone concerned in it.

She could hardly determine what her own expectation of its event really was, and she earnestly tried to drive away the hope that Edward would not marry Lucy after all. What Mrs. Ferrars would say and do, though there could not be a doubt of its nature, she was anxious to hear; and still more anxious to know how Edward would conduct himself. For *him* she felt much compassion; for Lucy very little—and it cost her some pains to procure that little—and for the rest of the party none at all.

As Mrs. Jennings could talk on no other subject, Elinor soon saw the necessity of preparing Marianne for its discussion. No time was to be lost in making her acquainted with the real truth, and in endeavouring to bring her to hear it talked of by others, without betraying that she felt any uneasiness for her sister, or any resentment against Edward.

Elinor's office was a painful one. She was going to remove what she really believed to be her sister's chief consolation—to give such particulars of Edward as she feared would ruin him forever in her good opinion—and to make Marianne, by their similar situations, which to <u>her</u> fancy would seem strong, feel all her own disappointment over again. But unwelcome as such a task must be, it was necessary, and Elinor therefore hastened to perform it.

She was very far from wishing to dwell on her own feelings, or to represent herself as suffering much. Her narration was clear and simple; and though it could not be given without emotion, it was not accompanied by violent agitation, nor grief. *That* belonged rather to the hearer, for Marianne listened with horror, and cried excessively. Elinor, it seemed, was the comforter of others in her own distresses as well as in theirs. All the comfort that could be given by assurances of her own composure of mind, and a very earnest vindication of Edward from every charge but of poor judgment, was readily offered.

But Marianne for some time would give credit to neither. Edward seemed a second Willoughby; and acknowledging as Elinor did, that she *had* loved him most sincerely, could she feel less than herself? As for Lucy Steele, she considered her so totally incapable of attaching a sensible man, that she could not be persuaded at first to believe, and afterwards to pardon, any former affection of Edward for her.

Her first communication had reached no farther than to state the fact of the engagement, and the length of time it had existed. Marianne's feelings had then broken in, and put an end to all regularity of detail; and for some time all that could be done was to sooth her distress, lessen her alarms, and combat her resentment. The first question on her side, which led to farther details, was—

"How long has this been known to you, Elinor? Has he written to you?"

"I have known it these four months. When Lucy first came to Barton Park last November, she told me in confidence of her engagement."

At these words, Marianne's eyes expressed the astonishment which her lips could not utter. After a pause of wonder, she exclaimed—

"What!—while attending me in all my misery, has this been on your heart?—and I have reproached you for being happy!"

"I did not want you to know that I was the very opposite."

"Four months!" cried Marianne. "So calm! So cheerful! How have you borne it?"

"By feeling that I was doing my duty. My promise to Lucy obliged me to keep it a secret. I owed it to her, therefore, to avoid giving any hint of the truth; and I owed it to my family and friends not to create in them any concern for me which it could not be in my power to explain."

Marianne seemed much struck.

"I have very often wished to tell you and mother," added Elinor. "Once or twice I nearly attempted it."

"Four months! And yet you loved him?"

"Yes. But now I can think and speak of it with little emotion. I would not have you suffer on my account; for I assure you I no longer suffer materially myself. I have many things to support me. I am not conscious of having provoked the disappointment by any imprudence of my own, and I have borne it as much as possible without spreading it farther. I forgive Edward for all essential misconduct. I wish him very happy; and I am so sure of his always doing his duty. Though now he may harbour some regret, in the end he will be overcome. Lucy does not lack sense, and that is the foundation on which everything good may be built. And after all, Marianne, depending entirely on any particular person for one's happiness is a very poor idea indeed. Edward will marry Lucy, and time and habit will teach him to forget that he ever thought another woman superior to *her*."

"If such is your way of thinking," said Marianne, "if the loss of what is most valued is so easily to be made up by something else, your resolution, your self-command, are perhaps, a little less to be wondered at."

"I understand you. You do not suppose that I have ever felt much. For four months, Marianne, I have had all this on my mind, without being at liberty to speak of it to a single creature; knowing that it would make you and my mother most unhappy whenever it was explained to you, yet unable to prepare you for it in the least. It was told me—it was in a manner forced on me by the very person herself whose prior engagement ruined all my prospects; and told me, as I thought, with triumph. This person's suspicions, therefore, I have had to oppose, by endeavouring to appear indifferent where I have been most deeply interested. And it has not been only once; I have had her hopes and exultation to listen to again and again. I have known myself to be divided from Edward forever, without hearing one circumstance that could make me less desire the connection. Nothing has proved him unworthy; nor has anything declared him indifferent to me. I have had to contend against the unkindness of his sister, and the insolence of his mother, and have suffered the punishment of an attachment without enjoying its advantages. And all this has been going on at a time when, as you too well know, it has not been my only unhappiness. If you can think me capable of ever feeling, surely you may suppose that I have suffered *now*. The composure of mind with which I have brought myself at present to consider the matter has been the effect of constant and painful exertion."

Marianne was quite subdued.

"Oh! Elinor," she cried, "you have made me hate myself forever. How barbarous have I been to you! You, who have been my only comfort, who have borne with me in all my misery, who have seemed to be only suffering for me! Is this my gratitude! Is this the only payment I can offer you?"

In such a frame of mind as she was now in, Elinor had no difficulty in obtaining whatever promise she required. Marianne agreed never to speak of the affair to anyone with the least appearance of bitterness—to meet Lucy without betraying the smallest increase of dislike to her—and even to see Edward himself, if chance should bring them together, without any change in her usual cordiality. These were great concessions; but where Marianne felt that she had injured, no reparation could be too much for her to make.

She admirably kept her promise of being discreet. She listened to all that Mrs. Jennings had to say upon the subject, with an unchanging complexion, agreed with everything, and was heard three times to say, "Yes, ma'am." She listened to her praise of Lucy with only moving from one chair to another, and when Mrs. Jennings talked of Edward's affection, it cost her only a spasm in her throat. Such advances towards heroism in her sister made Elinor feel equal to anything herself.

The next morning brought a farther trial, in the form of a visit from their brother, who came to talk over the dreadful affair, and bring them news of his wife.

"You have heard, I suppose," said he with great solemnity, as soon as he was seated, "of the very shocking discovery that took place under our roof yesterday."

They all nodded; it seemed too awful a moment for speech.

"Your sister," he continued, "has suffered dreadfully. Mrs. Ferrars too—in short, it has been a scene of such distress; but I will hope that the storm may be weathered without our being, any of us, quite overcome. Poor Fanny! She was in hysterics all yesterday. But I would not alarm you too much. Donavan says there is nothing materially wrong; her constitution is a good one, and her resolution equal to anything. She has borne it all with the fortitude of an angel! She says she never shall think well of anybody again; and one cannot wonder at it, after being so deceived! Meeting with such ingratitude, where so much kindness had been shown, so much confidence had been placed! It was quite out of the benevolence of her heart, that she had asked these young women to her house; merely because she thought they deserved some attention, were harmless, well-behaved girls, and would be pleasant companions. Otherwise we both wished very much to have invited you and Marianne to be with us, while your kind friend there was attending her daughter. And now to be so rewarded! 'I wish with all my heart,' says poor Fanny in her affectionate way, 'that we had asked your sisters instead of them.'"

Here he stopped to be thanked; which being done, he went on.

"What poor Mrs. Ferrars suffered, when first Fanny broke it to her, is not to be described. While she with the truest affection had been planning a most eligible connection for him, was it to be supposed that he could be all the time secretly engaged to another person! Such a suspicion could never have entered her head! If she suspected *any* attachment elsewhere, it could not be in *that* quarter. '*There*, to be sure,' said she, 'I might have thought myself safe.' She was quite in agony. We consulted together, however, as to what should be done, and at last she determined to send for Edward. He came. But I am sorry to relate what ensued. All that Mrs. Ferrars could say to make him put an end to the engagement was of no avail. Duty, affection, everything was disregarded. I never thought Edward so stubborn, so unfeeling, before. His mother explained her plan to have him marry Miss Morton, and told him that she would give him the Norfolk estate, which brings in a good thousand a year. She even offered, when matters grew desperate, to make it twelve hundred; and in opposition to this, if he still persisted in this low connection, represented to him the certain poverty that must attend the match. His own two thousand pounds she protested should be his all; she would never see him again; and so far would she be from affording him the smallest assistance, that if he were to enter into any profession with a view of better support, she would do all in her power to prevent his advancing in it."

Here Marianne, in indignation, clapped her hands together, and cried, "Gracious! Can this be possible?"

"Well may you wonder, Marianne," replied her brother, "at the obstinacy which could resist such arguments as these. Your exclamation is very natural."

Marianne was going to retort, but she remembered her promises, and forbore.

"All this, however," he continued, "was urged in vain. Edward said very little; but what he did say was in the most determined manner. Nothing would prevail on him to give up his engagement. He would go through with it, cost him what it might."

"Then," cried Mrs. Jennings, with blunt sincerity, no longer able to be silent, "he has acted like an honest man! I beg your pardon, Mr. Dashwood, but if he had done otherwise, I should have thought him a rascal. I have some little concern in the business, as well as yourself, for Lucy Steele is my cousin, and I believe there is not a better kind of girl in the world, nor one who more deserves a good husband."

John Dashwood was greatly astonished; but his nature was calm, not open to provocation, and he never wished to offend anybody, especially anybody of good fortune. He therefore replied, without any resentment—

"I would by no means speak disrespectfully of any relation of yours, madam. Miss Lucy Steele is, I dare say, a very deserving young woman, but in the present case you know, the connection must be impossible. And to have entered into a secret engagement with a young man under her uncle's care, the son of a woman especially of such very large fortune as Mrs. Ferrars, is perhaps altogether a little extraordinary. In short, I do not mean to reflect upon the behaviour of any person whom you have a regard for, Mrs. Jennings. We all wish her extremely happy, and Mrs. Ferrars's conduct throughout the whole, has been such as every conscientious, good mother, in like circumstances, would adopt. It has been dignified and fair. Edward has drawn his own lot, and I fear it will be a bad one."

Elinor's heart hurt for Edward, who had braved his mother's threats for a woman who could not reward him.

"Well, sir," said Mrs. Jennings, "and how did it end?"

"I am sorry to say, ma'am, in a most unhappy rupture—Edward is dismissed forever from his mother's notice. He left her house yesterday, but where he is gone, or whether he is still in town, I do not know; for *we* of course can make no inquiry."

"Poor young man! What is to become of him?"

"What indeed, ma'am! It is a melancholy consideration. Born to the prospect of such affluence! I cannot conceive a situation more deplorable. The interest of two thousand pounds—how can a man live on it! When to that is added the recollection that he might, but for his own folly, within three months have been in the receipt of two thousand five hundred a year (for Miss Morton has thirty thousand pounds), I cannot imagine a more wretched condition. We must all feel for him; and the more so, because it is totally out of our power to assist him."

"Poor young man!" cried Mrs. Jennings. "I am sure he would be very welcome to stay at my house; and so I would tell him, if I could see him. It is not fit that he should be living on his own now, at lodgings and taverns."

Elinor's heart thanked her for such kindness towards Edward.

"If he would only have done as well by himself," said John Dashwood, "as all his friends were disposed to do by him, he might now have been in his proper situation, and would have needed nothing. But as it is, it must be out of anybody's power to assist him. And there is one thing more preparing against him, which must be worse than all—his mother has determined, with a very natural kind of spirit, to settle *that* estate upon Robert immediately, which might have been Edward's on proper conditions. I left her this morning with her lawyer, talking over the business."

"Well!" said Mrs. Jennings, "that is *her* revenge. Everybody has a way of their own. But I don't think mine would be to make one son independent because another had plagued me."

Marianne got up and walked about the room.

"Can anything be more galling to the spirit of a man," continued John, "than to see his younger brother in possession of an estate which might have been his own? Poor Edward! I feel for him sincerely."

A few minutes more concluded his visit; and with repeated assurances to his sisters that he really believed there was no material danger in Fanny's indisposition, and that they need not therefore be very uneasy about it, he went away. The three ladies were unanimous in their sentiments on the present occasion, as far at least as it regarded Mrs. Ferrars's conduct, the Dashwoods' and Edward's.

Marianne's indignation burst forth as soon as he left the room; and as her vehemence made reserve impossible in Elinor, and unnecessary in Mrs. Jennings, they all joined in a very spirited critique.

CHAPTER 38

Mrs. Jennings was very warm in her praise of Edward's conduct, but only Elinor and Marianne understood its true merit. *They* only knew how little he stood to gain in exchange for friends and fortune. Elinor gloried in his integrity; and Marianne forgave all his offences in compassion for his punishment. But it was not a subject on which either of them were fond of dwelling. Elinor avoided it upon principle, as Marianne's positive assurances of Edward's continued affection for herself made her hope more than she ought. Marianne's courage soon failed her, as trying to converse upon the topic always left her more dissatisfied with herself than ever, by the comparison it necessarily produced between Elinor's conduct and her own.

She felt all the force of that comparison; but not as her sister had hoped, to urge her to regain her previous fortitude. Instead, she felt it with all the pain of continual self-reproach, regretted most bitterly that she had behaved so unwisely; but it brought only the torture of penitance, without the hope of change. Her mind was so much weakened that she still believed present exertion was impossible, and therefore it only dispirited her more.

Nothing new was heard by them, for a day or two afterwards, of affairs in Harley Street, or Bartlett's Buildings. But Mrs. Jennings had resolved from the first to pay a visit of comfort and inquiry to her cousins as soon as she could; and nothing but the hindrance of more visitors than usual had prevented her going to them.

The third day following the discovery of the secret engagement was so fine, so beautiful a Sunday as to draw many to Kensington

Gardens, though it was only the second week in March. Mrs. Jennings and Elinor were of the party; but Marianne, who knew that the Willoughbys were again in town, and had a constant dread of meeting them, chose to stay at home rather than venture into so public a place.

An intimate acquaintance of Mrs. Jennings joined them soon after they entered the Gardens, and Elinor was not sorry that by her continuing with them, and engaging all Mrs. Jennings's attention, she was herself left to quiet reflection. She saw nothing of the Willoughbys, nothing of Edward, and for some time nothing of anybody who could be interesting to her. But at last, she found herself, with some surprise, approached by Miss Steele, who expressed great satisfaction in meeting them, and on receiving encouragement from the particular kindness of Mrs. Jennings, left her own party for a short time, to join theirs. Mrs. Jennings immediately whispered to Elinor—

"Get it all out of her, my dear. She will tell you anything if you ask. You see I cannot leave Mrs. Clarke."

It was lucky, however, for Mrs. Jennings's curiosity, and Elinor's too, that she would tell anything *without* being asked, for nothing would otherwise have been learned.

"I am so glad to meet you," said Miss Steele, taking her familiarly by the arm, "for I wanted to see you of all things in the world." Then lowering her voice, "I suppose Mrs. Jennings has heard all about it. Is she angry?"

"Not at all, I believe, with you."

"That is a good thing. And Lady Middleton, is *she* angry?"

"I cannot suppose it possible that she should be."

"I am monstrous glad of it. Good gracious! I have had such a time of it! I never saw Lucy in such a rage in my life. She vowed at first that she would never decorate my new bonnets, nor do anything else for me again, so long as she lived; but now she is quite come around, and we are as good as ever. Look, she made me this bow for my hat, and put in the feather last night. There now, *you* are going to laugh at me too. But why should I not wear pink ribbons? I do not care if it is the Doctor's favourite colour. I am sure, for my part, I should never have known he *did* like it better than any other colour, if he had not happened to say so. My cousins have been teasing me so much! I declare sometimes I do not know how I put up with it."

She had wandered to a subject upon which Elinor had nothing to say, and therefore soon judged it expedient to find her way back again to the first.

"Well, but, Miss Dashwood," speaking triumphantly, "people may say what they choose about Mr. Ferrars's declaring he would not have Lucy; and it's quite a shame for such ill-natured reports to be spread abroad. Whatever Lucy might think about it herself, you know it was no business of other people to say it was certain."

"I never heard anything of the kind hinted at before, I assure you," said Elinor.

"Oh! Did you not? But it *was* said, I know very well, and by more than one; for Miss Godby told Miss Sparks that nobody in their senses could expect Mr. Ferrars to give up a woman like Miss Morton, with thirty thousand pounds to her fortune, for someone with nothing at all; and I had it from Miss Sparks myself. And besides that, my cousin Richard said himself, that when it came to the point, he was afraid Mr. Ferrars would break the engagement. When Edward did not come see us for three days, I could not tell what to think myself; and I believe in my heart Lucy gave it all up for lost. We came away from your brother's on Wednesday, and we saw nothing of Edward at all on Thursday, Friday, and Saturday. This morning he came, just as we got home from church; and then it all came out, how he had been sent for Wednesday to Harley Street, and been talked to by his mother and all of them, and how he had declared before them all that he loved nobody but Lucy, and nobody but Lucy would he have. And how he had been so worried by what passed, that as soon as he had went away from his mother's house, he had got upon his horse, and rid into the country somewhere or other; and how he had stayed at an inn all Thursday and Friday, on purpose to get the better of it. And after thinking it all over and over again, he said it seemed to him as if, now that he had no fortune, it would be quite unkind to keep her bound to the engagement, because it must be for her loss, for he had nothing but two thousand pounds, and no hope of anything else; and if he was to choose the church as his profession, as he had been thinking, he could get nothing but a curacy, and how was they to live upon that? He could not bear to think of her doing no better, and so he begged, if she had the least mind for it, to put an end to the matter directly, and leave him to find his way alone. I heard him say all this as plain as could possibly be. And it was entirely for *her* sake, and upon *her* account, that he said a word about breaking it off, and not for his own sake. I will take my oath he never dropped a syllable of being tired of her, or of wishing to marry Miss Morton, or anything like it. But, to be sure, Lucy would not listen to such talk; so she told him directly (with a great deal about sweet and love, you know, and all that—Oh, la! one can't repeat such things, you know)—she told him directly, she had not the least mind in the world to be off, for she could live with him upon very little, and whatever he might have, she should be very glad to have it all, you know, or something of the kind. So then he was monstrous happy, and talked on some time about what they should do, and they agreed he should take orders directly, and they must wait to be married till he found a position. And just then I could not hear anymore, for my cousin called from below to tell me Mrs. Richardson was come in her coach, and would take one of us to Kensington Gardens; so I was forced to go into the room and interrupt them, to ask Lucy if she would like to go, but she did not care to leave Edward; so I just run upstairs and put on a pair of stockings, and came off with the Richardsons."

"I do not understand what you mean by interrupting them" said Elinor; "you were all in the same room together, were you not?"

"No indeed! Not us. La! Miss Dashwood, do you think people talk of love when anybody else is around? Oh! For shame—to be sure you must know better than that," she laughed. "No, no; they were in the drawing room together, and all I heard was only by listening at the door."

"What?" cried Elinor. "Have you been repeating to me what you only learned yourself by listening at the door? I am sorry I did not know it before; for I certainly would not have allowed you to give me particulars of a conversation which you ought not to have heard. How could you behave so unfairly to your sister?"

"Oh, la! There is nothing in *that*. I only stood at the door, and heard what I could. And I am sure Lucy would have done just the same by me. A year or two back, when Martha Sharpe and I had so many secrets together, she would hide in a closet, or behind a partition, on purpose to hear what we said."

Elinor tried to talk of something else, but Miss Steele could not be kept more than a couple of minutes from what was foremost in her mind.

"Edward talks of going to Oxford soon," she said, "but now he is lodging at Pall Mall. What an ill-natured woman his mother is, an't she? And your brother and sister were not very kind! However, I shan't say anything against them to *you*; and to be sure they did send us home in their own carriage, which was more than I expected. And for my part, I was all in a fright for fear your sister should ask us for the needlebooks she had gave us a day or two before; but however, nothing was said about them, and I took care to keep mine out of sight. Edward has got some business at Oxford, he says, so he must go there for a time; and after *that*, as soon as he can find a bishop, he will be ordained. I wonder what curacy he will get! Good gracious!" she giggled. "I'd lay my life I know what my cousins will say, when they hear of it. They will tell me I should write to the Doctor, to get Edward the curacy of his new living. I know they will; but I am sure I would not do such a thing for all the world.—'La!' I shall say, 'I wonder how you could think of such a thing. *I* write to the Doctor, indeed!'"

"Well," said Elinor, "it is a comfort to be prepared against the worst. You have got your answer ready."

Miss Steele was going to reply on the same subject, but the approach of her own party made another more necessary.

"Oh, la! Here come the Richardsons. I had a vast deal more to say to you, but I must not stay away from them not any longer. I assure you they are very genteel people. He makes a monstrous deal of money, and they keep their own coach. I have not time to speak to Mrs. Jennings about it myself, but pray tell her I am quite happy to hear she is not in anger against us, and Lady Middleton the same. If anything should happen to take you and your sister away, and Mrs. Jennings should want company, I am sure we should be very glad to come and stay with her for as long a time as she likes. I suppose Lady Middleton won't ask us anymore this go round. Goodbye; I am sorry Miss Marianne was not here. Remember me kindly to her."

After this, she had time only to pay her farewell compliments to Mrs. Jennings, before her company was claimed by Mrs. Richardson: and Elinor was left in possession of knowledge which might feed her powers of reflection some time, though she had learned very little more than what had been already foreseen in her own mind. Edward's marriage with Lucy was firmly determined on, and the time of its taking place remained as absolutely uncertain as she had concluded it would be. Everything depended, exactly in accordance with her expectation, on his getting that preferment, of which, at present, there seemed not the smallest chance.

As soon as they returned to the carriage, Mrs. Jennings was eager for information; but as Elinor did not wish to spread intelligence that had been so unfairly obtained, she confined herself to the brief repetition of such simple particulars, as she felt assured that Lucy, for the sake of her own importance, would choose to have known. The continuance of their engagement, and the means that were to be taken for promoting its end, was all her communication; and this produced from Mrs. Jennings the following natural remark—

"Wait for his having a living!. We all know how *that* will end; they will wait a twelvemonth, and finding no good comes of it, will set down upon a curacy of fifty pounds a year, with the interest of his two thousand pounds, and what little Mr. Steele and Mr. Pratt can give her. Then they will have a child every year! Lord help 'em! how poor they will be! I must see what I can give them towards furnishing their house.

The next morning brought Elinor a letter by the two-penny post, from Lucy herself. It was as follows—

Bartlett's Buildings, *March*. I hope my dear Miss Dashwood will excuse the liberty I take of writing to her; but I know your friendship for me will make you pleased to hear such a good account of myself and my dear Edward, after all the troubles we have went through lately, therefore will make no more apologies, but proceed to say that, though we have suffered dreadfully, we are both quite well now, and as happy as we must always be in one another's love. We have had great trials, and great persecutions, but however, at the same time, gratefully acknowledge many friends, yourself not the least among them, whose great kindness I shall always thankfully remember, as will Edward too, who I have told of it. I am sure you will be glad to hear, as likewise dear Mrs. Jennings, I spent two happy hours with him yesterday afternoon. He would not hear of our breaking the engagement, though earnestly did I, as I thought my duty required, urge him to it for the sake of prudence, and we would have parted forever on the spot, had he consented to it; but he said it should never be, he thought nothing of his mother's anger, while he could have my affections; our financial prospects are not very bright, to be sure, but we must wait, and hope for the best. He will be ordained shortly, and should it ever be in your power to recommend him to anybody that has a living to bestow, am very sure you will not forget us, and dear Mrs. Jennings too, trust she will speak a good word for us to Sir John, or Mr. Palmer, or any friend that may be able to assist us. Poor Anne was much to blame for what she did, but it turned out all right, so I say nothing; hope Mrs. Jennings won't think it too much trouble to give us a call, should she come this way any morning, 'twould be a great kindness, and my cousins would be proud to know her. I beg to be most gratefully and respectfully remembered to her, and to Sir John, and Lady Middleton, and the dear children, when you chance to see them, and love to Miss Marianne."

As soon as Elinor had finished it, she performed what she concluded to be its writer's real design, by placing it in the hands of Mrs. Jennings, who read it aloud with many comments of satisfaction and praise.

"Very well indeed! How prettily she writes! That was quite proper to let him be off if he would. That was just like Lucy. Poor soul! I wish I *could* get him a living with all my heart. She calls me dear Mrs. Jennings, you see. She is as good-hearted a girl as ever lived. Very well, upon my word. That sentence is very prettily turned. Yes, yes, I will go and see her sure enough. How attentive she is, to think of everybody! Thank you, my dear, for showing it me. It is as pretty a letter as ever I saw, and does Lucy's head and heart great credit."

CHAPTER 39

The Miss Dashwoods had now been in town for more than two months, and Marianne's impatience to be gone increased every day. She sighed for the air, the liberty, the quiet of the country, and fancied that if any place could give her ease, Barton must do it. Elinor was hardly less anxious than herself to return, but she was conscious of the difficulties of so long a journey, which Marianne could not be brought to acknowledge. She began, however, seriously to turn her thoughts towards their departure, and had already mentioned their wishes to their kind hostess, who resisted them with all the eloquence of her goodwill, when a plan was suggested which appeared to Elinor as more serviceable than any other. The Palmers were going to Cleveland about the end of March, for the Easter holidays; and Mrs. Jennings, with both her friends, received a very warm invitation from Charlotte to go with them. It was repeated with so much real politeness by Mr. Palmer himself as, combined with the very great amendment of his manners towards them since her sister had been known to be unhappy, convinced her to accept it with pleasure.

When she told Marianne what she had done, however, her first reply was not very auspicious.

"Cleveland!" she cried, with great agitation. "No, I cannot go to Cleveland."

"You forget," said Elinor, gently, "that it is not so very near Combe Magna."

"But it is in Somersetshire—I cannot go into Somersetshire."

Elinor would not argue the propriety of overcoming such feelings; she only endeavoured to counteract them by working on others. She represented it, therefore, as a measure which would determine the time of her returning to that dear mother, whom she so much wished to see, in a more eligible, more comfortable manner, than any other plan could do, and perhaps without any greater delay. From Cleveland, which was within a few miles of Bristol, the distance to Barton was not more than one day, though a long day's journey; and their mother's servant might easily come there to accompany them on the journey. As there could be no occasion for their staying more than a week at Cleveland, they might now be at home in little more than three weeks' time. As Marianne's affection for her mother was sincere, it must triumph, with little difficulty, over the imaginary evil she had earlier mentioned.

Mrs. Jennings pressed them very earnestly to return with her again from Cleveland. Elinor was grateful for the attention, but it could not change their plans; and their mother's approval being readily obtained, everything relative to their return was arranged as far as it could be. Marianne found some relief in determining the hours that were yet to divide her from Barton.

"Ah! Colonel, I do not know what you and I shall do without the Miss Dashwoods," said Mrs. Jennings to him when he first called on her, after their leaving her was settled—"for they are quite resolved upon going home from the Palmers. How forlorn we shall be when I come back! We shall sit and gape at one another, as dull as two cats."

Perhaps Mrs. Jennings was hoping, by this vigorous sketch of their future boredom, to provoke him to make an offer of marriage to Elinor, and if so, she had soon afterwards good reason to think her object gained. When Elinor moved to the window, he followed her to it with a look of particular meaning, and conversed with her there for several minutes. The effect of his discourse on the lady could not escape her observation. Though she was too honourable to listen, and had even changed her seat, on purpose that she might *not* hear, to one close by the piano forte on which Marianne was playing, she could not keep herself from seeing that Elinor changed colour, and was too intent on what he said, to continue her drawing. Still farther in confirmation of her hopes, in the interval of Marianne's turning from one piece to another, some words of the Colonel's inevitably reached her ear, in which he seemed to be apologising for the badness of his house. This set the matter beyond a doubt. She wondered indeed at his thinking it necessary to do so; but supposed it to be the proper etiquette. What Elinor said in reply she could not distinguish, but judged from the motion of her lips that she did not think *that* any material objection, and Mrs. Jennings commended her in her heart for being so honest. They then talked on for a few minutes longer without her catching a syllable, when another lucky stop in Marianne's performance brought her these words in the Colonel's calm voice:

"I am afraid it cannot take place very soon."

Astonished and shocked at so unlover-like a speech, she was almost ready to cry out, "What should hinder it?" She checked her desire, confined herself to this silent observation—

"This is very strange! Surely he need not wait to be older."

This delay on the Colonel's side, however, did not seem to offend or mortify his fair companion in the least, for on their moving different ways, Mrs. Jennings very plainly heard Elinor say with a voice which showed her to feel what she said—

"I shall always think myself very much obliged to you."

Mrs. Jennings was delighted with her gratitude, and only wondered, that after hearing such a sentence, that the Colonel should be able to leave them, as he immediately did, and go away without making any reply! She had not thought her old friend could have made so indifferent a suitor.

What had really passed between them was to this effect—

"I have heard," said he, with great compassion, "of the injustice your friend Mr. Ferrars has suffered from his family; for if I understand the matter right, he has been entirely cast off by them because of his engagement with a very deserving young woman. Have I been rightly informed? Is it so?"

Elinor told him that it was.

"The cruelty," he replied, with great feeling, "of dividing, or attempting to divide, two young people long attached to each other, is terrible—Mrs. Ferrars does not know what she is doing—what she may drive her son to. I have seen Mr. Ferrars two or three times in Harley Street, and am much pleased with him. He is not a young man with whom one can be acquainted in a short time, but I have seen enough of him to wish him well for his own sake, and as a friend of yours, I wish it still more. I understand that he intends to be a clergyman. Will you be so good as to tell him that the living of Delaford, now available, as I am informed by this day's post, is his, if he thinks it is worth accepting. The more recent occupant, I believe, did not make more than 200 pounds per year, and though it is certainly capable of improvement, I fear, not to such an amount as to afford him a very comfortable income. Such as it is, however, my pleasure in presenting it to him will be very great. Pray assure him of it."

Elinor's astonishment could hardly have been greater, had the Colonel been really making her an offer of his hand. Her emotion was such as Mrs. Jennings had attributed to a very different cause; but her gratitude for the particular friendship which prompted Colonel Brandon to this act was strongly felt and warmly expressed. She thanked him for it with all her heart, spoke of Edward's principles and disposition with that praise which she knew them to deserve; and promised to undertake the commission with pleasure, if it were really his wish to delegate so agreeable an office to another. But, at the same time, she could not help thinking that no one could perform it as well as himself. But Colonel Brandon seemed so desirous of its being told to him through her, that she would not on any account oppose him. Edward, she believed, was still in town, and fortunately she had heard his address from Miss Steele. She could undertake therefore to inform him of it, in the course of the day. After this had been settled, Colonel Brandon began to talk of his own advantage in securing so respectable and agreeable a neighbour; and *then* he mentioned with regret that the house was small and indifferent; an inconvenience which Elinor, as Mrs. Jennings had supposed her to do, made very light of, at least as far as regarded its size.

"The smallness of the house," said she, "I cannot imagine any inconvenience to them, for it will be in proportion to their family and income."

"This little rectory *can* do no more than make Mr. Ferrars comfortable as a bachelor," the Colonel continued. "It cannot enable him to marry. I am sorry to say that my patronage ends with this. If, however, by any unforeseen chance it should be in my power to serve him farther, I must think very differently of him from what I now do, if I am not as ready to be useful to him then, as I sincerely wish I could be at present. What I am now doing indeed seems nothing at all, since it can advance him so little towards what must be his principal, his only object of happiness. His marriage must still be a distant good; at least, I am afraid it cannot take place very soon—"

Such was the sentence which, when misunderstood, so justly offended the delicate feelings of Mrs. Jennings; but after this narration of what really passed between Colonel Brandon and Elinor, while they stood at the window, the gratitude expressed by the latter on their parting may perhaps appear, in general, not less proper than if it had arisen from an offer of marriage.

CHAPTER 40

"Well, Miss Dashwood," said a smiling Mrs. Jennings as soon as the gentleman had withdrawn, "I do not ask you what the Colonel has been saying to you; for though I *tried* to keep out of hearing, I could not help catching enough to understand his business. And I assure you I never was more pleased in my life, and I wish you joy with all my heart."

"Thank you, ma'am," said Elinor. "It *is* a matter of great joy to me; and I feel the goodness of Colonel Brandon most sensibly. There are not many men who would act as he has done. I never was more astonished in my life."

"Lord! my dear, you are very modest! I ain't the least astonished at it in the world, for I have often thought there was nothing more likely to happen."

"You judged from your knowledge of the Colonel's general benevolence; but even you could not foresee that the opportunity would so very soon occur."

"Opportunity!" repeated Mrs. Jennings—"Oh! As to that, when a man has once made up his mind to such a thing, somehow or other he will soon find an opportunity. Well, my dear, I wish you joy again and again; and if ever there was a happy couple in the world, I think I shall soon know where to look for them."

"You mean to go to Delaford after them, I suppose," said Elinor, with a faint smile.

"Aye, my dear, that I do, indeed. And as to the house being a bad one, I do not know what the Colonel is thinking, for it is a good a one as ever I saw."

"He spoke of its being out of repair."

"Well, and whose fault is that? Why don't he repair it?—who should do it but himself?"

They were interrupted by the servant's coming in to announce the carriage being at the door; and Mrs. Jennings immediately preparing to go, said —

"Well, my dear, I must be going. I do not ask you to go with me, for I dare say your mind is too full to care for company; and besides, you must long to tell your sister all about it."

Marianne had left the room before the conversation began.

"Certainly, ma'am, I shall tell Marianne of it; but I shall not mention it at present to anybody else."

"Oh! very well," said Mrs. Jennings, rather disappointed. "Then you would not have me tell it to Lucy, for I am thinking of going as far as Holborn today."

"No, ma'am, not even Lucy, if you please. One day's delay will make little difference; and till I have written to Mr. Ferrars, I think it ought not to be mentioned to anybody else. I shall do *that* directly. It is important that no time should be lost with him, for he will, of course, have much to do relative to his ordination."

This speech at first puzzled Mrs. Jennings exceedingly. Why Mr. Ferrars was to be written to in such a hurry she could not immediately comprehend. A few moments' reflection, however, produced a very happy idea, and she exclaimed—"Oh! I understand you. Mr. Ferrars is to be the man. Well, so much the better for him. Aye, to be sure, he must be ordained quickly; and I am very glad to find things are so well between you. But, my dear, is not this rather out of character? Should not the Colonel write himself? Surely he is the proper person to do it."

Elinor did not quite understand the beginning of Mrs. Jennings's speech; neither did she think it worth inquiring into; and therefore only replied to its conclusion.

"Colonel Brandon is so delicate a man that he rather wished someone else would announce his intentions to Mr. Ferrars than himself."

"And so *you* are forced to do it. Well, *that* is an odd kind of delicacy! However, I will not disturb you. You know your own concerns best. So goodbye, my dear. I have not heard of anything to please me so well since Charlotte gave birth."

And away she went, but returning again in a moment —

"I have just been thinking of Betty's sister, my dear. I would be very glad to get her such a good mistress. But whether she would do for a lady's maid, I am sure I can't tell. She is an excellent housemaid, and works very well at her needle. However, you will think of all that at your leisure."

"Certainly, ma'am," replied Elinor, not hearing much of what she said, and more anxious to be alone than to continue the conversation.

How she should begin—how she should express herself in her note to Edward, was now all her concern. The particular circumstances between them made it difficult to tell him something any other person would have been able to say easily. She feared to say too much or too little, and sat deliberating over her paper, with the pen in her hand, till interrupted by the entrance of Edward himself.

He had met Mrs. Jennings at the door on her way to the carriage, as he came to leave his farewell card. She had invited him to enter by saying that Miss Dashwood was within, and wanted to speak with him.

Elinor had just been thinking that however difficult it might be to express herself properly by letter, it was at least preferable to giving the information by word of mouth, when her visitor entered, to force her upon this greatest exertion of all. Her astonishment and confusion were very great on his so sudden appearance. She had not seen him since his engagement became public, and therefore not since his knowing her to be acquainted with it. He too was much distressed, and they sat down together in a state of embarrassment. Whether he had asked her pardon for his intrusion on first coming into the room, he could not recollect; but determining to be on the safe side, he made his apology as soon as he could say anything, after taking a chair.

"Mrs. Jennings told me," said he, "that you wished to speak to me, at least I understood her so—or I certainly should not have intruded on you in such a manner. I should, however, have been extremely sorry to leave London without seeing you and your sister, as it is not probable that I should soon have the pleasure of meeting you again. I am going to Oxford tomorrow."

"You would not have gone, however," said Elinor, recovering herself, and determined to get over what she so much dreaded as soon as possible, "without receiving our good wishes, even if we had not been able to give them in person. Mrs. Jennings was quite right in what she said. I have something important to tell you of, which I was on the point of communicating in writing. I have been given a most agreeable assignment," she said, breathing rather faster than usual as she spoke. "Colonel Brandon, who was here only ten minutes ago, has asked me to say that he wishes to offer you the living of Delaford, and only wishes it were more valuable. Allow me to congratulate you on having so respectable and kind a friend, and to join in his wish that the living—it is about two hundred a-year—were much more considerable, and such as might better enable you to establish all your views of happiness."

What Edward felt, as he could not say it himself, it cannot be expected that anyone else should say for him. He was astonished at receiving such unexpected news, and excited by the communication; but he managed to say only these two words —

"Colonel Brandon!"

"Yes," continued Elinor, gathering more courage, as some of the worst was over; "Colonel Brandon means it as a token of his concern for what has recently passed—for the cruel situation in which the unfortunate conduct of your family has placed you, and likewise as a proof of his high esteem for your general character, and his particular approval of your behaviour on the present occasion."

"Colonel Brandon giving *me* a living! Can it be possible?"

"The unkindness of your own relations has made you astonished to find friendship anywhere."

"No," replied he, with sudden consciousness, "not to find it in *you*; for I cannot be ignorant that to you, to your goodness, I owe it all. I feel it—I would express it if I could—but, as you well know, words often fail me."

"You are very much mistaken. I do assure you that you owe it entirely, at least almost entirely, to your own merit, and Colonel Brandon's recognition of it. I have had no hand in it. I did not even know, till I understood his plan, that the living was available; nor had it ever occurred to me that he might have had such a living within his power to bestow. As a friend of mine, of my family, he may perhaps—indeed I know he *has*, still greater pleasure in bestowing it; but, upon my word, you owe nothing to me."

Truth obliged her to acknowledge some small share in the gift, but she acknowledged it with hesitation, which probably made him even more suspicious. For a short time he sat deep in thought, after Elinor had ceased to speak; at last, and as if it were rather an effort, he said —

"Colonel Brandon seems to be a man of great worth and respectability. I have always heard him spoken of as such, and your brother, I know, thinks much of him. He is undoubtedly a sensible man, and in his manners perfectly a gentleman."

"Indeed," replied Elinor, "I believe that you will find him, upon further acquaintance, all that you have heard him to be. As you will be such very near neighbours, for I understand the parsonage is almost close to the mansion-house, it is particularly important that he *should* be all this."

Edward made no answer; but when she had turned away, gave her a look so serious, so earnest, as seemed to say that he might hereafter wish the distance between the parsonage and the mansion-house much greater.

"Colonel Brandon, I think, is staying in St. James's Street," said he, soon afterwards, rising from his chair.

Elinor told him the number of the house.

"I must hurry away then, to give him those thanks which you will not allow me to give *you*; to assure him that he has made me a very— an exceedingly happy man."

Elinor did not offer to detain him; and they parted, with a very earnest assurance on *her* side of her unceasing good wishes for his happiness in every change of situation that might befall him; on *his*, with more of an attempt to return the same good will, though without the power of expressing it.

"When I see him again," said Elinor to herself, as the door shut him out, "he will be the husband of Lucy."

And she sat down to reconsider the past, recall the words, and endeavour to comprehend all the feelings of Edward; and, of course, to reflect on her own with discontent.

When Mrs. Jennings came home, her mind was so occupied by the important secret in her possession that she brought it up as soon as Elinor appeared.

"Well, my dear," she cried, "I sent you up the young man. Was that the right thing to do? I suppose you had no great difficulty in getting him to accept your proposal?"

"He seemed very pleased by it."

"Well, and how soon will he be ready? For it seems all to depend upon that."

"Really," said Elinor, "I know so little of these kind of forms, that I can hardly even guess the time, or the preparation necessary; but I suppose two or three months will complete his ordination."

"Two or three months!" cried Mrs. Jennings; "My dear, how calmly you talk of it! Can the Colonel wait two or three months? Though one would be very glad to do a kindness for poor Mr. Ferrars, I do think it is not worthwhile to wait two or three months for him. Sure, somebody else might be found that would do as well; somebody that has already taken orders."

"I assure you, ma'am, that Colonel Brandon's only object is to be of use to Mr. Ferrars."

"Lord bless you, my dear! Surely you do not mean to persuade me that the Colonel only marries you for the sake of giving ten guineas to Mr. Ferrars!" The misunderstanding could not continue after this; and an explanation immediately took place, by which both gained considerable amusement for the moment, without any material loss of happiness to either.

"The parsonage is but a small one," said she, after the first expression of surprise and satisfaction was over, "and very likely *may* be out of repair; but to hear a man apologising, as I thought, for a house that to my knowledge has five sitting rooms on the ground-floor, and I think the housekeeper told me, could make up fifteen beds! And to you too, who had been used to living in Barton Cottage! It seemed quite ridiculous. But, my dear, we must encourage the Colonel to do something to the parsonage, and make it comfortable for them, before Lucy goes to it."

"But Colonel Brandon does not seem to have any idea of the living's being enough to allow them to marry."

"The Colonel is a ninny, my dear; because he has two thousand a-year himself, he thinks that nobody else can marry on less. Take my word for it, that, if I am alive, I shall be paying a visit at Delaford Parsonage before the end of September; and I am sure I shan't go if Lucy ain't there."

CHAPTER 41

Edward, having carried his thanks to Colonel Brandon, proceeded with his happy news to Lucy; and such was the excess of his joy by the time he reached Bartlett's Buildings that she was able to assure Mrs. Jennings, who called on her again the next day with her congratulations, that she had never seen him in such spirits before in her life.

She joined Mrs. Jennings most heartily in her expectation of their being all comfortably together in Delaford Parsonage by the end of September. She was more than happy to give Elinor that credit which Edward gave her, and she spoke of her friendship for them both with most grateful warmth. She was ready to acknowledge all their obligation to her, and openly declared that no exertion for their good on Miss Dashwood's part, either present or future, would ever surprise her, for she believed her capable of doing anything in the world for those she really valued. As for Colonel Brandon, she was not only ready to worship him as a saint, but was moreover truly anxious that he should be treated as one in all worldly concerns. She felt that his tithes should be raised to the utmost, and secretly resolved to avail herself, at Delaford, as far as she possibly could, of his servants, his carriage, his cows, and his poultry.

It had been more than a week since John Dashwood called in Berkeley Street, and since that time no notice had been taken by them of his wife's indisposition, beyond one verbal inquiry, so Elinor began to feel it necessary to pay her a visit. This was an obligation, however, which went not only against her own inclination, but which had no support or encouragement from her companions. Marianne was very intent on preventing her sister's going at all; and Mrs. Jennings, though her carriage was always at Elinor's service, so very much disliked Mrs. John Dashwood, that not even her curiosity to see how she looked after the late discovery, nor her strong desire to offend her by taking Edward's side, could overcome her unwillingness to be in her company again. The consequence was, that Elinor set out by herself to pay a visit, for which no one could really have less inclination, and to run the risk of a conversation with a woman whom neither of the others had so much reason to dislike.

Mrs. Dashwood was denied; but before the carriage could turn from the house, her husband accidentally came out. He expressed great pleasure in meeting Elinor, told her that he had been just going to call in Berkeley Street, and assured her that Fanny would be very glad to see her. He invited her to come in. They walked upstairs into the drawing room, but nobody was there.

"Fanny is in her own room, I suppose," said he, "I will go to her, for I am sure she will not have the least objection in the world to seeing *you*—very far from it indeed. *Now* especially there cannot be— but however, you and Marianne were always great favourites.—Why did Marianne not come?"

Elinor made what excuse she could for her.

"I am not sorry to see you alone," he replied, "for I have a good deal to say to you. This living of Colonel Brandon's—can it be true?—has he really given it to Edward?—I heard it yesterday by chance, and was coming to inquire about it."

"It is perfectly true. Colonel Brandon has given the living of Delaford to Edward."

"Really!—Well, this is very astonishing!—no relationship!—no connection between then!—and now that livings fetch such a price!—what was the value of this?"

"About two hundred a year."

"I suppose that the case may probably be *this*. Edward is only to hold the living till the person to whom the Colonel has given it to is old enough to take it. Aye, aye, that is the truth, depend upon it."

Elinor contradicted it, however, by relating that she had herself been asked to convey the offer from Colonel Brandon to Edward, and therefore must understand the terms on which it was given,.

"It is truly astonishing!" he cried, after hearing what she said. "What could be the Colonel's motive? He could have made a much more financially prudent decision."

"He had a very simple motive—to be of use to Mr. Ferrars."

"Well, well, Edward is a very lucky man! You will not mention the matter to Fanny, however; for though I have broken it to her, and she bears it vastly well, she will not want to hear it talked of. Mrs. Ferrars," he added, lowering his voice to the tone becoming so important a subject, "knows nothing about it at present, and I believe it will be best to keep it entirely concealed from her for as possible. When the marriage takes place, I fear she must hear of it all."

"But why is such a precaution necessary? Though Mrs. Ferrars cannot have the smallest satisfaction in knowing that her son has money enough to live upon, for *that* must be quite out of the question; yet why, after her recent behaviour, is she supposed to feel anything at all? She is done with her son, she has cast him off forever, and has made all those over whom she had any influence cast him off likewise. Surely, after doing so, she cannot be affected by any impression of sorrow or joy on his account—she cannot be interested in anything that befalls him. She would not be so weak as to throw away the comfort of a child, and yet retain the anxiety of a parent!"

"Ah! Elinor," said John, "your reasoning is very good, but it is founded on ignorance of human nature. When Edward's unhappy match takes place, depend upon it his mother will feel as much as if she had never discarded him. Therefore, every circumstance that may accelerate that dreadful event must be concealed from her as much as possible. Mrs. Ferrars can never forget that Edward is her son."

"You surprise me; I would think it must nearly have escaped her memory by *this* time."

"You wrong her exceedingly. Mrs. Ferrars is one of the most affectionate mothers in the world."

Elinor was silent.

"We are thinking *now*," said Mr. Dashwood, after a short pause, "that *Robert* will marry Miss Morton."

Elinor, smiling at the grave and decisive importance of her brother's tone, calmly replied —

"The lady, I suppose, has no choice in the matter?"

"Choice! How do you mean?"

"I only mean that I suppose, from your manner of speaking, it must be the same to Miss Morton whether she marries Edward or Robert."

"Certainly there can be no difference, for Robert will now for all intents and purposes be considered the eldest son. They are both very agreeable young men—I do not know that one is superior to the other."

Elinor said no more, and John was also for a short time silent. His reflections ended thus —

"Of *one* thing, my dear sister," kindly taking her hand, and speaking in an awful whisper, "I may assure you: and I *will* do it, because I know it must gratify you. I have good reason to think—indeed I have it on the best authority, or I should not repeat it, for otherwise it would be very wrong to say anything about it—that, in short, whatever objections there might be against you marrying Edward, it would have been far preferable to her. I was exceedingly pleased to hear that Mrs. Ferrars considered it in that light—a very gratifying circumstance, you know, to us all. 'It would have been beyond comparison,' she said, 'the least evil of the two.' But all that is quite out of the question—not to be thought of or mentioned; as to any attachment, you know—it never could be—all that is in the past. But I thought I would just tell you of this, because I knew how much it would please you. Not that you have any reason to regret, my dear Elinor. There is no doubt of your doing exceedingly well—quite as well, or better, perhaps, all things considered. Has Colonel Brandon been with you lately?"

Elinor had heard enough, if not to gratify her vanity and raise her self-importance, then to agitate her nerves and fill her mind. She was therefore glad to be spared from the necessity of saying much in reply herself, and from the danger of hearing anything more from her brother, by the entrance of Mr. Robert Ferrars. After a few moments' chat, John Dashwood, recollecting that Fanny was yet uninformed of his sister's being there, left the room in search of her; and Elinor was left to improve her acquaintance with Robert, who, by the happy self-complacency of his manner while enjoying so unfair a division of his mother's love and liberality, was confirming her most unfavourable opinion of his head and heart.

They had scarcely been two minutes by themselves, before he began to speak of Edward; for he too had heard of the living, and was very curious about the subject. Elinor repeated the particulars of it, as she had given them to John, and their effect on Robert, though very different, was not less striking than it had been on *him*. He laughed most heartily. The idea of Edward's being a clergyman, and living in a small parsonage house, amused him beyond measure; and when to that was added the fanciful imagery of Edward reading prayers, and publishing marriage announcements, he could conceive nothing more ridiculous.

Elinor, while she waited in silence, and immovable seriousness, the conclusion of such folly, could not restrain her eyes from being fixed on him with a look that spoke all the contempt she felt. It was a look, however, very well bestowed, for it relieved her own feelings, and he did not even notice it. He was recalled from wit to wisdom, not by any reproof of hers, but by his own sensibility.

"We may treat it as a joke," said he at last, recovering from his affected laugh, "but upon my soul, it is a most serious business. Poor Edward! He is ruined forever. I am extremely sorry for it—for I know him to be a very good-hearted man; as well-meaning a fellow perhaps, as any in the world. You must not judge him, Miss Dashwood, by *your* slight acquaintance. Poor Edward! His manners are certainly not the happiest in nature. But we are not all born, you know, with the same abilities. Poor fellow! to see him in a circle of strangers!—to be sure it was pitiable enough!—but, upon my soul, I believe he has as good a heart as any in the kingdom; and I declare and protest to you I never was so shocked in my life, as when the news all burst forth. I could not believe it. My mother was the first person who told me of it, and I, feeling myself called on to act with resolution, immediately said to her, 'My dear madam, I do not know what you may intend to do on the occasion, but as for myself, I must say, that if Edward does marry this young woman, *I* never will see him again.' That was what I said immediately—I was most uncommonly shocked indeed!—Poor Edward!—he has shut himself out forever from all decent society!—but as I directly said to my mother, I am not in the least surprised at it; from his style of education it was always to be expected. My poor mother was half frantic."

"Have you ever seen the lady?"

"Yes, once; while she was staying in this house, I happened to drop in for ten minutes; and I saw quite enough of her. The most awkward country girl, without style or elegance, and almost without beauty. I remember her perfectly. Just the kind of girl I should suppose likely to captivate poor Edward. I offered immediately, as soon as my mother related the whole to me, to talk to him myself, and convince him not to go through with it; but it was too late *then*, I found, to do anything. Had I been informed of it a few hours earlier, I think it is most probable that something might have been done. I certainly should have represented it to Edward in a very strong light. 'My dear fellow,' I would have said, 'consider what you are doing. You are making a most disgraceful connection, one your family unanimously disapproves.' I cannot help thinking, in short, that means might have been found. But now it is all too late. He must starve, you know; that is certain; absolutely starve."

He had just settled this point with great composure when the entrance of Mrs. John Dashwood put an end to the subject. But though *she* never spoke of it outside her own family, Elinor could see its influence. She even proceeded as far as to be concerned to find that Elinor and her sister were so soon to leave town, as she had hoped to see more of them; an exertion in which her husband, who entered the room with her, seemed to see everything that was most affectionate and graceful.

CHAPTER 42

One other short call in Harley Street, in which Elinor received her brother's congratulations on their travelling so far towards Barton without any expense, and on Colonel Brandon's being to follow them to Cleveland in a day or two, completed her visits to the brother and sisters in town. She received a weak invitation from Fanny, to come to Norland whenever she should happen to be in the neighborhood, which of all things was the most unlikely to occur. John told Elinor he would come to see her soon at Delaford, which was all that foretold any meeting in the country.

It amused her to observe that all her friends seemed determined to send her to Delaford; a place in which, of all others, she would now least choose to visit or wish to reside. Not only was it considered as her future home by her brother and Mrs. Jennings, but even Lucy, when they parted, gave her a pressing invitation to visit her there.

Very early in April, and tolerably early in the day, the two parties from Hanover Square and Berkeley Street set out from their respective homes to meet, by appointment, on the road. For the convenience of Charlotte and her child, they were to be more than two days on their journey, and Mr. Palmer, travelling more quickly with Colonel Brandon, was to join them at Cleveland soon after their arrival.

Marianne, few as had been her hours of comfort in London, and eager as she had long been to leave it, could not bid adieu to the house in which she had for the last time enjoyed those hopes and that confidence in Willoughby, which were now extinguished forever, without great pain. Nor could she leave the place in which Willoughby remained busy in new engagements, and new schemes, in which *she* could have no share, without shedding many tears.

Elinor's satisfaction at the moment of removal was more positive. She had no such object for her lingering thoughts to fix on, and left no creature behind from whom it would give her a moment's regret to be divided forever. She was pleased to be free from the persecution of Lucy's friendship, she was grateful for bringing her sister away unseen by Willoughby since his marriage, and she looked forward with hope to what a few months of tranquillity at Barton might do towards restoring Marianne's peace of mind, and confirming her own.

Their journey was safely performed. The second day brought them into the cherished, or the prohibited county of Somerset, for as such was it dwelt on in turn in Marianne's imagination; and on the afternoon of the third they drove up to Cleveland.

Cleveland was a spacious, modern-built house, situated on a sloping lawn. It had no park, but the pleasure grounds were tolerably extensive. Like every other place of the same degree of importance, it had its open shrubbery, and closer wood walk, and a road of smooth gravel winding round a plantation led to the front. The lawn was dotted over with timber; the house itself was under the guardianship of the fir, the mountain-ash, the acacia, and a thick screen of tall poplars.

Marianne entered the house, her heart swelling with emotion from the consciousness of being only eighty miles from Barton, and not thirty from Combe Magna; and before she had been five minutes within its walls, while the others were busily helping Charlotte show her child to the housekeeper, she left it again, stealing away through the winding shrubberies. Her eye wandered over a wide tract of country to the southeast, resting fondly on the farthest ridge of hills in the horizon, and she fancied that from their summits Combe Magna might be seen.

In such moments of precious misery, she rejoiced in tears of agony to be at Cleveland; and as she returned by a different route to the house, feeling all the happy privilege of country liberty, of wandering from place to place in free and luxurious solitude, she resolved to spend almost every hour of every day while she remained with the Palmers in the indulgence of such solitary rambles.

She returned just in time to join the others as they left the house, on an excursion through its more immediate premises; and the rest of the morning was easily whiled away, in lounging round the kitchen garden, examining the bloom upon its walls—in dawdling through the greenhouse, where the loss of her favourite plants, unwarily exposed, and nipped by the lingering frost, raised the laughter of Charlotte—and in visiting her poultry yard, where in the disappointed hopes of her dairy-maid, by hens forsaking their nests, or being stolen by a fox, or in the rapid decease of a promising young brood, she found fresh sources of merriment.

The morning was fine and dry, and Marianne had not planned for any change of weather during their stay at Cleveland. With great surprise therefore, did she find herself prevented by rain from going out again after dinner. She had depended on a twilight walk to the Grecian temple, and perhaps all over the grounds, and an evening merely cold or damp would not have deterred her from it; but a heavy rain even *she* could not fancy pleasant weather for walking.

Their party was small, and the hours passed quietly away. Mrs. Palmer had her child, and Mrs. Jennings her needlework. They talked of the friends they had left behind, arranged Lady Middleton's engagements, and wondered whether Mr. Palmer and Colonel Brandon would get farther than Reading that night. Elinor, however little concerned in it, joined in their discussion, and Marianne soon procured herself a book.

Nothing was lacking on Mrs. Palmer's side that constant and friendly good-humour could do to make them feel welcome. The openness of her manner more than atoned for that lack of elegance which made her often deficient in the forms of politeness. Her kindness, recommended by so pretty a face, was engaging; her folly, though evident, was not offensive because it was not conceited, and Elinor could have forgiven everything but her laugh.

The two gentlemen arrived the next day to a very late dinner, making a pleasant addition to the party, and a very welcome change to their conversation, which had slowed during a long morning of the same continued rain. Elinor had seen so little of Mr. Palmer, and in that little had seen so much variety in his manners to her sister and herself, that she knew not what to expect to find when he was with his own family. She found him, however, perfectly the gentleman in his behaviour to all his visitors, and only occasionally rude to his wife and her mother. She found him very capable of being a pleasant companion, and only prevented from being so always by a tendency to believe himself superior to other people in general, particularly to Mrs. Jennings and Charlotte. The rest of his character and habits were marked, as far as Elinor could perceive, with no traits at all unusual in his sex and time of life. She liked him much better than she had expected.

Of Edward, or at least of some of his concerns, she now received news from Colonel Brandon, who had been in Dorsetshire. He talked to her a great deal of the parsonage at Delaford, described its deficiencies, and told her what he meant to do to address them. His behaviour to her in this as well as in every other particular, his open pleasure in meeting her after an absence of only ten days, his readiness to talk with her, and his interest in her opinion, might very well justify Mrs. Jennings's persuasion of his attachment. It would have been enough, perhaps, had not Elinor still, as from the first, believed Marianne his real favourite. She watched his eyes, while Mrs. Jennings thought only of his behaviour; and while his looks of anxious concern about Marianne's feeling, in her head and throat the beginning of a heavy cold, entirely escaped the latter lady's observation, *she* could discover in them the needless alarm of a lover.

Two delightful twilight walks on the third and fourth evenings of her being there, not merely on the dry gravel of the shrubbery, but all over the grounds, and especially in the most distant parts of them, gave Marianne a violent cold. Prescriptions poured in from all quarters, and as usual were all declined. Though heavy and feverish, with a pain in her limbs, a cough, and a sore throat, it was with difficulty that Elinor prevailed on her, when she went to bed, to try one or two of the simplest of the remedies.

CHAPTER 43

Marianne got up the next morning at her usual time; to every inquiry replied that she was better, and tried to prove herself so, by engaging in her usual employments. But a day spent in sitting shivering over the fire with a book in her hand which she was unable to read, or in lying on a sofa, did not do much for her continued recovery. When, at last, she went early to bed, more and more indisposed, Colonel Brandon was only astonished at her sister's composure, who, though attending and nursing her the whole day, against Marianne's inclination, and forcing proper medicines on her at night, felt no real alarm.

A very restless and feverish night, however, disappointed her expectations. When Marianne, after persisting in rising, confessed herself unable to sit up, and returned voluntarily to her bed, Elinor was very ready to adopt Mrs. Jennings's advice of sending for the apothecary.

He came, examined his patient, and though encouraging Miss Dashwood to expect that a very few days would restore her sister to health, allowed the word "infection" to pass his lips, giving instant alarm to Mrs. Palmer on her baby's account. Mrs. Jennings, who had been inclined from the first to think Marianne's complaint more serious than Elinor, now urged the necessity of her immediate removal with her infant; and Mr. Palmer, though treating their fears as unnecessary, found the anxiety of his wife too great to be withstood. Her departure therefore was fixed on; and, within an hour after Mr. Harris's arrival, she set off, with her little boy and his nurse, for the house of a near relation of Mr. Palmer's, who lived a few miles on the other side of Bath. Mrs. Jennings, with a kindness of heart which made Elinor really love her, declared her resolution of not stirring from Cleveland as long as Marianne remained ill, and of endeavouring, by her own attentive care, to supply to her the place of the mother she had taken her from; and Elinor found her on every occasion a most willing and active helper, desirous to share in all her fatigues, and often, by her better experience in nursing, of material use.

Poor Marianne could no longer hope that tomorrow would find her recovered; and the idea of what tomorrow would have produced, but for this unlucky illness, made every ailment more severe. On that day their journey home was to have begun, and, attended the whole way by a servant of Mrs. Jennings, they were to have taken their mother by surprise the following day. The little that she said was to lament this inevitable delay; though Elinor tried to raise her spirits, and make her believe, as she then really believed herself, that it would be a very short one.

The next day produced little or no alteration in the state of the patient. Their party was now further reduced; for Mr. Palmer was persuaded at last by Colonel Brandon to perform his promise of following her; and while he was preparing to go, Colonel Brandon himself, with a much greater exertion, began to talk of going likewise. Here, however, the kindness of Mrs. Jennings interposed most acceptably; for to send the Colonel away while his love was in so much uneasiness on her sister's account, would be to deprive them both, she thought, of every comfort. Therefore she told him at once that his staying at Cleveland was necessary to herself, that she should want him to play cards in the evening, while Miss Dashwood was above with her sister.

Marianne was of course kept in ignorance of all these arrangements. She knew not that she had been the means of sending the owners of Cleveland away, in about seven days from the time of their arrival. It gave her no surprise that she saw nothing of Mrs. Palmer; and as it gave her likewise no concern, she never mentioned her name.

Two days passed from the time of Mr. Palmer's departure, and her situation continued the same. Mr. Harris, who visited every day, still talked boldly of a speedy recovery, and Miss Dashwood was equally hopeful; but the expectation of the others was by no means so cheerful. Mrs. Jennings had determined very early that Marianne would never get over it, and Colonel Brandon, who was chiefly of use in listening to Mrs. Jennings's fears, was not in a state of mind to resist their influence. He tried to reason himself out of fears which the different judgment of the apothecary seemed to render absurd; but the many hours of each day in which he was left entirely alone, were but too favourable for the entertainment of every melancholy idea, and he could not expel from his mind the persuasion that he should see Marianne no more.

On the morning of the third day however, the gloomy anticipations of both were almost done away; for when Mr. Harris arrived, he declared his patient materially better. Her pulse was much stronger and every symptom more favourable than on the preceding visit. Elinor, confirmed in every pleasant hope, was all cheerfulness; rejoicing that in her letters to her mother, she had pursued her own judgment rather than her friend's, in making very light of the indisposition which delayed them at Cleveland, and almost fixing on the time when Marianne would be able to travel.

But towards the evening Marianne became ill again, growing more heavy, restless, and uncomfortable than before. Her sister, however, still hopeful, was willing to attribute the change to nothing more than the fatigue of having sat up to have her bed made. Carefully administering the medicines prescribed, she saw her with satisfaction sink at last into a slumber, from which she expected the most beneficial effects. Her sleep, though not as quiet as Elinor wished to see it, lasted a considerable time; and anxious to observe the result of it herself, she resolved to sit with her during the whole of it. Mrs. Jennings, knowing nothing of any change in the patient, went unusually early to bed. Her maid, who was one of the principal nurses, was resting in the housekeeper's room, and Elinor remained alone with Marianne.

The repose of the latter became more and more disturbed; and her sister, who watched with unremitting attention her continual change of posture, and heard the frequent but inarticulate sounds of complaint which passed her lips, was almost wishing to rouse her from so painful a slumber when Marianne, suddenly awakened by some accidental noise in the house, started hastily up, and with feverish wildness, cried out —

"Is mama coming?"

"Not yet," replied the other, concealing her terror, and helping Marianne lie down again; "but she will be here I hope, before long. It is a great way, you know, from here to Barton."

"But she must not go round by London," cried Marianne, in the same hurried manner, "I shall never see her, if she goes by London."

Elinor perceived with alarm that she was not quite herself, and while attempting to sooth her, eagerly felt her pulse. It was weaker than ever; and Marianne, still talking wildly of mama, convinced Elinor to send instantly for Mr. Harris, and to dispatch a messenger to Barton for her mother. She decided to consult with Colonel Brandon, and hastened down to the drawing room, where she knew he was generally to be found at this hour.

It was no time for hesitation. Her fears and her difficulties were immediately before him. He listened in silent despondence, then offered himself as the messenger who should fetch Mrs. Dashwood. Elinor thanked him with brief, though fervent gratitude, and while he went to hurry off his servant with a message to Mr. Harris, and an order for post-horses directly, she wrote a few lines to her mother.

The comfort of such a friend at that moment as Colonel Brandon—how gratefully was it felt! A companion whose judgment would guide, whose attendance must relieve, and whose friendship might sooth her mother! As far as the shock of such a summons *could* be lessened, Colonel Brandon's presence, his manners, and his assistance, would lessen it.

He, meanwhile, whatever he might feel, acted with all the firmness of a collected mind, made every necessary arrangement with the utmost urgency, and calculated with exactness the time in which she might look for his return. Not a moment was lost in delay of any kind. The horses arrived, even before they were expected, and Colonel Brandon only pressed her hand with a look of solemnity before hurrying into the carriage. It was then about twelve o'clock, and she returned to her sister's apartment to wait for the arrival of the apothecary, and to watch by her the rest of the night. It was a night of almost equal suffering to both. Hour after hour passed away in sleepless pain and delirium on Marianne's side, and in the most cruel anxiety on Elinor's, before Mr. Harris appeared. The servant who sat up with her, for she would not allow Mrs. Jennings to be called, only tortured her more, by hints of what her mistress had always thought.

Marianne's ideas were still, at intervals, fixed incoherently on her mother, and whenever she mentioned her name, it gave a pang to the heart of poor Elinor, who, reproaching herself for having trifled with so many days of illness, and looking for some immediate relief, fancied that all relief might soon be in vain, that everything had been delayed too long, and pictured to herself her suffering mother arriving too late to see this darling child, or to see her rational.

She was on the point of sending again for Mr. Harris, or if *he* could not come, for some other advice, when the former—but not till after five o'clock—arrived. His opinion, however, made some little amends for his delay, for though acknowledging a very unexpected and unpleasant alteration in his patient, he would not allow the danger to be material, and talked of the relief which a fresh mode of treatment must bring. He promised to call again, in the course of three or four hours, and left both the patient and her anxious attendant more composed than he had found them.

With strong concern, and with many reproaches for not being called to their aid, did Mrs. Jennings hear in the morning of what had passed. Her former worries, now with greater supporting evidence, left her no doubt of the eventual outcome. Though trying to speak comfort to Elinor, her conviction of her sister's danger would not allow her to offer the comfort of hope. Her heart was really grieved. The rapid decay, the early death of a girl so young, so lovely as Marianne, must have struck a less interested person with concern. On Mrs. Jennings's compassion she had other claims. She had been for three months her companion, was still under her care, and she was known to have been greatly injured, and long unhappy. The distress of her sister too, particularly a favourite, was before her. As for their mother, when Mrs. Jennings considered that Marianne might probably be to *her* what Charlotte was to herself, her sympathy was very sincere.

Mr. Harris was punctual in his second visit, but he came to be disappointed in his hopes of what the last would produce. His medicines had failed, the fever was unabated, and Marianne was only more quiet—not more herself. Elinor, catching all, and more than all, his fears in a moment, proposed to call in further advice. But he judged it unnecessary; he had still something more to try, some fresh application, of whose success he was almost as confident as the last, and his visit concluded with encouraging assurances which reached the ear, but could not enter the heart, of Miss Dashwood. She was calm, except when she thought of her mother, but she was almost hopeless; and in this state she continued till noon, scarcely stirring from her sister's bed, her thoughts wandering from one image of grief, one suffering friend to another, and her spirits oppressed to the utmost by the conversation of Mrs. Jennings, who did not hesitate to attribute the severity and danger of this attack to the many weeks of previous indisposition which Marianne's disappointment had brought on. Elinor felt all the reasonableness of the idea, and it gave fresh misery to her reflections.

About noon, however, she began to fancy, to hope she could perceive a slight amendment in her sister's pulse. She waited, watched, and examined it again and again. At last, with an agitation more difficult to bury under exterior calmness than all her foregoing distress, ventured to communicate her hopes. Mrs. Jennings, though forced to acknowledge a temporary revival, tried to keep her young friend from indulging a thought of its continuance. Elinor told herself likewise not to hope. But it was too late. Hope had already entered; and feeling all its anxious flutter, she bent over her sister to watch—she hardly knew for what. Half an hour passed away, and the favourable symptom was seen. Others even arose to confirm it. Her breath, her skin, her lips, all flattered Elinor with signs of improvement, and Marianne fixed her eyes on her with a rational though weak gaze. Anxiety and hope now oppressed her in equal degrees, and left her no moment of tranquillity till the arrival of Mr. Harris at four o'clock—when his assurances, his congratulations on a recovery in her sister even surpassing his expectation, gave her confidence, comfort, and tears of joy.

Marianne was in every respect materially better, and he declared her entirely out of danger. Mrs. Jennings, perhaps satisfied with the partial justification of her forebodings which had been found in their late alarm, allowed herself to trust in his judgment, and admitted with cheerfulness the probability of an entire recovery.

Elinor could not be cheerful. Her joy was of a different kind, and led to anything rather than to happiness. Marianne restored to life, health, friends, and to her doting mother, was an idea to fill her heart with sensations of exquisite comfort, and expand it in fervent gratitude, but it led to no outward demonstrations of joy, no words, no smiles. All within Elinor's breast was satisfaction, silent and strong.

She continued by the side of her sister with little intermission the whole afternoon, calming every fear, satisfying every inquiry of her enfeebled spirits, supplying every succour, and watching almost every look and every breath. The possibility of a relapse would of course, in some moments, occur to remind her of what anxiety was—but when she saw on her frequent and minute examination, that every symptom of recovery continued, and saw Marianne at six o'clock, sink into a quiet, steady, and to all appearance comfortable, sleep, she silenced every doubt.

The time was now approaching when Colonel Brandon might be expected back. At ten o'clock, she trusted, or at least not much later, her mother would be relieved from the dreadful suspense in which she must now be travelling towards them. The Colonel too! Oh! How slow was the progress of time which yet kept them in ignorance!

At seven o'clock, leaving Marianne still sweetly asleep, she joined Mrs. Jennings in the drawing-room to tea. Of breakfast she had been kept by her fears, and of dinner by their sudden reverse, from eating much. The present refreshment, therefore, with such feelings of content as she brought to it, was particularly welcome. Mrs. Jennings would have persuaded her at its conclusion to take some rest before her mother's arrival, and allow *her* to take her place by Marianne; but Elinor had no sense of fatigue, no capability of sleep at that moment, and she was not to be kept away from her sister an unnecessary instant. Mrs. Jennings therefore attending her upstairs into the sick chamber, to satisfy herself that all continued right, left her there again to her thoughts, and retired to her own room to write letters and sleep.

The night was cold and stormy. The wind roared round the house, and the rain beat against the windows; but Elinor, all happiness within, paid it no attention. Marianne slept through every blast, and the travellers—they had a rich reward in store for every present inconvenience.

The clock struck eight. Had it been ten, Elinor would have been convinced that at that moment she heard a carriage driving up to the house; and so strong was the persuasion that she *did*, in spite of the *almost* impossibility of their having already arrived, that she moved into the adjoining dressing-closet and opened a shutter, to be satisfied of the truth. She instantly saw that her ears had not deceived her. The flaring lamps of a carriage were immediately in view. By their uncertain light she thought she could discern it to be drawn by four horses; and this, while it told the excess of her poor mother's alarm, gave some explanation to such unexpected rapidity.

Never in her life had Elinor found it so difficult to be calm, as at that moment. The knowledge of what her mother must be feeling as the carriage stopped at the door—of her doubt, her dread, perhaps her despair—and of what *she* had to tell! With such knowledge it was impossible to be calm. All that remained to be done was to be speedy; and therefore staying only till she could leave Mrs. Jennings's maid with her sister, she hurried downstairs.

The bustle in the vestibule, as she passed along an inner lobby, assured her that they were already in the house. She rushed forwards towards the drawing room—she entered it, and saw only Willoughby.

CHAPTER 44

Elinor, starting back with a look of horror at the sight of him, obeyed the first impulse of her heart in turning instantly to leave the room. Her hand was already on the knob when he hastily advanced, and saying, in a voice rather of command than supplication —

"Miss Dashwood, for half an hour—for ten minutes—I entreat you to stay."

"No, sir," she replied with firmness, "I shall *not* stay. Your business cannot be with *me*. The servants, I suppose, forgot to tell you that Mr. Palmer was not in the house."

"Had they told me," he cried with vehemence, "that Mr. Palmer and all his relations were with the devil, it would not have turned me from the door. My business is with you, and you alone."

"With me!"—in the utmost amazement—"well, sir—be quick—and if you can—less violent."

"Sit down, and I will be both."

She hesitated; she knew not what to do. The possibility of Colonel Brandon's arriving and finding him there crossed her mind. But she had promised to hear him, and her curiosity was piqued. She walked silently towards the table and sat down. He took the opposite chair, and for half a minute not a word was said by either.

"Please be quick, sir" said Elinor impatiently—"I have no time to spare."

He was sitting in an attitude of deep meditation, and seemed not to hear her.

"Your sister," said he, with abruptness, a moment afterwards—"is out of danger. I heard it from the servant. God be praised! But is it true?—is it really true?"

Elinor would not speak. He repeated the inquiry with yet greater eagerness.

"For God's sake tell me, is she out of danger, or is she not?"

"We hope she is."

He rose up, and walked across the room.

"Had I known as much half an hour ago—But since I *am* here"—speaking with forced liveliness as he returned to his seat—"what does it signify?—For once, Miss Dashwood—it will be the last time, perhaps—let us be cheerful together. I am in a fine mood for cheerfullness. Tell me honestly"—a deeper glow spread over his cheeks—"do you think me most a scoundrel or a fool?"

Elinor looked at him with greater astonishment than ever. She began to think that he must have been drinking. The strangeness of such a visit, and of his manners, made no sense otherwise; and with this impression she immediately rose, saying —

"Mr. Willoughby, I advise you at present to return to Combe. I am not at leisure to remain with you longer. Whatever your business may be with me, it will be better recollected and explained tomorrow."

"I understand you," he replied, with an expressive smile, and a voice perfectly calm. "Yes, I am very drunk. A pint of porter with my cold beef at Marlborough did the job well."

"At Marlborough!" cried Elinor.

"Yes—I left London this morning at eight o'clock, and the only ten minutes I have spent out of my carriage since that time were for a brief luncheon at Marlborough."

The steadiness of his manner, and the sharpness of his eye as he spoke, convinced Elinor that whatever other unpardonable folly might bring him to Cleveland, he was not brought there by intoxication. She said, after a moment's recollection,

"Mr. Willoughby, you *ought* to feel, and I certainly *do*—that after what has passed—your coming here in this manner requires a very particular excuse. What do you mean by it?"

"I mean," said he, with serious energy, "if I can, to make you hate me one degree less than you do *now*. I mean to offer some kind of explanation, some kind of apology, for the past—to open my whole heart to you, and by convincing you, that though I have been always a blockhead, I have not been always a rascal, to obtain something like forgiveness from Mar—from your sister."

"Is this the real reason of your coming?"

"Upon my soul it is," was his answer, with a warmth which brought all the former Willoughby to her remembrance, and in spite of herself made her think him sincere.

"If that is all, you may be satisfied already, for Marianne *does*— she has *long* forgiven you."

"Has she!" he cried, in the same eager tone. "Then she has forgiven me before she ought to have done it. But she shall forgive me again, and on more reasonable grounds. *Now* will you listen to me?"

Elinor nodded.

"I do not know," said he, after a pause of expectation on her side, and thoughtfulness on his own, "how *you* may have accounted for my behaviour to your sister, or what diabolical motive you may have attributed to me. Perhaps you will hardly think better of me. It is worth the attempt however, and you shall hear everything. When I first became acquainted with your family, I had no other intention, no other view than to pass my time pleasantly while I was obliged to remain in Devonshire, more pleasantly than I had ever done before. Your sister's loveliness and interesting manners could not but please me; and her behaviour to me almost from the first was astonishing, when I reflect on what it was, and what *she* was, that my heart should have been so unaware! But at first, I must confess, my vanity only was elevated by it. Thinking nothing of her happiness, and only of my own amusement, giving way to feelings which I had always been too much in the habit of indulging, I endeavoured, by every means in my power, to make myself pleasing to her, without any design of returning her affection."

Miss Dashwood at this point, turning her eyes on him with the most angry contempt, stopped him, by saying —

"It is hardly worthwhile, Mr. Willoughby, for you to relate, or for me to listen any longer. Such a beginning as this cannot be followed by anything. Do not let me be pained by hearing anything more on the subject."

"I insist on your hearing the whole of it," he replied. "My fortune was never large, and I had always been extravagant, always in the habit of associating with people with higher incomes than myself. Every year since my coming of age, or even before, I believe, had added to my debts; and though the death of my old cousin, Mrs. Smith, was to set me free, yet that event being uncertain, and possibly far distant, it had been for some time my intention to establish myself by marrying a woman of fortune. To attach myself to your sister, therefore, was not a thing to be thought of; and with a meanness, selfishness, cruelty—which no indignant, no contemptuous look, even of yours, Miss Dashwood, can ever condemn as much as I deserve—I was acting in this manner, trying to engage her regard, without a thought of returning it. But one thing may be said for me, even in that horrid state of selfish vanity, I did not know the extent of the injury I had planned, because I did not *then* know what it was like to love. But have I ever known it? Had I really loved, could I have sacrificed my feelings to vanity, to greed? Or could I have sacrificed hers? But I have done it. To avoid a comparative poverty, which her company would have deprived of all its horrors, I have, by raising myself to affluence, lost everything that could make it a blessing."

"You did then," said Elinor, a little softened, "believe yourself at one time attached to her."

"To have resisted such attractions, to have withstood such tenderness! Is there a man on earth who could have done it? Yes, I found myself, by degrees, becoming sincerely fond of her. The happiest hours of my life were spent with her, when I felt my intentions were strictly honourable, and my feelings blameless. Even *then*, however, when fully determined to propose to her, I allowed myself most improperly to put off, from day to day, the moment of doing it, from an unwillingness to enter into an engagement while my financial circumstances were so desperate. Then I discovered that Mrs. Smith had somehow or other been informed, I imagine by some distant relation, whose interest it was to deprive me of her favour, of a connection—but I need not explain myself farther," he added, looking at her with an heightened colour and an inquiring eye, "you have probably heard the whole story long ago."

"I have," returned Elinor, colouring likewise, and hardening her heart anew against any compassion for him, "I have heard it all. And how you will explain away any part of your guilt in that dreadful business, I confess is beyond my comprehension."

"Remember," cried Willoughby, "from whom you received the account. Could it be an impartial one? I acknowledge that her situation and her character ought to have been respected by me. Her affection for me deserved better treatment, and I heartily wish it had never happened. But I have injured more than her; and I have injured one, whose affection for me (may I say it?) was scarcely less warm than hers; and whose mind—Oh! How infinitely superior!"

"Your indifference, however, towards that unfortunate girl—I must say it, unpleasant to me as the discussion of such a subject may well be—your indifference is no apology for your cruel neglect of her. Do not think yourself excused by any weakness, any natural defect of understanding on her side, in the cruelty so evident on yours. You must have known, that while you were enjoying yourself in Devonshire, pursuing fresh schemes, always happy, she was reduced to the extremest indigence."

"But, upon my soul, I did *not* know it," he warmly replied. "I had inadvertently neglected to tell her my whereabouts, but common-sense might have told her how to find it out."

"Well, sir, and what said Mrs. Smith?"

"She accused me of the offence, at once, and my confusion may be guessed. The purity of her life, the formality of her notions, her ignorance of the world—everything was against me. The matter itself I could not deny, and vain was every endeavour to soften it. She was previously disposed, I believe, to doubt the morality of my conduct in general, and was moreover discontented with the very little attention, the very little portion of my time that I had bestowed on her while visiting. In short, it ended in a total breach. By one measure I might have saved myself. She offered to forgive the past if I would marry Eliza. That could not be—and I was formally dismissed from her favour and her house. The night following was spent by me in deliberating on what my future conduct should be. The struggle was great—but it ended too soon. My affection for Marianne, my thorough conviction of her attachment to me—it was all insufficient to outweigh that dread of poverty, or get the better of those false ideas of the necessity of riches, which I was naturally inclined to feel, and expensive society had increased. I persuaded that I had no other option than to marry a wealthy woman. A heavy scene however awaited me, before I could leave Devonshire; I was engaged to dine with you on that very day, some apology was therefore necessary for my breaking the engagement. But whether I should write this apology, or deliver it in person, was a point of long debate. To see Marianne, I felt would be dreadful, and I even doubted whether I could see her again, and keep my resolution, but I went, I saw her, and left her miserable—hoping never to see her again."

"Why did you come in person, Mr. Willoughby?" said Elinor, reproachfully; "a note would have answered every purpose. "

"It was necessary to my own pride. I could not bear to leave the country in a manner that might lead you, or the rest of the neighbourhood, to suspect any part of what had really passed between Mrs. Smith and myself, and I resolved therefore on calling at the cottage, on my way to Honiton. The sight of your dear sister, however, was really dreadful; and to heighten the matter, I found her alone. You were all gone, I do not know where. I had left her only the evening before, so fully, so firmly resolved within myself on doing right! A few hours were to have engaged her to me forever; and I remember how happy were my spirits, as I walked from the cottage to Allenham, satisfied with myself, delighted with everybody! But in this, our last interview of friendship, I approached her with a sense of guilt. Her sorrow, her disappointment, her deep regret, when I told her, that I was obliged to leave Devonshire so immediately—I never shall forget it; combined, too, with such reliance, such confidence in me! Oh, God! What a hard-hearted rascal I have been!"

They were both silent for a few moments. Elinor first spoke.

"Did you tell her that you would soon return?"

"I do not know what I told her," he replied, impatiently; "less than was due to the past, beyond a doubt, and in all likelihood much more than was justified by the future. I cannot think of it—it won't do. Then came your dear mother to torture me farther, with all her kindness and confidence. I was miserable. Miss Dashwood, you cannot have an idea of the comfort it gives me to look back on my own misery. I owe such a grudge to myself for the stupid, rascally folly of my own heart, that all my past sufferings under it are only triumph and exultation to me now. Well, I went, left all that I loved, and went to those to whom, at best, I was only indifferent. My journey to town—travelling with my own horses, and therefore so tediously—no creature to speak to—my own reflections so cheerful—when I looked forward everything so inviting!—when I looked back at Barton, the picture so soothing!—oh!—it was a blessed journey!"

He stopped.

"Well, sir," said Elinor, who, though pitying him, grew impatient for his departure, "and this is all?"

"All! No, have you forgotten what happened in town? That infamous letter. Did she show it to you?"

"Yes, I saw every note that passed."

"When the first of hers reached me (as it immediately did, for I was in town the whole time), my feelings were very, very painful. Every line, every word was, in the hackneyed metaphor which their dear writer, were she here, would forbid, a dagger to my heart. To know that Marianne was in town was in the same language a lightning bolt. Lightning bolts and daggers!"

Elinor's heart, which had undergone many changes in the course of this extraordinary conversation, was now softened again.

"Marianne's note, by assuring me that I was still as dear to her as in former days—that in spite of the many, many weeks we had been separated, she was as constant in her own feelings and as full of faith in the constancy of mine as ever, awakened all my remorse. I say awakened, because time and London, business and pleasure had in some measure quieted it, and I had been growing into a fine hardened villain, fancying myself indifferent to her, and choosing to believe that she too must have become indifferent to me. I talked to myself of our past attachment as a mere idle, trifling business, shrugging up my shoulders in proof of its being so, and silencing every reproach by secretly saying now and then, 'I shall be heartily glad to hear she is well married.' I still felt that she was infinitely dearer to me than any other woman in the world, and that I was using her infamously. But everything was then just settled between Miss Grey and me. To retreat was impossible. All that I had to do was avoid you both. I sent no answer to Marianne, intending by that means to preserve myself from further notice; and for some time I was even determined not to call in Berkeley Street. But at last, judging it wiser to affect the air of a cool, common acquaintance than anything else, I watched you all safely out of the house one morning, and left my name."

"Watched us out of the house!"

"You would be surprised to hear how often I watched you, how often I was on the point of approaching you. I have entered many a shop to avoid your sight, as the carriage drove by. Lodging as I did in Bond Street, there was hardly a day in which I did not catch a glimpse of one or other of you; and nothing but the most constant watchfulness on my side, a most invariably prevailing desire to keep out of your sight, could have separated us so long. I avoided the Middletons as much as possible, as well as everybody else who was likely to prove an acquaintance in common. Not aware of their being in town, however, I blundered on Sir John, I believe, the first day of his coming, and the day after I had called at Mrs. Jennings's. He asked me to a party, a dance at his house in the evening. Had he *not* told me that you and your sister were to be there, I should have felt it too certain a thing to trust myself near him. The next morning brought another short note from Marianne—still affectionate, open, confiding—everything that could make *my* conduct most hateful. I could not answer it. I tried, but could not frame a sentence. But I thought of her, I believe, every moment of the day. If *you* can pity me, Miss Dashwood, pity my situation as it was *then*. With my head and heart full of your sister, I was forced to play the happy lover to another woman! Those three or four weeks were worse than all the rest. Well, at last, as I need not tell you, you were forced on me: and what a sweet figure I cut! What an evening of agony it was! Marianne, beautiful as an angel, on one side, calling me Willoughby in such a tone! Oh God! Holding out her hand to me, asking me for an explanation with those bewitching eyes fixed on my face! And Sophia, jealous as the devil, on the other hand, looking all that was—Well, it does not matter; it is over now. Such an evening! I ran away from you all as soon as I could, but not before I had seen Marianne's sweet face as white as death. *That* was the last, last sight I ever had of her. It was horrid! Yet when I thought of her today as really dying, it was a kind of comfort to me to imagine that I knew exactly how she would appear to those who saw her last in this world. She was before me, constantly before me, as I travelled, looking just as pale as she did then."

A short pause of mutual thoughtfulness followed. Willoughby, rousing himself, broke it thus —

"Well, let me make haste and be gone. Your sister is certainly better, certainly out of danger?"

"We are assured of it."

"Your poor mother too! Doting on Marianne."

"But the letter, Mr. Willoughby, your own letter; have you anything to say about that?"

"Yes, yes, *that* in particular. Your sister wrote to me again, you know, the very next morning. You saw what she said. I was breakfasting at the Ellison's, and her letter, with some others, was brought to me there from my lodgings. It happened to catch Sophia's eye before it caught mine; and its size, the elegance of the paper, the hand-writing, altogether, immediately made her suspicious. Some vague report had reached her before of my attachment to a young lady in Devonshire, and what had passed within her observation the preceding evening had identified the young lady, and made her more jealous than ever. Affecting that air of playfulness, therefore, which is delightful in a woman one loves, she opened the letter directly, and read its contents. She was well paid for her boldness. She read what made her miserable. Her misery I could have handled, but her contempt, her malice—at all events it must be appeased. And in short, what do you think of my wife's style of writing? Delicate, tender, truly feminine—was it not?"

"Your wife! The letter was in your own handwriting."

"Yes, but I had only the credit of copying such sentences as I was ashamed to put my name to. The original was all her own, her own happy thoughts and gentle diction. But what could I do? We were engaged, everything in preparation, the day almost decided upon—but I am talking like a fool. Preparation! Day! In honest words, her money was necessary to me, and in a situation like mine, anything was to be done to prevent an end to the engagement. After all, what did it matter to my character in the opinion of Marianne and her friends, in what language my answer was given? The result would be the same. My business was to declare myself a scoundrel, and whether I did it with a bow or a wave was of little importance. 'I am ruined forever in their opinion,' said I to myself; 'I am shut out forever from their company; they already think me an unprincipled fellow, and this letter will only make them think me a black-hearted one.' Such were my reasonings as, in a sort of desperate carelessness, I copied my wife's words, and parted with my last reminders of Marianne. Her three notes—unluckily they were all in my pocket-book, or I would have denied their existence, and hoarded them forever; I was forced to give them up, and could not even kiss them. And the lock of hair—that too I had always carried about me in the same pocket-book, which was now searched by her with the most passionate intesity—the dear lock—all, every memento was torn from me."

"You are very wrong, Mr. Willoughby, very blameable," said Elinor, while her voice, in spite of herself, betrayed her compassionate emotion. "You ought not to speak in this way, either of Mrs. Willoughby or my sister. You have made your own choice. It was not forced on you. Your wife has a claim to your politeness, to your respect, at least. She must be attached to you, or she would not have married you. To treat her with unkindness, to speak of her slightingly, will not help Marianne, nor can I suppose it a relief to your own conscience."

"Do not talk to me of my wife," said he with a heavy sigh. "She does not deserve your compassion. She knew I had no regard for her when we married. Well, married we were, and came down to Combe Magna to be happy, and afterwards returned to town. And now do you pity me, Miss Dashwood? Or have I said all this to no purpose? Am I—be it only one degree—am I less guilty in your opinion than I was before? My intentions were not always wrong. Have I explained away any part of my guilt?"

"Yes, you have certainly removed something—a little. You have proved yourself, on the whole, less faulty than I had believed you. You have proved your heart less wicked, much less wicked. But I hardly know—the misery that you have inflicted—I hardly know what could have made it worse."

"Will you repeat to your sister when she is recovered, what I have been telling you? Let me be a little lightened too in her opinion as well as in yours. You tell me that she has forgiven me already. Let me be able to fancy that a better knowledge of my heart, and of my present feelings, will draw from her a more spontaneous, more natural, more gentle, less dignified forgiveness. Tell her of my misery and my penitence, tell her that my heart was never inconstant to her, and if you will, that at this moment she is dearer to me than ever."

"I will tell her all that is necessary to what may comparatively be called your justification. But you have not explained to me the particular reason of your coming now, nor how you heard of her illness."

"Last night, in Drury Lane, I ran into Sir John Middleton, and when he saw who I was he could not resist the temptation of telling me what he knew ought to vex me horridly. As bluntly as he could speak it, therefore, he told me that Marianne Dashwood was dying of a fever at Cleveland—a letter that morning received from Mrs. Jennings declared her danger most imminent—the Palmers all gone off in a fright, etc. I was too shocked to be able to pass myself off as uncaring. His heart was softened in seeing mine suffer; and much of his ill-will was done away. When we parted, he almost shook me by the hand while he reminded me of an old promise about a pointer puppy. What I felt on hearing that your sister was dying—and dying, too, believing me the greatest villain on Earth, scorning, hating me in her last moments—for how could I tell what horrid motives might have been assumed? *One* person I was sure would represent me as capable of anything. What I felt was dreadful! My resolution was soon made, and at eight o'clock this morning I was in my carriage. Now you know all."

Elinor made no answer. Her thoughts were silently fixed on the irreparable injury which idleness, extravagance, and luxury had made in the mind, the character, and the happiness of a man who had a naturally open and honest disposition, and an affectionate temper. Vanity, while seeking its own guilty triumph at the expense of another, had involved him in a real attachment, which extravagance, or at least its offspring necessity, had required to be sacrificed. Each faulty propensity, in leading him to error, had led him likewise to punishment. The attachment was likely to prove a source of incurable unhappiness to himself. From thoughts of this kind she was recalled at the end of some minutes by Willoughby, who, rousing himself from thoughts at least equally painful, started up in preparation for going, and said,

"There is no use in staying here; I must be off."

"Are you going back to town?"

"No; to Combe Magna. I have business there. From there to town in a day or two. Goodbye."

He held out his hand. She could not refuse to give him hers; he pressed it with affection.

"And you *do* think something better of me than you did?" said he, letting it fall, and leaning against the mantlepiece, as if forgetting he was leaving.

Elinor assured him that she did; that she forgave, pitied, wished him well—was even interested in his happiness—and added some gentle counsel as to the behaviour most likely to promote it. His answer was not very encouraging.

"As to that," said he, "I must just endure my life as well as I can. Domestic happiness is out of the question. If, however, I am allowed to think that you and yours feel an interest in my fate and actions, it may be the means—it may put me on my guard—at least, it will be something to live for. Marianne, to be sure, is lost to me forever. I shall now go away and live in dread of one event."

"What do you mean?"

"Your sister's marriage."

"That cannot make her any more lost to you than she is now."

"But she will be gained by someone else. And if that someone should be the very he whom, of all others, I could least bear—but I must be going. Goodbye; God bless you!"

And with these words, he almost ran out of the room.

CHAPTER 45

Elinor, for some time after he left her, for some time even after the sound of his carriage had died away, remained too overwhelmed by what she had just heard to think even of her sister.

Willoughby—he whom only half an hour ago she had abhorred as the most worthless of men—Willoughby, in spite of all his faults, excited a degree of compassion for the sufferings produced by them. This made her think of him as now separated forever from her family with a tenderness, a regret, rather in proportion to his wishes than to his merits.

When at last she returned to the unconscious Marianne, she found her just waking, refreshed by so long and sweet a sleep. Elinor's heart was full. The past, the present, the future—Willoughby's visit, Marianne's safety, and her mother's expected arrival, threw her altogether into an agitation of spirits which kept off every indication of fatigue, and made her only fearful of betraying herself to her sister. Within half-an-hour after Willoughby's leaving the house, she was again called downstairs by the sound of another carriage. Eager to save her mother from every unnecessary moment's horrible suspense, she ran immediately into the hall, and reached the outer door just in time to receive and support her as she entered it.

Mrs. Dashwood, whose terror as they drew near the house had produced almost the conviction of Marianne's being no more, had no voice to inquire after her, no voice even for Elinor; but *she*, waiting neither for salutation nor inquiry, instantly gave the joyful relief. Her mother, catching it with all her usual warmth, was in a moment as much overcome by her happiness as she had been before by her fears. She was supported into the drawing-room between her daughter and her friend. There, shedding tears of joy, though still unable to speak, she embraced Elinor again and again, turning from her at intervals to press Colonel Brandon's hand, with a look which spoke at once her gratitude, and her conviction of his sharing with herself in the bliss of the moment. He shared it, however, in a silence even greater than her own.

As soon as Mrs. Dashwood had recovered herself, to see Marianne was her first desire; and in two minutes she was with her beloved child, rendered dearer to her than ever by absence, unhappiness, and danger. Elinor's delight, as she saw what each felt in the meeting, was only checked by a concern of its robbing Marianne of farther sleep. Mrs. Dashwood could be calm, could be even prudent, when the life of a child was at stake, and Marianne, satisfied in knowing her mother was near her, and conscious of being too weak for conversation, submitted readily to the silence and quiet prescribed by every nurse around her. Mrs. Dashwood *would* sit up with her all night, and Elinor, in compliance with her mother's request, went to bed. But the rest was kept off by irritation of spirits. Willoughby, "poor Willoughby," as she now allowed herself to call him, was constantly in her thoughts; she would not but have heard his vindication for the world, and first blamed, then forgave herself for having judged him so harshly before. But her promise of relating it to her sister was invariably painful. She dreaded the telling of it, dreaded what its effect on Marianne might be. She doubted whether after such an explanation she could ever be happy with another, and for a moment, wished Willoughby a widower.

The shock of Colonel Brandon's errand at Barton had been much softened to Mrs. Dashwood by her own previous alarm; for so great was her uneasiness about Marianne that she had already determined to set out for Cleveland on that very day, without waiting for any farther intelligence. She had so far settled her journey before his arrival that the Careys were then expected every moment to fetch Margaret away, as her mother was unwilling to take her where there might be infection.

Marianne continued to mend every day, and the brilliant cheerfulness of Mrs. Dashwood's looks and spirits proved her to be, as she repeatedly declared herself, one of the happiest women in the world. Elinor could not hear the declaration, nor witness its proofs without sometimes wondering whether her mother ever recollected Edward. But Mrs. Dashwood was led away by the exuberance of her joy to think only of what would increase it. Marianne was restored from danger, and in her recovery she had yet another source of joy unthought of by Elinor. It was thus imparted to her, as soon as any opportunity of private conference between them occurred.

"At last we are alone. My Elinor, you do not yet know all my happiness. Colonel Brandon loves Marianne; he has told me so himself."

Her daughter, feeling by turns both pleased and pained, surprised and not surprised, was all silent attention.

"You were never like me, dear Elinor, or I should wonder at your composure now. Had I sat down to wish for any possible good to my family, I should have fixed on Colonel Brandon's marrying one of you as the object most desirable. And I believe Marianne will be the most happy with him of the two."

Elinor was half inclined to ask her reason for thinking so, but her mother must always be carried away by her imagination on any interesting subject, and therefore instead of an inquiry, she passed it off with a smile.

"He opened his whole heart to me yesterday as we travelled. It came out quite unawares, quite undesignedly. I, you may well believe, could talk of nothing but my child; he could not conceal his distress. I saw that it equalled my own, and he perhaps thinking that mere friendship would not justify such sincere sympathy—or rather not thinking at all, I suppose—made me acquainted with his earnest, tender, and constant affection for Marianne. He has loved her, my Elinor, ever since first seeing her."

Here, however, Elinor perceived, not the language, not the professions of Colonel Brandon, but the natural embellishments of her mother's active imagination, which made everything delightful to her, as it chose.

"His regard for her, infinitely surpassing anything that Willoughby ever felt or feigned, has subsisted through all the knowledge of dear Marianne's unhappy feelings for that worthless young man! Without selfishness—without encouraging a hope— could he have seen her unhappy with another? Such a noble mind! Such openness, such sincerity! No one can be deceived in *him*."

"Colonel Brandon's character," said Elinor, "as an excellent man, is well established."

"I know it is," replied her mother seriously, "or after such a warning, *I* should be the last to encourage such affection, or even to be pleased by it. But his coming for me as he did, with such active, such ready friendship, is enough to prove him one of the worthiest of men."

"His character, however," answered Elinor, "does not rest on *one* act of kindness, which his affection for Marianne would have surely motivated. To Mrs. Jennings, to the Middletons, he has been long and intimately known; they equally love and respect him; and even my own knowledge of him, though recently acquired, is very considerable. So highly do *I* value and esteem him, that if Marianne can be happy with him, I shall be as ready as yourself to think our connection the greatest blessing to us in the world. What answer did you give him? Did you allow him to hope?"

"Oh! My love, I could not then talk of hope to him or to myself. Marianne might at that moment be dying. But he did not ask for hope or encouragement. His was an involuntary confidence, an irrepressible confession to a friend—not an application to a parent. Yet after a time I *did* say, for at first I was quite overcome, that if she lived, as I trusted she might, my greatest happiness would lie in promoting their marriage. Since our arrival, since our delightful security, I have repeated it to him more fully, and have given him every encouragement in my power. Time, a very little time, I told him, will do everything. Marianne's heart is not to be wasted forever on such a man as Willoughby. His own merits must soon secure it."

"To judge from the Colonel's spirits, however, you have not yet made him equally hopeful."

"No. He thinks Marianne's affection too deeply rooted for any change in it except after a great length of time; and even supposing her heart again free, is too unsure of himself to believe, that with such a difference of age, and disposition, he could ever convince her. There, however, he is quite mistaken. His age is only so much beyond hers, as to be an advantage, as to make his character and principles fixed; and his disposition, I am well convinced, is exactly the very one to make your sister happy. And his person, his manners too, are all in his favour. My partiality does not blind me; he certainly is not as handsome as Willoughby but, at the same time, there is something much more pleasing in his countenance. There was always a something, if you remember, in Willoughby's eyes at times, which I did not like."

Elinor could *not* remember it; but her mother, without waiting for her assent, continued—"And his manners, the Colonel's manners, are not only more pleasing to me than Willoughby's ever were, but they are of a kind I well know to be exactly what Marianne prefers. Their gentleness, their genuine attention to other people, and their manly unstudied simplicity, is much more in accord with her real disposition, than the liveliness, often artificial, and often ill-timed, of the other. I am very sure myself, that had Willoughby turned out as really amiable, as he has proved himself not to be, Marianne would yet never have been as happy with *him*, as she will be with Colonel Brandon."

She paused. Her daughter could not quite agree with her, but her dissent was not heard, and therefore gave no offence.

"At Delaford, she will be within an easy distance of me," added Mrs. Dashwood, "even if I remain at Barton. In all probability, for I hear it is a large village, indeed there certainly *must* be some small house or cottage close by, that would suit us quite as well as our present situation."

Poor Elinor! Here was a new scheme for getting her to Delaford! But her spirit was stubborn.

"His fortune too! For at my time of life you know, everybody cares about *that*—and though I neither know, nor desire to know, what it really is, I am sure it must be a good one."

Here they were interrupted by the entrance of a servant, and Elinor withdrew to think it all over in private, to wish success to her friend, and yet, in wishing it, to feel a pang for Willoughby.

CHAPTER 46

Marianne's illness had not been long enough to make her recovery slow; and with youth, natural strength, and her mother's presence, it proceeded so smoothly as to enable her to move, within four days after the arrival of the latter, into Mrs. Palmer's dressing-room. When there, at her own particular request, for she was impatient to pour forth her thanks to him for fetching her mother, Colonel Brandon was invited to visit her.

His emotion in entering the room, in seeing her altered looks, and in receiving the pale hand which she immediately held out to him, was such as in Elinor's guess, must arise from something more than his affection for Marianne, or the consciousness of its being known to others. She soon discovered in his melancholy eye and varying complexion as he looked at her sister, the probable recurrence of many past scenes of misery to his mind, brought back by that resemblance between Marianne and Eliza already acknowledged, and now strengthened by the hollow eye, the sickly skin, the posture of reclining weakness, and the warm acknowledgment of peculiar obligation.

Mrs. Dashwood, not less watchful of what passed than her daughter, but with a mind very differently influenced, and therefore watching to very different effect, saw nothing in the Colonel's behaviour but what arose from the most simple and self-evident sensations. In the actions and words of Marianne she persuaded herself to think that something more than gratitude already dawned.

At the end of another day or two, Marianne growing visibly stronger every twelve hours, Mrs. Dashwood, urged equally by her own and her daughter's wishes, began to talk of returning to Barton. On *her* measures depended those of her two friends; Mrs. Jennings could not leave Cleveland during the Dashwoods' stay, and Colonel Brandon was soon brought, by their united request, to consider his own time there as equally determinate, if not equally indispensable. At his and Mrs. Jennings's united request in return, Mrs. Dashwood was prevailed on to accept the use of his carriage on her journey back, for the better accommodation of her sick child, The Colonel, at the joint invitation of Mrs. Dashwood and Mrs. Jennings, engaged with pleasure to redeem it by a visit at the cottage, in the course of a few weeks.

The day of separation and departure arrived; and Marianne, bidding Colonel Brandon farewell with the cordiality of a friend, was carefully assisted by him into the carriage. Mrs. Dashwood and Elinor then followed, and the others were left by themselves, to talk of the travellers, and feel their own boredom, till Mrs. Jennings was summoned to her chaise to take comfort in the gossip of her maid for the loss of her two young companions; and Colonel Brandon immediately afterwards went his solitary way to Delaford.

The Dashwoods were two days on the road, and Marianne bore her journey on both without essential fatigue. Everything that the most zealous affection, the most solicitous care could do to render her comfortable, was offered by each watchful companion, and each found their reward in her comfort and calmness of spirits. To Elinor, the observation of the latter was particularly grateful. She, who had seen her week after week so constantly suffering, oppressed by anguish of heart which she had neither courage to speak of, nor fortitude to conceal, now saw, with a joy, which no other could equally share, an apparent composure of mind, which, in being the result as she trusted of serious reflection, must eventually lead her to contentment and cheerfulness.

As they approached Barton, indeed, and entered on scenes, of which every field and every tree brought some peculiar, some painful recollection, she grew silent and thoughtful, and turning away her face from their notice, sat earnestly gazing through the window. But here, Elinor could neither wonder nor blame. No sooner had they entered their common sitting-room, than Marianne turned her eyes around it with a look of resolute firmness, as if determined at once to accustom herself to the sight of every object with which the remembrance of Willoughby could be connected. She said little, but every sentence aimed at cheerfulness, and though a sigh sometimes escaped her, it never passed away without a smile. After dinner she would try her piano. She went to it; but the music on which her eye first rested was an opera, procured for her by Willoughby, containing some of their favourite duets, and bearing on its outward leaf her own name in his handwriting. That would not do. She shook her head, put the music aside, and, after running over the keys for a minute complained of feebleness in her fingers, and closed the instrument again; declaring, however, with firmness as she did so, that she should in the future practise often.

The next morning produced a continuance of these happy symptoms. With a mind and body alike strengthened by rest, she looked and spoke with more genuine spirit, anticipating the pleasure of Margaret's return, and talking of the dear family party which would then be restored, of their mutual pursuits and cheerful company as the only happiness worth having.

"When the weather is settled, and I have recovered my strength," she said, "we will take long walks together every day. We will walk to the farm at the edge of the down, and see how the children are doing; we will walk to Sir John's new plantations at Barton Cross, and the Abbeyland; and we will often go to the old ruins of the Priory, and try to trace its foundations as far as we are told they once reached. I know we shall be happy. I know the summer will pass happily away. I mean never to be later in rising than six, and from that time till dinner I shall divide every moment between music and reading. I have formed my plan, and am determined to enter on a course of serious study. Our own library is too well known to me to be resorted to for anything beyond mere amusement. But there are many works well worth reading, at the Park; and there are others which I know I can borrow from Colonel Brandon. By reading only six hours a day, I shall gain in the course of a year a great deal of instruction which I now feel myself to lack."

Elinor honoured her for a plan which originated so nobly as this. Her smile, however, changed to a sigh when she remembered that her promise to Willoughby was yet unfulfilled, and feared she had something to communicate which might again unsettle the mind of Marianne, and ruin at least for a time this fair prospect of busy tranquillity. Choosing therefore to delay, she resolved to wait till her sister's health was more secure before she attempted it. But the resolution was made only to be broken.

Marianne had been two or three days at home before the weather was fine enough for an invalid like herself to venture out. A soft, genial morning appeared, and Marianne, leaning on Elinor's arm, was allowed to walk as long as she could without fatigue, in the lane near the house.

The sisters set out at a pace as slow as the feebleness of Marianne required. They had gone only so far beyond the house as to admit a full view of the hill, the important hill behind, when, pausing with her eyes turned towards it, Marianne calmly said—

"There, exactly there," pointing with one hand, "on that projecting mound—there I fell; and there I first saw Willoughby."

Her voice sunk with the word, but presently reviving she added—

"I am thankful to find that I can look with so little pain on the spot! Shall we ever talk on that subject, Elinor? I *can* talk of it now, I hope."

Elinor tenderly invited her to speak on.

"As for regret," said Marianne, "I am done with that, as far as *he* is concerned. I do not mean to talk to you of what my feelings have been for him, but what they are *now*. At present, if I could be satisfied on one point—if I could be allowed to think that he was not *always* acting a part, not *always* deceiving me; but above all, if I could be assured that he never was so *very* wicked as my fears have sometimes fancied him, since the story of that unfortunate girl—"

She stopped. Elinor joyfully treasured her words as she answered—

"If you could be assured of that, you think you should be at peace."

"Yes. My peace of mind is doubly involved in it, for not only is it horrible to suspect a person of such designs, but how must it make me appear to myself? That a most shamefully unguarded affection could expose me to—"

"How then," asked her sister, "would you account for his behaviour?"

"I would suppose him—Oh! how gladly would I suppose him, only fickle—very, very fickle."

Elinor said no more. She was debating within herself about beginning her story directly, or postponing it till Marianne was in stronger health. They crept on for a few minutes in silence.

"I am not wishing him too much good," said Marianne at last with a sigh, "when I wish his secret reflections may be no more unpleasant than my own. He will suffer enough in them."

"Do you compare your conduct with his?"

"No. I compare it with what it ought to have been; I compare it with yours."

"Our situations have little similarity."

"Do not, my dearest Elinor, let your kindness defend what I know your judgment must condemn. My illness has made me think— it has given me leisure and calmness for serious recollection. Long before I was enough recovered to talk, I was perfectly able to reflect. I considered the past; I saw in my own behaviour since the beginning of our acquaintance with him last autumn, nothing but a series of imprudence towards myself, and lack of kindness to others. I saw that my own feelings had prepared my sufferings, and that my lack of wisdom had almost led me to the grave. My illness, I well knew, had been entirely brought on by myself, by such negligence of my own health, as I had felt even at the time to be wrong. Had I died, it would have been self-destruction. I did not know my danger till the danger was removed; but with such feelings as these reflections gave me, I am surprised at my recovery—at the very eagerness of my desire to live. Had I died, in what peculiar misery would I have left you, my nurse, my friend, my sister! You, who had seen all my fretful selfishness; who had known all the murmurings of my heart! How should I have lived in _your_ remembrance! Mother too! How could you have consoled her? I cannot express my own abhorrence of myself. Whenever I looked towards the past, I saw some duty neglected, or some failing indulged. Everybody seemed injured by me. The kindness, the unceasing kindness of Mrs. Jennings, I had repaid with ungrateful contempt. To the Middletons, the Palmers, the Steeles, to every common acquaintance even, I had been insolent and unjust; with a heart hardened against their merits, and a temper irritated by their very attention. To John, to Fanny,—yes, even to them, little as they deserve, I had given less than their due. But you, you above all, even more than Mother, had been wronged by me. I, and only I, knew your heart and its sorrows; yet, to what did it influence me? Not to any compassion that could benefit you or myself. Your example was before me: but to what purpose? Was I more considerate of you and your comfort? No; I turned away from every exertion of duty or friendship; scarcely allowing sorrow to exist but with me, regretting only *that* heart which had deserted and wronged me, and leaving you, for whom I professed an unbounded affection, to be miserable for my sake."

Here ceased the rapid flow of her self-reproving spirit; and Elinor, impatient to soothe, though too honest to flatter, gave her instantly that praise and support which her frankness and her contrition so well deserved. Marianne pressed her hand and replied—

"You are very good. The future must be my proof. I have laid down my plan, and if I am capable of adhering to it, my feelings shall be governed and my temper improved. They shall no longer worry others, nor torture myself. I shall now live solely for my family. You, my mother, and Margaret, must henceforth be all the world to me; you will share my affections entirely between you. From you, from my home, I shall never again have the smallest incitement to move; and if I do mix in other society it will be only to show that my spirit is humbled, my heart changed, and that I can practise the civilities, the lesser duties of life, with gentleness, and forbearance. As for Willoughby, to say that I shall soon or that I shall ever forget him, would be a lie. His memory can be overcome by no change of circumstances or opinions. But it shall be regulated, it shall be checked by religion, by reason, by constant employment."

She paused, and added in a lower voice, "If I could but know *his* heart, everything would become clear."

Elinor, who had now been for some time reflecting on the propriety or impropriety of speedily embarking on her narration, without feeling at all nearer decision than at first, heard this, and soon found herself beginning.

She prepared her anxious listener with caution; related simply and honestly the main points on which Willoughby based his apology; did justice to his repentance, and softened only his claims of present regard. Marianne said not a word; she trembled, her eyes were fixed on the ground, and her lips became whiter than even sickness had left them. A thousand inquiries sprung up from her

NSE AND SENSIBILITY FOR TEENS

heart, but she dared not urge one. She caught every syllable with panting eagerness; her hand unknowingly closely pressed her sister's, and tears covered her cheeks.

Elinor, dreading her being tired, led her towards home; and till they reached the door of the cottage, easily guessing what her curiosity must be, though no question was suffered to speak it, talked of nothing but Willoughby. As soon as they entered the house, Marianne with a kiss of gratitude spoke two words through her tears: "Tell mama." She then walked slowly upstairs.

CHAPTER 47

Mrs. Dashwood rejoiced in his being cleared from some part of his guilt; she was sorry for him and wished him happy. But the feelings of the past could not be recalled. Nothing could restore him with a faith unbroken—a character unblemished, to Marianne. Nothing could do away the knowledge of what the latter had suffered at his hand, nor remove the guilt of his conduct towards Eliza. Nothing could return him, therefore, to the place he formerly occupied in her heart and mind.

Had Mrs. Dashwood, like her daughter, heard Willoughby's story from himself—had she witnessed his distress, and been under the influence of his countenance and his manner, it is probable that her compassion would have been greater. But it was neither in Elinor's power, nor in her wish, to rouse such feelings in another, by her explanation. Reflection had given calmness to her judgment, and sobered her own opinion of what Willoughby deserved. She wished, therefore, to declare only the simple truth, and lay open such facts as were really due to his character, without any embellishment of tenderness.

In the evening, when they were all three together, Marianne began voluntarily to speak of him again; but that it was not without effort.

"I wish to assure you both," said she, "that I see everything—as you can wish me to do."

Mrs. Dashwood would have interrupted her instantly with soothing tenderness, had not Elinor, who really wished to hear her sister's unbiassed opinion, by an eager sign, encouraged her to remain silent. Marianne slowly continued—

"It is a great relief to me—what Elinor told me this morning—I have now heard exactly what I wished to hear." For some moments her voice was lost; but, recovering herself, she added, and with greater calmness than before: "I am now perfectly satisfied, I wish for no change. I never could have been happy with him, after knowing, as sooner or later I must have known, all this. I should have had no confidence in him."

"I know it—I know it," cried her mother. "Happy with such a man! With one who had so injured the peace of the dearest of our friends, and the best of men! No—my Marianne has not a heart to be made happy with one who would act in this manner! Her conscience, her sensitive conscience, would have felt all that the conscience of her husband ought to have felt."

Marianne sighed, and repeated—"I wish for no change."

"You consider the matter," said Elinor, "exactly as a good mind and a sound understanding must consider it; and I dare say you perceive, as well as myself, not only in this, but in many other circumstances, reason enough to be convinced that your marriage must have involved you in many certain troubles and disappointment. Had you married, you must have been always poor. His extravagance is acknowledged even by himself, and his whole conduct declares that self-denial is a word hardly understood by him. His demands and your inexperience together on a small, very small income, must have brought great distress. *Your* sense of honour and honesty would have led you, I know, when aware of your situation, to attempt all the thrift that would appear to you possible. Perhaps, as long as your frugality affected only on your own comfort, you might have been allowed to practise it—but how little could your best efforts do to stop the ruin which had begun before your marriage?"

Marianne's lips quivered. "Do you really think him selfish?"

"The whole of his behaviour," replied Elinor, "from beginning to end has been grounded on selfishness. It was selfishness which first made him play with your affections—which afterwards, when his own were engaged, made him delay the confession of it, and which finally carried him from Barton. His own enjoyment, or his own ease, was, in every particular, his ruling principle."

"It is very true. *My* happiness never was his object."

"At present," continued Elinor, "he regrets what he has done. And why does he regret it? Because he finds it has not done for him what he hoped it would. It has not made him happy. But does it thence follow that, had he married you, he would have been happy? The inconveniencies would have been different. He would then have suffered under financial distresses which, because they are removed, he now sees as nothing. He would have had a wife of whose temper he could make no complaint, but he would have been always poor; and probably would soon have learned to rank the innumerable comforts of an estate and good income as of far more importance, even to domestic happiness, than the temper of his wife."

"I have not a doubt of it," said Marianne; "and I have nothing to regret—nothing but my own folly."

"Rather say your mother's imprudence, my child," said Mrs. Dashwood. "*She* must be answerable."

Marianne would not let her proceed; and Elinor, satisfied that each felt their own error, wished to avoid any survey of the past that might weaken her sister's spirits. She therefore, pursuing the first subject, immediately continued—

"*One* observation may, I think, be fairly drawn from the whole of the story—that all Willoughby's difficulties have arisen from his behaviour to Eliza Williams. That crime has been the origin of every lesser one, and of all his present discontents."

Marianne agreed most warmly, and her mother was led by it to an enumeration of Colonel Brandon's injuries and merits. Her daughter did not look, however, as if much of it were heard by her.

Elinor, according to her expectation, saw on the two or three following days, that Marianne did not continue to gain strength as she had done; but while she still tried to appear cheerful and easy, her sister could safely trust to the effect of time upon her health.

Margaret returned, and the family was again quietly settled at the cottage, and if not pursuing their usual studies with quite so much vigour as when they first came to Barton, at least planning a vigorous resumption of them in future.

Elinor grew impatient for some tidings of Edward. She had heard nothing of him since her leaving London, nothing new of his plans, nothing certain even of his present situation. Some letters had passed between her and her brother, in consequence of Marianne's illness, and in the first of John's, there had been this sentence: "We know nothing of our unfortunate Edward, and can make no inquiries on so prohibited a subject, but conclude him to be still at Oxford," which was all the intelligence of Edward afforded her by the correspondence, for his name was not even mentioned in any of the following letters. She was not doomed, however, to be long in ignorance of his plans.

Their man-servant had been sent one morning to Exeter on business; and when he returned, this was his voluntary communication—

"I suppose you know ma'am, that Mr. Ferrars is married."

Marianne gave a violent start, fixed her eyes upon Elinor, saw her turning pale, and fell back in her chair in hysterics. Mrs. Dashwood was shocked to perceive by Elinor's countenance how much she really suffered, and in a moment afterwards, alike distressed by Marianne's situation, knew not on which child to bestow her principal attention.

The servant, who saw only that Miss Marianne had taken ill, had sense enough to call one of the maids, who, with Mrs. Dashwood's assistance, supported her into the other room. By that time, Marianne was rather better, and her mother leaving her to the care of Margaret and the maid, returned to Elinor, who though still much disordered, had so far recovered the use of her reason and voice as to be just beginning an inquiry as to the source of this news. Mrs. Dashwood immediately took all that trouble on herself: and Elinor had the benefit of the information without the exertion of seeking it.

"Who told you that Mr. Ferrars was married, Thomas?"

"I see Mr. Ferrars myself, ma'am, this morning in Exeter, and his lady too, Miss Steele as was. They was stopping in a carriage at the door of the New London Inn, as I went there with a message from Sally at the Park to her brother, who is one of the postboys. I happened to look up as I went by the chaise, and so I see directly it was the youngest Miss Steele; so I took off my hat, and she knew me and called to me, and inquired after you, ma'am, and the young ladies, especially Miss Marianne, and bid me I should give her compliments and Mr. Ferrars', their best compliments and service, and how sorry they was they had not time to come on and see you—but they was in a great hurry to go forwards, for they was going further down for a little while—but when they come back, they'd make sure to come and see you."

"But did she tell you she was married, Thomas?"

"Yes, ma'am. She smiled, and said how she had changed her name since she was in these parts. She was always a very affable and free-spoken young lady, and very civil behaved. So, I made free to wish her joy."

"Was Mr. Ferrars in the carriage with her?"

"Yes, ma'am, I just see him leaning back in it, but he did not look up; he never was a gentleman much for talking."

"Was there no one else in the carriage?"

"No, ma'am, only they two."

"Do you know where they came from?"

"They come straight from town, as Miss Lucy—Mrs. Ferrars told me."

"And are going farther westward?"

"Yes, ma'am—but not to bide long. They said they will soon be back again, and then they'd be sure and call here."

Mrs. Dashwood now looked at her daughter; but Elinor knew better than to expect them. She recognised the whole of Lucy in the message, and was very confident that Edward would never come near them. She observed, in a low voice, to her mother, that they were probably going down to Mr. Pratt's, near Plymouth.

Thomas's intelligence seemed over. Elinor looked as if she wished to hear more.

"Did you see them off, before you came away?"

"No, ma'am—the horses was just coming out, but I could not bide any longer; I was afraid of being late."

"Did Mrs. Ferrars look well?"

"Yes, ma'am, she said how she was very well; and to my mind she was always a very handsome young lady—and she seemed vastly contented."

Mrs. Dashwood could think of no other question, and Thomas was dismissed. Marianne had already sent to say that she should eat nothing more; Mrs. Dashwood's and Elinor's appetites were equally lost.

When the dessert and the wine were arranged, and Mrs. Dashwood and Elinor were left by themselves, they remained long together in a similarity of thoughtfulness and silence. Mrs. Dashwood feared to make any remark, and ventured not to offer consolation. She now found that she had erred in relying on Elinor's representation of herself; and justly concluded that everything had been expressly softened at the time, to spare her from an increase of unhappiness. She realized that in Elinor, though it showed in a very different way, she might have a daughter suffering almost as much as Marianne.

CHAPTER 48

Elinor now discovered the difference between the expectation of an unpleasant event, however certain the mind may be told to consider it, and certainty itself. She now found that, in spite of herself, she had always hoped, while Edward remained single, that something would occur to prevent his marrying Lucy. But he was now married, and she condemned her heart for believing in any other possibility than what had occurred.

That he should be married so soon, before (as she imagined) he could be ordained, and consequently before he could be in possession of the living, surprised her a little at first. But she soon saw how likely it was that Lucy, in her haste to secure him, should overlook everything but the risk of delay. They were married in town, and were now hastening down to her uncle's. What had Edward felt on being within four miles of Barton, on seeing her mother's servant, and on hearing Lucy's message!

They would soon, she supposed, be settled at Delaford, that place in which so much conspired to give her an interest—which she wished to be acquainted with, and yet desired to avoid. She saw them in an instant in their parsonage-house; saw in Lucy the active, contriving manager, uniting at once a desire of smart appearance with the utmost frugality, and ashamed to be suspected of half her economical practices—pursuing her own interest in every thought, courting the favour of Colonel Brandon, of Mrs. Jennings, and of every wealthy friend. In Edward, she knew not what she saw, nor what she wished to see—happy or unhappy—nothing pleased her—she turned away her head from every thought of him.

Elinor flattered herself that someone in London would write to them to announce the event, and give farther particulars; but day after day passed, and brought no letter, no tidings. Though uncertain that anyone was to blame, she found fault with every absent friend. They were all thoughtless or indolent.

"When do you write to Colonel Brandon, ma'am?" was an inquiry which sprung from the impatience of her mind to have something to go on.

"I wrote to him, my love, last week, and rather expect to see, than to hear from him again. I earnestly pressed his coming to us, and should not be surprised to see him walk in today or tomorrow, or any day."

This was something to look forward to. Colonel Brandon *must* have some information to give.

Scarcely had she so determined it, when the figure of a man on horseback drew her eyes to the window. He stopped at their gate. It was a gentleman, it was Colonel Brandon himself. Now she would hear more, and she trembled in expectation of it. But—it was *not* Colonel Brandon. Were it possible, she would say it must be Edward. She looked again. He had just dismounted; she could not be mistaken. It *was* Edward. She moved away and sat down. "He comes from Mr. Pratt's purposely to see us. I *will* be calm."

In a moment she perceived that the others were likewise aware of the mistake. She saw her mother and Marianne change colour; saw them look at her, and whisper a few sentences to each other. She would have given the world to be able to speak—but she had no utterance. Not a syllable passed aloud. They all waited in silence for the appearance of their visitor. His footsteps were heard along the gravel path; in a moment he was in the passage, and in another he was before them.

His countenance, as he entered the room, was not too happy. His complexion was white with agitation, and he looked as if fearful of his reception, and conscious that he merited no kind one. Mrs. Dashwood, however, met him with a look of forced complacency, gave him her hand, and wished him joy.

He coloured, and stammered out an unintelligible reply. When the moment of action was over, she wished that she had shaken hands with him too. But it was then too late, and she sat down again and talked of the weather.

Marianne had retreated as much as possible out of sight, to conceal her distress; and Margaret, understanding some part, but not the whole, took a seat as far from him as she could, and maintained a strict silence.

When Elinor had ceased to rejoice in the dryness of the season, a very awful pause took place. It was put to an end to by Mrs. Dashwood, who felt obliged to hope that he had left Mrs. Ferrars very well. In a hurried manner, he replied in the affirmative.

Another pause.

Elinor, resolving to exert herself, though fearing the sound of her own voice, now said—

"Is Mrs. Ferrars at Longstaple?"

"At Longstaple!" he replied, with an air of surprise. "No, my mother is in town."

"I meant," said Elinor, taking up some work from the table, "to inquire after Mrs. *Edward* Ferrars."

She dared not look up, but her mother and Marianne both turned their eyes on him. He coloured, seemed perplexed, and after some hesitation, said—

"Perhaps you mean—my brother—you mean Mrs. *Robert* Ferrars."

"Mrs. Robert Ferrars!" was repeated by Marianne and her mother, in an accent of the utmost amazement. Though Elinor could not speak, even *her* eyes were fixed on him with the same impatient wonder. He rose from his seat and walked to the window, apparently from not knowing what to do. He took up a pair of scissors that lay there, and while spoiling both them and their covering by cutting the latter to pieces as he spoke, said, in a hurried voice—

"Perhaps you do not know—you may not have heard that my brother has been married to—to the youngest—to Miss Lucy Steele."

His words were echoed with unspeakable astonishment by all but Elinor, who sat with her head leaning over her work, in a state of such agitation as made her hardly know where she was.

"Yes," said he, "they were married last week, and are now at Dawlish."

Elinor could sit no longer. She almost ran out of the room, and as soon as the door was closed, burst into tears of joy, which at first

280

she thought would never cease. Edward, who had till then looked anywhere rather than at her, saw her hurry away, and perhaps saw— or even heard—her emotion; for immediately afterwards he fell into a reverie, which no remarks, no inquiries, and no affectionate address of Mrs. Dashwood could penetrate. At last, without saying a word, he left the room, and walked out towards the village, leaving the others in the greatest astonishment and perplexity on a change in his situation so wonderful and so sudden—a perplexity which they had no means of lessening but by their own surmises.

CHAPTER 49

Unaccountable, however, as the circumstances of his release might appear to the whole family, it was certain that Edward was free: and to what purpose that freedom would be employed was easily determined by all; for after experiencing the blessings of *one* imprudent engagement, nothing less could be expected of him in the failure of *that*, than the immediate creation of another.

His errand at Barton, in fact, was a simple one. It was only to ask Elinor to marry him; and considering that he was not altogether inexperienced in such a question, it might be strange that he should feel so uncomfortable in the present case as he really did, so much in need of encouragement and fresh air.

How soon he had walked himself into the proper resolution however, how soon an opportunity of exercising it occurred, in what manner he expressed himself, and how he was received, need not be particularly told. This only need be said, that when they all sat down to table at four o'clock, about three hours after his arrival, he had secured his lady, engaged her mother's consent, and was not only in the rapturous profession of the lover, but one of the happiest of men. His situation indeed was more than commonly joyful. He had more than the ordinary triumph of accepted love to swell his heart and raise his spirits. He was released, without any reproach to himself, from an entanglement which had long formed his misery, with a woman whom he had long ceased to love—and elevated at once to that security with another, which he must have thought of almost with despair, as soon as he had learned to consider it with desire. He was brought from misery to happiness, and the change was openly spoken in such a genuine, flowing, grateful cheerfulness, as his friends had never witnessed in him before.

His heart was now open to Elinor—all its weaknesses, all its errors confessed, and his first boyish attachment to Lucy treated with all the philosophic dignity of twenty-four.

"It was a foolish, idle inclination on my side," said he, "the consequence of ignorance of the world. Though I left Longstaple with what I thought, at the time, was a most unconquerable preference for his niece, yet had I any employment I should very soon have outgrown the fancied attachment, especially by mixing more with the world, as in such a case I must have done. But instead of having anything to do—instead of having any profession chosen for me, or being allowed to choose any myself, I returned home to be completely idle; and for the first year afterwards, I had not even the nominal employment which belonging to the university would have given me, for I was not sent to Oxford till I was nineteen. I had therefore nothing in the world to do, but to fancy myself in love; and as my mother did not make my home in every respect comfortable— as I had no friend, no companion in my brother, and disliked new acquaintance, it was natural for me to be very often at Longstaple, where I always felt myself at home, and was always sure of a welcome. Accordingly, I spent the greatest part of my time there from eighteen to nineteen. Lucy seemed to be everything that was amiable and obliging. She was pretty too—at least I thought so *then*, and I had seen so little of other women, that I could make no comparisons, and see no defects. Considering everything, therefore, I hope, foolish as our engagement was, foolish as it has since in every way been proved, it was not at the time an unnatural, or inexcusable folly."

The change which a few hours had wrought in the minds and the happiness of the Dashwoods, was such—so great—as promised them all the satisfaction of a sleepless night. Mrs. Dashwood, too happy to be comfortable, knew not how to love Edward nor praise Elinor enough—how to be enough thankful for his release without wounding his honor, nor how at once to give them leisure for unrestrained conversation together, and yet enjoy, as she wished, the sight and company of both.

Marianne could speak *her* happiness only by tears. Comparisons would occur, regrets would arise; and her joy, though sincere as her love for her sister, was of a kind to give her neither spirits nor language. But Elinor, how are *her* feelings to be described? From the moment of learning that Lucy was married to another, that Edward was free, to the moment of his justifying the hopes which had so instantly followed, she was everything but tranquil. But when the second moment had passed—when she compared her situation with what so lately it had been—she was overcome by her own happiness, and it required several hours to give sedateness to her spirits, or any degree of tranquillity to her heart.

Edward was now to stay at the cottage at least for a week; for whatever other claims might be made on him, it was impossible that less than a week should be given up to the enjoyment of Elinor's company, or suffice to say half that was to be said of the past, the present, and the future. Though a very few hours spent in the hard labour of incessant talking will dispatch more subjects than can really be in common between any two rational creatures, yet with lovers it is different. Between *them* no subject is finished, no communication is even made, till it has been made at least twenty times over.

Lucy's marriage, the unceasing and reasonable wonder among them all, formed of course one of the earliest discussions of the lovers; and Elinor's particular knowledge of each party made it appear to her, in every view, as one of the most extraordinary and unaccountable circumstances she had ever heard. How they could be thrown together, and by what attraction Robert could be drawn to marry a girl of whose beauty she had herself heard him speak without any admiration—a girl already engaged to his brother, and on whose account that brother had been disowned by his family—was beyond her comprehension. To her own heart it was a delightful affair, to her imagination it was even a ridiculous one; but to her reason, her judgment, it was completely a puzzle.

Edward could only attempt an explanation by supposing, that perhaps at first accidentally meeting, the vanity of the one had been so worked on by the flattery of the other, as to lead by degrees to all the rest. Elinor remembered what Robert had told her in Harley Street, of his opinion of what his own mediation in his brother's affairs might have done, if applied to in time. She repeated it to Edward.

"*That* was exactly like Robert," was his immediate observation. "And *that*," he presently added, "might perhaps be in *his* head when the acquaintance between them first began. And Lucy perhaps at first might think only of procuring his good offices in my favour. Other designs might afterwards arise."

How long it had been carrying on between them, however, he was equally at a loss with herself to make out; for at Oxford, where he had remained by choice ever since leaving London, he had had no means of hearing of her but from herself, and her letters to the very last were neither less frequent, nor less affectionate than usual. Not the smallest suspicion, therefore, had ever occurred to prepare him for what followed; and when at last it burst on him in a letter from Lucy herself, he had been for some time, he believed, half stupified between the wonder, the horror, and the joy of such a deliverance. He put the letter into Elinor's hands—

"Dear Sir,—Being very sure I have long lost your affections, I have thought myself at liberty to bestow my own on another, and have no doubt of being as happy with him as I once used to think I might be with you. I can safely say I owe you no ill-will, and am sure you will be too generous to do us ill. Your brother has gained my affections entirely, and as we could not live without one another, we are just returned from the altar, and are now on our way to Dawlish for a few weeks, which place your dear brother has great curiosity to see, but thought I should first trouble you with these few lines, and shall always remain, your sincere well-wisher, friend, and sister, LUCY FERRARS. I have burned all your letters, and will return your picture at the first opportunity. Please destroy my scrawls; but the ring, with my hair, you are welcome to keep."

Elinor read and returned it without any comment.

"I will not ask your opinion of it as a composition," said Edward. "For worlds would not I have had a letter of hers seen by *you* in former days. In a sister it is bad enough, but in a wife! How I have blushed over the pages of her writing! I believe I may say that since the first half year of our foolish—business—this is the only letter I ever received from her, of which the substance made me any amends for the defect of the style."

"However it may have come about," said Elinor, after a pause, "they are certainly married. And your mother has brought on herself a most appropriate punishment. The independence she settled on

Robert, through resentment against you, has put it in his power to make his own choice; and she has actually been bribing one son with a thousand a year to do the very deed which she disinherited the other for planning to do. She will hardly be less hurt, I suppose, by Robert's marrying Lucy, than she would have been by your marrying her."

"She will be more hurt by it, for Robert always was her favourite. She will be more hurt by it, and on the same principle will forgive him much sooner."

In what state the affair stood at present between them, Edward knew not, for no communication with any of his family had yet been attempted by him. He had left Oxford within twenty-four hours after Lucy's letter arrived, with only one object before him. He would do nothing till he were assured of his fate with Miss Dashwood; and by his rapidity in seeking *that* fate, it is to be supposed, in spite of the jealousy with which he had once thought of Colonel Brandon—in spite of the modesty with which he rated his own merits, and the politeness with which he talked of his doubts, he did not upon the whole expect a very cruel reception. It was his business, however, to say that he *did*, and he said it very prettily.

That Lucy had certainly meant to deceive, to go off with a flourish of malice against him in her message by Thomas was perfectly clear to Elinor; and Edward himself now thoroughly enlightened on her character, had no hesitation believing her capable of the utmost ill-nature. Though his eyes had been long opened, even before his acquaintance with Elinor began, to her ignorance and a lack of liberality in some of her opinions, they had been equally imputed, by him, to her lack of education; and till her last letter reached him, he had always believed her to be a well-disposed, good-hearted girl, and thoroughly attached to him. Nothing but such a persuasion could have prevented his putting an end to an engagement which, long before the discovery of it laid him open to his mother's anger, had been a continual source of regret to him.

"I thought it my duty," said he, "regardless of my feelings, to give her the option of continuing the engagement or not, when I was renounced by my mother, and stood to all appearance without a friend in the world to assist me. In such a situation as that, where there seemed nothing to tempt the greed or vanity of any living creature, how could I suppose, when she so earnestly, so warmly insisted on sharing my fate, whatever it might be, that anything but the most disinterested affection was her motive? And even now, I cannot comprehend on what motive she acted, or what fancied advantage it could be to her, to be fettered to a man for whom she had not the smallest regard, and who had only two thousand pounds in the world. She could not foresee that Colonel Brandon would give me a living."

"No, but she might suppose that something would occur in your favour; that your own family might in time relent. And at any rate, she lost nothing by continuing the engagement, for she has proven that it did not affect her inclination nor her actions. The connection was certainly a respectable one, and probably gained her esteem among her friends; and if nothing more advantageous occurred, it would be better for her to marry *you* than to be single."

Edward was of course immediately convinced that nothing could have been more natural than Lucy's conduct, nor more self-evident than the motive of it.

"Your behaviour was certainly very wrong," said Elinor, "because—to say nothing of my own conviction—our relations were all led away by it to fancy and expect *what*, as you were *then* situated, could never be."

He could only plead an ignorance of his own heart, and a mistaken confidence in the force of his engagement.

"I was simple enough to think, that because my *faith* was plighted to another, there could be no danger in my being with you; and that the consciousness of my engagement was to keep my heart as safe and sacred as my honour. I felt that I admired you, but I told myself it was only friendship; and till I began to make comparisons between you and Lucy, I did not know what I felt. After that, I suppose, I *was* wrong in remaining so much in Sussex, but I convinced myself I was doing no injury to anybody but me."

Elinor smiled, and shook her head.

Edward heard with pleasure of Colonel Brandon's being expected at the Cottage, as he really wished not only to be better acquainted with him, but to have an opportunity of thanking him for giving him the living of Delaford. *Now* he felt astonished himself that he had never yet been to the place. But so little interest had he taken in the matter, that he owed all his knowledge of the house, garden, condition of the land, and rate of the tithes, to Elinor herself, who had heard so much of it from Colonel Brandon, and heard it with so much attention as to be entirely mistress of the subject.

One question after this only remained undecided between them, one difficulty only was to be overcome. They were brought together by mutual affection, with the warmest support of their real friends; their intimate knowledge of each other seemed to make their happiness certain—and they only wanted something to live upon. Edward had two thousand pounds, and Elinor one, which, with the Delaford living, was all that they could call their own; for it was impossible that Mrs. Dashwood should advance anything, and they were neither of them quite enough in love to think that three hundred and fifty pounds a year would supply them with the comforts of life.

Edward was not entirely without hopes of some favourable change in his mother towards him; and on *that* he rested for the remainder of their income. But Elinor had no such confidence; for, since Edward would still be unable to marry Miss Morton, and his choosing herself had been spoken of in Mrs. Ferrars's flattering language as only a lesser evil than his choosing Lucy Steele, she feared that Robert's offence would serve no other purpose than to enrich Fanny.

About four days after Edward's arrival, Colonel Brandon appeared, to complete Mrs. Dashwood's satisfaction, and to give her the dignity of having, for the first time since her living at Barton, more company with her than her house would hold. Edward was allowed to retain the privilege of first-comer, and Colonel Brandon therefore walked every night to his old quarters at the Park, from whence he usually returned in the morning, early enough to interrupt the lovers' first tête-à-tête before breakfast.

A three weeks' residence at Delaford, where, in his evening hours at least, he had little to do but calculate the disproportion between thirty-six and seventeen, brought him to Barton in a temper of mind which needed all the improvement in Marianne's looks, all the kindness of her welcome, and all the encouragement of her mother's language, to make it cheerful. Among such friends, however, and such flattery, he revived. No rumour of Lucy's marriage had yet reached him; he knew nothing of what had passed, and the first hours of his visit were consequently spent in hearing and in wondering. Everything was explained to him by Mrs. Dashwood, and he found fresh reason to rejoice in what he had done for Mr. Ferrars, since eventually it promoted the interest of Elinor.

It would be needless to say that the gentlemen advanced in the good opinion of each other, as they advanced in each other's acquaintance, for it could not be otherwise. Their resemblance in good principles and good sense, in disposition and manner of thinking, would probably have been sufficient to unite them in friendship, without any other attraction; but their being in love with two sisters, and two sisters fond of each other, made that mutual regard inevitable and immediate, which might otherwise have awaited the effect of time and judgment.

The letters from town, which a few days before would have made every nerve in Elinor's body thrill with rapture, now arrived to be read with less emotion than mirth. Mrs. Jennings wrote to tell the wonderful tale, to vent her honest indignation against the jilting girl, and pour forth her compassion towards poor Mr. Edward, who, she was sure, had quite doted upon the worthless hussy, and was now, by all accounts, almost broken-hearted, at Oxford. "I do think," she continued, "nothing was ever carried on so sly; for it was but two days after Lucy called and sat a couple of hours with me. Not a soul suspected anything of the matter, not even Nancy, who, poor soul, came crying to me the day after, in a great fright for fear of Mrs. Ferrars, as well as not knowing how to get to Plymouth; for Lucy, it seems, borrowed all her money before she went off to be married. I was very glad to give her five guineas to take her down to Exeter, where she is thinking of staying three or four weeks with Mrs. Burgess, in hopes, as I tell her, to fall in with the doctor again. And I must say that Lucy's crossness not to take her along with them in the chaise, is worse than all. Poor Mr. Edward! I cannot get him out of my head, but you must invite him to Barton, and Miss Marianne must try to comfort him."

Mr. Dashwood's strains were more solemn. Mrs. Ferrars was the most unfortunate of women—poor Fanny had suffered agonies— and he considered the existence of each, under such a blow, with grateful wonder. Robert's offence was unpardonable, but Lucy's was infinitely worse. Neither of them was ever again to be mentioned to Mrs. Ferrars; and, even if she might hereafter be induced to forgive her son, his wife should never be acknowledged as her daughter, nor be permitted to appear in her presence. The secrecy with which everything had been carried on between them was treated as enormously heightening the crime, because had any suspicion of it occurred to the others, proper measures would have been taken to prevent the marriage; and he called on Elinor to join with him in regretting that Lucy's engagement with Edward had not rather been fulfilled, than that she should thus be the means of spreading misery farther in the family. He thus continued—

"Mrs. Ferrars has never yet mentioned Edward's name, which does not surprise us; but, to our great astonishment, not a line has been received from him on the occasion. Perhaps, however, he is kept silent by his fear of offending, and I shall therefore give him a hint, by a line to Oxford, that his sister and I both think a letter of proper submission from him, addressed perhaps to Fanny, and by her shown to her mother, might not be taken amiss; for we all know the tenderness of Mrs. Ferrars's heart, and that she wishes for nothing so much as to be on good terms with her children."

This paragraph was of some importance to the prospects and conduct of Edward. It convinced him to attempt a reconciliation, though not exactly in the manner pointed out by their brother and sister.

"You may certainly ask to be forgiven," said Elinor, "because you have offended; and I should think you might *now* venture so far as to profess some apology for having ever formed the engagement which drew on you your mothers anger."

He agreed that he might.

"And when she has forgiven you, perhaps a little humility may be convenient while acknowledging a second engagement, almost as imprudent in *her* eyes, as the first."

He had nothing to say against it, but still resisted the idea of a letter of proper submission; and therefore, to make it easier to him, it was resolved that, instead of writing to Fanny, he should go to London, and personally intreat her good offices in his favour. "And if they really *do* help," said Marianne, "to bring about a reconciliation, I shall think that even John and Fanny are not entirely without merit."

After a visit on Colonel Brandon's side of only three or four days, the two gentlemen left Barton together. They were to go immediately to Delaford, that Edward might have some personal knowledge of his future home, and assist his patron and friend in deciding on what improvements were needed to it; and from thence, after staying there a couple of nights, he was to proceed on his journey to town.

CHAPTER 50

After a proper resistance on the part of Mrs. Ferrars, just so violent and so steady as to preserve her from that reproach which she always seemed fearful of incurring, the reproach of being too amiable, Edward was admitted to her presence, and pronounced to be again her son.

Her family had recently been exceedingly fluctuating. For many years of her life she had had two sons; but the crime and annihilation of Edward, a few weeks ago, had robbed her of one; the similar annihilation of Robert had left her for a fortnight without any; and now, by the restoration of Edward, she had one again.

In spite of his being allowed once more to live, however, he did not feel the continuance of his existence secure till he had revealed his present engagement; for the publication of that circumstance he feared might give a sudden turn to her approval, and send him off as rapidly as before. With apprehensive caution therefore it was revealed, and he was listened to with unexpected calmness. Mrs. Ferrars at first reasonably endeavoured to dissuade him from marrying Miss Dashwood, by every argument in her power. She told him that in Miss Morton he would have a woman of higher rank and larger fortune; and saying that Miss Morton was the daughter of a nobleman with thirty thousand pounds, while Miss Dashwood was only the daughter of a private gentleman, with no more than *three*; but when she found that, though perfectly admitting the truth of her representation, he was by no means inclined to be guided by it, she judged it wisest, from the experience of the past, to allow it.

Therefore, after such an ungracious delay as she owed to her own dignity, and as served to prevent every suspicion of good will, she issued her decree of consent to the marriage of Edward and Elinor. What she would do towards augmenting their income was next to be considered, and the amount of ten thousand pounds was offered. It was as much as was desired, and more than was expected by Edward and Elinor. Mrs. Ferrars herself, by her shuffling excuses, seemed the only person surprised at her not giving more.

With an income quite sufficient to their wants thus secured to them, they had nothing to wait for after Edward was in possession of the living, but the readiness of the house, to which Colonel Brandon, with an eager desire for the accommodation of Elinor, was making considerable improvements. After waiting some time for their completion—after experiencing, as usual, a thousand disappointments and delays, from the unaccountable laziness of the workmen—the ceremony took place in Barton church early in the autumn.

The first month after their marriage was spent with their friend at the Mansion house, from whence they could superintend the progress of the Parsonage, and direct everything as they liked on the spot; could choose papers, guide the installation of shrubberies, and add a porch. Mrs. Jennings's prophecies, though rather jumbled together, were fulfilled. She was able to visit Edward and his wife in their Parsonage by the end of September, and she found in Elinor and her husband, as she really believed, one of the happiest couples in the world. They had in fact nothing to wish for, but the marriage of Colonel Brandon and Marianne, and rather better pasturage for their cows.

They were visited on their first settling by almost all their relations and friends. Mrs. Ferrars came to inspect the happiness which she was almost ashamed of having authorised; and even the Dashwoods paid for a journey from Sussex to do them honour.

"I will not say that I am disappointed, my dear sister," said John, as they were walking together one morning before the gates of Delaford House—"*that* would be saying too much, for certainly you have been one of the most fortunate young women in the world, as it is. But, I confess, it would give me great pleasure to call Colonel Brandon brother. His property here, his place, his house, everything in such respectable and excellent condition! And his woods! I have not seen such timber anywhere in Dorsetshire, as there is now standing in Delaford Hanger! And though, perhaps, Marianne may not seem exactly the person to attract him, yet I think it would altogether be adviseable for you to have them now frequently staying with you, for as Colonel Brandon seems a great deal at home, nobody can tell what may happen. When people are much thrown together, and see little of anybody else, you may as well give her a chance."

But though Mrs. Ferrars *did* come to see them, and always treated them with the pretense of decent affection, they were never insulted by her real favour and preference. *That* was due to the folly of Robert, and the cunning of his wife; and it was earned by them before many months had passed. The selfishness of the latter, which had at first drawn Robert into the scrape, was the principal instrument of his deliverance from it; for her respectful humility, attentions, and flatteries, as soon as the smallest opening was given for their exercise, reconciled Mrs. Ferrars to his choice, and re-established him completely in her favour.

The whole of Lucy's behaviour in the affair, and the prosperity which crowned it, therefore, may be held forth as a most encouraging instance of what an earnest, unceasing attention to self-interest will do in securing every advantage of fortune, with no other sacrifice than that of time and conscience. When Robert first sought her acquaintance, and privately visited her in Bartlett's Buildings, it was only with the view imputed to him by his brother. He merely meant to persuade her to give up the engagement; and as there could be nothing to overcome but the affection of both, he naturally expected that one or two interviews would settle the matter. In that point, however, and that only, he erred. Though Lucy soon gave him hopes that his eloquence would convince her in *time*, another visit, another conversation, was always wanted to produce this conviction. Some doubts always lingered in her mind when they parted, which could only be removed by another half hour's discourse with himself. His visits were by this means secured, and what followed is already known. Instead of talking of Edward, they came gradually to talk only of Robert—a subject on which he had always more to say than on any other, and in which she soon betrayed an interest even equal to his own. In short, it became speedily evident to both, that he had entirely supplanted his brother. He was proud of his conquest, proud of tricking Edward, and very proud of marrying privately without his mother's consent. They spent some months in great happiness at Dawlish; for she had many relations—and he drew several plans for magnificent cottages. From thence returning to town, they procured the forgiveness of Mrs. Ferrars by the simple expedient of asking for it. The forgiveness at first, indeed, as was reasonable, included only Robert. Lucy still remained some weeks longer unpardoned. But perseverance in humility of conduct, and messages, in self-condemnation for Robert's offence, and gratitude for the unkindness she was treated with, procured her in time the haughty notice which overcame her by its graciousness, and led soon afterwards, by rapid degrees, to the highest state of affection and influence. Lucy became as necessary to Mrs. Ferrars as either Robert or Fanny; and while Edward was never cordially forgiven for having once intended to marry her, and Elinor, though superior to her in fortune and birth, was spoken of as an intruder, *she* was in everything considered, and always openly acknowledged, to be a favourite child. They settled in town, received very liberal assistance from Mrs. Ferrars, were on the best terms imaginable with the Dashwoods, and setting aside the jealousies and ill-will continually existing between Fanny and Lucy, in which their husbands of course took a part, as well as the frequent domestic disagreements between Robert and Lucy themselves, nothing could exceed the harmony in which they all lived together.

What Edward had done to forfeit the right of eldest son might have puzzled many people to find out. What Robert had done to earn it might have puzzled them still more. It was an arrangement, however, justified in its effects, if not in its cause; for nothing ever appeared in Robert's style of living, or of talking, to give a suspicion of his regretting the extent of his income, as either leaving his brother too little, or bringing himself too much. If Edward might be judged from the ready discharge of his duties in every particular, from an increasing attachment to his wife and his home, and from the regular cheerfulness of his spirits, he might be supposed no less contented with his lot, no less free from every wish of an exchange.

Elinor's marriage divided her as little from her family as could well be contrived, without rendering the cottage at Barton entirely useless, for her mother and sisters spent much more than half their time with her. Mrs. Dashwood's wish of bringing Marianne and Colonel Brandon together was hardly less earnest, though rather more liberal than what John had expressed. It was now her primary goal. Precious as was the company of her daughter to her, she desired nothing so much as to give up its constant enjoyment to her valued friend; and to see Marianne settled at the Mansion house was equally the wish of Edward and Elinor. They each felt his sorrows and their own obligations, and Marianne, by general consent, was to be the reward of all.

With such a confederacy against her—with a knowledge so intimate of his goodness—with a conviction of his fond attachment to herself, which at last, though long after it was observable to everybody else, burst on her—what could she do?

Marianne Dashwood was born to an extraordinary fate. She was born to discover the falsehood of her own opinions, and to counteract, by her conduct, her most favourite maxims. She was born to overcome an affection formed as late in life as at seventeen, and with no sentiment superior to strong esteem and lively friendship, voluntarily to give her hand to another!. *That* other, a man who had suffered no less than herself under the event of a former attachment—whom, two years before, she had considered too old to be married—and who still sought the safeguard of a flannel waistcoat!

But so it was. Instead of falling a sacrifice to an irresistible passion, as once she had fondly flattered herself with expecting—instead of remaining even forever with her mother, and finding her only pleasures in study, as afterwards in her more calm and sober judgment she had determined on—she found herself, at nineteen, submitting to new attachments, entering on new duties, placed in a new home, a wife, the mistress of a family, and the patroness of a village.

Colonel Brandon was now as happy as all those who best loved him believed he deserved to be. In Marianne he was consoled forever past affliction; her regard and her company restored his mind to animation, and his spirits to cheerfulness. Marianne found her own happiness in forming his. She could never love by halves; and her whole heart became, in time, as much devoted to her husband as it had once been to Willoughby.

Willoughby could not hear of her marriage without a pang; and his punishment was soon afterwards complete in the voluntary forgiveness of Mrs. Smith, who, by stating his marriage with a woman of character as the source of her clemency, gave him reason to believe that had he behaved with honour towards Marianne, he might at once have been happy and rich. That his repentance of misconduct, which thus brought its own punishment, was sincere, need not be doubted; nor that he long thought of Colonel Brandon with envy, and of Marianne with regret. But that he was forever inconsolable—that he fled from society, or contracted a habitual gloom of temper, or died of a broken heart, must not be depended upon—for he did neither. He lived to frequently enjoy himself. His wife was not always out of humour, nor his home always uncomfortable. In his breed of horses and dogs, and in sporting of every kind, he found no inconsiderable degree of domestic felicity.

For Marianne, however—in spite of his incivility in surviving her loss—he always retained that decided regard which interested him in everything that befell her, and made her his secret standard of perfection in woman. Many a rising beauty would be slighted by him in after days as bearing no comparison with Mrs. Brandon.

Mrs. Dashwood was prudent enough to remain at the cottage, without attempting to move to Delaford; and fortunately for Sir John and Mrs. Jennings, when Marianne was taken from them, Margaret had reached an age highly suitable for dancing, and not very ineligible for being supposed to have a lover.

Between Barton and Delaford, there was that constant communication which strong family affection would naturally dictate. Among the merits and the happiness of Elinor and Marianne, let it not be ranked as the least considerable, that though sisters, and living almost within sight of each other, they could live without disagreement between themselves, or producing coolness between their husbands.

ABOUT THE AUTHOR

Gerry Baird lives in Utah. He is an avid Jane Austen fan, and when he's not writing he spends his time playing piano and guitar. He is a self-help junkie, a proud father of three, and a lover of inspiring stories.

30807023R00176

Printed in Great Britain
by Amazon